Portrait

of a

GIRL RUNNING

J . B . C H I C O I N E

Straw
Hill
Publishing

strawhillpublishing@jbchicoine.com

Cover art: original watercolor painting—*Portrait of a Girl Running*—by J.B. Chicoine
Cover and interior design and art by Straw Hill Design

ISBN-13: 978-0615887340
ISBN-10: 0615887341

Printed in the United States of America

⁂ ACKNOWLEDGMENTS

SO MANY PEOPLE HAVE BEEN INVOLVED WITH WRITING this novel, either directly or indirectly, by providing feedback or encouragement. I originally wrote it for my husband's amusement back in 2006, and since then it has undergone extensive revisions and restructuring.

I'd like to thank my sister Diana for finding something positive to say about it after I made her slog through the first draft of over 150k words. Your ongoing support has meant the world to me.

Thank you Craig A. Chicoine, for your tireless feedback and suggestions. Also, my other beta readers, Liza Carens Salerno, Carol Newman Cronin, Lindsey Hanchett, Laura Martone, Susan Mills, Claire Dawn, and those who offered support and helpful comments, Scott Daniel, Glenn Rawlinson, Beth Zygiel, Peggy Heinrich, Donna Morris, Ann Ireland, Emmaline Hoffmeister, Diane Dalton. Special thanks to Lisa Porter for your keen psychological insights.

Many, many thanks to my writing partner, Robynne Marie Plouff. I have lost track of how many times you've read this story—you helped me shape it into something fit for human consumption.

Most of all, thanks to my Todd—all my stories are for you, but especially this one. Thank you for all your complexities, for a personality I can dissect a hundred different ways and still come up with complete characters that delight and inspire me!

Portrait

of a

GIRL RUNNING

CHAPTER 1

HAD THE WIND BEEN BLOWING OUT TO SEA, LEILA would have let the draft carry the ashes out over the ocean in one little puff and been done with it, but she had, on a previous occasion, the misfortune of not calculating wind direction and ended up with a face full of powdery remains. She had since learned to stand upwind before shaking the contents of the large, folded handkerchief. Giving her fist a hard look, she squatted in the ankle-deep surf, unfurling her fingers.

Just get it over with!

Keeping the cloth high enough to prevent the ebbing water from wetting its hem, she dumped the contents—about as much as might fill a tablespoon. It drifted away in a little clump. A good swish would fix that. Once it dispersed, she waited until the surf drew it out, tumbling it along with sand and flotsam that shimmered as it roiled. She shook the handkerchief and folded it back into a compact square, then tucked it in the hip pocket of her loose-fitting cut-offs. She wondered how many tablespoons remained. Might she cry if she stood there long enough?

Not waiting for the pang in her chest to erupt as tears, she faced the five-mile return stretch of Long Island's Robert Moses State Park, walked a few yards and then picked up her pace, sprinting from a jog to a full-out run. Too quickly, her diaphragm ached, though it wasn't the run that winded her. Slowing, she arched her back to catch her breath and stopped. An offshore wind pushed wisps of hair from her forehead as she faced the surf. All eternity stretched out above and before her in shades of blue and gray—ultra-marine, cerulean, Payne's gray—and even a swipe of ochre. What a grand paintbrush, strokes of perfection. Oh, the vastness of it! She didn't ponder anything as lofty as God, only the magnitude of promises—especially those made under duress and later second-guessed.

As an image of her father flashed behind closed eyelids, Leila's chest tightened with each heartbeat. She drew in a constricted breath, pushing back the surge of panic—*Just keep running*—and continued down the beach.

Waves crashed to her right, firming the shoreline as she ran. The Atlantic's roar drowned out the increasing hordes of city dwellers—their transistor radios and squealing children—even the odor of tropical ointments, cigarettes, and greasy fries, but it couldn't deafen the pounding in her ears. She focused on her rhythmic breathing. If she ran fast enough, the jarring percussion of bare feet against compacting sand might numb the more acute pain in her heart. If she stayed focused on what lay in the distance, she wouldn't stumble over immediate obstacles.

Leila ran west, to the edge of Fire Island, and then doubled back to where she started. Near sunset, cool ocean air rolled in. She slowed to a jog, untied the long shirtsleeves from around her hips, and headed toward the dunes, slipping her arms into sleeves. Asphalt seared her feet, as she sprinted across the causeway. Sprays of sand twirled upward and danced around the parking lot. Most cars had exited. Her body buzzed with fatigue; sweet exhaustion that she hoped would yield deep, dreamless sleep.

Gulls overhead called out, guiding her to the pavement's far side. They dashed at discarded French fries beside her '67 Volkswagen Beetle—and its flat tire. If not for her bare feet, she would have given it a firm kick. At that moment, the sound of blues blared from a nearby car. She smiled at the irony of it, at how her otherwise dependable little car had done her wrong.

Everything would be exactly where she had placed it, the tire iron, the jack, and the spare, all tucked neatly in their places.

"You need a hand?"

It wasn't as if she hadn't noticed the approaching blues-playing car as she popped the front hood, but she ignored it, hoping she exuded a more-than-competent vibe.

She tugged the tire and grumbled, "Nope," without turning enough to get a look at the driver. "I got it."

The recording track changed.

"You sure?" he asked as the familiar blues riff grabbed her attention. "'Cause you're getting the front of your white shirt all black."

Intent on the song, she gave her shirt a dismissive glance as the tire teetered half-in and half-out of the trunk. She raised a brow in his direction and the words just slipped out—"That sounds sort of like 'Cross Road Blues,' but different."

"Yeah, it's called 'Crossroads'."

She turned just enough to note the make and color of his car. Two-door Saab. Dark green. Dented front fender. Cracked windshield. "Well, that sure isn't Robert Johnson."

He chuckled. "No, it's Clapton—Cream's version."

"Oh, right," she said, a little embarrassed that she hadn't deduced it on her own. "I guess I'm more familiar with the older stuff."

His brow rose and his mouth stayed agape. She had caught him off guard. That didn't keep him from pulling into the parking spot at her passenger side.

Crap! She let the tire hit the pavement. *That's what you get for talking to strangers.*

Music continued playing when he shut off the engine. She backed away from her trunk and again inspected the front of her shirt. One button hung by a thread. She yanked it and tucked it in her pocket.

Get a good look at him, in case you have to give the police a description.

He repositioned his cap visor toward the back. Hazel eyes flashed as he tucked a lock of dark, chin-length hair behind his ear. His straight nose looked as red as her thighs, and his square jaw, rough as sand. He appeared as sun-weary and disheveled as she did.

"It looks like you have everything under control," he said, "but why ruin your shirt? Let me just give you a hand."

Just remember, all men are pigs, her father had told her— like the warning that 'stoves are hot'—there was truth to it, but she had yet to test the extent to which it applied. Just the same, she did not intend to do any testing in an all-but-abandoned parking lot. And, she had little hope of employing her other dad's warning, often accompanied by a wink— *Whatever you do, don't flash those dimples,* as if she had any control over the way they graced her cheeks even when she spoke.

She sized him up. A little taller than her, maybe five-ten, but if she caught him off guard, she could implement a few practiced maneuvers and disarm him—at least bring him to his knees. After that, with a build like his, taking to flight would be her best bet. She felt more than confident of her ability to outrun him.

Rather than sidle past, she provided him ample room and positioned herself strategically behind his car—noted his license number—and watched. She had been around far more men than women in her seventeen years, and so she rarely paid particular attention to one man as being more handsome than another, though most had at least one appealing characteristic, if only a sweet singing voice. But the man changing her tire seemed a compilation of all the best features she had ever seen.

He lifted her tire without effort as she scanned his car's interior. On the back seat, a small Styrofoam ice chest lay atop worn upholstery. Beside it, a camera and long lens pushed back the flap of a professional-looking carrying case. No trash, but a carpenter's tape measure and several cassettes cluttered the dashboard and a few shavings amidst sawdust were visible through the hatchback. A pair of miniature sneakers hung from the rearview mirror. Harmless stuff. Nothing alarming.

"Are you visiting or just moved?" He snagged her attention.

"What?"

His jaw tipped toward her rear window. "Your dump permit—it hasn't expired."

Leila cringed. *Ridiculous oversight.*

He spun the tire iron. "We don't have dump decals around here. You must be from upstate or out of state."

"What—nobody likes dump picking on Long Island?"

"Well, I'm sure there's some pretty good pickin's out in the Hamptons, nicer beaches too. But then I would have to wonder what you're doing here." His playful grin twisted to a wince as his arm bulged with exertion over a stubborn nut. He looked back at her, waiting for a response.

She folded her arms. Her usual stance. "I moved to the Island a few weeks ago."

"Oh yeah? Where from?"

It seemed a harmless enough question. "New Hampshire."

"You don't sound like you're from N'Hampsha'." He winked, mimicking the distinct intonation of the state's natives.

A wash of optimism eroded a layer of caution. "You know New Hampshire?"

"Some. I went to school in Hanover for a little while."

"Dartmouth?"

"Yeah. But just for a semester."

"What did you study?"

The flat tire hit the ground. "Nothing I wanted to commit to."

If he were trying to impress her, he ought not mention that he had dropped out of such a prestigious institution. In fact, the way he went about changing her tire, without any puffed-up posturing, even the way he wore a loose-fitting T-shirt when something skintight would better show off his physique, argued against arrogance, self-absorption, or any intent to impress her. His whole demeanor bespoke modesty and a defiance of her father's warning. All the more reason to keep her guard up.

He rolled and lifted the spare into place and seemed content for a minute. She doubted that would end his conversational efforts.

Once he had the nuts back in place and tightened, he cast her a curious glance. Was he hoping she might take a little initiative? Leila tucked a wayward strand of chestnut hair back into her long braid and held her reticent ground. She could have come up with something clever to say but didn't want to encourage him. He smiled and nodded as if granting whatever made her comfortable. She doubted he would leave it at that. He did not disappoint.

"So, why did you move from beautiful New Hampshire to this rat race?"

She shrugged. "That is a big question. Why does anyone move from paradise to, well, whatever you want to call Long Island?"

He paused, as if giving her response weighty consideration.

"Family. Job .... Or lack of options," he said, flashing a glance that penetrated, even in its brevity.

"So, which was it?"

He stood, leaning the tire iron against the flat. "Lack of options. What about you?"

"Same thing."

"Then I guess we both come by the blues honestly."

"Well, honestly, the blues are all I've ever known."

"You're too young for that."

"I wish that were true." She unfolded her arms and reached for the tire iron.

He didn't push the issue. He simply deposited the flat and jack in the trunk.

"Got a rag?" he asked.

"Oh, yeah. Sorry," she said, joining him. "Here."

He wiped his hands and replaced the rag. "There's some really great jazz and blues clubs in the area. Have you been to any of them?"

She smiled at the memories he evoked. "Not recently."

"Well, there's a place down on Merrick Road, east of here, the Blues Basement." He repositioned his cap's visor. "They play a bunch of the old stuff with some new twists. It's pretty good. There's a lot of local talent that are regulars. You ought to check it out sometime."

"Didn't that used to be the Owl's Nest?"

He smiled at her mention of it. "Yeah, I think it was, right up till the last few years. A lot of the old guys have died out, but some of the new ones do a pretty good job."

"So, you like the newer renditions?"

A slow but full smile lit his face as he slipped his hands into his front pockets. His eyes flickered. "I like the old *and* the new."

They faced each other, each leaning against their own car. The sun dipped below the horizon, and seagulls called out as the music tape ran silent. Neither moved.

He didn't seem like a pig, though she didn't dare ignore the warning. Perhaps he just had a better handle on keeping his piggyness at bay when changing tires for stranded young ladies. Or perhaps he might be genuinely kind.

"It wouldn't have been much fun changing my tire with sunburn," she said. "Thanks for doing it for me."

"No problem."

A gull swooped, distracting them for a moment. When their eyes again met, neither moved. The only thing that stirred was her stray lock of hair. She drew in a long breath.

He spoke up. "Maybe, we could meet up at a club sometime?"

Her eyes shifted.

He rebounded. "Or whatever you might be comfortable with."

"That sounds like a lot of fun." She bit her lip. "But ... this just isn't a very good time for me."

"Okay," he said, as if it were all the same to him.

Rather than turning and climbing into her car, as she should, she looked at him as if she were formulating a further response. She said nothing.

He removed his hat, swept his hair back, and extended his hand. "I'm Ian."

She leaned into the formal introduction.

"Leila," she said, withdrawing quicker than she would have liked. "I've never met anyone named Ian."

"I've never met anyone named Leila."

"Well ... thanks again for the help."

"It was my pleasure," he said, but she didn't give him a chance to say anything more. She rounded her car and slipped into the front seat with keys in hand, feeling his stare. As she started the engine, he tapped her passenger window and then retreated to the front seat of his Saab as she cranked the handle. He returned with the cassette tape that had been playing.

"It's just a bunch of stuff I compiled. You might enjoy it," he said, handing it to her along with a business card. "Just in case a better time comes along."

She read the card. *Ian Brigham—Photographer-at-Large— Portraits & On Location Photography.* She grinned, thinking of her father. He used to call her 'Leila-at-Large.' She liked the coincidence.

CHAPTER 2

L EILA STRETCHED AS SHE SAT UP IN BED, SCANNING HER room. The business card tucked in the dresser mirror paused her attention. She padded over to the dresser and fingered the card without removing it. At least her trip to the beach had yielded something more than simply satisfying a ritual. No, nothing would come of her encounter with the man who had changed her tire, but she had forgotten how nice it was to make a little conversation with a grown man— that is, one with all his teeth.

She refocused to the reflection of her closed closet. Time to complete another ritual. In three steps, she opened the door, reached for the brass canister on the top shelf, and returned it to the dresser where it would spend another day. If it hadn't been for the urn's contents and all it represented, she might have plucked the card and made a phone call, but as it was, she glared at the square box of her father's remains. She lost track of how many times she had carried out the ash-scattering ritual over the past six months. Whenever she visited a new place, she unwrapped the ashes, made a deposit, and looked forward to the day when she would fulfill the least of her promises. The ritual was not the immediate burden; what to do with the urn of remaining ashes in the meantime presented her with an uncomfortable dilemma.

She didn't put much weight in theories of an afterlife, but since so many seemed convinced of it, she didn't think it safe to discard the idea entirely. In fact, it only became a concern each night before she climbed into bed. Uninterred human remains in the very same room, perhaps watching, contributed to her restless nights. Her discomfort had given birth to her nightly ritual—placing the canister in the closet in the evening and setting it back on her dresser each morning.

Leila straightened the urn and then turned her back on it, again scanning her room. This was where her father had slept when they lived here briefly about ten years ago. Her father's best friend—her other dad—Joe, used to sleep in the downstairs apartment with his dad, Artie. Leila hadn't minded the sofa. She had slept in so many places that anything better than blankets on the floor was bliss. Besides, she hadn't been the only one who'd had uncomfortable accommodations. Poor Joe, all six feet, three inches of him had to sleep on a cot in Artie's closet-sized spare room, competing with a lifetime collection of music memorabilia. But most of the time, Joe hung around in their upstairs apartment. Both Joe and Leila had complicated father-child relationships. Even now, Artie didn't hear from Joe a whole lot. Neither did she.

Leila dressed in shorts and a T-shirt. Twenty minutes later, after a quick cup of tea, she trotted down the enclosed, exterior staircase that emptied onto cracked concrete. Bright light filtered through her squint as morning humidity filled her lungs. Turning right, she followed a short path to her landlord's front door, although, in the strictest sense, Artie was not her landlord at all.

She tapped his front door as a formality, more of a courtesy, to warn the elderly man of her arrival as if he weren't already waiting.

"Good morning, Artie," she called. She would find him at the kitchen table with his cup of coffee and *Newsday*, as always.

"G'morning, Angel," he said, two rows of straight teeth securely in place and gleaming white against his black skin and peppered chin.

"Anything I can get you this morning?"

"You know I got everything I need," he said, same as every morning. "You just be careful and don't talk to none of them fools on the corner."

"Don't worry, I won't," she said, same as every morning. "I'll be back by eight."

In reality, hardly anyone hung out on the corner by the convenience mart at the hour Leila passed by, and after a short time, word had already spread that she was the white chick living over Artie's place, which meant she was hands-off. She wondered how many neighbors she would see in school come September. How many knew she played blues with a bunch of old men?

Although she started off slow, by the end of the street, concrete blurred beneath her feet. The air smelled bitter. Jogging in place, she waited for the light to turn and then continued on to the overpass. In a short distance, she quickened her pace, hoping to beat the tremulous clanking of the Long Island Rail Road. Of course it was safe to run beneath it, but all that thunderous weight above seemed a defiance of bad odds that always caught up. With the railway behind her, the next few blocks passed quickly.

Three miles south, at the fringes of Millville's lower village, mature hardwood trees canopied the streets, giving the neighborhoods a cooler feel than the newer, northern developments, but better than that, she disappeared into the whiteness of middle-class South Millville.

Turning a corner onto another shady lane, her pace slowed at a yard-sale sign. A small, wood-framed drawing table near the sidewalk stood out amidst household bric-a-brac. She stopped and ran her hand over it. Perhaps this table had made a difference in a former artist's work. She envisioned the patinated wood in the corner of her apartment—pictured herself sitting at it with her watercolors. Perhaps they would flow better upon such a serious and well-worn foundation.

"How much?" Leila asked.

The householder squinted. "You run past here every day."

"That's right."

"What's the tag say?"

"Says fifteen. Will you take eight?" Leila asked, now handling a pair of size-eight sneakers, lightly worn.

"I don't know ...."

Leila stroked the table again. "There wouldn't happen to be any art supplies that go along with this, would there?"

"Yeah, just behind it." The woman pointed to a shallow wooden case with brass latches.

Leila's heart leapt, beating faster than at a full run. She lifted the lid as if it were a treasure chest. At the sight that greeted her, she could have heard an angelic chorus. Tube after tube of Windsor Newton pigments lined up alongside a dozen or so half-pans of watercolors and a neat bundle of brushes—rounds, flats, fine point. She pulled one and held it to the light. Kolinsky sable. Putting on her best poker face, she prepared for a stare down.

"I'll give you fifteen if you throw in the box and the sneakers."

The woman smiled. "You paint, do you?"

Leila shrugged. "I try."

"You plan on carrying all that away right now?"

Leila pulled a small wad from her sock, peeled off five ones and another bill. "I'll give you ten now and five when I pick it up in an hour."

The woman's mouth twisted as Leila's gaze intensified. The woman flinched. "Deal."

Leila smiled all the way down the dead-end street. Perhaps her streak of bad luck had ended.

She slipped through a severed chain-link fence onto the Millville Memorial High School athletic field and track where she ran another two miles.

🌿CHAPTER 3

TWENTY MINUTES BEFORE SAM GOODY'S RECORD store closed for the night, Leila glanced at the clock as she restocked LP records. She worked as many hours as she could before September, when school started. Sure, more money came in handy, but if Ian happened to shop at the mall and ever came looking for more music, the long shifts increased her chances of seeing him. The fact that his card indicated he lived in Millville only heightened her hopes. On the other hand, she didn't need the complication of an older guy—or *any* guy. Besides, by the end of her long days, she was too tired to even entertain the thought of a real-life romance. Tonight was a case in point. She had worked a twelve-hour shift. Her eyes burned and her feet ached. She only wanted to go home and climb in bed—not cook a romantic dinner and pry some guy off her. Of course, that didn't mean she wouldn't indulge a fantasy, but even then, her fantasies culminated with imaginary conversations about art and life, not sex.

Leila grabbed another stack of LPs, monitoring the mall's dwindling traffic. Outside the store, a few giggling teenagers tripped past, followed by a brown-jacketed man. He slowed. *Oh, please keep walking.* She yawned and refocused on the jazz and blues titles, tucking one album behind the next. When she raised her eyes, brown corduroy headed down her aisle. *Terrific.* She nudged a heavy box aside, allowing the late shopper to pass. He did not. He hovered nearby, one hand tucked in his jeans pocket as the other flipped LP after LP to the front of the bin. He grumbled, rubbing his unshaven jaw. Frowning, he glanced at her. The sooner she offered assistance, the sooner he would be gone.

"May I help you find something?"

Between his brows, two permanent creases extended to his forehead. He folded his arms across his blazer and then removed his glasses to better glower as he read her nameplate.

"*Lee-lah*," he said, mispronouncing her name.

She sensed facetiousness and should have let his blunder ride. Instead, she smiled. "It's *Leila*, with a long A. Like the song."

As if catching a whiff of something unfamiliar, but not altogether repugnant, he flinched.

"Well, *Leila*," he repeated with irate emphasis. "It's obvious you don't carry Robert Johnson."

"Yes, I know. It's a shame really, that some of the lesser-known or short-lived artists kind of get overlooked." She cast a glance over her shoulder as if about to divulge top-secret information and said with some disgust, "We don't even stock Artie Sparks."

His ice-blue eyes squinted. "Oh, and I suppose you're Sam Goody's Delta blues expert, are you?"

His remark struck her as funny, though she sensed it best not to let on that she knew far more about any genre of blues than she cared to—more than any teenage girl ought to be burdened with.

She kept her smile pasted in place. "I'm just the new hireling, low-girl-on-the-totem-pole, so I suppose that makes me a blues expert of sorts."

He squinted harder and let out a snort. The bridge of his nose disappeared into an ominous hedge of eyebrow. His pale eyes gathered swirls of stormy gray. Her confidence and smile thinned as he towered over her.

"I'd be happy to put in a special order for some Robert Johnson," she said, turning toward the checkout before he could shoot a rebuke. "It would be here by Friday."

"Fine, then. Do it." He turned and headed toward the exit.

"I just need your name and phone number," she called out after him.

"Don't worry. I'll be back." His words landed like a threat.

Leila submitted the order, fabricating a name and phone number. Just for good measure, she ordered whatever else Robert Johnson had released. Even if her cranky customer never returned, Johnson should have his rightful place amongst his peers.

On Friday, when the tall, disgruntled man returned, asking for her by name, Leila retrieved the albums and he purchased them all.

"Thank you," he said with his usual scowl. He did not have altogether unappealing features for a middle-aged man, though if he smiled occasionally he might even be handsome, sort of the way Vincent Price—host of *Creature Features*—might be considered handsome in real life.

Leila hoped never to lay eyes on Disgruntled Man again. Unfortunately, he returned week after week, asking for her by name. He no longer mispronounced it, but that was poor compensation for speaking in little more than grunts and snorts. She wished he would ignore her, but the way he focused on her—on searching out her eyes—demanded her attention and creeped her out. If he was trying to intimidate her, she would not back down. She had learned that much from her father. "It's all in the eyes," he would say, "if you look away, you lose." She had even practiced the arch of her father's brow, just for effect. The ambiguity of a polite smile was her own twist.

More times than not, she had to place a special order, doing so under his assigned pseudonym, Farty Limburger. She never bothered to ask for his real name. In fact, she found him more tolerable with his ridiculous alias. Ornery as he was, at least he broke up the monotony of her routine. Their encounters usually ended in a standoff; his stare devolving to a glare while her polite, unyielding eyes smiled. The day she presented him an out-of-production Artie Sparks album, an almost-smile chinked his curmudgeonly armor.

CHAPTER 4

*P*IANO *SCALES UNDULATING FROM ROOMS WITH doors that shut, leaving Leila in a crowded hall where faceless bodies swirl around her. A voice from behind. Half-clothed and disoriented, she spins in a vacuum of white light and wakes in a sweat, her heart charged with panic.*

That dream—not quite a nightmare until the end—recurred during the early morning before Leila's first day of school. She half-expected it, even though she had prepared everything ahead of time, from transferring school records, to acquiring her class schedule, and making arrangements to shower in the gym locker room after her run to school. Even with all the anxiety of attending a new school, the classroom setting and school routine had become a stabilizer in her otherwise unpredictable life. As much as she wished to be free of it, she craved its framework.

Leila rolled out of bed. In two steps she entered her living room and passed her small sofa. Three more steps landed her in front of her efficiency range. Ten minutes later and sipping tea, she stood in front of the large window above the table overlooking Artie's front yard. In another five minutes, she dressed and twisted her hair into a knot, securing it with a bamboo chopstick. She then checked off her list: brush teeth, stock backpack—notebooks, lunch, clean towel and change of clothes. Counting off each step down the stairway to

Artie's apartment, she continued her morning routine.

With asphalt underfoot, she picked up her pace, slipping into an altered state, a place where physical exertion—pain, even—displaced her emotional torments. Distance was her goal, not speed. Distance between her and some thing—some obscure shadow that took on the face of doctors, nurses, and hospice workers, the intrusive teachers and well-intentioned busybodies. Leila knew nothing of endorphins, neither was she swayed by self-help rhetoric and anti-drug advocates. She only knew running eased the pain, if not masked it altogether.

As Leila rounded the high school track a final time, her life gradually caught up. Her pounding heart had little to do with exertion. Despite all her preparations, apprehension rushed in as she snatched her backpack from the bleacher. She sucked in confidence as she hurried toward the building and pushed through double doors to the back corridor, and then entered the dark alcove at the back of the gym.

In an adjoining glassed-in cubicle-of-an-office, Ms. Thorpe, head of the phys ed department, leaned against her metal desk, twirling a whistle on a lanyard. Her official red-and-gray athletic attire expanded to their limit, clinging like plastic wrap but without a hint of cellulite. When she stood erect, nothing jiggled. Even the *Warriors* insignia that stretched and distorted across her voluminous bust dared not joust. So much woman packed into barely five feet.

Thorpe stepped into the doorway, consuming most of it. Her black skin merged into the shadow of a silhouette. "Make sure you clean up after yourself."

"Yes, Ma'am." Leila slipped into the locker room.

She arranged her clean underwear on the bench and hung a plain blouse inside the locker. Re-securing the bun atop of her head, she stepped into the stream of hot water. Gym shower stalls were all alike. Small monochromatic tiles. A white curtain separated her from all the uncertainties outside. Her lily-of-the-valley-scented soap mingled with the antiseptic odor of bleach, until its floral aroma permeated her shower stall. It reminded her of running in New Hampshire, of shaded roadside patches where the dainty flower grew.

As she stepped out, the scent trailed. With time to spare, Leila dried, dressed, and extracted the stick from her hair that unfurled to her waist. She brushed the thick handful back and twisted it up and behind into a knot, then reinserted the stick. Giving her padlock a spin, she checked her watch. No hurry.

Intent on making a good impression, she veered toward the office and poked her head inside.

"Thank you again for letting me come in early to use the shower," she said.

"You're welcome."

At first, Leila didn't notice the person standing at the back corner of the office, at a door adjoining another room. In fact, she might not have noticed him at all if he hadn't shifted his weight. With that one quiet motion, he caught her eye. He wore his hair in a ponytail with no hat, but it was him—the man who had changed her tire.

"Leila Sanders, this is our track coach, Coach Brigham," Thorpe said.

Leila's heart pounded.

Ian Brigham's mouth opened and then closed as his complexion drained color. His eyes darted. He offered only a nod.

"Hi," she said.

He tensed, returning a neutral, "Hello."

Both glanced at Thorpe who appeared oblivious to their conflict, which had in seconds mounted to unbearable.

"Well, I gotta run," Leila blurted and turned away. She glanced back at Ian through the glass-encased cubicle. He looked as if he had just been slapped in the face.

❧ CAUGHT IN THE GIRL'S GAZE, IAN BRIGHAM STOOD dumbfounded. He wanted to acknowledge their acquaintance but couldn't. Heck, he could scarcely look her in the eye, let alone own up to having hit on a seventeen-year-old. As his metabolism stabilized, every implication of Leila's presence rushed at him.

Ever since he changed her tire, Ian had hoped to see her again, which was unlike him—a date that didn't pan out was forgotten. Yet, he had even frequented the Blues Basement on the chance she might show up. Likely, she would have remembered him, though he didn't take that for granted. And yet now, there she was, walking away after fully recognizing him. In some prolonged sleight of time and motion, a summer's worth of fantasy exited through the double doors into the corridor.

Thorpe and her assistant, Karen Weiss had talked about the 'Girl Runner,' but it never occurred to him to ask her name. Even a little forewarning would have gone a long way in mitigating some of the awkwardness. At least he could have acknowledged Leila in a more dignified way.

Thorpe interrupted his musing. "So, what do you think of her?"

It took a moment to process her question. "You say she runs every day?"

"To and from school."

Karen Weiss entered the office, saying, "I suppose that was her. What do you think, Ian?"

He knew Karen well enough to measure his response. "Until I see her run, it's hard to say."

"She has the right build, even better than Miranda. Perhaps this will be the year," Weiss said.

"We'll see." Brigham slipped into the boys' office adjoining Thorpe's. Weiss followed as he yanked his chair and sat.

"I've been waiting three years for this," Karen said, leaning against his desk, her tanned thigh only inches away. "The girls need a team of their own."

"Please don't quote the federal statute again, Karen. You're preaching to the choir. You think I want a repeat of last year?"

"Miranda was your best runner."

"She wasn't our best, but I'll grant you, she was good—

besides, you know that wasn't the concern. I simply don't want to expend more energy on the gender issue than on drills and meets."

Karen huffed. "It's no longer a matter of allowing girls to play on a boys' team. It's a matter of the school board finally funding a separate girls' team."

"You're barking up the wrong tree, Karen," Ian said, scooting his chair away from her. "It's Thorpe's husband who's on the school board. Go hound her."

"You are simply no fun at work, Ian," she said, nudging her calf against his bare knee as she peeked out the door. She stood and then leaned over him, whispering, "Are we still on for tonight?"

"Um, sure," he said, already uncertain about exactly why they had rekindled the relationship after a summer-long reprieve. He had assumed it would feel as comfortable as slipping into an old T-shirt, but it didn't fit the way he remembered. It occurred to him that perhaps they never 'fit' in the first place. In fact, by the time June had rolled around at the end of the last school year, Karen had cooled things off. Just before she left for vacation in Connecticut, she had suggested they date others over the summer. Ian supposed she already had someone else in mind. He told her it didn't matter, though perhaps it bothered him more than he had anticipated. She left a void—he couldn't deny that. And he did like her most of the time, even if her eyes glazed over at the mention of art or photography. Of course, it didn't hurt that she was cute, nicely built, and wore her shorts short, not to mention she was also daring, fun loving, and energetic in bed. Yet the superficiality that once seemed good enough now left him empty. Besides that, he could never convince her that an evening at the Blues Basement constituted a good time.

As soon as Karen left, Ian stretched back in his chair and nudged his office door shut. The one person occupying his thoughts more than he cared to admit had just walked out of the gym on her way to homeroom. How could he have so grossly miscalculated Leila's age? Not that she looked even close to her mid-twenties, but she sure didn't carry herself like the typical seventeen- or eighteen-year-old. And of all things, she was a new student at Millville Memorial High School.

🌿CHAPTER 5

A S SOON AS LEILA STEPPED INTO THE HALL, HER recurring dream came rushing in—swarms of faceless bodies darting at her, spinning her around until she lost any sense of direction. All she could think of was Ian Brigham.

Even though their first encounter had been brief, she hated that she hadn't been able to stop thinking about him. She wasn't like those other boy-crazy girls who fell for every cute guy that came along. Guys did not impress Leila. They provided the illusion of stability, like a rickety chair—useful to an extent but unreliable. She would rather stand. Yet meeting Ian had tricked her into hoping, or at least into imagining.

The one man she dared build a fantasy around—painting him into her imaginary life-by-the-lake, complete with photography and art studios in a quaint cottage—had sneaked his way in the backdoor and stood just out of reach. He now fit the category of another recurring dream; someone—some vaguely significant person—always beyond her grasp. Her body throbbed and heated with embarrassment, excitement, and even shame—she didn't have time to over analyze why. That would have to wait.

Bumping shoulders and elbows as she pushed her way through the crowd, Leila squinted at her crumpled schedule. Laughter punctuated the murmur of voices, fading as the halls cleared. Following a few stragglers, she bounded up the stairway. Not until she had run the length of the second story did she realize she had taken a wrong turn. She spun as the bell clamored. Her sneakers chirped against the polished floors as she sprinted to the opposite end of the long corridor, where light from a distant window reflected off the floor, dimming everything around it. Panting, she neared the open door of Mr. Myles' homeroom to the sound of an alphabetic recitation. Adrenaline shot to her fingertips.

"... Rabinowitz. Rodriguez. Ryan. Sanchez. Sanders— *Sanders*—"

Leila cringed at her name. Students froze in morbid silence like no other homeroom she had ever attended. All eyes shifted to her and back to Mr. Myles.

A face smiled from a seat in the row nearest the door. The front and corner desk in front of him remained unoccupied. The boy gestured, mouthing, "*Sanders*?"

Leila slipped into the corner chair, catching a glimpse of her teacher's profile as he turned away, facing the long row of windows. Her stomach turned as he stiffened and drew in a deep, stuttering breath. He continued roll call, his grumbling voice prickling her skin. "Schultz. Sterns. Stilwell ...," and finished up with, "Tanner, Thompson, and Trombley."

He clapped the roll-call book shut and spun around. Before she even saw his face, she recognized her Sam Goody customer from hell.

He paced along the windowed side of the room, his tennis shoes silencing his steps as he moved from the front of the room to the back and again to his desk. He did not spare any of the drama she had grown accustomed to. For a paycheck she tolerated him, but the balance now shifted. As he skulked toward her, she struggled to bring her sight to his. *If you look away, you lose.*

He stood before her, eyes brimming with disapproval, stolid and icy as ever.

"You're a *newcomer* and a *late* one, at that!"

Leila shifted to sit erect and maintained her gaze.

"No one shows up late to my classroom. Perhaps you

didn't realize that, Miss *Leila* Sanders," he said, emphasizing her first name with recognition.

Despite her thumping chest, Leila didn't flinch or squirm. "It's not my custom to be late, Mr. Li—" Limburger nearly slipped from her lips. She corrected, "*Myles*," unintentionally emphasizing his name, the way he had hers.

His eyes widened and then squinted as if they might spew flames. "There are *consequences* to being late to my classroom, Miss Sanders! Do you understand what that means?"

"I'm sure it means I'll pay for this in ways I can't even imagine."

His brow rose a mere fraction and with it, the corner of his mouth. A distinct frown reversed his almost-smile. "Be careful, Miss Sanders. As any of your classmates will inform you, you are not off to a good start."

As he walked back to his desk, she quaked from her core to every fiber of her clothes.

Myles announced, "Complete these contact cards and pass them to the front." He placed a stack on each first desk and lingered at Leila's before slapping it in front of her. He then returned to his desk and buried himself behind his *Rolling Stone* magazine.

Leila had done this dozens of times. It should have been straightforward and simple, but her hands sweat.

Last name. First name. Address. She quickly filled in the blanks.

Date of Birth: *May 3, 1960*

Phone number: *None*

Father: *Marcus Billings*. Oops … Erased *Billings* and rewrote—*Sanders*.

Father's Address: She sighed. *Same*.

Mother: Marilyn Sanders

Mother's Address: She fidgeted with the pencil, *Unknown*
Guardian: —

Emergency contact: Leila began writing *Artie Sparks*, but on second thought, Myles would recognize the name and think she was being insolent. With vigor, she erased Artie and rewrote *Arthur Spartan*, his legal name. Her animation drew Myles' attention. As he rose, he kept his eyes set upon her and began collecting cards from the front row.

He towered over the desk of each front-row student as Leila tucked her card under the pile. When he reached her desk, she kept her sights straight ahead at his oxford shirt beneath his corduroy jacket. As she placed the stack in Myles' outstretched hand, she met his eyes. The fluorescent bulbs blanched his high cheekbones and highlighted the streaked-gray hair that curled behind his ears. His receding hairline seemed consistent with a man in his fifties. Was his clean-shaven face simply a pretense of good grooming meant to impress on the first day of school?

Glaring back, he positioned her card at reading-glasses level, telescoping it to arm's length.

"Leila … Sanders …."

She held her breath. Just then, a perky girl appeared in the doorway. "I'm here to pick up the record cards for the office."

Myles frowned. "Just in time to suck all the fun out of that!"

He shoved the cards at the girl.

"Next on the agenda—locker assignments. As seniors, you are entitled to your very own locker this year. Unfortunately, too many parents in your community chose to procreate in 1960. Therefore, we have a locker shortage and two of you will have to share. The question is, which wretched souls will forfeit their long-awaited privacy?"

Again, he approached his morning target. Inhaling courage, Leila met his stare with a raised brow and cocked her head. A sinister smile curled his lips as he tore a paper in two and slapped one half on Leila's desk and the other on the boy's desk behind her. "And I don't want to hear any whining."

He then moved on to Sterns and Stilwell.

The bell rang. The good news was that homeroom had ended. The bad news was her first class, trigonometry, was with Mr. Myles.

Leila followed the sandy-haired boy to their shared locker.

He fumbled with the combination. "They say he's an acquired taste, but *I* don't know anyone who's acquired it."

She forced a smile, looking up from his Jethro Tull T-shirt to his face.

He grinned. "I thought for sure we were going to see a massacre on the first day of school. Man, you have no idea what you walked into—don't no one come into *any* of his classes late."

"He's just a big bag of wind."

"Sure he is, but he's the kind of wind that can make your life hell. Don't you see? He's going to have it in for you for the rest of the year. The last kid he targeted ended up pissing his pants right in class."

Leila rolled her eyes. "Great."

"Oh, in case you didn't know, I'm Kyle—you know, Schultz, behind you."

"Yeah, I'm Leila."

"Huh. Leila—like the Clapton song?"

"It's spelled different."

He shook his head. "You're definitely new here."

"More or less."

He squinted. "You run past my house every day."

She shrugged. "Maybe."

"Huh." He shut the locker. Neither of them had deposited anything. "Well, it's back to Mr. Myles again."

He rolled his eyes and grinned. One corner of his mouth curled up and the other curled down. He had a boyish face. If he hadn't been so tall, she might have mistaken him for a freshman.

"Fortunately," he continued, "after math, I won't have to see him again until tomorrow."

A petite and pretty girl with blond, Farrah Fawcett hair came up behind him, slipping her arms around his waist.

He turned and kissed her quickly. "You'll make me late!"

The girl glanced at her.

"This is Leila. She's new. This is Maryanne."

"His *girlfriend*." She looked Leila up and down, raising an unimpressed brow. "Where are you from?"

"New Hampshire."

She smirked. "I guess so."

"Well, gotta run," Leila said.

Kyle kissed Maryanne and pushed her away. "Seriously Annie, you're going to make me late."

When Leila reentered the class on time, Mr. Myles scowled. "*You …,*" he exhaled with disdain and then returned to his reading.

His seat assignment landed her at the exact desk she had claimed in homeroom with Schultz again behind her.

"Welcome to trigonometry," Myles stated and began to scratch out formulas on the blackboard.

While keeping her guard up, Leila copied numbers and letters that made no sense. She had barely passed geometry and even now had trouble remembering any of it.

After a minute, Kyle's breath tickled the back of her neck as he whispered, "What would happen if I pulled that chop stick out of your hair?"

Myles flinched. His head cocked and his scribbling paused. Leila's eyes widened.

Mr. Myles whirled around and braced himself against his desk as if restraining a full-blown tantrum. "Yes, Miss *Leila* Sanders, we'd *all* like to know what would happen if Mr. Schultz pulled that chopstick from your hair."

She blinked. *He can't be serious.*

He grabbed a wooden ruler and slapped it against his palm. "Well, Miss Sanders? Answer the question!"

She cleared her throat. "Well, sir, I'd have to injure Mr. Shultz with it. You'd confiscate it because I used it as a weapon. I'd be sent to the office and possibly suspended." She paused. "At the very least, I'd have no way to eat my lunch."

A glint shot from Myles eyes—the same she had seen at the store—a begrudging sanction of her wit, though she doubted he meant to let on.

He came to the front of her desk and tilted his head.

"So, you *do* understand how things work, Miss Sanders."

He walked past her to Kyle's side.

Myles' ruler snapped against the desk. "Is this how it's going to be, Schulz?"

"No sir, I'm sorry. It won't happen again."

🦋 A YOUNG WOMAN WEARING A LONG DENIM SKIRT and gauzy peasant blouse greeted Leila at her classroom door, pressing her palms together and bowing in guru fashion. "Welcome."

Leila averted her eyes, making her way to an obscure seat in the far corner.

After the bell rang, Miss Michaels drew in a cleansing breath and smiled. "Good morning, my fellow artists and creative spirits."

A boy, sitting in front of Leila, toked an imaginary joint and passed it to his snickering friend.

With the grace of a ballerina, Miss Michaels distributed sketch tablets from student to student, her long skirt floating behind. "You probably noticed the wine bottle, softball, and Kleenex box on the table in the middle of the room. Today, I just want you to sketch what you see. There is no right or wrong interpretation."

Leila eyed the objects, comparing their relative angles. If only she were as good at interpreting mathematical abstractions of angles as she was at visually sizing them up and transferring them to paper. By the time she had turned twelve years old, Leila had mastered the cylindrical bend of beer cans and bottles, the disk shape of lounge tables, and cubic angles of amplifiers and keyboards. Her favorite was the freestyle curvature of an open, empty guitar case. If nothing else was available, she always had her left hand or a foot or the figures and faces of those surrounding her, those in her father's blues band.

She liked sketching, but she loved painting. Running provided inspiration for painting—as opposed to simply sketching. Early morning transits offered long shadows, contrasting vibrant light, and rich color. Yet, as much as she loved painting, she struggled with it. Oils and acrylic weighted her brush and congealed like Elmer's glue, but watercolors, for as much as they defeated her attempts at getting them under control, begged her persistence. She had hoped that being free to pursue painting, rather than piano lessons, would bring better results. To an extent, it had, but her slow going brought frustration.

Leila's pencil took over as her mind buzzed. Miss Michaels hovered from one pupil to the next as she made her rounds toward the back of the classroom. As Miss Michaels approached, Leila covered her work.

"May I?" the teacher asked.

With hesitation, Leila revealed her drawing—not so much a sketch as a precise depiction of the objects on the table.

"Very nice, Leila," she whispered. "My, but you certainly do get carried away with details."

That was an understatement.

LEILA SAT ON THE TOP BLEACHER, TUCKED AWAY from the breeze and read over her math homework. With all the stress of trigonometry—the formulas and the teacher—she could never catch up with all the abstract concepts, let alone keep up. And this was just day one. Her last semester in New Hampshire was a blur, and math had always been a jumble of numbers. Her only recourse was to study and study hard. She bit into her peanut butter and jelly sandwich, cramming as much math as she could for the remainder of her lunch session.

An irregular stream of boys distracted her. Taking to the track, they jogged counterclockwise, followed by Coach Brigham. She sat up straight, her pulse in her ears as he laid his clipboard on the bench and turned toward his students.

The boys progressed around the track. Some jogged side by side. Few seemed to be exerting themselves. Kyle, the front runner, passed each jogger in the sporadic line. He seemed to be the only one running. All the others moved along at a sloppy trot.

As she studied Kyle's body—the consistent way his muscles contracted and released, the way his head held a fixed gaze—she pulled the drawing pad from her bag. Sketching, she tried to capture movement.

As Kyle rounded the curve, Coach Brigham came up alongside him. The other boys relinquished the track, letting the two runners pass. Kyle and his coach ran in unison, their gait synchronized as they exchanged a few words. Within a few strides their cadence fell and rose to their own tempo.

For the next half lap, Leila sat, mesmerized. Although taller with an athletic build, Kyle contrasted boyishly with Ian and his well-developed upper physique. Yet Brigham's thigh and calf muscles were compact and wiry, compared to the thick, long and powerful-looking legs carrying Kyle. As they completed their first lap, Brigham veered off and slowed to a jog. As he passed the bench, he inhaled. The arch of his back straightened as his line of sight met Leila. Her chin rose with acknowledgment. It was futile to avoid him, but she didn't look forward to another awkward encounter.

The outside warning bell rang. Leila packed up and came down from the bleachers ahead of the gym class. Coach Brigham lagged behind. The boys began their procession back toward the locker room, each passing Leila, one by one. Last in the lineup, Kyle came up alongside her, panting.

"Hey," he said, shyer than before.

"Hi, Kyle."

"Listen, I'm sorry for kind of getting you in trouble with Myles. I didn't mean anything by it."

"Don't sweat it. Besides, I don't really think it was me who was in trouble. What are you, one of his worst students or something?"

"No—actually, I'm probably his best. He hates handing out an A, so I'm pretty much at the top of his blacklist."

"How long has that been going on?"

"Since I was a freshman."

"So what am I? A new way to keep you in line?"

Kyle shrugged.

"Yeah, well, keep me out of it, if you don't mind."

His pace faltered. "I said I was sorry."

"It's okay, I just don't like getting off to a bad start."

He began jogging backwards. "So, we're cool?"

She offered a smile. "Sure."

"See ya 'round." Kyle broke back into a full jog toward the gym.

🌿 LEILA HEADED TO THE ONE CLASS THAT RANKED worse than math. Phys ed. Why did gym teachers always assume that "runner" meant "athlete"—that physically fit meant coordinated? Taking her time as she strolled the corridor leading to the gym lobby, she paused at the sight of black-and-white photographs hanging at eye level.

Many of the photos depicted intense moments of athletic victory and disappointment. The portrayal of students in unguarded interactions at school events impressed her, not only in their candor but their composition. She had been reading up on basic design and the arrangement of subjects in art. The photos executed the principles with creativity. Ian Brigham's signature did not surprise her. If only they could spend time, sharing their creative interests. She shuffled off to gym class only to encounter more frustration.

Whacking a tennis ball around the court was a waste of time and a pointless display of Leila's incoordination. She may have been able to run, but she could not hit a ball of any sort, with any device. If it required synchronizing with someone else, it was even worse. When that someone was a popular girl—Maryanne to be specific—it could not get any worse. Unless she had a spectator.

Ms. Thorpe shook her head as Leila made contact with one ball in ten. At first, Maryanne smiled but soon cringed every time Leila swung at the ball and missed. With pleading gestures, Maryanne appealed to Ms. Thorpe.

Miss Weiss intervened. "No, no! Like this—" she said, relieving Leila of her racket.

Contentedly, Leila watched as Weiss served and

Maryanne returned an impressive volley. They played for a few minutes, and then Coach Brigham came off the track field just before the warning bell. Miss Weiss arched her back, delivering a showy serve and smiled at Ian.

🐚 BRIGHAM RETREATED TO HIS OFFICE WHILE THE last-period students changed in their locker rooms. He overheard Karen Weiss and Thorpe debating in the girls' cubicle.

"… She may not have large-motor coordination—" Thorpe asserted.

Weiss interrupted, "You mean she's a spaz."

"—but given the fact that she runs everyday, she must have amazing endurance," Thorpe said and then called out, "What's more important Brigham—conditioning and endurance, or coordination?"

He did not want to weigh in with any opinion on Leila, but they likely wouldn't relent. "C'mon, you know both are required."

"That's right," Thorpe said with satisfaction, redirecting her comments to Weiss. "If there's an inherent strength, coordination can be trained if it's due to a lack of confidence. I think that's her only problem."

In fact, Leila could run. Ian had seen that himself. He photographed many people on the beach back in July, but not until he later developed the film did he realize one of them had been her. She had style and grace worthy of the lens, but he hadn't clocked her. That, however, was not his lament. It wasn't as if he needed the entire day to come to the proper conclusion. He already knew the stance he needed to take. If only he felt more resolved. He had a hard time considering her as just another silly teenage student, like so many "teenyboppers" that Thorpe teased him about. They were cute kids honing their newfound flirting skills. He understood adolescence and respected the girls. None of them had ever posed any temptation—until Leila. He would stay in his office, hoping to avoid her at least until tomorrow.

Thorpe called out. "Leila, step on in here."

"Ma'am?"

"What does your knapsack weigh? About five pounds?"

"I don't know."

"Drop that thing on the scale over here." Thorpe beckoned, "Brigham, check this out."

Ian braced himself for the sight of Leila as he stepped into the adjoining doorway. As Thorpe pushed the counterbalance further and further over, Leila looked him in the face, as if inviting acknowledgment of more than just a first-day-at-school acquaintance. He could return only a faint smile.

He glanced at her backpack. It tipped eleven pounds.

"My lord," Thorpe said, "I'd hate to be a bug on the sidewalk you run home on! What on earth do have in there?"

"Homework. Mostly math stuff."

Weiss leaned to double-check the weight, shrugging it off as if it were of no account.

"And look at those spindly things!" Thorpe said, pointing at her legs. Although she wore modest athletic shorts, Leila pressed her knees together. Her hands dropped to her thighs as she glanced at her lower body.

Brigham couldn't help comparing Weiss' tan, muscular, and well-defined legs to the relaxed taper of Leila's thighs as they curved into her calves. They didn't look at all spindly to him, not there in the gym office and certainly not on that July afternoon, in her short cutoffs. If the sight of Leila in front of him didn't now bring a flush to his face, the vivid memory did. He glanced at Karen who could read his attraction all too well. Her jealousy showed on her pinched face.

Leila blushed as she hoisted her bag and slung it over her shoulder.

"Gotta run." Leila gave him a disappointed look and then disappeared into the corridor.

Chapter 6

CLARENCE MYLES UNFOLDED HIS *ROLLING STONE* magazine, letting out a snort. Elvis Presley was not a month dead, but already Myles found the media coverage annoying, and now the King had invaded yet another magazine cover. He wasn't sure why he even bothered with the subscription these days—though the sheer width of the paper provided an effective shield when he wished for solitude during those few minutes before and after students filed in for homeroom. He glanced at his watch. Ten blissful, tranquil minutes remained.

His coffee cup steamed as he brought it behind the paper and to his lips. The closed door clicked, drawing his attention. He adjusted his glasses and peered over his magazine at Miss Leila Sanders. For all of his posturing yesterday, she was an unexpected twist to his pre-class morning. Most of his students were standard issue, but there was something about Leila. He had a few favorites, though he prided himself on not letting on. Given her propensity for subtly challenging him, he would have to be extra vigilant. It wasn't that her countenance was insolent so much as unimpressed—which was exactly what impressed him and exactly why his stern posture must not waver.

Without acknowledging his frown, she claimed her seat and pulled out her trigonometry textbook.

"Homework is supposed to be done at home," he grumbled.

"It's not homework. I'm just brushing up before class."

"Trying to impress me, are you?"

"I don't care about impressing you."

He scrutinized her demeanor. She had attitude, but he didn't sense disrespect. Just the same, he retorted, "You should care about impressing me."

"Well, I don't."

"Then I expect you'll be my worst student."

"And I expect you'll be my worst teacher."

"The most hated perhaps, but make no mistake—I'll be the best teacher you've ever had."

Apparently still unimpressed, she continued her stare long enough to make her point before returning to her textbook.

Even after students filed in and her face was one of the many avoiding his notice, he caught her indulging a furtive peek. Their eyes locked. He forced a sneer and looked away. When homeroom ended all but Leila cleared the room.

Myles pushed back into his seat, folding his arms across his chest and squinted. "Don't you have some girly thing to do in the hallway or restroom?"

"No."

He again adjusted his glasses for effect. "You are encroaching on my private time."

Leila frowned, but didn't budge.

He raised his voice. "Join your fellow urchins in the hallway!"

Leila rose, meeting his cautionary stare as she laggardly resigned herself to the hall, like an errant child defying a stern parent, testing his follow through.

This one will be an interesting challenge—I like her.

AFTER LEILA'S LAST-PERIOD STUDY HALL, SHE POKED her head into the gym office. Ms. Thorpe was not in her usual place, neither was Miss Weiss anywhere around. Leila stepped inside, passed the desk and a bag of volleyballs beside the adjoining closed door and read the plaque—Boys Office. She straightened her back and tapped.

"It's open."

Leila cracked the door. Ian stretched back in his chair, hands behind his hatless head. He glanced at her, did a double take and sat erect.

"Leila," he said in a quick exhalation.

"Sorry. Is this a good time?"

"Uh … yeah." He came to his feet, his complexion washed out under the florescent lights.

She stepped inside. "I mean, will we have a little privacy?"

His eyes darted. She hoped the distance she kept between them would put him at ease. With a nod, he leaned against the desk, his arms across his chest.

"Yeah," he said, "I was hoping we could talk."

She closed the door most of the way, leaving it ajar. As he took a breath, Leila took the initiative.

"I really wanted to call you this summer …."

"Leila—"

"Let me finish. After that whole awkward thing yesterday morning, I sort of wish I had called. It probably wouldn't have taken us long to figure out I was going to be a student here. I guess then we could have avoided all that—"

"Leila," he cut in again, drawing an unsteady breath. "I owe you an apology. I was honestly under the impression you were older—I mean, the car, the nightclub thing—the blues—you just didn't fit the teen profile. If I thought you were underage or in high school I never would have asked you out."

If he meant to defuse the situation, his eyes pleaded contrary to his words.

"I can see where I might have given you the wrong impression," she said.

He shifted, a flush coloring his face.

She continued, "If I had known that you—"

At that moment, in their tentativeness, the door swung open. Karen Weiss glanced at Leila with wide then narrowing eyes, reserving the raised brow for Ian. "Am I interrupting something?"

"No," Ian said. "We were just talking—"

"Oh yes." Weiss zoomed in on Leila. "How is our little runner? Has Coach Brigham been encouraging you to try out for track?"

Leila shot a look at Brigham. "Track?"

"You know," Weiss continued, "it's never too early to start training."

Leila cocked her head. She hadn't considered that Coach Brigham might have had some other agenda. "Actually, he hadn't quite got to that yet."

"Really?" Weiss cast dubious eyes at Brigham. "Well, you really should try out. And don't let the fact that it's an all-boy team put you off. We'll never get a girls' team unless more girls show an interest." With a challenging tone, Weiss continued, "You might have heard we had a girl on the team last year. Miranda did very well, and I'm sure there'll be even more schools that will allow you to compete this year."

Taken aback, Leila directed her dismay at both Brigham and Weiss. "You think I'm interested in the track team?"

"Why wouldn't you be interested? You're a runner." Weiss said.

"Running and being a part of a team are entirely different."

Weiss smirked. "Perhaps you're just afraid you're not good enough."

Ian interrupted, "She runs every day. Of course she's good enough."

Leila flashed scorn. "Okay, what neither of you seems to understand is that I don't care whether I'm good enough."

The two coaches exchanged confounded looks.

"I don't have time for this," Leila said, giving Ian a final disappointed glare and left.

ON THE LAST LEG OF LEILA'S RETURN RUN FROM school, she rounded her street corner, slowing from a jog to a walk. A concrete path split Artie's yard and led her to the front stoop where she deposited her backpack before stepping into his apartment.

"Hi, Artie …," she called out.

"Afta'noon, Angel," he responded in his southern drawl.

She leaned against the kitchen doorway and smiled. "You need anything before I start my homework?"

"Nope, I'm all set."

"You sure?"

"Yes, ma'am."

"Then, I'll check back before I head off to work, okay?"

"That'd be fine ...."

Leila planted a kiss on his bristly black head. Letting the screen door slam behind her, she grabbed her pack and rounded the corner to the stairway. She opened her mailbox affixed to asbestos siding and snatched a postcard from Amsterdam.

"Joe ...." She hustled up the stairs, forgetting to count off each step. As she entered her living room, light from the kitchen spilled from the front window, illuminating the words.

She smiled. "Miss you too, Joe—" and repressed a burning, teary-eyed sensation.

Gulping a glass of water, she headed to her bedroom and eyed the box of ashes from several angles. She shifted it as if to align it more perfectly. From behind it, she plucked Ian's business card and read it for the hundredth time. One phone call and perhaps she could have finally had a friend—too late for that. Besides, men didn't like to stay "just friends." She had seen that over and over again, all through her growing-up years.

A 'friend' would show up to watch her father's band practice, but as soon as the lady had left for the night, Leila heard all the talk about how she'd get laid within a week. It usually took only days—sometimes that very night, and Leila only knew that because of all the innuendo, if not outright details, the following day. Her dad and Joe were no exceptions, but they'd had a rule against bringing women home. Had they honestly thought she didn't know why one of them wouldn't come home some nights? She may not have caught on at seven years old, and she hadn't quite understood by nine, but by eleven, she had a pretty good idea that it had something to do with sex—even if at that age the concept was vague.

Leila tucked Ian's card back in the mirror. She returned to the kitchen and emptied her pile of books onto the table. This year, it seemed her workload and the sheer weight of books had doubled. Having eighth-period study hall three days a week would help. If only she didn't have to alternate that with gym twice a week. The burden of books she would be toting home on Tuesdays and Thursdays made her cringe. One more reason to hate gym.

For an hour, she perused trigonometry, and with a quick check of the clock, grabbed her keys and the postcard.

"Artie," she shouted as she burst through his door. "Before I leave, I want to show you the card Joe sent."

He smiled a big, toothy grin and held it toward the light. "Read it to me."

"He says, 'Amsterdam loves the blues—and they seem to like me too! Got a new gig that should carry me through the end of the year. I miss you more than you know ... Love, Joe'."

The smile never left Artie's face as he said, "I taught him everything he knows."

Leila smiled, placing the card on the table in front of him. She had grown accustomed to the ritual of their exchanges. Although she would have enjoyed some variation in their conversation, there was something reassuring in its predictability. She hadn't yet figured out if it was social nerves or if at eighty-five his mind was going. Just the same, he let her ramble on about flat tires, customers from hell, gym teachers, cute boys and the Ogre Myles.

"Like father, like son," she said.

"And you won't find a better guitarist north of Mississippi—not even across the Atlantic Ocean."

"Except you, of course." She kissed the top of his head.

"Don't you be flatterin' me, Angel—now, you git on off to work."

🌊 CHAPTER 7

A SSUMING SHE HAD BEEN A TOPIC OF DISCUSSION among the phys ed staff, Leila took her time changing into her gym shorts and lagged behind the class as they filed out to the track. She suspected a not-so-secret agenda.

Clutching her clipboard, Ms. Thorpe announced, "Today we will establish a basis to determine the progress of each girl, between now and the end of the semester." Her voice carried, even when she spoke at a normal volume. "Begin by taking your at-rest pulse, proceed to some basic stretches and then begin running the track. After each lap, I will record your pulse rate."

At least the track collaborators, Brigham and Weiss, had not shown up. Leila breathed easier. After mimicking her fellow pupils' stretches, she moved with the rest of the girls as they hit the track. Finding a comfortable middle ground, she brought her speed up a notch so as not to disappoint Ms. Thorpe, and then maintained that pace.

Ahead of Leila, Maryanne ran with another three girls— the stereotypical popular girls. They bantered amongst themselves as each vied for position. Leila trailed behind. Rounding the 400-meter mark to complete one lap, each girl slowed with her fingers to her wrist, already counting off and comparing pulse rates. Each paused long enough to report to Ms. Thorpe and to notice that Coach Brigham had made an appearance along with Miss Weiss. Leila came up next, not nearly so eager as each girl ahead of her. She refused to look at either teacher.

"Rate?" Thorpe demanded.

Leila poked at her wrist, unable to find her pulse.

Thorpe shoved the clipboard at the coach and grabbed Leila's wrist, counting off as she looked at her watch. Her brow shot up. Thorpe frowned. "You know a large portion of your grade in this class is based on effort, don't you Sanders?"

"I guess."

"Then I want to see some effort out there!"

"Yes, ma'am."

Leila pulled back out into the stream of girls, feeling Weiss and Brigham's stare. The other girls clumped into groups of threes and fours as Leila ran alone. As she came up behind each group, she slowed her speed and passed without drawing much attention.

At the half-lap mark, she caught up to the forerunners again and held back, maintaining her posterior position. Her rhythm choked. Her economizing gait would give away her lack of enthusiasm and so she loped alongside the popular girls and pulled away from them as she rounded the bend the second time.

Again, Leila had difficulty locating her pulse. As she approached Thorpe, she shrugged. "One-ten?"

Thorpe's eyes and nostrils flared as she thrust her hand to Leila's throat, pressing her finger deep into her neck. Leila's eyes widened—now she had no trouble feeling her artery.

Thorpe again glowered. "You think this class is a waste of your time?"

Leila glanced at Brigham and back at Thorpe. "No ma'am, I don't."

"Don't lie to me, Sanders." She shook her finger. "You think because you run every day, and because you're probably in better physical condition than every girl in this class, that you shouldn't have to exert yourself!"

Leila did not respond but for her now increasing pulse.

Thorpe had the attention of her entire class.

"Admit it!" Thorpe's hand settled firmly on one hip as she poked her finger at Leila. "You would much rather use this time to catch up on your homework!"

"Yes ma'am."

Thorpe squinted until her eyes nearly disappeared. Leila braced herself.

"I'll tell you what," Thorpe exhaled. "I'll cut you a deal. You get out on that track and run—I mean give it all you've got—you run to my satisfaction and quit when I say quit, and you don't have to show up for my gym class for the rest of this semester."

Leila squinted back, fixing her gaze. "But I need to pass gym or I won't graduate."

"You'll get a passing grade."

Leila weighed the stakes. Any unwanted attention paled when compared to freedom from humiliation in gym class, not to mention extra time to complete assignments before her run home. And no more Weiss. "I need to pass with an A."

You look away, you lose.

Thorpe's eye twitched. "Then earn it! and you've got a deal."

Leila started on the track slowly, breathing from her diaphragm. She relaxed her shoulders and arms as her clenched fists unfurled. Picking a row clear of any runners, she gained momentum. Her breathing steadied as she established a consistent rhythm, holding her pace for a half lap. Each foot stroke blurred her awareness of the other girls, and her mind cleared as she overtook them without a glance.

Rather than put distance behind her, Leila thrust forward into some other consciousness, running toward something beyond escaping gym or impressing Ian. She fixed on it, on the thud of each foot stroke against the immovable plane beneath her. Her own breath and pounding heart muted.

She was flying.

She didn't know how long or far she ran, but when her exertion exceeded her lung capacity, she slowed simultaneously with Thorpe's whistle. "Class over!"

Maryanne and her friends moved, glancing back at Leila as they made their way toward the gym, exchanging cupped whispers.

Leila took the final 300-meters at a leisurely run and then tapered to a jog. The three gym teachers exchange words, though Brigham's eyes remained upon Leila. Thorpe just smiled as she puffed her chest, turned, and then strutted toward the school building behind Weiss and the last of the popular girls. Brigham headed out to meet Leila on the track.

She walked, now breathing hard and arching her back—exhilarated rather than tired.

She called out, "Did you want to check my pulse?"

Brigham smiled and shook his head. He walked toward her as she headed his way.

"Did Thorpe pass me?" she said when they met up.

"How can you even ask that?"

They continued alongside each other, toward the building.

Leila looked at him sideways. "So, now I suppose you're going to try and recruit me for track."

"Can you blame me? I'm the track coach, that's what I'm supposed to do." He looked much better outdoors—his relaxed smile had returned and so had his natural color.

"Well, you're going after the wrong girl," she said. "I have no interest in running track."

"But why? You're a natural."

"Lots of reasons."

He looked straight at her. "Would you care to share?"

"Aside from the fact that I'm probably the least competitive person you'll ever meet, this just isn't a good time for me, that's all," she said, avoiding his eyes.

"Is that what you always say when you're too scared to follow through?"

Leila had used the 'not-a-good-time-for-me' line on him before—in fact, she used it often when hoping to sidestep uncomfortable issues without divulging too much.

"I'm not scared to follow through when something's in my best interest." She now met his gaze. "But as far as I can see, this is only in your best interest."

He smiled as if caught. "Sure, it'd be great to coach someone like you—with your potential, I mean—but think of what it would do for this school. Your participation would likely push the board to fund a girls' track team."

"I have been to so many schools that I couldn't care less who gets what team." She kicked at some loose gravel as they walked. "And I'm not so self-centered to think I'd have any impact on anyone or anything."

"You sell yourself short, not to mention your future."

She smirked. "And now you're going to tell me I'd get a scholarship for running? Yeah, well, maybe in another twenty years when anyone finally gives a hoot about girls' sports—hell, I don't even care about girls' sports. Or any sports for that matter."

He stopped walking and faced her. She paused with him.

"Then what do you care about?"

"I care about getting through this school year without drawing any attention to myself."

"It's a little late for that. Tomorrow you'll be the talk of the school."

Leila rolled her eyes. "Why can't a girl just run and be left alone?"

"Why would a girl *want* to just run and be left alone?"

"What—now you wanna be my shrink?"

"I want to be your coach."

"I don't need a coach."

"What do you need?"

She looked directly at him. "What you can't give me." She started walking again.

"Okay, Leila, listen—what's your bottom line?"

"What do you mean?"

"I'm willing to negotiate."

She laughed. "What?"

"What's it going to take to get you on the team?"

"You mean, like a bribe."

"You already proved you have a price. What is it in this case?"

She shook her head. "Yeah, well, Thorpe caught me off guard—I didn't have a chance to think it through."

"Just the same, you do have a price."

"I can't believe you."

"Sure you can."

She smirked. "Bribing me to run track is the most ridiculous thing I've ever heard."

"Is it?"

"Okay, I'll do it for a million dollars."

"Be serious."

"You be serious."

He sighed. "Okay, just think about it—will you at least consider it?"

"And you'll get off my case, and keep Miss Weiss and Thorpe off my case too?"

"If you'll think about it—yeah."

"Okay, I'll think about it—but don't get your hopes up. I'm only stringing you along to get you off my back."

He threw a hand up and backed off with a grin. "A maybe is good enough for now."

As they left the track, Leila thought of only one thing she wanted from him—from anyone, for that matter. She just wanted a friend. Could she ask for something so simple without it turning into something too complicated? She could certainly test his boundaries with some friendly conversation.

"I meant to tell you," she said, "I really like that tape you gave me."

"Tape? Oh, yeah ...," Ian chuckled. "I forgot about that. I thought I just misplaced it or something."

"Or maybe you thought you gave it to some other girl?" she grinned. "You probably have a whole truckload that you dole out to ladies in distress."

"And thanks to me, there are quite a number of spinsters enjoying the blues as we speak."

"Including Miss Weiss?"

"No. Not Miss Weiss."

Leila smiled. She couldn't help liking him. She would

have liked to needle him a little more on Miss Karen Weiss, but she had other curiosities. "So, given that you're the track coach, how much photography do you actually do? I mean, are you primarily a photographer and then a coach or the other way around?"

He flashed surprise and hesitated. "I guess I'm a photographer ... I mean, that's primarily what I want to be. Coaching is just what I do."

"Well, you have business cards."

"Yeah, I've sold some pieces, but I'm nowhere near the point of supporting myself with it."

"I really like your work in the gym lobby."

"Oh yeah?"

"They're really intense. I almost feel embarrassed for your subjects."

His eyes sparked. "Why embarrassed?"

"You caught them with some pretty stark emotion written all over them."

"I know. I'm never entirely comfortable with that."

They paused at the school entrance. "Do you ever photograph people who actually know you're photographing them?"

"I've done some portraits."

"But not like school-picture portraits."

"No, nothing like that."

"More intimate?"

"I suppose you could say that." His folded arms contracted across his clipboard.

She sensed his discomfort and veered toward something more neutral. "The ones in the lobby—did you crop them to tighten your composition, or did you frame them in your lens that way?"

"A little of both." He smiled, his breath irregular. "You have an artistic eye."

She shrugged. "Maybe."

"Are you an artist?"

"Sort of."

"What medium do you work in?"

"Pencil. I'm trying out watercolor but struggling."

"That's a hard medium."

"Yeah, but I like the challenge."

"That doesn't surprise me."

She turned to look at him, catching him as he studied her face the way a portraitist does. As if in pain, he looked away.

Leila spoke her heart, "I'd love to see more of your work, sometime."

He tensed and drew a long breath. "Leila," he said, now evading her stare, "As much as I'd like that, I really wouldn't be comfortable with it."

She knew why, but tried to make light. "Why? You're not insecure about your work, are you?"

"My insecurities—"

Ms. Thorpe burst through the doors. "We've made some headway, have we?"

Ian gave a quick and noncommittal shrug, as Leila huffed with irritation, not so much at Thorpe's question but at the interruption. Leila pushed past them both, in a hurry to retrieve her books.

WHY CAN'T I JUST LOOK FOR A FRIEND MY OWN age? Kids at school seemed to do it all the time—make friends, go to parties, hang out at lunchtime. They made it seem so easy—getting along and sharing interests. Leila couldn't remember exactly when it had dawned on her that she hadn't any friends her own age. She had overheard other kids talking about playing after school, but for the longest time she thought they meant playing an instrument—like in a band.

It hadn't felt like isolation at the time, after all, her father had rarely left her unattended—either he or Joe or another trusted member of the band had always kept her nearby. She had learned how to stay quiet and out of the way, not only during band practice, but when her father went into a mood, sometimes for weeks. She knew how to entertain herself, and her isolation felt normal at the time—now it just felt lonely.

❧CHAPTER 8

W HEN CLARENCE MYLES ENTERED THE FACULTY
lounge, conversation lulled. He cut a path through
several teachers, including Thorpe, Michaels,
Brigham, and Weiss, avoiding all eye contact. If the lounge
hadn't housed the only refrigerator short of the cafeteria—
and lunch staff rated even lower than faculty—he would have
bypassed it altogether. He yanked open the buzzing old
Frigidaire. His pesto-slathered chicken breast between two
slices of French bread, and a bit of last night's brie cheese,
would be worth a return visit at noon. Too bad his lunch
couldn't include a few swallows of Merlot.

Myles filled his coffee mug and moved toward the door as
Miss Michaels resumed the conversation, chirping, "... she's
such a free spirit, it's no wonder her feet barely touched the
ground. At any rate, it looks good for the track team this year
with Kyle Schultz and now Leila Sanders. She's bound to be
a star runner."

Myles paused, casting a glance at Weiss who kept her eyes
on Brigham—not as if that were anything new, but she didn't
stare with her usual lust. Brigham stood, without reaction.

Thorpe chimed in, "She certainly has the self-discipline
for it, running to and from school every day. Problem is she's
not exactly a team player, this one." She jabbed Brigham.
"You're going to have a real challenge on your hands."

Myles' brow shot up. He applauded his own intuition,

finding a degree of satisfaction in learning that the rare student who had made an impression on him was, in fact, exceptional in some way—perhaps even a nonconformist, as uninterested in playing nice with the establishment as he was. At seventeen, not likely but, in her case, conceivable.

"Do you think we'll get a girls' track team out of it?" Andrea Michaels stirred the pot.

Miss Weiss, lingering to the side and unable to contain herself, finally blurted what everyone knew she would: "Title Nine states—"

Another faculty member cut her off. "Spare us the Title-Nine lecture, Karen."

"Karen's right, though," Brigham spoke up. "And if Leila Sanders forces the issue, once and for all—good."

All eyes fell on Thorpe who remained silent as Brigham brushed past Myles and walked out.

No one bothered to ask Myles' opinion lest he snarl and make some snide remark about frail egos, pointless administrative debates, unilateral budget cuts or policy fanaticism. Over the past nearly thirty years of teaching and having been involved with previous school systems, even serving on a school board in Philadelphia, he had a particular dislike for administration-versus-faculty politics. He admired that Brigham seemed to share his distaste. In fact, Ian Brigham was probably the only staff member with whom he had exchanged more than a few perfunctory words.

Last year, during the first week of September, Brigham—the newcomer to the faculty at Millville High School—had noticed the *Rolling Stone* magazine under Myles' arm. He casually mentioned an article, highlighting some blues or jazz.

Myles had asked, "Do you play or just listen?"

In a manner consistent with blues modesty, Ian replied, "I mostly listen, but I noodle some blues on my guitar."

Myles respected that Brigham had left to the imagination whether he could really belt it out or had understated his ability.

"What about you? Do you play or just listen?"

"Sax," Myles replied, ending the exchange.

A month later, Myles had heard that Ian, conscripted to jam with the school rock band during the finale at the homecoming dance, had significantly minimized his ability.

🐚IGNORING POST-RUN WHISPERS AND GAWKS, LEILA sat in homeroom, listening to the drone of announcements over the public address system. Although Mr. Myles read as usual, she sensed something amiss. He hadn't attempted to engage her in any way, but his utter stillness begged she look at him.

His gaze had already settled upon her and when their eyes met, he arched one brow. Although it raised the hair on her arms, she kept her eyes on his. Did he expect her to recoil? She refused to look away. His expression morphed. It wasn't quite an almost-smile, in fact, the curve of his mouth did not change nor did the narrowing of his eyes. Perhaps it was as subtle as dilating pupils or an imperceptible twitch—it didn't matter; something passed between them and neither could take it back.

🐚IN ART CLASS, MISS MICHAELS SET OUT THE watercolors. It should have been an easy exercise, but Leila's brush, paints, and water wrestled on the paper, creating an uneven, splotchy mess. At home they behaved better, but in class, with Miss Michaels hovering, Leila's hand cramped. She tore off the top page and began again with a little better result. She then flipped the page back and proceeded to sketch her instructor, a lax image upon which to embellish. She laid out all the angles, taking special note of the lighting so she could later add detail.

When time came for Miss Michaels to review the class' progress, Leila flipped back to the day's lesson and received her teacher's usual commendation. Even though it sounded canned, it was better than her father's less-than-enthusiastic praise, a means of buying from her another hour of silent drawing in the corner. Anything to keep her content as the band worked on their sound.

LEILA WOKE WITHOUT THE ALARM ON SATURDAY morning. She rolled to glance at the clock. Six-ten. She had hoped to sleep in on one of her only days off, but even in her dim, shade-drawn room, she couldn't drift back to sleep. It might have been a dream that woke her or over-stimulation from her first week at school. Either way, she lay awake but did not want to get out of bed. If she had someone to take care of her, to bring her breakfast or lunch in bed, someone to clean her house and pick up groceries, perhaps she might stay in her room for days at a time the way her father sometimes had. It hadn't happened frequently—most of the time he had more energy and enthusiasm for life than anyone she had ever known, but when he plummeted, he hit hard and it scared her.

"Don't worry, he'll snap out of it," Joe would always say, but it had scared him, too. Those were the times when Joe stepped in and played father. Sometimes, she wished Joe were her father, with his kind and accepting ways. In his opinion, she could do no wrong. Not that he spoiled her, but he was more the nurturer, band-aiding scraped knees and pinning her artwork to the walls, picking her up from school, the one who more often said, "Love you, Baby."

Her father could be fun, too, but that was on his way 'up.' That's when he got along with everyone. His moods were easy and less intense. He smiled more and seemed satisfied with Leila's piano progress, but once he hit the ceiling—and that sometimes lasted weeks and weeks—his expectations of her would grow and so would his restlessness. They would soon be moving. And then he would crash.

Leila inched her way from under her sheet onto her tummy and to the edge of the bed. She reached for the shade. With a tug, it furled with repeating thumps, illuminating the room as if she had flipped the light switch.

She flopped to her back. An irregular crack ran through rough ceiling plaster and formed the crooked smile of an abstract face. Every ceiling she had ever slept under hid a hundred different faces waiting to smile or frown or scream in horror, depending on the light. As she stared, her sinuses burned and her vision blurred. She waited for a tear—enough to wipe away—but the waters always receded. Pushing herself to sit at the end of her bed, she gazed at her reflection in the dresser mirror.

"Just keep busy," she said under her breath. Her focus shifted to Ian Brigham's card at the corner of her mirror, then to the postcard from Joe, and down to the vacant dresser top. Commencing her morning ritual, she replaced the canister where it would spend another day. After prying off the lid, she peeked inside at the measuring spoon sitting atop ashes. Time for another excursion. She bent, peering at Ian's card to read the address, and then brought Joe's postcard to the kitchen table. While she waited for water to boil, she wrote:

> *Dear Joe,*
>
> *Thanks for the postcard—Artie really liked it too. We're glad things are going well. And thanks for the money you wired—you didn't have to send so much, I'm actually getting by really well. I think Artie is doing pretty good too, but sometimes he forgets things, and I think his cough might be getting worse, but don't worry. I still spend every Saturday night playing with him and Buddy. I love listening to his guitar—he sounds just like you.*
>
> *School is great. I'm making lots of new friends. I hope you'll be able to make it home for my graduation. Have you met anyone special yet? I bet there's lots of pretty ladies in Amsterdam or Paris, or Vienna, or wherever you are now. I hope when you do find someone, she won't be just a groupie.*
>
> *Here's a little painting for you. I think I'm finally getting the hang of it. Remember how you used to hang all my drawings on the refrigerator ... I miss that ... I miss you. Please call sometime soon.*
>
> *Love, Leila*

She sealed it in an envelope and scribbled the address. A half hour later, she jogged to the nearest mailbox where it began its journey to Amsterdam, but who knew how long before it would find Joe—sometimes it took days, even weeks to make contact, like when her father had died.

From the mailbox, she continued her journey to the high school and then farther south. Most of the streets in this part of Millville ended at or ran along one of the canals that emptied into the Great South Bay. Now that early September had arrived, she could venture to the village beach without worrying about bystanders crowding the waterfront.

Nearing the beach, she passed an empty track and softball field. The parking lot was empty, although a few villagers sat at picnic tables. Leila paused at the sight of a mother pushing her toddler on the beachside swing set. Had her mother ever played with her that way? As much as she would have liked to imagine it, she didn't dare. Fantasies like those solidified images that made her mother seem real—she was better off not missing what she never knew, real or imagined.

Leila walked her way out to the end of the jetty and watched for a break in the light water traffic where boats entered and exited the mouth of the canal near the yacht club. A rainbow of color floated atop the water, narrowing and widening, and breaking her reflection. She tugged the folded handkerchief from her pocket and stared at the ashes—each time she prepared for the ritual, the heap of ash scooped into the handkerchief increased in volume. She let out a sigh as she sat, checked the wind direction, and then emptied it without ceremony.

On the beach, the squeals and laughter of children stirred something churning within her—a longing, like a child, watching her favorite ball float out to sea. As soon as she felt the burning, she came to her feet, walked the jetty back to the sand and started her run home. On second thought, perhaps she would run a lap on the beach track. It reminded her of the community center track where she had first started running at around nine or ten years old. It neighbored an apartment they lived in with a window overlooking the track, which was the only reason her father permitted her out of his reach. After her father fell sick, she never asked permission and ran when and wherever she liked.

❧ STANDING IN FRONT OF ARTIE'S RANGE, LEILA turned pork chops in his iron skillet. Any waft of frying food drew Buddy from next door. "We go way back to Prohibition days," Artie had told her. "Got ourselves in a mess with the Klan and had to migrate." Buddy had confirmed it with a head-wagging "Oooeee!" Since they had to leave everything behind, she was glad that in their old age they still had each other.

The door to Artie's apartment creaked and then slammed shut. "Mmm, Mmm—sure smells good in here," Buddy bellowed.

Leila set a platter of chops on the table where Artie already sat. "Might as well join us," he said, as always.

Leila ate with them and listened. Most of the conversation consisted of repeating what each had just said, only louder, but neither old man seemed to mind. It didn't matter to Leila—she had already heard most of it anyway.

"Did you get that amp fixed yet?" Buddy shouted.

"You know I haven't," Artie snapped back at him. "Nothing's preventing you from bringing yours. If you put your hearing aid in it wouldn't matter if the volume don't work so good."

Buddy laughed, his large belly jiggling as he shoveled in another mouthful.

By eight o'clock, they started tuning up. Leila sat at the piano, stroking uneven ivories. A wave of melancholy settled in her chest and weighted her hands. Buddy plucked his bass as if it were the fibers of her heart. When Artie hummed a few chords, her fingers responded, striking one key and then another. She closed her eyes and imagined her dad. As Artie bent a few notes, the twang of it conjured images of Joe. Before tears had a chance to form, she answered their chords with a few notes. She didn't think much about how she played—not like when her dad had sat beside her, drilling her on scales and chords. Now, the music came automatically. By nine o'clock, a few other locals showed up with guitars and another visitor grabbed bongos from the closet. By nine-thirty or ten, music rolled over and under, weaving its way into the laughter and chatter.

Near midnight, Leila went to the kitchen for a glass of water and returned to the doorway, her gaze scanning the room. Two black, octogenarian Mississippi refugees, one Cuban, a Puerto Rican, and several other locals sat amidst dilapidated furniture, laughing and playing. They all talked so fast and loud. She couldn't help smiling at the lot of them. Was this as close as she would come to fitting in? In a way she did fit—just like with her father's band. The biggest difference was the lack of cigarette haze, on account of Artie's lungs; though the scent of pot smoke drifted in from the porch when someone came or went. Although she knew most of the guys by name they still stared and seemed to wonder at her. She felt conspicuous, like a kitten raised amidst a litter of pups.

She sidled up to Artie, between Buddy and Pedro.

"I'm calling it a night," she said and patted his sparse hair.

Buddy tipped his chin toward her. "Where's my sugar?"

Leila thumped his head. He feigned injury.

"G'night, Angel," one after another said as she left.

She climbed into bed. Music wafted through the floorboards, enveloping her in a comforting blues lullaby—like when she was a child, falling asleep to the sound of the band.

&~CHAPTER 9

E VERY MORNING LEILA WOKE, BLANKETED WITH SO
many restrictions, and each day she longed to shed their
weight. So much of her growing up felt undisciplined at
the time, when in fact unstated rules had controlled her life.
Don't disrupt the quiet. Don't talk about home at school.
Don't tell that you have two fathers—one black, one white—
and no mother. Don't ask about your mother. Don't wake
Dad. Don't get caught drawing unless you've practiced
piano. Don't make friends—you'll be moving as soon as you
get attached. Don't pass up an opportunity to eat. Don't trust
authority. And most of all, Don't trust men you don't know.

If her classmates realized she now lived on her own
without any supervision, coming and going as she pleased,
they would envy her freedom. Yet she lived like a creature
born in captivity, afraid to leave her cage—afraid someone
might find out.

"They'll put you in foster care," her father had warned, as
if that would expose her to the worst abuses, to the horrors he
had suffered as a displaced child. He never elaborated on the
horrors, but when she was older, Joe told her that her dad had
been molested in ways a young girl shouldn't even know
about. She never doubted the truth of her father's fear and
had adopted it as her own. But now, what was the worst that
could happen? After all, she wasn't a four-year-old. Would
the courts place her in an unsafe environment? Would they

make an issue of her unsupervised status, now, only eight months from her eighteenth birthday? She could wiggle her way through all the loopholes and out of danger—perceived or real—but like a child trying to conquer a fear of heights, she could not bring herself to step too near the edge without retreating to the safety of rules.

Dread settled in her core, weighing down her body as she lay in bed, contemplating her Sunday—her life. Why did her peers seem to be having all the fun, while she remained trapped in limbo between adolescence and adulthood? Indeed, her father had left her the legacy of adulthood but none of the privileges.

"Get out of bed." Instead, she rolled over and pulled the sheet over her head. She scowled at the thought of going for a run. If she hadn't resorted to running as a way to manage her stress, she wouldn't have drawn unwanted attention; she wouldn't have been noticed, not by Thorpe and Weiss, and not by Ian Brigham. And she wouldn't be regretting the price she had put on her privacy simply to get out of gym class. And she certainly wouldn't be contemplating what she might be willing to sacrifice for Ian Brigham.

When lying in bed became more uncomfortable than confronting her day, she rose and went to the refrigerator. After removing a bottle of orange juice, she shut the door and stared at her calendar, at the repeating cycle of days. Summer was like remission—all happy and hopeful but bound to end, and end it did. As she sipped from the bottle, she flipped the pages forward to May and let them settle back to the previous months.

From the kitchen, she took six steps to her new drawing table, glanced at her despicable sneakers by the door and then sat. Within a half hour, she had laid the wash for the portrait of Miss Michaels. If she built up the layers without turning the paint to mud, it might even look like her teacher—at least a fair representation. As she added detail, she recalled her exchange with Ian regarding his photography.

Leila knew how risky it felt to show someone—someone

whose opinion mattered—something into which she had poured her heart. She had lived with the artistic temperament —with insecure musicians—her whole life, and she understood that levels of confidence and self-acceptance varied from very insecure to arrogant. She knew where in the lineup she fell, but what about Ian? She sensed that he was not far ahead of her, but where did he draw the line between what he exhibited and what he reserved? Or did he draw a line between those whom he allowed in and those he excluded? She wanted to be on the intimate side of the boundary, seeing not just some sanitized version of his work, but the entire body of it. What inspired and drove him? Did his artistic ego match the creative boldness she had seen in his photographs at school?

The bigger question was, what value would Ian place on exposing himself if she were to press him? The notion made her wish for his uncensored reaction, forbidding him opportunity to overthink or rethink, to revise, or edit. Such a proposition could not take place in the school setting and not with Karen Weiss anywhere around.

As she waited for the paint to dry, Leila pulled out her sketch of Kyle Schultz running and the subsequent drawing of Ian Brigham.

🌿 IAN LINGERED BETWEEN HIS SHEETS. HAVING SPENT too many nights in Karen's waterbed, he now relished his firm mattress and the solitude of his own room on a Sunday morning. As he rolled over, a stream of light walked a slow path across the floor and turned his oak dresser a warm gold. The hardwood planking throughout the house had sold him on the fixer-upper. Even though he had a little better than minimal experience with carpentry when he rescued her from foreclosure, she had allowed him to practice on her, yielding to his eager desire to learn and do her justice. Yes, he thought of his pretty cottage in feminine terms. Petite and unassuming, unappreciated for years, the ugly sister withering between two domineering and over-indulged edifices. Ian took pride in bringing out her potential. She would repay his kindness. After all, he had spent the last of his savings—and the last two summers—salvaging her.

Wearing only his jeans and sipping coffee, he ambled from the kitchen to the foyer and into his studio. Light poured from floor-to-ceiling windows overlooking his backyard, where the canal offered an illusion of privacy. He would forgo a morning sail, and even his morning jog. A few hours in the darkroom better suited his mood.

In complete darkness, feeding a strip of film into the canister required full concentration—a reprieve from thinking. When he flipped the light switch back on, his pondering returned.

It had been nearly two weeks since he had picked up where he left off with Karen Weiss, but already he had too easily allowed the whims of opportunity and convenience to draw him back into the relationship. In many ways, they were again at square one, full of passion yet emotionally tentative. In such a short time, she had become uncomfortably possessive. Now Ian hoped the flames of the relationship would extinguish like all of his past liaisons. Nevertheless, like a kettle swirling with emotion, a flame ignited under his desire for intimacy—true intimacy—yet he was unsure if it was Karen or Leila stirring the pot.

He popped a blues tape in the player and cranked up the bass. As he stood before his workstation, tossing a film canister from hand to hand, he eyed a sheet of thumbnails that lay out from the night before. Setting the undeveloped film aside, he fingered a negative strip that corresponded with the proof sheet on the table. Holding it up to the light, he breathed in restraint, then set that strip aside.

Catching the graceful yet elusive movements of a runner—not just a jogger—challenged him. Although he often photographed many of his student runners—that they might see where to improve their posture or pronation—it was altogether different to capture a body in motion for the sake of composition and art. That was what he had been after on the beach back in July. He examined a couple of alternate strips, but the one that inspired him begged another look. He again picked it up. It seemed almost hot to his touch, but that did not prevent him from bringing it to the darkroom.

There were about a dozen shots. The angle started off head-on and progressed to side views, the last two from behind as his subject passed by. He positioned the film in the enlarger and cropped the background. As gradations of black and white became distinguishable, Leila in motion emerged from beneath the developer solution where her body gained definition. She was not casually jogging; she was in a full-out run, beautifully proportioned and balanced. Her face lacked the strain of exertion, and her eyes nearly closed.

Ian's stomach tightened. Candid shots of runners often evoked strong emotion when developing them for the first time, yet scrutinizing Leila's form felt voyeuristic. Perhaps he had crossed a line, broken some unspoken photographer's rule. He stepped back, awash in the heat of guilt, quickly clipping her images to the drying line without a final inspection.

He stepped back into his studio where the fresher afternoon air cooled his bare chest. His stomach gurgled as he headed to the kitchen. Leftover pizza did not look as appealing as beer. He pulled a Heineken from the six-pack and chugged a bottle. Unquenched, he grabbed another and then headed back to his studio.

At his worktable, he stood over the thumbnail proof sheet from the Girl Running file, analyzing Leila's stride. She had such potential as a runner, and he sensed, as an individual. What compelled her to run with such determination? What 'lack of options' had sent her from New Hampshire to Long Island? He hoped he would have the opportunity to find out.

Downing his beer, he left the proof sheet on the table and returned to the refrigerator, feeling the effects of his two ales. He elected to eat pizza first and washed it down with more beer. As he headed back to his studio, the doorknocker tapped softly.

Ian was not expecting anyone. Karen knew he would be

home, likely working in the darkroom, which meant he did not want to be disturbed. Although they frequently shared her bed, Karen had never been to his house, and he dreaded that it might be her, pushing the next boundary. Just as well—now was as good an opportunity as any to readjust their relationship, if not end it. He hoped for the latter. He took one more gulp as he braced himself before pulling the door open.

Ian's heart lunged. "Leila ...."

She looked at the beer bottle before speaking. "Is this a bad time?"

It took a moment to respond, "Um ...."

A few wisps framed her flushed cheeks. "I'm sorry, I should have called first."

"No ... this is, uh ... this is a good time," he said, making no move to invite her in.

"I'm sorry. I'm intruding." She backed off from the doorway. "We can just talk tomorrow."

"No. No, this is fine, uh, come on in." Ian glanced at his beer and folded his arms across his bare chest.

She stepped into the foyer, into the light pouring in from his studio. She wore the same white shirt as in July, with its sleeves rolled to her forearm. Light caught her unbuttoned front, revealing a white undershirt with a low scoop neck.

He closed the door as his heart pounded. "Let me just go put something on."

In his kitchen, he drank down the last of his beer and grabbed a denim shirt from the back of a chair. Returning to the foyer, he fumbled with a middle button or two.

Leila fidgeted then tucked her fingers in her jeans pockets. "I suppose you're wondering why I'm here."

"Yeah." He imagined any number of reasons why she might show up on his doorstep. He worked at another button and stepped back, thinking of a hundred ways to maintain control of the situation.

"Well ...." Her eyes shifted and so did her sandaled feet. "I made a decision, and I want to cut a deal."

Ian's brow lifted. "You do?"

"Yes."

"Okay …."

She breathed deep, tightly wrapping her arms around her middle. "I want to see your photography."

"My photography?"

"Yes. And not just the stuff you show everyone else. I want to see it all—even the stuff you don't think is very good. And your early work, too."

"Why my photography?"

"I want to get to know you—as an artist, I mean."

In all his years of taking pictures, her request was a first. Any interest a girl or woman had shown in his photography was usually more a means of seducing him than getting to know him. Not that they hadn't appreciated his talent—some did, but they seemed to consider his artistic bent as merely an enhancement of his packaging.

"I don't know, Leila." He studied her face for some hidden agenda. "Do your parents even know you're here?"

Her eyes wandered and then came back to his. "No. But my parents aren't a problem."

"Well, they may not seem like a problem right now, but it could end up being a big problem for me."

"You think I'm just some ridiculous seventeen-year-old who isn't concerned with consequences?"

"No. I'm just not comfortable with this—with how your parents might feel."

She pursed her lips and stared at the floor. When she finally looked back up, her eyes begged reassurance, as if she needed him to confirm his own trustworthiness.

"What?" he asked, hoping she would divulge the weight of what her eyes conveyed.

Her arms relaxed and dropped to her side. She rubbed her thighs. "I don't have parents."

"What do you mean?"

"I mean my mother left fifteen years ago and my father's dead."

The impassive delivery of her words diluted their import, and yet explained why she seemed mature beyond her years and fit the profile, the fantasy he had built around her. He wanted her to be a woman of depth. At the same time, he wished she were some silly girl with a crush, someone he could dismiss.

He asked, "Well, who's your guardian?"

She tucked her hands back in her pockets. "I don't exactly have one."

"You're being rather cryptic. Why don't you just tell me what's on your mind?"

Her dimples deepened but not with a smile. "Show me your photography first."

Perhaps she had calculated their respective vulnerabilities and considered them an even trade. But what of the consequences? Was she capable of the discretion he imagined—that he wished of her?

"I don't know, Leila."

"Okay," she said, again folding her arms tightly. "It was just an idea. I guess I'll see you Monday, then."

She began to turn away.

"Wait," he said. His chest contracted with anxiety and expanded with excitement. The thought of inviting her in dissipated the consequences. Three beers convinced him that he would be careful and still enjoy her company.

"If I show you my photography, you'll run track?"

"If you show me whatever I want to look at, then yes."

"Will you tell me what's really going on with you?"

"We'll see."

He nodded, sealing the deal.

What on earth am I doing? He pushed the studio door wide open. Mid-afternoon light streamed in the back window, washing the room in a luminous haze. A series of portraits hung in a row—his safe, commercial work with a wider appeal. Leila smiled, her shoulders lifting with the wonder of a child. Her eyes roved beyond his small gallery, back toward his work area and studio. She licked her lip and looked at him, as if again seeking permission.

"Go ahead," he said, directing her to the first portrait.

As she stepped forward, he gave her a wide berth and stood off to the side. Now that she was in, he didn't want to crowd her into hurrying.

All the displayed photographs were black and white. She moved from picture to picture, spending a minute on each. Long minutes. Her expression changed as her eyes moved about the subject. As she studied his work, he studied the subtle variations in the contours of her mouth, the way she dipped and raised her daintily carved chin.

Many of his subjects were women, most of them beautiful, some smiling, not necessarily seductive but pensive. The males he photographed varied in age and demeanor.

"I really like the backlighting on this one." She pointed to a little boy and the highlights in his hair, like a halo. She stroked the line of his cheek. "And the reflective light here, the way it softens his face."

"What do you think of the contrast? Do you think I went too far with it? You know, too dramatic for a portrait of a child?"

"I like contrast. I think it works." She moved on to the next.

Tracing the lines of arms and legs, bent at opposing angles, she said, "I like the way these are interacting, and the way the reflection here sort of goes off into negative space."

Ian smiled at her astute observations.

"May I?" she asked, gesturing toward his work area.

He stepped aside, more eager than he had anticipated. "Go ahead. It's part of the deal, I guess."

She walked past a tripod, light stand, and umbrella positioned halfway toward the tall windows at the back of the room that extended to the rear of the house. In front of the window, a small piano stool sat amidst a draped white sheet that formed a reflective backdrop. The setting glowed.

Ian's eyes darted toward the Girl Running proof sheet, left out at his workstation.

"How far back do your photos go?" she asked.

"To my first photo, the first real picture I took on purpose. It's a gate in a brick wall with early evening light. Here, I'll show you …."

Ian opened the large file cabinet at the far side of his worktable. He pulled a folder, removed a small photo, and then discreetly placed that folder on top of the Girl Running proof sheet. The small color snapshot he handed Leila had faded over the years, yet the bricks glowed beside the white, sun-washed gate.

"It's not a great photograph," he said, "but it was the first time I really discerned tonal values and what light could do. After that I couldn't stop."

"Is that what you were doing at the beach that afternoon, taking advantage of the light?"

"Yeah," he said, again impressed. "How did you know?"

"I saw your camera in the backseat of your car."

He nodded with satisfaction—she was indeed observant. Could she also discern his growing admiration and that he was having difficulty remembering her age?

"May I see the pictures you took that day?"

"Uh … yeah." Ian retrieved his Beach folder.

She fingered the Girl Running file tab, shifting the folder just enough to expose the label and the sheet beneath it. "Do you photograph all the runners on your team?"

Oh boy—no turning back now.

"I do," he said, inhaling composure. "However, any runner who happens to pass in front of my lens is liable to end up in my darkroom."

"Of course." She lifted the folder in which to replace the small color photograph, further exposing the thumbnails depicting her.

"Yeah … funny thing …," he preempted, "I happened to photograph a girl on the beach that afternoon."

Leila lifted the folder, examining the dozen miniature frames.

"So you did," she said, now squinting. She glanced at Ian. "Is this me?"

"Yes. I didn't realize it until I developed it. Although I have to admit, there did seem to be something familiar about you. I guess I just assumed it was our common interest in music and connection to New Hampshire."

She did not react. Ian hoped she didn't think he was some sort of stalker. She cocked her head, adjusting the angle of the paper and pointed to the first one in the series, the one he had developed that afternoon.

She said, "I like this one."

His jaw relaxed. "I do, too."

Leila smiled as she replaced the sheet and took the Beach folder from his hand. "May I?" she asked, moving toward the open drawer to return it to its place. "Do you mind if I thumb through some of these others?"

Even though she had put him more at ease, his heart sped. He was eager to show her the rest of his work. "Sure, go ahead."

She stared at the A divider. She didn't pull every file— only ones that seemed to interest her. "You like architecture."

"Yeah."

"And boats."

"Mostly sailboats."

"You sail?"

"I do." He did better than simply sail. He had taught tourists on New Hampshire lakes—during those years when he had worked full-time at any odd job: waiting tables in resort towns, caretaking on wealthy estates, playing handyman—while attending a community college.

"I've always wanted to learn how to sail."

He wanted to offer but didn't. "Then I'm sure you will one day."

When she arrived at the back of the top drawer—at the Ms—she perused the Mount Washington file with interest. He was particularly proud of the photography from his winter hiking trips, and it pleased him that she spent a fair amount of time on them.

"Have you ever been to the Presidential Range?" he asked.

"I hiked Tuckerman's Ravine with my dad once. But we only made it to Hermit Lake. I've always wondered how it would feel to look out from the top."

"It's indescribable—especially in the winter."

She gazed off. "Someday. Even if I never climb the mountain, I'm going to move back to New Hampshire, for sure."

How had Leila managed to say all the right things—hit upon so much of what he had wanted in a woman, in a relationship, and now, she too hoped to move back to New Hampshire someday.

Oh, stop it! She's only seventeen. You're giving her too much credit.

Leila returned her attention to the cabinet, moving to the next drawer and the files behind N. After spending not a few minutes on Nautical, her hand moved to Nudes. Ian held his breath. It had been a while since he added anything to that folder, and it wasn't as if he had forgotten about them, but not until that moment did he consider the implications of her seeing them. He cringed at the thought of the school board. Miss Michaels might explore nudes as art in the classroom with few if any repercussions, but these were photographs of naked women, and Leila was about to view them in his home studio. With him. Alone. Perhaps she would pass over them. She didn't. Without a word, she pulled the entire folder and laid it on the table.

Color rose in her cheeks as she examined each with the same fascination as the foregoing.

"I love this composition," she said.

Ian's smile twitched.

He had shot them in the studio with carefully planned light. Many focused on just one or two views of the body, curving and intertwining at various angles, all premeditated yet natural. In fact, many required scrutiny to ascertain just what aspect of the body he shot. Their sensuality existed not so much in their parts as in their pose, in what they implied and in what lay beyond. Leila viewed many of the photos from alternate angles as if they might transform into something altogether different. Where did it take her imagination?

"Who are they?" she asked.

"I hired models."

"No girlfriends?"

"No," he stated without hesitation, his hands tensely pocketed. "I've never photographed my girlfriends like that … not that I've never photographed them nude … I mean, I just … I don't …." *Idiot!*

Leila smirked. "Never mind." She closed the file and placed it in the drawer.

Ian had spent over an hour holding his breath as he watched Leila move from photograph to photograph. His mouth dried. He needed another beer. "It feels very warm in here. Would you like something to drink?"

Leila wiped her neck. "Yeah. It's kinda hot in here."

Ian exited and then returned with two glasses of ice water, one half-emptied. They sipped in silence alongside each other, staring out the big windows as he rattled ice in his glass. Had he made a mistake inviting her in and allowing her free access to his work—to the nudes file?

"What are you thinking?" she asked without turning.

He glanced at her profile, at her hair loosely twisted at the back of her head and at her flushed cheeks. "I'm thinking that if the school board knew you were here looking at nude photographs … I'd be in some pretty hot water."

"And how would they find out?"

He sighed. Of course she wouldn't tell, why would she? "I'm just saying …."

"I do realize you're out on a limb, Ian."

The brunt of skepticism shot from his sideways glance.

She continued, "If it makes you feel any better, I'm out on a limb, too."

"Really?" *I doubt it.*

She blurted, "I'm a minor and I've been living on my own. I don't have a parent, and I don't have a guardian. If someone were inclined, they could make a big deal of it and I'd end up a ward of the state."

He rubbed the side of his face. "How long have you been on your own?"

"Since my dad died last December."

His eyes shifted with slow comprehension and finally came back to Leila. "That was less than a year ago."

"Yeah."

"What about your mother?"

"Don't have one. She took off before my third birthday."

He moved toward her. "How did your dad die?"

Leila inhaled and held her breath as she said, "Cancer. It took a couple years."

Ian shook his head. "I'm so sorry—my dad died when I was a freshman in college … I know how hard that is."

"How did he—?"

"Car crash."

"That's sudden. It must have been hard."

"Yeah, it kinda blew my whole world apart."

Her brow furrowed as if she were calculating. "You were a freshman—at Dartmouth?"

"Yeah."

"Is that why you dropped out?"

"Yeah. No more funding."

"You never said what you majored in."

He snorted. "I was supposed to be a doctor—just like Dad."

"He didn't leave you any money to finish your education?"

"It all went in the civil law suit."

"I don't understand."

"He was drunk—killed a woman."

Leila sighed. "Whoa."

He couldn't believe he had just divulged to her what he had never told anyone. Why did he feel compelled to confide in her? "Yeah. And he wanted to tell me how to run my life …?"

Leila's watering eyes gripped him with such intensity— his empathy for her intermingling with his own repressed grief. He wasn't sure which was more disconcerting—the pang of emotion or the fact that young Leila stirred it. He shrugged, a fake smile curbing the significance of it. "I didn't want to be a doctor anyway, that was my dad's idea—though I would have liked an MFA."

"What about your mom?"

"My parents divorced when I was eleven. She's in Chicago, married to some big-wig hospital executive." He laughed as though none of it mattered, then looked back at her. Somehow, she had managed to make her confession about him.

"Never mind that," he craved knowledge of her. "How are you making it?"

"My dad and I devised a plan so that I could live on my own. I work, and my other dad helps out."

"Your other dad?"

"My dad's best friend. He lives in Amsterdam, I mean, that's where his post office box is."

"You mean, Netherlands, or upstate?"

"The country. He and my dad broke up—that is, the band broke up—a couple years before the diagnosis."

"They were musicians?"

"Yeah. Blues. Seems like we were on the road most of the time, or between gigs."

"You traveled with your father's band?"

Leila chuckled. "Only during school vacations. Crazy, huh? I can't tell you how many years it took before I realized that wasn't normal."

Ian stared, trying to comprehend what she had just divulged. Now the blues made sense, and her familiarity with nightclubs, and her ease with men. In fact, Leila was not the typical teenage girl.

"Who took care of you while your father was sick?"

"Me."

"Who took care of your dad?"

"Me," she stated matter-of-factly. "Until hospice stepped in. That's why I had to move. They pretty much had me all set up to go into foster care. As soon as he died, I relocated across the state border, from Vermont to New Hampshire— you know how slow inter-state bureaucracy is. I just got lost in the system."

"No one ever questioned who you were or where you came from?"

"I stayed low-keyed, moved to New London, a quiet little college town where landlords are accustomed to renting to young women. It was easy. Even when I started at the high school after Christmas vacation, I was surprised at how easy it was to fall between the cracks. If you don't make trouble, it's amazing how people will believe what they want. Add a move to Long Island six months later, and my trail fizzles into obscurity."

"Wouldn't it have been easier to simply go into foster care?"

Leila shrugged. "Maybe. But my dad scared the crap out of me with stories about how bad that could go—said it would give me nightmares for the rest of my life, like it did him."

She stared off for a moment, a slow grimace forming. When her gaze returned to his, she had more the countenance of a woman than a child.

"So we worked on a plan, and he made me promise to follow through."

"Jeez, Leila." The ramifications of her loss began to register. The pang in his core returned. "I'm so sorry."

"It's okay. I'm okay." She would have been convincing but for the way she pursed the quiver from her lips and her eyes darted.

If he moved only inches, she would have been in his arms. He tucked his hands back in his pockets. "When do you turn eighteen?"

"May."

"Is that why you don't want to run track? You're afraid someone will find out before you're legal?"

"Come spring, it won't really matter I guess. I'm just more

comfortable living quietly below the radar." Her eyes moved to his, and although he did not close the gap between them, she seemed nearer. "Besides that, I'm not competitive and I've never been a team player. I don't like participating."

She tipped her chin toward him. His jaw and loins tensed.

"Leila," he breathed her name, full of caution as he stepped back, one arm restraining the other across his chest.

If Leila had stepped a hair closer or initiated a kiss, Ian might have wavered in his determination to keep his hands to himself.

Leila turned away. "May I see your darkroom?"

"Uh—I suppose," he said, part relieved and part distrusting his own self-control in close quarters. Then he remembered the photographs of her hanging to dry. "I ought to warn you, though. Just before you got here I was working on one of those pictures of you running at the beach."

"Really?"

He pushed the door open and turned on the light.

"Yeah." He rubbed his forehead. "I'm afraid I didn't have a chance to hide the evidence."

"Evidence of what?" She stood before the drying line and glanced at him with a smile and went back to scrutinizing each shot.

He chuckled. "I think I'll refrain from answering that on grounds I might incriminate myself."

"I'll bet," she said and turned to him.

Even in the stuffy, too-warm room, goose bumps rose on his torso. He wished Leila would quit looking into his eyes as if reading his thoughts. With any other woman, he would not hesitate to stroke her face, drawing her in to sample her willingness—though in most cases it was she who tested his—it had been that way since his thirteenth birthday. He felt far more comfortable letting a woman set the pace. Intimacy rarely felt urgent. But in this moment, he wanted Leila in a way he had never experienced. Perhaps it was her innocence that tempted him. If he touched her, grazed her arm or her cheek, could he stop himself from taking what he had no right to?

"What do you think of them?" he asked, moving past her, keeping a safe distance.

"I like them. I mean, I've never seen myself running. I look far less awkward than I imagined." A rosy blush colored her cheeks. "I have to admit, it's pretty flattering."

He refrained from the flirtation of his usual banter and kept silent as she sidled past and moved from photo to photo.

"May I have this one?" she asked, unclipping a shot of her body in midair.

"Of course."

She examined it a moment longer and then moved over to his equipment. He gave her a brief rundown of the enlarger and different chemical baths and how they worked. They ended up back in front of the drying line. From there, he stepped into the doorway.

"So, aside from the subject," she said, moving past him and back out into his work area, "What inspires you most?"

"Lighting," he said as she stood between him and the glowing rear windows. "The light has to be just right."

She turned to face the shaft of light. It bathed her in luminance.

He continued, "Late afternoon or early evening is best."

"Like this time of day?" Her face filled with all the expectation of a virgin—he knew the look so well.

"Exactly like this." His breath caught in his chest. Their eyes met. Hers traveled all over him as if begging him near her. He approached and stood before her. She parted her lips and drew in a deep breath.

"Sit," he whispered.

Leila lowered herself to the stool, her gaze fixed upon his face. Touching only the stick restraining her loosening hair, he released the thick tresses, which tumbled over her shoulders. She sank her fingers in and drew her hair back, catching and reflecting the sun. He stood over her for a moment longer. He needed to move quickly before he lost the light.

"Would you take off your sandals?"

They slipped from her feet. He reached for his camera.

"And the blouse—would you mind?"

The shirt slid from her porcelain arms onto to the floor, exposing her tank top as he shot frame after frame. He could not catch his breath as his lens unleashed her beauty. For a moment, he lowered his camera and stared.

"You are so beautiful," he said, under his breath. She blushed.

"Arch your back a little." He clicked. "And dip your chin."

She obeyed.

"Turn toward me." He moved closer, swept her hair to one side, and backed away.

She kept her eyes on him and seemed to interpret his movements, submitting to his subtle gestures. Each adjustment of the lens was a caress, each shot a kiss. He lingered in the sensuality of her body and prolonged the intimacy of all they had shared, if only through his lens.

He finished off the first roll in black and white, while the light remained strong and intense. The sun had begun to set and the shadows fell longer as the light changed hue. He switched to a camera loaded with color film for picking up the subtleties of dwindling light and shot another entire roll.

As though he had spent the past hour in foreplay, he ached. There would be no culmination. She would soon be gone and he would have to shelve their afternoon like some inaccessible archive. His camera lowered. Neither spoke. The dim light extended the quiet. Leila's chest rose and settled matching his own heavy breathing as her eyes glistened. Her faint smile strained. Without a word, she stood and slipped into her sandals as Ian picked up her shirt and photo, handing them to her.

"Thanks for indulging me," he said, standing so close that she brushed against him as her arms slid into sleeves.

"I wish I could say anytime …."

He looked away, forcing himself to back off.

"So, when do I sign up?" she asked without a smile.

"Sign up?"

"You know, for track."

"You could at least pretend to be a little enthused."

"I don't recall you were particularly enthusiastic on your end of the deal, at least to begin with."

"Touché."

"So, do I start calling you Coach now or wait till I make the team?"

"Start whenever you want," he said, although he did not like the sound of the title on her lips.

"Then I guess I'll start tomorrow."

His beer had worn off and the full brunt of her words struck him. He hated the thought of tomorrow—of the moment she would step out of his house and become his student.

"Leila," he said, thinking he ought to stake the boundaries they had been pushing all afternoon.

"I know, Ian. This never happened, right?"

"I'm not saying that. It's just that this can't happen again."

"It would have been easier if I hadn't come. Is that what you wish?"

The tendons in his neck strained. He shook his head. There was no way around the wrongness of it all, no matter how right it felt. "I really need for you to leave now."

Her eyes welled as she whispered, "Okay, I'll let myself out."

She walked alone to the front of his studio as if she had somehow done something wrong. It felt reminiscent of a breakup, or worse yet, a one-night stand.

"Wait," he said, gaining on her. "Let me walk you out."

"You don't need to."

"I want to." He caught up.

"I hate my life." She wiped the corner of her eye.

He ushered her into the foyer, scrounging restraint. "This won't always be your life."

She half-smiled.

He reached out to stroke her arm but withdrew. "There's a

lot I want to say to you, but you know I can't."

"I know."

He nodded, his resolve wavering as he opened the front door. "Okay, then, I'll see you tomorrow."

"Okay."

She walked to the curb where she had parked her car, and not until she drove away did he close the door.

CHAPTER 10

THOUGHTS OF IAN QUICKENED LEILA'S STEP AS SHE ran to school the following morning. She would be careful not to linger in his company or meet his eyes too often. It would take only one look to confirm that it had all happened, though nothing really had happened. He had only shared his photography and shot a few pictures. No, he hadn't even touched her, though the back of his hand had brushed against her hair but only briefly, only to adjust it. That didn't really count—not if someone were to ask—yet remembering it gave her a shiver.

Leila pushed through the alcove door and glanced at the phys ed office but detected no noise or movement. Not until after her shower, as she passed back through the alcove, did she spot Miss Weiss sitting in the girls' office. Weiss stared at Leila without acknowledgment. Apparently Leila's impressive run had not warmed the woman's attitude. Had Ian told either of the girls' gym instructors that she would be trying out for track in the spring? Even if Miss Weiss did not yet know, had Leila given her reason to be so cold?

Leila's disconcertion intensified in math class as Myles paced, distributing results from Friday's quiz. Slapping paper after paper on desk after desk, he moved around the class until he arrived in front of Leila. He paused, sneering.

"I hope this is not indicative of what I can expect from you in the future, Miss Sanders."

An F filled nearly the entire page, sprawled atop red markings and slashes. Leila did not respond.

Myles moved on to Kyle, withholding his A+, making him snatch it from his teacher's grip.

Myles growled, "Don't get cocky, Shultz."

When their teacher had passed, Kyle whispered, "Wow, you really suck at math."

Leila ignored him.

After class ended, she approached Mr. Myles' desk as he scribbled. Her courage waned as she waited for his attention. He peered up over his glasses.

"What, Miss Sanders?" he said with a loud breath.

Sometimes Leila saw him as just another man, puffing himself up to look big and scary, and sometimes she experienced every bit of the intimidation he reveled in.

She held her breath. "I need extra help."

"What? You mean tutoring?"

"Yes."

"And whom would you have for a tutor?"

Her jaw shifted. "I don't know."

"Surely you don't expect me to."

"Good God, no."

"And I'm supposed to take time out of my busy schedule to arrange this tutoring?"

Leila shrugged.

"Miss Sanders, it has become quite obvious that you are simply not applying yourself."

Her anger deflated his size. "As if you have any idea how hard I work at applying myself."

"What I do know, Miss Sanders, is that your time and energy would be better spent on studying than running. You should seriously consider applying your wit to academics rather than challenging your instructor. Do I make myself clear?"

Although still sitting, he seemed to loom over her, larger than ever as the truth of his words bore down on her. She stared at him in defeat and then retreated.

Kyle lingered just outside the door. "Tutoring?"

"Eavesdropping?"

"Hard not to overhear. What exactly are you having trouble with?" he asked as Maryanne showed up, right on schedule.

"I'll figure it out," Leila said and headed to art class.

Her pencil would not obey, and her paints behaved even worse. Perhaps her father was right and Mr. Myles too. She ought to apply herself more and stay focused. Painting could easily be classified as a needless distraction, but she craved it as much as running. Perhaps she should abandon both and concentrate on graduating.

LEILA BUMPED ELBOWS WITH HER FORMER GYM classmates as she sidled past them on their way out of the alcove. *What a relief to not have to play tennis!* She sighed with silent satisfaction until she caught a passing glimpse of Miss Weiss in the office. Without drawing the woman's attention, Leila moved to the locker room. When she emerged in her running shorts and T-shirt, lugging her homework-laden backpack, Miss Weiss was backing out of the office.

"I'll see you tonight, then," Miss Weiss cooed, within Leila's earshot. Weiss spun around and spotted Leila. The woman's eyes flashed scorn. Leila should have immediately turned away, but astonishment held her fast a moment too long. Miss Weiss' expression morphed with a raised, challenging brow. Coming to her senses, Leila walked away with a lump in her throat.

How many other nights had Ian spent with Karen Weiss? Leila had no claim to him, but she had canceled out Miss Weiss as anyone of consequence. She couldn't imagine what Ian saw in such an abrasive person. But then, why wouldn't he be involved with someone? Leila blushed at her naïvety. Only a fool would think he had no woman in his life. After all, he was a grown man, and that's the way men were. Still, Ian cared for her, but perhaps he also cared for Karen Weiss—at least she could give him what men wanted.

🐚 IAN STEPPED INTO KAREN'S APARTMENT, GREETED BY the aroma of his favorite shrimp and pasta dinner. His favorite blues played in the background. She welcomed him with an icy Heineken and low-cut sundress.

"I thought I should be a little more open minded about your music." She slipped her arms around his waist and pressed herself against him. She smelled freshly showered and inviting.

"I really like this song," she whispered, her lips caressing his earlobe.

The hair raised on his arms. "Really? What about it do you like?"

"I like his voice and the rhythm. It's sort of ...," her voice dropped to a lusty whisper, "... earthy." Her hand slid to his hips, pulling him closer.

Gulping down his beer, Ian tried to focus on the reason why he had kept the date.

"You seem a little tense. Why don't you come, sit down, and eat." She massaged his shoulders.

He grabbed her hand. "Karen, I won't be staying."

She startled. "What do you mean?"

"I think that you and I shouldn't have gotten back together after this summer."

"What are you talking about?"

"I just don't think the two of us are right for each other."

"That's ridiculous! We have a great time together."

"Yes, but you have to admit, our relationship is pretty one dimensional."

She huffed. "So what if it revolves around sex? And great sex, I might add. What's wrong with that?"

"I just ... I want something more." Ian's saying it surprised even him. "And I just don't think we have enough in common to sustain that."

He anticipated that she likely expected some slight adjustment in their relationship, but her brows arched with surprise. She stepped back. "Are you saying that you think sex is the only thing we have in common?"

"Tell me that's not true."

"We both like sports."

"We don't even like the same sports."

"So what!"

"Karen, we have a lot of fun, but you can't honestly tell me that you see us in something long term."

"Long term is highly overrated," she shot back.

"I just feel like we're spinning our wheels." Ian tempered his tone, trying not to sound accusatory. "Although your noncommittal thing was fine to start with, I'm uncomfortable with it now."

"Fine. We'll commit."

"You don't want to commit to me Karen. And honestly, you're not the person I want to commit to."

She backed off. The fire in her eyes waned, and her arched brow furrowed.

"Karen, you have called the shots from the beginning. You made it very clear that this was just casual. You got a different boyfriend over the summer, and you take for granted that I'll come running whenever you call ...." He shook his head. "It was fun, but it's over."

Now, her eyes flared. "Well, this was working just fine for you before school started. So, what's changed? Have you got a thing for someone else? Perhaps one of your *students*?"

"I won't even respond to that." He turned and walked out.

"Ian!" she called out and then slammed the door behind him.

MR. MYLES' TENNIS SHOES SQUEAKED AS HE PACED. He enjoyed the added effect though it wasn't the sound that had his students on edge.

"In two weeks we will be halfway through the quarter, which of course means—" he prolonged their anticipation "—parent-teacher conferences."

He glanced at Leila who stared ahead, lips pursed and brow fixed with tension. No wonder, given her paltry efforts in class. He had hoped for more of her quick-witted participation. Myles strode toward her and paused at her desk, holding out the results of last week's quiz and frowned.

"I'm particularly looking forward to meeting the parents of students who will likely fail my class." For added impact, he slapped the D- onto her desk. "Less than two weeks, Miss Sanders."

Indeed, he was ever so curious about Miss Leila Sander's parents.

ᓚᡣ𐭩A WEEK CAME AND WENT. LEILA MET IAN ONLY IN passing, and he scarcely looked at her. Plagued with insecurity, she matched his restraint. Did she mean any more to him than Miss Weiss did? Their Sunday afternoon seemed more like one of her dreams, morphing and twisting until it bore only vague resemblance to real life. Could her time with him have been as good as she remembered?

On the morning that Leila handed in her forged conference-confirmation slip, a familiar foreboding set in. Leila could fudge a signature, in fact, she had honed that skill over the past nine months, but coming up with a real-live parent—well, a canister of ashes was as good as she could do. If only Artie weren't black. But even if he were white—age aside—she couldn't trust him to keep his mouth shut about the blues. He was no match for Mr. Myles. And her boss was out of the question. Even if they had that sort of rapport, Mr. Myles and he would each recognize the other from Sam Goody's. She went down the list of other older male acquaintances, Artie's friends, Buddy and Pedro, and resigned herself to a no-show.

Kyle did not help. Adding to her angst, he informed her that Coach Brigham thought it would be a good idea if she and Kyle started running together, that they could sharpen each other over the winter and be all the more conditioned come spring tryouts. She regretted coming across aloof, if not a little rude when she didn't jump at the chance, but she didn't feel like explaining.

The following day, the Thursday of the conferences, Leila's

stomach twisted as she sat, waiting for Myles' torture in homeroom or trigonometry, especially since her grades had made no improvement. She avoided eye contact. Miraculously, he did not single her out, which spiked her anxiety. Perhaps that was his intent. Or, perhaps he would have so many other parents to see that her parental absence would be unremarkable. Leila managed to push it out of mind for the remainder of the day, until she spotted Ian in the parking lot, just before starting her run home. She smoothed stray hairs from her face and smiled as he headed toward her. She met him halfway.

He grinned, rubbing the back of his neck. "Hi, Leila."

"Hello."

"So ...," he exhaled, "parent-teacher conferences tonight, huh?"

"Yeah." She adjusted the chopstick in her hair.

"How does that work in your situation?"

She shrugged. "I'm not sure, aside from the fact that my parents don't show up."

"You'd probably be surprised at how many parents don't show."

"Yeah, well, no offense, but isn't it more conspicuous when parents don't show up for math as opposed to gym?"

He conceded with a nod. "Does Myles have you worried?"

"Well, he seems to be the only one of my teachers who's even aware that parents will be coming tonight." She narrowed her brow. "What's the deal with Mr. Myles, anyway?"

"I don't know." Ian shook his head. "He's an odd one. Don't feel bad though, none of the faculty knows what to make of him either."

That was no consolation. She stared off.

"You know—" he drew her eyes back to his "—a lot of last-minute things come up in parents' lives. Sometimes they have to work an unexpected shift or their medical condition takes a turn for the worse. Life doesn't revolve around parent-teacher conferences or Mr. Myles."

"All that is true ...," she sighed. "It's just that Mr. Myles really gets under my skin."

"Yours and everyone else's."

"No, it's more than just him being annoying and hardheaded. We seem to have this weird thing working between us."

"How so?"

"It's hard to explain."

He smirked. "Hard to explain the way you and I are hard to explain?"

"Yuck. No." She did not find his remark as amusing as he did. "It's just that he'll know. He reads me, if that makes sense. He'll know for sure if I'm not being forthright."

"You mean, if you're lying."

His remark stabbed. "Ian, I'm not a liar. I know I don't always tell the whole truth, but in my core I'm not dishonest. I'm just guarded."

"Sorry, I didn't mean to imply that."

"It's okay. To tell you the truth, you're the only one I've really been honest with, except Artie, but I don't think he necessarily cares or remembers."

"Who's Artie?"

"The old guy I live above. He's my other dad's—Joe's— father. Maybe you've heard of Artie Sparks?"

"Sure. Delta Blues guitarist. Robert Johnson contemporary. Dropped off the scene in the late thirties."

"That's him."

His brow shot up. "Are you serious?"

"Yeah. He's sort of like my grandfather in an unrelated way."

"Why doesn't he play anymore?"

"He still plays, just not in clubs. He spent some time in rehab, but I think there was some other stuff involved too. I guess he just likes to keep a low profile, like me."

"Wow. I'd love to meet him sometime."

"Yeah, well, then you'd have to come to my house, and I don't think we're doing that. Are we?" The corner of her mouth curled.

His jaw squared. "No. We aren't."

They each stood with their arms folded. The standoff.

"This talking and then not talking is really weird, isn't it?" she said.

"Yeah. It is." He looked at her the way he had in his studio, drawing out the silence but closing the emotional distance. "And this isn't making it any easier."

"I should run, then." She began to turn.

"Wait. That reminds me. Has Kyle talked to you yet?" He extinguished the spark.

She rolled her eyes and smirked. "Yes."

"He's a good kid, you know. You could do a whole lot worse for a friend."

"He doesn't want to be my friend. He just wants to run."

"Well, how do you think friendships start?"

She shrugged. "My track record with starting friendships isn't all that great, so I guess I'm not really sure how it's supposed to work."

"Find out. Run with him."

She sighed. She didn't want Kyle for a friend. She wanted Ian.

🐉 BEFORE HEADING OFF TO WORK, LEILA SAT ON HER bed, holding the brass canister in her lap and opened it. The ashes appeared unchanged. Just a grayish, powdery mass with a few lumps. She wished the sight of them would evoke some apparition or supernatural sign from where she could gain insight or wisdom or just a little extra strength. Her wishes never yielded anything but overwhelming loss and a sense of isolation. She envied those who spoke of feeling their loved one's presence. Not once since his death did she sense her father's loving and watchful attendance, though even when he was alive, his love and attention felt conditional.

In a way, it was a relief not having her father around. She no longer worried about his approval, or if his charisma would wear thin and Joe would finally have his fill of the moods and broken promises. And she no longer worried if her father was really going to die. She had even given up all hope of ever finding or knowing her mother—that hope died along with her dad. It was a sad notion, more in theory than actuality, yet Leila couldn't miss what she never had. She only wondered how a mother could leave her child—that, and if the flaw was her mother's or Leila's. But there was no use pondering it.

CHAPTER 11

LEILA GATHERED HER BOOKS, GIVING MR. MYLES A stealthy glance as the rest of the class filed out of homeroom. Fatigue from a poor-night's rest weighed the books in her arms. She yawned, hoping to slink out of class undetected along with the others.

"Miss Sanders," Myles voice cut through the din of hustling students, shooting adrenaline through her veins. "Please remain."

Her stomach rolled as she slumped back into her seat.

When the class cleared, he peered over his glasses and nodded. "Please—"

He remained seated as she drew in a labored breath and approached his desk, hugging her books.

His eyes locked on hers. "I missed your parents last night."

"Yes, well," she summoned her best nonchalant tone, "it was pretty much impossible for them to be here."

"And why is that?"

"Well, my mother isn't around, and—"

"What does that mean, 'she isn't around'?"

"I don't know where she is. She left when I was little."

His squint registered no sympathy. "And your father? He could not make it because …?"

"He's …." Leila flinched and cleared her throat. She had difficulty mustering enough oxygen to say, "… he's sick."

Her pulse raced as her eyes shifted and Myles blurred. She hadn't intended to elaborate, but she divulged, "He has cancer." She gasped for breath, stumbling on the words, "He had a re—a relapse a couple of nights ago."

She cleared her throat. It had been a year ago, almost to the day, when her father came out of remission. She had found him writhing in pain and had to call the ambulance— the shriek of it rushed in on her, slashing through time, striking a chord of raw emotion. It mounted in her chest, threatening to strangle or erupt.

She averted her burning eyes and choked out the words, "I need to go—" and fled the room.

Lightheaded, she rushed past Kyle and pushed through the bathroom door. Her lungs swelled and compressed, hard and fast as she leaned over the bathroom sink.

"You're hyperventilating," a girl said from behind. "Get in the stall and sit."

Leila obeyed. The girl's hand pressed something cold and wet on the back of her neck, pushing her head between her knees.

"Breathe slow or you'll pass out," she said.

Leila couldn't breathe without sobbing. "I can't." She came off the stool and vomited into the toilet as she waved the girl away.

The bell rang. At once her mind and body shifted gears, as if returning to class would set her straight. She rinsed her mouth, wiped her face and pulled open the bathroom door.

Skidding into Myles' doorway without looking, she took her seat. Breathless and dazed, she wiped sweat from her forehead. Her ears rang and all surrounding noise receded.

As if far away, she heard her name, but it didn't register.

"Miss Sanders!"

Myles stood in front of her. He slowly came into focus. "Yes ...."

"You are late *and* failing," he said, his tone even yet grave as he slapped the weekly quiz onto her desk.

Her shoulders slumped.

He flung a gesture toward the door. "Get out."

"What?" she said in an exhalation.

"Get out of my classroom." His voice did not rise.

She involuntarily rolled her eyes as she stood, forgetting her books.

"Don't you dare roll your eyes at me!" He walked ahead of her to the doorway. As she passed him on her way out, he followed and slammed the door behind them.

Without touching her, he steered her to the corner between the wall and the rear window.

"What's the matter with you?" His voice softened.

"I think I'm sick."

He braced his hand against the wall, seeking eye contact. She had difficulty focusing, yet she detected concern.

He squinted. "Are you on something?"

"I'm not on anything."

"I don't like being lied to, Miss Sanders."

She looked him straight in the eye. "I'm not lying."

"Why didn't your father come?"

Leila's eyes moved to the floor and then the window.

"It's none of your business," she said, pushing his arm away and sidling past him. She didn't look back as she rushed through the rear stairwell door and bounded down the stairs and out the back exit. She ran toward the track but made it only to the far end of the bleachers before collapsing onto the first row.

She sat with her head between her knees, holding her stomach. A hundred-pound weight bore down between her shoulder blades, splitting her skull. She wanted to curl up and fall asleep and not think about Mr. Myles and not think about her father. If he had to die, why couldn't he have toughed it out another sixteen months? She was tired of still having to be his 'strong girl.'

As soon as tears moistened her knees, they dried up. She sat and arched her back. The sun warmed her face and eyelids.

"Leila!" Kyle called out, approaching with her math books.

"Jeez, what did he do to you?"

She didn't want to talk about it. "Nothing. He just reamed me out."

"Maryanne said you were puking your brains out after homeroom."

"I think I'm coming down with something."

"You don't look good. Maybe you should go home."

"Yeah ...," she whispered, massaging her neck.

"Do you have someone to come and pick you up?"

"No. I'll just walk."

"That's stupid. You look like you'd walk right out into traffic." Kyle scratched his head. "Come on. I'll get your backpack and then take you home."

Within a few minutes, she was sitting in his car.

"You drive to school?" she asked.

"Not usually. I live just down that dead end at the back of the field, but I've got a dentist appointment right after school." He put the car in gear and pulled out.

"What about Maryanne? Won't she have a hissy fit if she finds out?"

"She's not like that." Kyle stopped at the parking lot exit. "Which way?"

"North."

"Maryanne's a nice girl. You just don't know her."

"I'm not saying she isn't nice—she seems *perfectly* nice. It's just that I've known a lot of girls like her."

"So, what are you, prejudiced against all cheerleader types?"

"Yeah."

"Where do you get off being so judgmental? You don't even give people a chance. You don't have any friends—you don't even hang out with anyone or eat in the cafeteria."

"I'm just used to being alone."

Leila stared off at passing cars. How could Kyle understand why she behaved the way she did? And there was no use trying to fill him in.

The farther north they drove, the stiffer the silence.

"Did I miss a turn?" he asked.

"No, just keep heading north."

Kyle slowed at every street, glancing at her as if awaiting instruction to turn. When they crossed over into an all-black neighborhood, he said, "You live in North Millville?"

"Is that a problem?"

"No ... it's just a little weird, that's all." He glanced at her. "You have to admit it's a little weird."

"It's not weird. It's just where I live."

"Okay ...."

"Turn here. It's up there. The grayish one on the left with the little blue Beetle."

"Are you going to be okay?"

"Yeah," she said, too weary to say that she really didn't know, that she didn't want him to leave, that all she wanted was someone to hold her and tell her everything would be alright.

She tried to smile. "You'll find your way back out okay?"

"Yeah, no problem."

Leila climbed out. From the sidewalk, she leaned back in. "Thanks for the lift, Kyle. And tell Maryanne thanks for the wet towel."

CLARENCE MYLES RARELY SECOND-GUESSED THE WAY he handled his students. Many considered him harsh, he knew that. He also knew how to get results and had the track record to prove it. Only the rare student ever failed his class, and his students had the highest grade-point average in math at Millville high school. He would not allow someone like Kyle Shultz to skate by on easily made A's anymore than he tolerated mediocrity from those capable of better—clear and simple.

Most students reacted predictably. A little intimidation went a long way. In fact, his legendary status required only a grossly exaggerated story or two to earn him several years of compliance if not respect—or fear, as some interpreted it. Either way, his demands sharpened his students and years later, more than a few thanked him. Although someone like Leila Sanders had a great deal of potential, he accepted the possibility that she might never be a mathematical scholar. Nevertheless, he would not abide apathy and certainly not dishonesty.

What had Leila hoped to achieve by withholding information regarding her parents and forcing his hand, a hand he loathed to play? Her reaction was too barefaced to be fabrication, yet too calculated to be truthful. In fact, he had miscalculated how far to push her, and although he had saved face in front of his class, he had lost ground with a student he particularly liked and hoped to motivate. Myles could not define what had been violated, he only knew he could not let it pass without investigation.

He stood at the office counter. "Leila Sander's file. *Please*."

The secretary dropped a bulging folder in front of him. "I don't know how many schools this girl has been to, but she's a heavyweight."

Thumbing through the stack, he counted six different high school files. No extracurricular activities. Irregular attendance and grades that fluctuated, not just from subject to subject, but from quarter to quarter. No suspensions or other disciplinary problems. No notations. He picked up and read her information card. She was living with her father and no mother—and no telephone.

The secretary tapped her pencil beside him. "Are you done yet?"

He gathered the papers, withholding Leila's contact card and closed the folder.

"Yes. Thank you," he snarled as he exited.

"Hey! The card stays with the file!" she called out after him. Myles ignored her. The door shut behind him.

Leila had no home telephone number listed. Calling the emergency contact was pointless. Myles wanted the parent, the incontrovertible parent. That warranted a house call.

On his way north to his home in Farmingdale, Myles

stopped at a local convenience store for specific directions. As he steered through Leila's neighborhood, he surveyed his surroundings, glancing at black faces as he drove past. Modest homes lined the streets, some in good condition, but just as many in disrepair.

His Volvo pulled up to the curb in front of her house. A round-bellied man sat on the next-door porch and squinted as Myles climbed from his car. Myles acknowledged him with a nod and stepped through the chain-linked gate. A concrete walk split the tiny mowed yard. Stepping onto the front stoop, he rapped the asbestos shingle twice. A few seconds later, a small-framed black man opened the screen door and hobbled out. The sun deepened his wrinkles.

He scrutinized Myles sideways. "Can I help you?"

With the card in hand, Myles reciprocated with his own sideways stare. "I'm looking for Leila Sanders."

"Who's asking?"

"My name is Clarence Myles."

The toothless man smiled. "Clarence. I use to know a Clarence, everyone called him Larry. Anyone call you Larry?"

"No."

"Clarence Myles—" he rubbed his bristled head and coughed. "Oh, Mister Myles, da maff teacher …. Yes."

"And you are?"

"I'm Artie." He shrugged. "Sorry 'bout my teef. I didn't get around to putting 'em in today."

Myles smiled politely, though his patience had begun to wear. He glanced at the name on the card. "Would that be Arthur Spartan?"

"Don't nobody but da postman call me dat. I'm Artie Sparks." He held out his hand.

Myles clutched it firmly. "Artie Sparks? The blues guitarist?"

"Yes, sir." Artie smiled, his lips curling around his gums. "Dat's right—Angel says you know da blues."

"Angel?"

"Dat's what I call her, 'cause dat's what she is."

Myles had not envisioned Leila in any setting remotely like this. He scratched his neck.

"Well, Clarence—do you mind if I call you Clarence?"

"No." Myles did mind, yet he would tolerate it under the circumstances.

"Some blond boy brung her home dis mornin' and she been home all day. It ain't like her." As he turned back toward the house, he waved at his neighbor. "I sure hope she gonna be better for tomorrow night."

The old man kept his hand in the air as he stepped inside. "Good to meet'cha."

"Likewise." Myles stood for a moment longer. He glanced at the stairway toward which Artie had gestured, at the grinning fellow on the other side of the fence. Slowly he walked to the second-story entrance, now scrutinizing Leila's surroundings under new light.

"Artie Sparks," he said under his breath. *What else have you been withholding, Miss Leila Sanders?*

That she did not feel the need to drop names or impress him intrigued Myles, yet at the same time, her secrecy unsettled him. He had already sized her up as exceptional, but he might have underestimated her or at least her situation.

At the bottom of the stairwell, yellowed tape curled across the name Sanders on the mailbox. He climbed the stairs toward a dim light at the uppermost landing. Each step creaked as he ascended. Near the top, the muffled serenade of Billie Holiday greeted him. He almost smiled. Standing before a glass-paned door, he peered through sheer curtains that obscured much of what lay on the other side. What looked like a small love seat sat in the middle of a tiny room. Bright light poured in from the front of the house. His knuckle tapped the pane, rattling loose glass. A bit of window glaze crumbled onto his shoe. Something stirred on the sofa, and in a moment a figure rose and went to the back of the apartment. A moment later, the figure returned and cracked open the door.

Leila wrapped her sweater tightly. She pulled hair from her face and looked at him through pink and puffy eyes.

Myles swallowed, now regretting his harshness. "May I come in?"

"Do I have a choice?" Her voice lacked its usual strength or defiance.

"Please?"

She stepped aside, leaving the door cracked. He pushed it open and entered as Leila moved toward her bookcase. Tall stacks of cassette tapes teetered behind a framed picture beside the player. She hit the stop button.

Myles gave the room a cursory scan. In the kitchen her trigonometry textbook lay opened on the table. One chair sat beside it. On the sink sideboard, one cup and one plate dried on a towel. At his feet, only one pair of sneakers lay on the doormat and one jacket hung beside the door. Opposite where he stood, a small drawing table consumed the corner. Tacked sketches and paintings consumed the wall above it.

"I like your choice of music," he said, gesturing toward her stack of cassettes. "Do you mind?"

She neither consented nor refused, she simply shifted her weight. In three steps, Myles stood in front of her bookcase crammed with books and drawing pads in gradations of tallest to smallest. More books lay on the floor in a neat pile. Instead of perusing her music, he glanced at the picture, a faded photograph of two men—one black, one white—and a dimpled little girl standing on a beach. Leila around nine or ten years old.

"Family picture?" he asked.

She looked at him with eyes that seemed not to care. "Yeah."

He again scanned the room for any telltale sign of masculinity. Although the room did not bespeak overt femininity, he detected the faintest scent of lily-of-the-valley. Beside the bookcase, only a single door led out of the open living area—a bedroom door, wide open. A bottom-of-the-line cremation urn sat on her dresser. He sucked in a labored breath at the sight of it and its implication. His gaze returned to her. She half-rolled her eyes and slowly blinked, as if holding her eyes open required her last bit of energy. Myles' own strength drained at the thought of the inescapable truth.

He sighed. "How long has he been gone?"

Leila stiffened. Her eyes darted as if calculating. Did she really think he would not deduce the obvious?

Her chin quivered. "Nine months."

"Cancer?"

She nodded and looked away, pulling her sweater tighter around her waist.

Massaging his stubbled chin, he stared at her, putting all the pieces together. He hated what he had stumbled upon and the position it put him in. Even more, he hated the thought of a girl on her own, juggling adult responsibilities while suffering loss. And how did an old, worn-out blues musician come into play?

"And Artie?" he asked.

"What about Artie?" she snapped at him.

"Where does he fit in?"

"He's a friend of the family." She pulled her hair away from her face and met his eyes. He believed her. Leila's eyes always gave her away.

"And what about relatives?"

"Like I mentioned, my mom took off, and my dad—he was an orphan."

"Who's the other man in the picture?"

"Artie's son, my dad's best friend, Joe."

"Is Artie your legal guardian?"

Her eyes wandered and then came back to his. "No."

"Who is?"

"No one."

Myles sighed and Leila cringed. Truth or not, he didn't like her answers.

"Does anyone else know your situation?"

Leila frowned and turned away. Her reluctance reinforced his concern. He stepped closer and touched her shoulder, drawing her attention. With a raised brow, he insisted she reply.

Leila exhaled and mumbled, "Coach Brigham knows."

He had not anticipated that. Leila stared at him. Defiance shot from her eyes. Rather than risk shutting her down with intrusive questions about Coach Brigham, he rerouted. "Anyone else?"

"No."

He hated interrogating her as if she were incompetent, but he needed at least some reassurance. "How are you getting by?"

"I'm making ends meet. Joe helps out."

"You look skinny. Are you eating?"

She glared at him. "I've always been skinny. It's genetic."

"You turn eighteen in May?"

"Yes."

"Are you passing all your other classes?"

"Yes."

"You're still working at the mall?"

Her eyes narrowed with annoyance. "*Yes!*"

"Do you have days off?"

Her spark of defiance returned with ardor. "None of this is your business! I wish you'd just get out of here and leave me alone."

"It's too late for that," he said, immediately regretting his overly firm tone as she turned away. Had it been so long that he had forgotten how to be tender? He cleared his throat. "I just wanted to know if you have any time for yourself, time to rest up."

Her malleability surprised him as she glanced over her shoulder and responded with childlike trust. "I have weekends off."

"Good."

Exhaling reservation, he turned from her and walked the perimeter of the room as if inspecting her housekeeping, but mostly he needed a moment to think. Rounding the sofa, he glanced at her. She maintained a safe distance as he maneuvered to her art table and stood before it. A set of watercolors lay open beside a cup of gray water and a paper towel blotted with a spectrum of color. Her displayed work was good for her age. While it impressed him, he also understood the artistic temperament. Under the circumstances, it likely did not play in her favor. At the end of the neatly tacked row of her artwork was a black-and-white photograph of her, running. Who had shot that?

He shook his head. He had expected family dysfunction of some sort, but not this. He could not have imagined any of it, least of all the way Leila stirred his emotions. He thought of his daughter and his throat tightened. He needed another moment to collect himself, to get the choking sensation under control.

Leila appeared to be managing her life, but a young woman on her own, without tangible emotional or material support—apart from a toothless old musician—had obvious pitfalls. In spite of her aptitude for impressing him, did she have the resources to succeed, emotionally or otherwise? What was in her best interest? Myles himself had been victimized by bureaucratic bias. Not all arbitrary rules had an individual's best interest at heart. In his opinion, they had no heart. He hated to see her life further disrupted, but this was not a good situation. A child deserved a stable home with someone to care for her needs—he knew firsthand the fallout of instability. Shaking his head, he looked at Leila. He had stumbled onto her truth and stood judge over her life. Her eyes pleaded mercy and his insides softened.

"Are you going to tell?" she asked.

Her anguished face moved him. "If you got in a jam, would you tell me?"

"What do you mean?"

"I need your assurance that if you got into a bad situation, whatever that might be—that you would tell me—you'd let me help you." He had hoped to express himself without emotion but failed.

Leila's eyes welled and she turned away, wiping her face

as she nodded.

Silence consumed another minute as he weighed options and his own accountability. Finally, he said, "Provided you don't run into trouble ... for now ... no one needs to know."

She sniffed and wiped another tear but did not face him.

He firmed his posture and stated, "If you're going to graduate, you need to pass my class."

She cast him an irritated glance. "I'm perfectly aware of that."

He studied her one moment longer. "I'll see you Monday morning."

CHAPTER 12

ON MONDAY MORNING, ANNOUNCEMENTS CRACKLED over the PA system. Spirit-week agenda. Pep rallies. Costume day. And, of course, the homecoming parade, football game, and dance.

"... Featuring," Principal Boyd stated, "our very own rock band, the Tailgates ...."

Leila had no spirited feelings for this or any other school, and she had no intention of participating in spirit-week hoopla.

"You're going to wear a costume, aren't you?" Kyle nudged her, whispering from behind.

Leila rolled her eyes and ignored him the way Mr. Myles had been ignoring her all morning. She expected something would change between them, but his apparent lack of interest seemed the extent of it. Just the same, she stayed alert in case he changed his mind. Then homeroom dismissed and he called Kyle and Leila to his desk.

Both students exchanged wary looks and approached.

"Mr. Schultz, I have a mandatory extra-credit assignment for you."

Wiping his palms on his jeans, Kyle's weight shifted.

"Miss Sanders is—as of the results of last Friday's quiz— failing my class. Your assignment is to bring her grade up to a B average. Eighty percent will do. For every two points she's deficient of eighty percent, you will lose one point from your average."

"What!" Kyle exploded. "I could lose up to eight points off my grade."

Leila's jaw dropped. "What are you doing to me?"

Myles ignored her and continued addressing Kyle. "Exactly. The bonus is that if you succeed, I will bump your grade up to a ninety-nine percent."

"But she's a mathematical moron!" Kyle glanced at her. "No offense."

"Yes, she is. Therefore, I suggest you not waste any time."

Leila could not find words, but Kyle did. "You can't do this!"

Myles sprung to his feet and leaned into Kyle. "Oh, yes I can. And watch your tone. It's time you actually had to work for your grade."

Kyle backed down and glared at Leila. Cursing under his breath, he stormed out.

Leila remained, her mouth agape. "What are you trying to prove?"

"You wanted a tutor, now you have one. End of discussion." The old Myles had returned.

Again, the eye-roll. She stomped out of the room.

Kyle slammed their locker door as she approached. "You had to ask for a tutor."

"I'm sorry. I had no idea he would pull that. Isn't there some way you can get out of it?"

"What, are you nuts? Were you not in there?"

"I just need to brush up on my algebra and geometry a little."

"You can't be serious."

Leila shrugged.

He frowned. "And I suppose you barely passed those classes."

"D-minuses."

"Are you kidding me?"

"Well, the past couple of years haven't been very good for me."

He did not smile, not even a little.

She winced. "Why do you have to be so mean about it?"

"My grade's on the line. I can't afford to have you drag me down. I've got scholarships hanging in the balance."

Leila wilted. "I promise I'll study all the time, you'll see, you won't have to do hardly anything. I'll even give up running to school so I can spend more time on my formulas."

"Don't be stupid." He glanced at his watch and hustled back to Myles' class. They both flew into their seats just as the bell rang. Myles twitched a half-smile.

Rather than slapping her failing quiz results on her desk, Myles held it up for her to see and directed his comment to Kyle. "This is an unacceptable failure, Miss Sanders. I will be expecting a turnaround this week."

When Myles invaded her home, Leila had no idea just how things would change, but they would. Although his presence had agitated her, she craved something in his strength and boldness, something in which she found comfort. He had been fatherly in a way she never would have imagined him capable. At the same time, he now had information, information that gave him power. Control. She hated that. Ian had the same information, but she never sensed he had any desire to control her with it.

After math, Leila and Kyle made plans to meet outside the gym after eighth period to work out the details. Just before the agreed-upon time, she changed into her running shorts. The gym door groaned and she hurried into the alcove to meet Kyle in the hall, but instead she tripped headlong into Ian.

He steadied her. "Whoa. Big hurry today."

Leila withdrew. "Coach!"

"You doing okay?"

She wavered. "Yeah."

"I heard you might have had a rough weekend."

"Really? What did you hear?"

"That you looked like hell and Kyle had to take you home. Was it parent-teacher aftermath?"

"Interesting play on words."

Ian grinned.

"Myles paid me a visit at home. He—" just then, Kyle stuck his head between the glass-windowed alcove doors.

"There you are!" Kyle glanced from one to the other. "Should I come back?"

"Yeah, Kyle," Brigham said. "Just give us a minute."

"Sure thing, Coach." He stepped back out into the hall.

Ian maintained a respectable distance. "What happened?"

"Mr. Myles knows. All he had to do was look at me. He wasn't in my apartment for more than two minutes and he figured it out."

Ian's brow arched.

"I told you, we have this weird thing."

"What was his reaction?"

"If I stay out of trouble, he'll keep it to himself. He even sounded, I don't know, fatherly."

"Fatherly?"

"Yeah … and he knows that you know."

As if to ask how? Ian's eyes widened.

"I'm sorry. I told you, it's this weird thing we have. Besides, it didn't seem to faze him."

"How much does he know?"

"Only that you're aware of my situation."

"It doesn't matter." Ian's eyes softened. "Are you really doing okay?"

"I just think some things are beginning to catch up to me, but other than that …." She shrugged, forcing a smile.

They again stood at the impasse. He stepped closer and then caught himself. "You'd better run."

She nodded, the frustration in his eyes reflecting her own. She turned and pushed through the doors to where Kyle waited.

She pasted on a smile. "Okay, so what do you want to do?"

A couple of days a week she would drive to school and they would run track before classes. On those afternoons, they would study math at his house, given that it was less than a five-minute walk. Since Maryanne was cheerleading on Saturdays, they could put in some extra time at the track, early, before games.

෴KYLE STEPPED THROUGH THE CUT CHAIN-LINK fence early the next morning, spotting Leila across the field where she sat on the track bench. Yawning, he walked to meet her, his breath, heavy in the crisp, forty-five-degree air, and cold in his chest. He rubbed goosebumps beneath the sleeves of his hooded jacket.

The sun, low in the sky, set aflame maple trees lining the athletic fields. It appeared as though their tips had been dipped in crimson. He squinted. Could Leila be wearing only shorts and a sweatshirt?

"You must be freezing," he called out, toasty in his sweat pants.

"Not until I stopped moving and sat down." She shivered and stood as he approached. "This is what I normally wear. I warm up as I run."

Kyle stood before her. Leila was tall, but at six-four, he towered over her.

"Oh yeah?" his brows arched.

Leila started toward the track. "Let's go."

Kyle laughed. "You're killing me. Haven't you ever heard of a warm up?"

"Sure, I warm up as I jog, you know, before I start running."

He shook his head. "Girl, who taught you how to run?"

"Nobody."

"Stretches! We stretch first."

"Oh. Right. Like in gym class." Leila returned to the bench.

He shook his head. Coach was right, Leila was a virgin runner. "First we'll work on our quads."

"Quads? What are my quads?"

Sitting on the bench in front of her, he ran his hand up her outer thigh feeling goose bumps. "These are your quadriceps."

She gasped and Kyle grinned, drawing his hand back.

"Sorry," he said, comparing her legs to Maryanne's. His girlfriend had nicely shaped legs—they looked great in a cheerleading skirt—but at five-four, her legs didn't go on and on like Leila's.

"Just warn me next time," she said.

"I'm allowed a next time?"

"Don't be a pig."

He chuckled and demonstrated the quad stretches, then the hamstring stretch, and a few others she said she had never heard of. She mimicked each movement.

"Now we hit the track." He gestured and she followed. "We'll start off slow. You just keep pace with me."

Kyle took the outside lane on account of his longer stride and started off slow. As he pushed a little harder, she matched his speed. Kyle liked that she kept up. He enjoyed running with her even more than imagining it. Not that he had fantasized about her at length, but her mysterious ways intrigued him. So what if she seemed a little rude sometimes.

On the second lap, Kyle picked up his pace, monitoring her exertion. Coach Brigham had said she claimed to be noncompetitive. Testing her, Kyle slowed, hoping she might continue their previous pace or try to outrun him. When he pulled back, she lagged.

"Do you want to run faster?" he asked, hoping to egg her on.

"If you do."

"You think you can outrun me?"

"I don't know."

He stepped it up. Turning to face her, he ran backward. "You'd like to know though, wouldn't you?"

"I guess it doesn't really matter to me."

"I don't think you can."

Leila shrugged. "Who cares?"

He smiled. "Do you want to race me?"

"Don't be a jerk." She scowled and pulled back to a jog.

Alone and ahead of her, he stopped until she caught up. "So, you really aren't competitive?"

"Is that what this is? You want to test how competitive I am?"

"Well, believe it or not, track is competitive. You need to know how to compete. It's not like just getting out there and trying to run faster than everyone else. You start off in a line, but you're immediately vying for position. You may be a fast runner, but if you can't push your way into a slot as it opens up, you'll be heading up the rear." He had not meant to intimidate her, but her insecurity surfaced in the widening of her eyes.

She slowed to a walk. "I'm going to really suck at this."

"Don't say that. Come on." He tugged her arm and pulled her forward. "Let's run some more."

She acquiesced and they jogged for a minute longer.

He nudged her. "In a few weeks you are seriously going to want to whup me. You'll see."

🐾 MR. MYLES PULLED INTO HIS PARKING SPACE. AS HE climbed from his Volvo, two running figures caught his eye. The corner of his mouth curled with satisfaction at his astute match. How fortuitous that Kyle was as much Brigham's pawn as his own. In homeroom, he smirked at his two favorite students from behind his *Rolling Stone*. It was still unclear if the handsome young Brigham fit in somewhere beyond simply coaching. Myles had no intention of approaching him—not without solid knowledge or proof—or of divulging what he knew or at least presumed. Just the same, he had no problem putting Brigham on notice. When Myles had seen him in the staff lounge that morning, he had put a visual lock on Brigham and paid close attention to the young man's reaction. Brigham returned his stare, unintimidated. An interruption from Miss Michaels put an end to the face-off, but as soon as Myles stepped out of the lounge room, Brigham followed.

"Do you have something you want to say to me?" Ian asked.

Myles would not expose his hand, but he respected his colleague's forthrightness. "I see you've enlisted Kyle in your scheme to get a girls' track team."

"Is that what you think?"

"I think we both have our own agenda, and Kyle has become useful to us both. I know whose best interest I have at heart ...."

"Don't presume upon my motives, Mr. Myles. You don't know me," Ian said and walked away.

🍂 LEILA TURNED HER BUG DOWN THE DEAD-END lane, her shortcut, and glanced at Kyle. "I didn't know you live down here."

They drove under a canopy of mature oak and maple trees, all showing autumn color. Barberry bushes hedged either side of the narrow court. She pulled up in front of the large colonial that seemed right out of New England, with cedar shingles, trimmed shrubbery, and weedless lawn.

Kyle laughed. "You know, you've been running past my house practically every morning since last July."

She may not have noticed his house before, but apparently *she* had not been as inconspicuous in the white neighborhoods as she assumed. She followed Kyle up the brick pathway onto the stoop as he pushed the front door open. It squeaked and echoed as they stepped in onto hardwood floors.

"C'mon." He motioned for her to follow. Taking two steps at a time, he bounded up the staircase, ascending two half-flights of stairs. He slowed to walk up the third and then stepped into his room. It boasted as much floor space as Leila's entire apartment.

"Wow, this is nice," she said.

His double bed barely ate into the room, and a built-in desk nestled under a gabled window looking out over the back yard. A large shelf supported quite a few track-and-field trophies. Leila moved around the room with awe and paused in front of a large collection of albums.

"Wow, I never would have taken you as someone with such broadminded musical taste," she said.

"Oh, I'm full of surprises."

"So did your mother decorate your room?"

"What?"

"I mean, everything matches. And there's no poster of Farrah Fawcett."

"I'll have you know I picked plaid—it's not my fault that my mother went overboard with it," he said, crossing his arms. "And I wouldn't want you to think my room is always this clean. I knew you were coming so my mother made me get rid of my smelly socks and underwear."

Seating her at the desk beside him, he opened a notebook. "Okay, we're going to start with a few algebra equations so I can see where you're at." He handed her a sheet. "Reduce the equations to the lowest common denominator." Thus began their first tutoring session.

An hour later, on their way out to her car, he said, "Well, at least you're not a total math moron, just a little retarded. You'll be a math scholar in no time."

She forced a smile and shrugged. How could Kyle have so much on his side of the equation, while on the other side, she lived with such a deficit? It didn't add up.

He leaned against her driver's door. "So, Leila, what are you going to dress up as on Friday?"

She rolled her eyes. "What's the big deal with wearing a costume?"

"What's the big deal with not wearing one?"

"It just seems, well … it seems stupid."

"What are you saying? You think everyone who wears a costume is stupid?"

"Well, no … I've just never been into that whole thing."

"Why not?"

"I don't know. I guess we moved around too much."

"Well, you know, it's supposed to be fun. You know what fun is, right?"

She shot him a squint. "Yes."

"Sorry—just wasn't sure if fun fit into your whole antisocial profile."

"I'm not antisocial."

"Really?"

"Alright. I'm a little antisocial—you would be too if you'd been to so many different schools that you didn't even bother to keep track anymore."

His eyes widened. "Why'd you move around so much?"

A small bit of information seemed harmless enough. "My dad was a musician, always looking for a better gig, a better situation."

His brow flicked. "Seriously?"

"Actually, I'm in the witness protection program. If I divulge anything more, I put the lives of myself and my family in jeopardy, and I'd have to kill you."

He laughed and rolled his eyes. "You *are* a moron."

"*You're* a moron."

🐉CHAPTER 13

A DRAFTING EXERCISE SEEMED LIKE A GOOD IDEA TO Kyle. He explained it to Leila while puffing alongside her. Breath shot from his mouth. Brisk, early morning air chilled his neck.

"Drafting?" she puzzled.

"Yeah, it's when I run directly behind you to benefit from the reduction in wind resistance that you create as the leader. It's like if your little car is behind a big truck, it's easier to go faster," Kyle spoke in rhythm with his heavy breathing.

"But it still doesn't put you in front to win."

"Not initially, but it conserves some of my energy for the final push so that I can pass you and lead."

She nodded as he tucked behind her. He hoped that with no one at her side to regulate her pace, that Leila would push ahead. She did. Kyle kept up for a few paces, but within seconds the distance between them expanded. He didn't bother to reel her back. He grinned, realizing she was unaware of having defeated the purpose of the exercise. Several feet turned into yards—a quarter of the track later, she finally turned to him.

When Kyle caught up, he panted, "You are seriously fast."

Exertion colored her cheeks. "Sorry. I didn't mean to do that."

While they stretched to cool down, he kept glancing at her with a grin but said nothing. She ignored him. Perhaps she was even toying with him. He wished they could run together all day, rather than go to the homecoming game. Just the same, he looked forward to seeing Maryanne. She was one of the four girls nominated for homecoming queen, and he did not want to miss her big day.

As they walked back to his house under a canopy of ochre and crimson, he said, "You are going to homecoming, aren't you?"

Leila half-shrugged. "I hadn't planned on it."

"Aw, come on. You got through costume day. Your Stevie Wonder glasses were great."

"They were Ray Charles glasses."

"*Whoever*—I think you were even having fun with it by the end of the day."

"I guess it wasn't so awful."

"So you'll come?"

"Honestly Kyle, you don't know how uncomfortable it is, showing up alone. Besides, I have plans."

"Who says you'd be going alone? And what plans could you possibly have on a Saturday night?"

"You think I'm going to tag along with you and Maryanne? She'll love that. And I actually have friends that I hang out with on Saturday nights."

"Oh please," he chuckled. "What friends?"

"Older friends."

"Oh really?" No surprise there. "And what do you do with your *older* friends?"

"We ...." She twisted her mouth and wavered. "We jam."

He smirked, letting her step through the chain-link fence ahead of him. "Did you just say, you *jam*?"

"Yes. You know, when a group of musicians hang out and play for fun."

That surprised him. "I had no idea you were musical." He continued to smirk, unsure of her sincerity. "So, what do you *jam* on?"

"Piano."

"Are you any good?"

"What difference does that make?"

"You are good. I can tell, just like you're good at running."

"Yeah, well you'll never find out."

He kept smiling as they arrived in front of his house. "Can't you back out just this once? This is your last homecoming. I'm sure your *older* friends will understand."

She contorted her mouth as if reconsidering.

"Why don't you go home and get changed, and meet me back at my house before the game? And don't worry about Maryanne. She'll be fine. She'll hardly notice you're along."

Leila bit her lip. "Fine."

Kyle nudged her as she climbed into her car. "And would it kill you to wear your hair down for once?"

🙰 LEILA STOOD BEFORE HER MIRROR, COMBING OUT damp tresses. *I suppose it wouldn't kill you to wear your hair down.* She applied a few strokes of mascara and inspected the results. For the effort makeup took, it did make her pale eyes stand out. She wondered if Kyle would notice and hoped Maryanne wouldn't. It wasn't a date, but the idea of spending an afternoon with Kyle excited Leila. Maryanne, on the other hand, made her nervous—how would his girlfriend react to the intrusion? It was too late to reconsider the mascara, but she would forgo blush or lip-gloss.

Rather than give her a cool reception, Maryanne complimented Leila on her brown angora sweater and long locks. She even engaged Leila in small talk. Kyle, as expected, behaved as always—uninhibited, kissing Maryanne as though there was no onlooker. When the three arrived on the track, Maryanne tiptoed, reaching for a hug and kiss. Again, it was no passing kiss. Leila looked away, heated at their open display of affection bordering on passion. As Maryanne pranced onto the football field, Kyle's gaze followed the swish of her skirt.

"C'mon," Kyle said, heading to the home-team side.

A chill breeze whipped, stirring leaves and cheerleaders'

hems. Standing between the short chain-link fence and the bleachers, each pocketed their hands to ward off goose bumps. Leila straightened her back, her insides fluttering at the sight of students milling around the track and heading their way.

"Don't look so petrified," Kyle said, tipping his chin toward them. "They're only a bunch of morons like me."

Leila breathed deep and rolled her shoulders, trying to ease nerves.

"Hey, Kyle. Hi, Leila," they said as they passed by.

"Do I know them?" Leila asked, though she recognized one guy from Artie's neighborhood.

"Doesn't matter. They know you."

Leila tensed again. The nip in the air did nothing to cool the heat flooding her body.

"Didn't you know? You're Leila, the girl runner." He laughed. "Speaking of runners, here comes one now."

A boy with a bobbing gait and wearing a letter jacket headed toward them. Leila didn't recognize him.

"How ya doin', Kyle?" Deep dimples sank into his olive complexion. He stood about Leila's height, though his curly dark hair added several inches.

"Micah, how you doin'? This is Leila."

"Hi," he said. Heavy lids half-covered his glazed, brown eyes—she knew the look well.

"Micah's on the track team."

"Oh," she nodded. "Hi Micah."

"Micah is the Tailgate's lead guitarist, you know, in the band that's playing tonight."

"Oh."

Kyle nudged Micah. "I just found out Leila plays piano."

"Cool." Micah's head bobbed with approval. "What's your genre?"

"Mostly blues," she said.

"Wow, lady plays the blues." He grinned. "That's cool."

"Yeah," Kyle chimed in. "She's good, too."

Leila frowned and smacked his arm. "Shut up, Kyle. You

don't have any idea how I play."

Kyle shoved her. "Do too."

Another couple of kids joined them. Before long, she was one in the crowd. They moved onto the bleachers, about halfway up. Leila sat in front of Kyle, catching a whiff of pot when Micah sat beside her. The two boys speculated on the outcome of the game. It all sounded like trigonometry to her.

"So," Micah redirected the conversation to Leila. "You think you might try out for track?"

"I guess that's the plan."

"Cool." His head continued bobbing. "I hear you're pretty fast."

She shrugged, but Kyle jumped right in, "Man, you have no idea."

She tightened her lips, glaring.

He shot back, "God, Leila, it's not like it's some big secret." He returned to Micah. "We were running track this morning, and she—blew—me—away. We were trying out a drafting exercise. I was tailing her, moving at a steady clip— not full speed—but she didn't even know I was in the dust till she was a hundred meters ahead."

"Seriously ...," Micah bobbed.

"Yeah, yeah, yeah." She exhaled as her attention drifted, then snagged on the sight of Ian entering the field. His camera-bag strap cut diagonally across his T-shirt, tucked into just-snug-enough jeans. With his camera and telephoto lens in hand, he scanned the track perimeter. A large-busted cheerleader bounded toward him, her hips swaying as she invaded his personal space. She then twirled and bounded back toward the cheerleading squad. Ian veered off and followed her.

Kyle grabbed Leila's shoulder from behind and whispered in her ear, "I know. Doesn't she just make you sick?"

She jabbed his knee. "You're such a jerk."

Brigham shot a few pictures of posing cheerleaders and then headed toward the bleachers where the trio sat. As soon as he made it to the divider fence, Kyle sprung to his feet.

"I'll be right back."

Scaling down the bleachers, two benches at a time, he met Coach Brigham at the fence. Leila did not have a chance to panic before Micah asked her opinion on the British Blues Revolution.

"I'm not real familiar with it per se, but I like some of the Eric Clapton I've heard."

"Slowhand—he's like one of my idols. Him and Jimi Hendrix. That song 'Layla' is pretty cool, too."

"Yeah." She knew the title more than the actual song and tried not to sound uninterested—it was just that Ian and Kyle were so distracting. She knew what they were talking about. Kyle's animation and then Ian's smile and nod gave it away.

Micah grew quiet. Leila tightened her clasped hands. Why was Kyle taking so long? Micah seemed nice enough, but she hadn't bargained for sitting alone beside him. How could she be so at ease with grown men, while most teenage boys seemed like a foreign species?

"So, Micah," she cut the silence, "do you know any good blues riffs?"

"Are you kidding me? They're pretty much the entire foundation of rock."

Leila smiled at the familiarity of his words—perhaps he wasn't so foreign after all.

"Hey, would you like to hear some Clapton tonight?" He grinned.

"Yeah," she said, though it didn't really matter to her. "That'd be great."

Down at the foot of the bleachers, Ian looked up, bringing his camera to his eye. Twisting the lens, he shot a couple frames. She broke out in a full-dimpled grin. His camera lowered and he smiled back.

Micah's fingers twitched across his imaginary guitar. Many of Leila's 'older friends' had a similar twitch.

Kyle returned, sitting beside Leila, and continued his teasing. Before she knew it, the game had begun. At halftime, Principle Boyd crowned Maryanne's rival Deirdre, the buxom cheerleader, as queen. Ian caught it all on film. By the time the game started back up, Leila had lost track of Ian until she spotted Miss Weiss leading him, along with Leila's gaze, just behind the bleachers. Leila's neck craned. She couldn't grasp the drift of their exchange as people milled around and passed in front of them, but there wasn't a whole lot of space between Ian and Miss Weiss. The two stepped farther out of sight. Leila tried to focus on the game. Although she understood little of it, she soon found herself rooting for the home team. When they won, she applauded the victors, but the opposing team's defeat stole her smile.

Although Maryanne took her own defeat cheerfully, a pang of disappointment sent Leila to her side.

"I don't know," she said to Maryanne, "but do you think it's possible the judges might have been swayed by her unruly boobs?"

Maryanne burst out laughing. Kyle smirked.

Bare branches raked the sun as it dropped into the treetops. Although the air had warmed halfway through the game, the chill again set in. Kyle replaced his jacket over Maryanne's shoulders. Micah had disappeared at halftime—said he had to set up sound equipment, but on their way into the school building, Leila saw him behind the score shack smoking a joint.

When they entered the gym, a few students had already gathered for the dance and stood around the black-skirted bandstand. The familiar sound of tuning instruments sent a tingle of pleasure up her spine.

Mr. Williams, the band teacher, assisted Micah with the amplifier connections and fiddled with the pickups on their guitars. Lead, backup, and bass guitars, drums, and piano. Leila migrated away from her group and toward the bandstand. She missed this element of her past, though not too long ago she couldn't wait to leave it behind. The bassist reminded her of Joe—tall and handsome and light-skinned for someone considered black. He passed her a nod of recognition—in fact, she had seen him around her neighborhood. He seemed to appreciate the attention and played a few licks while keeping his eyes on her. Musicians—they just loved an audience.

Before long, Principal Boyd introduced the Homecoming Queen and King. With applause, he invited the Tailgates onto the stage. The lights dimmed as a rear spotlight beamed on the lead guitarist, Micah, backlighting the frizz of his curly hair. Ian was right there with his camera. Deirdre and the captain of the football team took center floor for the Homecoming King and Queen's dance. Maryanne grabbed Kyle's hand and leaned over to Leila.

"Check this out. His mother is a ballroom dance instructor," she said and dragged him in front of the stage with the other runners-up. Kyle took the lead, maneuvering Maryanne, spinning and twisting her petite body. He was even more graceful on the dance floor than he was on the track.

To complete the warm up, Micah coaxed a few more dancers on to the floor with a quick tempo. Leila closed her eyes. The sounds transported her to a hundred nights in dozens of garages and basements, each note plucking a bittersweet chord. Her trained ear scrutinized their sound. Initially, their timing was off. Micah's voice sounded pitchy, but as they heated up, they pulled it together and synchronized well. Then he went into a zone, contorting his body and face as his fingers zipped up and down the frets, playing Hendrix. Hours went into Micah's agility, but he made it look easy. As her attention moved from player to player, she analyzed their form and technique, comparing them to those she had grown up around.

As familiar as it all felt, it struck Leila odd; she had rarely seen any band play for an audience. She knew the sound of recorded music, warm-ups, and practice, but only one time did a more lenient nightclub manager allow her to sneak from the backroom and sit in a dark corner near the bandstand. The opportunity had thrilled her. On that long-ago night, in some small way, she grasped what drove her father. Micah had the same drive as he played. That look lingered when he glanced up between songs and smiled right at her.

He then moved into some Lynyrd Skynyrd as she scanned the perimeter of the gym just in time to spot Karen Weiss in a tight red dress. She grabbed Ian's lethargic hand. He shook his head, giving her no second chance before he walked away. The sight of some rift between them sent Leila into distraction. She scarcely noticed Micah clearing his throat as he stepped up to the mic.

His head bobbed. "Here's a little Clapton, from Derek and the Dominos ...."

Leila vaguely recognized the high-pitched riff as Micah launched into another zone. The audience rallied. He drew it out several more times, leading into the vocals.

Kyle nudged her with a loud whisper, "Hey, Micah's singing your song."

"Shush."

Micah improvised on the tempo and slowed his hand as he hit the notes leading into the first line of "Layla." Although she couldn't make out all the lyrics, she understood just enough to ignite a fire in her chest that spread to her cheeks.

As he sang the refrain, a chill shot up her spine and she glanced at Ian. Their eyes met. Had the song evoked the same reaction in him? Leila braced herself for the next chorus. Her self-consciousness suspended in the minutes that passed. The refrain came again and again. She could have sworn another hundred pairs of eyes stared. When the song finally ended, the entire gymnasium came to their feet in an ovation. Leila stood too, wiping a tear. Kyle whistled from behind and nudged her as she clapped. Micah announced a short break.

"You okay?" Kyle asked.

"Yeah. I just wasn't expecting that."

"Seriously moving stuff, huh? Is he good or what?"

"He's very good."

"Bet that first verse about running and hiding, and your foolish pride, really got to you, huh?"

She shrugged. She would have to listen to the lyrics again to catch all the words, but she had the feeling Ian already knew them by heart.

She pulled at her turtleneck. "I'm going to get some air."

Leila pushed through the side exit, catching a whiff of the cool night and the scent of cigarettes wafting from glowing dots near the parking lot. As the door closed, an overhead light shone on Ian. She matched not only his folded arms but his unsteady gaze until their eyes fixed. Again, the torment. Each forced a smile.

Ian spoke. "That was quite a performance."

"Yes." Leila kept her eyes on his, biting her lip.

He exhaled, his hand rubbing his short-sleeved bicep. His weight shifted toward her just as the door pushed open.

Micah stepped out between them. "Hey."

"Outstanding performance, Micah," Ian said. "You did Clapton proud."

"Thanks man." Micah bobbed and glanced at Leila.

She fidgeted with her earlobe. "It was very moving. You got me all choked up."

"Yeah, I know," he said, his gaze cast to her feet and then her face. "I saw you, you know, at the end. That's like a serious compliment."

She smiled, careful to limit her eye contact with either of them.

Micah piped up. "I was wondering if you wanted to dance, I mean, they're just playing a Dire Straits tape, but ...."

"Sure, if you don't mind dancing with a spaz."

"No, I'd like to dance with a spaz," he bobbed and opened the door. As she stepped inside, he poked his head back out, saying a few words to Coach Brigham.

Leila and Micah joined several other couples at the center of the floor. "Sultans of Swing" played softly in the background. While everyone else danced faster, Micah, placed both hands on her waist, setting a slow pace. She would have been more comfortable with the old-fashioned, hand-in-hand stance Joe had taught her, but she had no choice other than to settle her hands on his shoulders. As they swayed, there was something familiar and disarming about Micah, about the way he moved to the music, something in the way his T-shirt, moist with perspiration, felt inoffensive beneath her hand. The way he smelled of marijuana.

She knew Micah. She knew he stayed up practicing a technique or song for hours until he perfected it. He had foregone sleep, food and human conversation as though music filled his every need. Her father would have approved of Micah.

As they danced, he spoke up, "So, um … do you read music, play by ear, or improvise?"

"I never really learned to read music too well. I guess I only know how to play by ear and improvise."

"Seriously. That's cool."

Leila shrugged. Sometimes she wished she had applied herself to the more disciplined aspect of playing, the way her father wanted. "So what, you can improvise," he would say, unimpressed, "but you'll never amount to anything if you can't read." Joe, on the other hand liked to show off her knack for the impromptu, and the band found her adorable. Adorable—that's what adults say to kids doing their darndest, whether or not they were any good.

"I really like this song, 'cause it's about a bunch of musicians," Micah said.

Leila smiled. He felt oh, so familiar.

His hand crept up her back. "I really like your sweater. It's soft."

She stared over his shoulder. "Thanks."

"So, do you play a lot?"

"Every Saturday night."

"Cool … So, would you get completely freaked out if I, like, asked you to play some blues with us later? 'Cause Steve, ya know, our pianist, got wasted and he's pukin' out back. And besides, pretty much everyone will be gone by then, and it would be really cool if you played."

Leila tossed her head and laughed. "You're kidding, right?"

"No."

Leila's eyes widened and she drew back.

Micah added, "I mean, you know, if you don't want to, that's cool too, 'cause lots of people don't like playing for an audience. I just thought, you know, 'cause it's blues, and there won't be hardly anyone still hanging around, and Coach Brigham is gonna mess around with us too—"

At the mention of Coach Brigham, Leila's pulse hastened a smile to her lips. "He plays?"

"Yeah, real sweet acoustic blues guitar."

She could have guessed Ian played. Part of her wanted to surprise and impress him. Leila couldn't keep from smiling.

"So, you'll do it?" Micah said.

She shook her head. "Oh, no, I couldn't."

"C'mon, you gotta know some Allman Brothers or something."

In fact, Leila did. The tape Ian had given her was laced with it. Better than that, she knew Robert Johnson, B.B. King, Lightning Hopkins, Muddy Waters and the like. For Pete's sake, she played with authentic blues musicians every Saturday night and she had no trouble keeping up. Sometimes she had even crept into the lead. And the thought of messing around with Ian—she couldn't stop smiling.

"Seriously, we gotta have a pianist," he said, nudging her.

"Well, I guess I could try and play just a little."

"Cool." He nodded as the song ended. He walked off toward the stage, continuing his head-bob.

As Leila rejoined Maryanne and Kyle at the edge of the dance floor, her lungs constricted. What had she just gotten herself into?

Kyle pulled her aside. "I think Micah's got a thing for you."

She shrugged him off. "So are you guys sticking around?"

"Oh yeah," he said. "You should've been here for last year's finale. Coach Brigham played, too. It was great."

Leila cringed. It's just the blues. She was probably more familiar with them than anyone there, except perhaps Micah and Ian, but perhaps even more than them. Round and around she psyched herself, twisting her stomach into a knot. Besides, this was just a group of high school students—much easier to impress than her father.

Leila listened for the next hour, paying even more attention to the tone of the band and how they carried their tempo. She imagined where she might interject a chord or carry along the melody, if she were playing.

"You don't look so good, Leila," Kyle said as Micah segued into something with heavy blues influence. The crowd had not thinned the way Leila hoped.

"I'm fine …," she said. Time for fretting ended. Micah smiled at her and nodded. Ian had already taken a seat beside the piano where he tweaked his tuning.

She braced herself, came to her feet, and then headed toward the stage. Wiping her clammy hands over her jeans, she stepped up onto the bandstand. Her stomach rolled. As she pulled up to the piano, Ian shot her a double take. His wide eyes flashed away as he fidgeted with his pick.

"Didn't I mention I mess around on the piano a little?" she said loud enough for only him to hear.

He shook his head, repressing a smile.

Micah leaned toward her. "Go ahead and fool with the piano a little. Mr. Williams says the action seems stiff—try it out."

Leila played a few scales, hitting all the octaves. The bass resonated from the soundboard and through the floor. Her fingers moved over the ivories. The mellow tone of chord progressions steadied her breathing and her hands. Glancing at Ian, her smile twitched.

He asked, "Do you think you can play any of that stuff from the tape?"

"The one you misplaced?"

"Yeah, that one."

"I've learned them all, actually," she said, pushing up angora sleeves and flicking her hair back.

Ian nodded. Micah led with something upbeat. The piano lead-ins were simple and clean and easy to start her off. The drummer and bass guitarist jumped in. Everything Leila had ever learned energized her fingers as she hammered out a few safe chords, peppered with vibratos she learned from her father, masking some of her stumbling. After a few minutes she easily dueled with Ian in a lively piano-guitar dialogue. Playing a few standard guitar licks, Micah joined Brigham with corresponding riffs. The tall handsome bassist from the neighborhood pulled it all together. Micah then moved to her side, picking up on her cues—visual and musical—as their playing merged into a duet. Micah kept the phrases basic. He led her along and occasionally drew her out, testing her playfulness. He made her look good. Micah and Ian passed the lead between them, each bantering with Leila and then joined back in with the group.

Leila lost track of how long they played. Joe would have been proud of her for trying something so out of her safe routine. Her father would have criticized how her timing was sometimes off. He would have cringed at her hesitations.

Micah finally took the initiative to wind things down, signaling the drummer who tapered the tempo. Drumsticks reverberated off cymbals that drowned with applause. The remaining students in the audience thinned as the band packed up.

Leila closed the fallboard and swiveled on the piano bench as Ian laid his guitar in its case. Neither looked at the other.

"See ya around," the bassist nudged Leila as he left the stage.

She offered him a smile. "You ought to come by Artie's some time."

The bassist grinned as Micah approached and sat on the bench beside her. "Thanks a lot, Leila. That was amazing!"

She twisted her hair up off her neck, wishing for a breeze. "Well, thanks for picking up the slack where I messed up."

"Are you kidding me?" Micah bobbed. "You were great, wasn't she, Coach?"

Ian looked her straight in the face. Perspiration glistened at his brow. "You were good. Very good."

Leila hoped Micah was too stoned to notice the way their stares lingered.

"Well, anyway, it was fun," she said, coming to her feet, wiping her hands over her back pockets.

Ian rose with her. "It was a good time, Micah—"

"Well, I've really gotta run," she said, without giving Micah a chance to say anything more.

She came off the stage ahead of Ian. Across the gym, Karen Weiss hung back at the front exit, looking directly at them.

Leila turned to him. "Ian—"

He shot a glance at Miss Weiss and tensed. "Leila, we should just say goodnight."

"As opposed to …?"

His eyes darted.

"Sorry," she said. "I know. Goodnight, Coach."

He turned and headed to the side exit. Leila left through the back alcove. As she stepped through the door, she stumbled upon Kyle and Maryanne making out in such a heated passion that they didn't even notice her until she was passing by.

"Jeez, Leila—a little warning would be nice," Kyle said, pulling his hand from under Maryanne's sweater. Neither made a move to follow her.

"Sorry." Leila blushed and exited.

The elation she experienced on stage disappeared as soon as she stepped into the dark. She looked up into crisp, black skies, expecting the awesomeness she had grown accustomed to in New Hampshire. It seemed half the stars had disappeared, relinquishing their brightness above an over-lit island. Or perhaps they had simply fallen from the sky. Nothing ever stayed the same, not even something as consistent as the unchanging heavens.

CHAPTER 14

L EILA PASSED THROUGH THE SCHOOL CORRIDORS ON Monday morning, weaving through the blue jeans-and-T-shirted obstacle course. Unsolicited greetings hurried her all the faster to homeroom. As the first to arrive, she sat alone with Mr. Myles.

"Well Miss Sanders," he said, peering over his magazine as usual, "you continue to surprise me."

She pitched him an inquisitive look.

"You failed to mention that you're an improvisational pianist."

How had he so quickly found out? "There are a lot of things you don't know about me."

"Admittedly so. Yet, for someone trying to fly beneath the radar, I am a little taken aback by such risky behavior ...." His words hung in midair like a bass note as students began entering.

What had he meant by that? She hated the way he forced her to second-guess decisions—if not poorly-thought-out impulses. Not that she hadn't been second-guessing since the moment she stepped onto the bandstand. But now, thanks to Mr. Myles, she had to reconsider it all over again.

How could playing the piano be risky? It wasn't as if her performance had been publicized on a billboard. And who cared, anyway? Though in the back of her mind, Miss Weiss concerned her. But even still, she had been careful with Ian, hadn't she? And so what if she had made a few friends and some from her neighborhood recognized her? Okay, there might be a problem with Micah—she could tell he liked her. But he hadn't asked her out, so she didn't have to make up some lame excuse or tell him she didn't want to go out with someone like her father, or that she was in love with Coach Brigham. Besides all that, her father couldn't make her move again, now that she was settled. And the state didn't care whom she played piano with. Nevertheless, the same old withdrawal pulled her away from the normalcy she craved. As always, being a regular teenager felt as risky as ever.

When Kyle sat behind her, he gave her a good-natured nudge. She didn't respond.

"What's with you?" he asked.

"Nothing."

"Okay, I'm sorry we didn't walk you back to your car."

"It doesn't matter. I'm fine."

In math, she passed Friday's quiz with a sixty-six percent, lifting some of her pessimism, until Myles announced the upcoming, semi-quarterly exam. Kyle let out a heavy sigh. They would have to step up their studies.

🐉 AFTER MATH, KYLE ARRIVED AT THEIR LOCKER, JUST behind Leila. Sure, she had said she was fine, but things had gone so well on Saturday that he expected a different post-homecoming Leila. At least a friendlier or more relaxed or happier Leila. She exchanged her textbooks and went to shut the door when he grabbed it, blocking her escape. "What's the hurry?"

"No hurry," she said, but her eyes darted past him.

"You had fun at homecoming, didn't you?"

"Sure."

"You were a regular social butterfly."

She ignored his comment. "So, what are we going to do about Friday's exam?"

"We should probably double up—study every afternoon, starting today."

"Okay, just as long as we're done in time for my job."

He nudged her, hoping to lighten her up. "You know what that means! We get to run every morning too."

"Okay, well, I gotta go," she said and ducked under his arm into the stream of students.

He scratched his head as she disappeared down the hall.

That afternoon, Leila was just as aloof. He played along, equaling her detachment, focusing strictly on the lessons. Just the same, her sullenness perplexed and even irritated him.

KYLE TRAILED A FEW STEPS BEHIND LEILA AS THEY walked from his house to the track in silence. Now that the temperature had dropped, she had finally resorted to wearing sweatpants instead of shorts, but she still had the cutest wiggle to her rear end. Admiring her derrière, he assessed her mood. As they stretched, he winked and coaxed her smile.

"I'm all for comfort," he said. "I just miss those long gams."

She gave him a friendly slap. Perhaps her mood had subsided.

"So where did you learn to play piano?" Kyle ventured as they took to the track. "Did your parents make you take lessons or what?"

Her rhythm faltered. "My dad taught me."

"That's right, he's a musician. Does he play anything besides piano?"

"Guitar and percussion."

"Cool. So who are the guys you jam with, anyway?"

She didn't answer right away. "Just some old-timers."

"So when you say old, how old do you mean?"

"Pretty old. Artie's in his eighties."

Now his rhythm faltered. "Wow! Okay, so, do you realize how weird that is? I mean, not necessarily weird in a bad way. Just really out of the ordinary."

"I guess. That's just what I grew up with."

"Really?"

She picked up her pace. "So didn't your parents make you

take some sort of music lessons?"

"I wish! My mother, being a dance instructor and all, made me take lessons and from her no less," he said, keeping up. "It's a wonder I'm as well-adjusted as I am."

"Yeah, well, I'm really impressed with the way you dance. I dance like a backup singer."

Kyle chuckled at how she nailed her self-description. "So, back to your dad."

"What about my dad?" She looked at him askance and then dashed ahead of him in a full run, forbidding further questions. She sure knew how to end a conversation. He didn't bother to catch up. Over the next several days, he let her set the pace of their dialogue and their pace on the track, keeping conversation light and impersonal.

🦎 ON FRIDAY AFTERNOON, KYLE AND MICAH EXITED the school building together. Micah had been asking about Leila all week long, so Kyle had a pretty good idea of what his friend had in mind when they met up with her. The three chatted for a minute and then Micah directed his attention to Leila. That was Kyle's cue. He lagged behind but couldn't help eavesdropping.

Micah cleared his throat. "So, Leila, I was wondering if you want to get together and jam sometime."

"To tell you the truth—" she squirmed "—I've just got too much going on right now."

She didn't even temper her refusal with, 'I would really like to but … ', or offer the easy let down, 'Maybe when things slow down a little ....' She didn't even bother with 'Gosh, I'm sorry .... '

Micah's head bobbed and his shoulders slumped. "Okay … sure, that's cool ...."

Leila walked away, leaving them both behind. Kyle took for granted his steady girlfriend until disappointment and bewilderment furrowed Micah's brow. Saying anything would rub it in.

She continued her brisk walk as Kyle caught up. As she

stepped through the chain-link fence, he said, "Jeez, Leila. That was pretty cold."

Equaling his irritated stare, she turned. "Give me a break."

He was tired of giving her a break. "I don't believe you."

"You know what? I've got a splitting headache and I'm not in the mood for this," she said, and although she didn't break into a run, she left him behind. When she headed for her car instead of his house, the day's lesson was off.

"Fine," he said under his breath. What was her problem anyway?

LEILA'S HEAD SPLIT. EVERYTHING MIGHT SPILL OUT IF she had to say another word to anyone. Was following in her father's moody footsteps inevitable? The bewilderment in Kyle's eyes matched the way she had felt when trying to understand her father's withdrawals. If it weren't for Joe, she didn't know what she would have done. But then, even he couldn't hack it anymore. Why had he stuck around as long as he did? If only her father's cancer had been diagnosed sooner, Joe never would have left. And she hadn't been allowed to say anything about the cancer until it came back. By then, Joe had changed. Sure, he sent money and postcards and even called occasionally, but he didn't sound the same. With three thousand miles between them, how could it ever be the same again? Just the same, if he had called that afternoon, she would have begged him to come home.

🪶 CHAPTER 15

KYLE SAT ON HIS FRONT STOOP, HIS GAZE FIXED AT the intersection down his street, waiting for Leila's little blue bug. Perhaps she wouldn't even bother to show up after yesterday's rift, but right on time, she turned the corner.

As she climbed from her car, her smile seemed forced. He didn't feel like forcing conversation on top of it. Without a word, he met her at the curb and they began their walk to the track. They remained silent until they slipped through the hole in the fence.

"I don't blame you if you don't want to talk to me," she said.

"Hey, I'm not the one who gets all tight lipped."

"You're upset with me."

"Yeah, that's right. I am."

Kyle waited for her to pursue it while they stretched and then moved on to the track. They started a slow jog. After a minute, she spoke. "Are you going to tell me why?"

"Yeah, I'll tell you why. For starters, I can't believe the way you blew Micah off."

"I didn't blow him off."

"You did too! He was crushed. You, of all people, should know how sensitive musician types are."

Leila's shoulders dropped and she nearly tripped. "Yeah, well, I just don't need to get involved with some *musician-type* guy."

Her pace increased. So did Kyle's as he breathed in puffs. "I don't believe you! Did you even hear what you just said and how stupid that sounds coming out of your mouth?"

Her breathing outpaced her stride. "Being a musician or jamming with one is far different from being in a relationship with one."

"What is that supposed to mean?"

"It means, to men—to musicians like Micah—their music is more important to them than anything or anyone."

"Well what exactly are you expecting from him? I mean, he barely knows you, and already he's singing you songs. What more do you want from the poor guy?"

"Yeah, well, singing to someone or writing them a song does not compensate for not being there."

"For God's sake Leila, the guy just wants to play music with you. It's not like he wants to marry you." He looked at her, confounded. "What are you even talking about, anyway?"

Leila pushed ahead. While they still had air and were able to converse, he would push her boundaries.

"Leila," he softened his tone. "We're not talking about Micah, are we?"

She did not respond but for the pain clouding her eyes. "Are you going to tell me what's going on at home, Leila? What is it? Is your father a drunk or something?"

As soon as the words left his mouth, he sensed she was building to the point of breaking out in a full-blown run. As she pushed ahead, he continued to sprint alongside her. She increased her pace but could not shake him.

He grabbed her arm. "Leila!"

She jerked out of his grip. Her body came to an abrupt standstill. He stopped just ahead.

She blurted, "Did it ever occur to you that there are things I just don't want to talk about, things that you don't need to know …? So why don't you just get off my back and let's run."

She charged past him, running at a fast clip for about a

hundred yards. Kyle did not take off after her. He stood dumfounded and then set out walking in her direction. What had he unleashed?

She approached the long stretch of the track and veered off, heading toward the short chain-link fence. As she gripped it, her chest heaved. She turned to face him, her anguished eyes seeking his. He started toward her as she clutched the linked fence behind, her body rocking.

"What is it Leila? Why don't you just tell me?"

She drew in a breath. "My father's not a drunk. He died almost a year ago." She seemed to be waiting for his response, but he had none. Her words had not begun to sink in when she continued, "I live on my own, by myself, in a place I don't want to be, with people I scarcely know, just trying to make the best of it. Until I met you, I'd never even had a glimpse at a life like you have. Two parents living in a nice home, probably the one you've always lived in, with friends you've known all your life. Having friends your own age instead of a bunch of old musicians." She barely paused to breathe. "Hanging around smelly nightclubs or someone's dilapidated garage as your father and the guys drink beer and work on their sound. Always looking for a better gig someplace else, in some state halfway across the country."

She kicked the fence behind her. "Always, I love you, but always the music first. All the apologies and the promises that we'll settle down, live in a house. I went from being the band mascot and gopher to a nursemaid."

Kyle stepped forward as tears streamed down her face.

"Yeah, I'm a difficult person to be around. I don't know the first thing about making friends."

He pulled her close. The tighter he held her, the harder she cried.

Holy crap. He tried to sort through everything she had just divulged. As her body heaved, his own throat tightened and his eyes burned. As he pieced together all the parts of the puzzle that previously did not fit, he understood why she did not want a relationship with Micah. Why she seemed always on edge around kids her own age. Why she was sick after parent-teacher conferences. He now had an inkling of why she lived where she did. And why she was always running.

Kyle did not withdraw until her breathing slowed and she pulled back just enough to retrieve a paper towel from her pocket. She blew her nose. Saying nothing, he stroked loose hairs from her face. She evoked the tenderest feelings. As she leaned into him again, his lips brushed her forehead.

"Let's go back to my house," he whispered. With his arm across her back, he led her off the field.

In his room, Kyle shoved aside books and papers on his desktop and pushed up the sash of the gabled window above it. He pulled himself out onto the roof overlooking his backyard and then offered his hand. Leila followed.

Brisk air ruffled the trees that blossomed with full autumn color. Noonday sun warmed the roof shingles. They sat close, looking out over a small brick patio. The emotional crescendo had fallen and Leila sat quietly. Kyle had questions, and although he waited for her to take the initiative, it occurred to him that she might be waiting for him.

"I'm really sorry about your father," he said.

Leila acknowledged his words with a stiff smile.

"How did he die?"

"Cancer."

"What about your mom?"

"Never knew her." Leila stared straight ahead, pursing her lips.

"Wow."

"Have I completely freaked you out?"

"Are you kidding me?" His hand found hers. "No way! You're like the most interesting person I've ever met."

Her dimples deepened with a smile and her eyes met his. She had a very different look than Maryanne, but she was just as pretty—prettier when she wore her hair down. At the thought of his girlfriend, he became aware of Leila's hand beneath his and withdrew, planting both hands behind him. "So, does anyone else know?"

"Ian—I mean, Coach Brigham and Mr. Myles know."

"Oh crap! Myles knows?"

"Yes." This time, she gave details, filling in the formerly vague elements of Myles' place in their relationship. The alliance forced upon him and Leila now made sense.

"So what's the deal with Brigham?" His arms wrapped around bent knees.

Leila's eyes widened. "What do you mean?"

"Well, I was just wondering if you had a thing for him, or something."

"Why would you say that?"

"For one thing, all the girls do. And that day when the two of you were talking in the gym—I don't know, it seemed like you were talking about more than just track."

Leila shrugged and looked straight ahead. "He was just concerned about the Friday thing, when I went home sick."

"Yeah—but you do have a thing for him, don't you?"

She said nothing.

"'Cause, I've been trying to figure out why you're even trying out for track. I mean, it's pretty obvious that you're not into it. So, I'm thinking, you must have a thing for Coach Brigham. What else could it be?"

Leila sighed. "I actually met him at the beach last summer, just after I arrived on Long Island. He knows I'm on my own. He was pretty horrified to find out that I was only seventeen and going to the school where he's the coach."

Now his eyes widened and then he frowned. "So, he's got a thing for you, too."

"Why do you say that?"

"I've seen the way he looks at you. Even at homecoming, when he was taking pictures of you on the bleachers—there was definitely something between you two." He glanced at her. "And that's not all. You should have seen the look on his face when Micah was singing 'Layla'."

She stared off as Kyle continued, "And you seriously have a thing for him, too. And it's not just a crush."

Leila now looked straight at him. "I do. I guess you think

that's pretty pathetic."

"You know he could get in a lot of trouble."

"Of course I know that. That's why we try to avoid each other."

"That's what you call trying to avoid each other?"

"Don't be laying a guilt trip on me, Kyle. You don't know how it feels to be alone."

"Sorry," he said. The last thing he wanted was to push her away. "So, you live where you do because you can't afford to live anywhere else?"

"Sort of. It's a long story."

"Then tell me about the old guys you play with. What kind of music?"

"We play mostly Delta blues, a bunch of old-time Southern guitar. A lot of harmonica. Artie, the old guy I live above, was actually pretty famous in his day. Any hardcore-blues musician knows his work."

"It's kind of cool that they let you play with them."

"Yeah, it is, but they're pretty laid back. I think they just like having someone young around. Besides, I cook him dinner every Saturday night."

"Is that what you're doing tonight?"

"Yup."

"'Cause you know, Maryanne is out of town with her parents this weekend, and I'm going to be all alone ...."

Leila giggled for the first time in days. "You want to come with me, Kyle?"

"You know I do. If you don't think they'd mind."

"Actually, I think Artie would like to finally meet you."

"He knows about me?"

"Of course he does. You're the 'tall, handsome boy'."

CARRYING A FULL SACK OF GROCERIES, KYLE followed Leila as they approached Artie's front stoop. Catching his breath, he wiped his free hand on his jeans and steadied his nerves.

Artie flung the door wide open and smiled with big

choppers. "This must be Kyle."

"It sure is," Leila said.

Kyle extended his hand, juggling the groceries. "Hello, sir."

The old man's hand looked frail and felt cool but gripped with surprising strength. As they stepped inside, Kyle surveyed the dim apartment. It was odd that an old man living alone had so many chairs eating up so little floor space.

Artie grinned. "Now, you go on and get a pop from the icebox."

Pop? Icebox? Sidling past the sofa, Kyle followed Leila into the outdated kitchen.

"Set the groceries on the table," she said.

He placed the paper sack on Formica, which sat atop chipped linoleum.

Leila handed him a root beer soda. "Take it back out and go sit with Artie. I'll get dinner started."

"Are you serious?"

"He's an old man. He won't bite you."

"Yeah, but did you see the teeth on him?"

Leila laughed as he took a deep breath and exited. Artie looked at him sideways and patted the worn cushion beside him.

Kyle sank into the sofa. His knees jutted upward.

"Well, son, what do you play?"

Kyle gulped a breath. "I only play records."

"What? No instrument?"

"No, sir."

"Well, you got two hands, don't'cha?"

"Yes, sir."

"I heard you can dance, so you can keep time and hit something can't'cha?"

"Yes, sir."

"Then go on over to that closet and fetch the bongos."

Kyle leaned forward, placed his soda on a scuffed coffee table, and pried himself from the cushions.

As he opened the closet door, the scent of Vicks and mothballs greeted him. He hoped he wouldn't have to go digging. To his relief, amidst crammed overcoats and boxes, a set of bongos lay on the floor beside a guitar.

He returned to the sofa and this time sat on the edge of the cushion, balancing the small set of drums between his knees. Meanwhile, Artie had picked up his guitar and began picking.

A gristly old black man thundered in, belly first. The door slammed behind him. The near-ancient man squinted hard, looking Kyle up and down.

"We have a guest," Artie said. "Kyle."

Full lips parted in a big smile. "So this is Kyle."

By the time dinner was over, Kyle leaned back in his chair along with the others, talking and laughing. Within an hour, several other regulars showed up, and by nine o'clock, all were tuned up and ready to jam. Leila took to the piano bench. Kyle claimed a chair opposite Buddy, who grinned at him the whole time. Unsure of how to proceed, Kyle fidgeted with the bongos.

"Just keep time with the bass. You think you can do that?" Buddy said.

Kyle did his best, encouraged by Leila's occasional glance. It didn't take long before he warmed up, alternating between the bass and tenor drum. He even experimented with half and quarter beats. As he watched Artie playing his harmonica while strumming his guitar, something about the combination made Kyle's hands more responsive. It was impressive, how so much emotion came from one small instrument.

Around half-past midnight, Artie asked Leila for a glass of water and then directed his attention to Kyle.

"You'd like to play the harp, wouldn't'cha son?" he said.

"Yes, sir."

"Go on over to that chifforobe."

Kyle set aside the bongos and stood in front of the doorless cabinet where a couple guitar cases leaned against its interior.

"In the bottom drawer, there. Fetch that there little box in the corner."

Kyle brought it over to Artie and sat at his side.

Artie pushed it back at Kyle. "If you don't learn on it, you have to give it back. See there, it's got instructions and everything."

"Yes, sir, I sure will. I'll definitely learn to play it. Thank you."

"Hey, Kyle," Leila said. "Don't you have an eleven-thirty curfew?"

"Holy crap," he said glancing at his watch. "Oh, man, I gotta call my mother!"

Three minutes later, after an even-tempered reaming out, Leila drove Kyle home.

"Are you in big trouble?" she asked.

"Oh yeah," he said, smiling. "But this was seriously worth it."

This was the most extraordinary thing Kyle had ever done in his entire starchy, white-middle-class life.

🐾 KYLE COULD HARDLY WAIT TO SEE LEILA ON Monday morning, their first post-weekend encounter. Even though his parents had grounded him for two weeks, and Maryanne was more upset about it than he was, he still smiled every time he thought of playing with Leila and Artie and the Boys. He had practiced on the harmonica every spare minute and couldn't wait to show off.

As soon as he sat in homeroom, he nudged Leila with his harmonica.

"Check this out," he said. Momentarily caught up, he played a scale.

"Mr. Schultz," Myles thundered.

"Oh crap."

"Please bring that up here."

Kyle shuffled to Myles' desk, wincing at the possibility of losing his harp. "Mr. Myles, I am so sorry, I swear, you will never see this or hear from it in your class again. Please don't take it away from me."

"Hand it over."

Kyle hesitated, and then placed it in his outstretched palm.

Myles weighed it in his hand and flipped it over, examining it closely. "How did you come by this instrument?"

"A friend gave it to me."

"Really. Well that friend must like you very much. Do you have any idea what I'm holding?"

"A harmonica."

"A harmonica? This is not just a harmonica. It's a Hohner Marine Band, diatonic harp. An old one. And a clean one at that. Someone must like you very much." Myles cast a glance behind Kyle, as if he deduced that Leila had been a party to it. "You'd better take very good care of it."

Myles slapped it back in Kyle's hand.

"Yes, sir."

At their locker, Leila smiled as Kyle demonstrated his first accomplishments on the harmonica. Behind Leila, Maryanne approached and he tucked the harp back into his pocket.

"I'd better get going," Leila said.

"Hey, Annie." Hoping she might have softened, he moved in closer. "Baby, tell me you're not going to stay mad at me. I just can't stand it."

He couldn't read her silence, but she allowed him to stroke her hair. "Please let me make it up to you."

She stared into his eyes, unwavering. "Do you have feelings for Leila?"

"What do you mean, like romantic feelings?"

"Yeah."

Kyle couldn't believe she even needed to ask. "I like her, sure, but I don't feel anything for her like I do about you. You're the one I want, Annie. You know that."

He pulled her close and hoped his kiss would reassure her. She didn't respond at first, but he knew how she liked to be kissed, and that seemed to do the trick.

🦅CHAPTER 16

T WO WEEKS INTO NOVEMBER, THE COLD STALLED, ushering in an Indian Summer. Only a few leaves clung to the trees. It reminded Leila of the February she once spent in Mississippi, when the temperature continuously hovered above freezing. The pungent aroma of decomposing foliage permeated the humid air.

Saturday marked the end of Kyle's two-week sentence, although his parents still allowed him to run with and tutor Leila. But more significantly, Saturday marked his one-year anniversary with Maryanne. It always amazed Leila when any teenage couple lasted more than a few months. So, if Maryanne made Kyle happy, and she seemed to, then fine. Just the same, Leila would miss her exclusive time with him, likely to Maryanne's relief. She had given Leila the cold shoulder for the past two weeks, perhaps because Leila and Kyle now shared a musical interest, that Leila spent time with Kyle while Maryanne couldn't, or that Maryanne worried that Leila and he might have something going on.

As usual, Kyle and Leila spent an early morning on the track. As they wound down, he invited her back to his room. "I have something really special I want to show you."

Music played in the background as they sat on his bed, facing each other. Kyle handed her a velvet box. Her eyebrows rose in anticipation as she cracked the lid; it sprung back revealing a ruby-encrusted heart of gold.

"Wow," she gasped.

"It's her birthstone. You think she'll like it?"

"She'd be crazy not to …." Leila fingered the ornament, making it twinkle. "I can't even imagine what it would be like to get something this nice from a boyfriend."

"What do you mean? I'm sure you've gotten a lot of nice presents from boyfriends."

"Yeah, well that would require actually having a boyfriend."

"Are you kidding me? A pretty girl like you?"

Leila's ears burned at the word pretty. Her stomach fluttered. She chuckled. "Well, there was Billy Peterson in third grade—he even tried to kiss me, but I punched him in the gut."

"Seriously? That's the only time you've been kissed?"

"Well, there was the drummer who drank too much and tried to kiss me. My dad beat the crap out of him."

"Really? How old were you?"

"Around fourteen. After that, my dad made me take a self-defense class so I could beat the crap out of men, myself."

"Jeez, remind me never to try and kiss you."

Leila laughed. She doubted she would put up a struggle.

"So, like, you're even a virgin when it comes to kissing?" He shook his head, as if a seventeen-year-old girl who hadn't been kissed was unfathomable. "I mean, I'm, you know, I haven't actually done it, but I've gotten in a whole lot of kissing, and then some—"

"You're a virgin?"

"That's a girl word. Guys can't be virgins."

"Oh, right," she rolled her eyes. "Guys have either *done it* or *not done it*."

"That's right. Maryanne is the virgin."

"But not you, even though you haven't *done it*." Leila passed the box back.

"That's right. I mean, sure I'd like to … I'm a teenage guy after all. But I don't push her." Kyle looked at the symbol of his devotion. "I really care for her."

Leila envied the tenderness beaming from Kyle's eyes. How would it feel to be his girlfriend? To be the recipient of such a gift? How would his lips feel on hers, kissed the way she had seen him kiss Maryanne? Her stomach rolled at the thought, pushing blood to her neck and cheeks.

Kyle looked up at her as she bit her lip. Their eyes met and she lingered a moment too long. Her gaze flashed away. Had he read her thoughts? Could he tell her heart was pounding out of her chest?

"What was that about?" he said.

"I um …." She forced herself to look at him, but the frisson had not cooled. "I just think it's really sweet what you're doing. Maryanne is really lucky."

Kyle swallowed hard, his eyes still on hers. Even in their mutual discomfort—seeing the same expression she had seen on Ian's face—neither looked away.

"So," Leila hoped to squash the tension. "Where are you taking her?"

He fidgeted with the box. "Out to dinner, at Surf and Turf."

"Oooo … expensive."

"Yeah," he said. "She's worth it."

Leila sat up straight and breathed deep. Kyle continued to fumble with the box, his face flushed.

Snapping it shut, he rose from the bed and turned his back on her. "Well, I promised I would pick her up at noon."

Leila stood. "I can let myself out. Are we still on for tomorrow morning?"

"Yeah. Dress warm. It's supposed to turn cold."

🐚 KYLE'S BODY ACHED WITH FATIGUE AS HE ROLLED out of bed. His head throbbed as if he had a hangover, but even if he wanted to cancel his run with Leila, it was too late. Besides, he had no way to contact her. Fortunately, when she showed up, she was in a quiet mood. As they started down the street, each exhalation clung to the frigid air.

"Well? How did it go?" she finally said as they stepped

through the fence.

"It went fine," he nodded, trying to spike his enthusiasm.

"Fine? Is that all? Just fine?"

"No, it was great—I mean, it was really great." He could not bring himself to look at her.

By any seventeen-year-old-guy standard, it had gone better than great. Maryanne cried at the sight of the necklace. He braved the words "I love you," even though afterward, he wondered if he had said it more to convince himself.

"Well? What did she think of the necklace?" Leila pressed.

"She loved it."

"So, that's it?"

"Yeah," he said, but that was by no means all of it. When he brought Maryanne home, she had led him down to her parents' boathouse on the canal, the way she often did, but this time, she had a lot more in mind.

Leila nudged him. "Yeah, next thing you know, the two of you will be engaged and it will be happily-ever-after."

He tried to muster a chuckle but had trouble coming up with even a smile. The memory of how wrong it had all gone choked his humor, though the deficiency had nothing to do with Maryanne. It had everything to do with Leila, how he hadn't been able to stop thinking of her all evening. How he had missed her during dinner, how he had imagined what the necklace would have looked like around Leila's neck. He had pushed those thoughts out of mind—just too much time spent with Leila, lately. But the worst of it happened later, in the most intimate moment—when images of Leila, not Maryanne, involuntarily flooded his mind. How could he betray Maryanne in his heart, the girl he had just told 'I love you'?

Self-loathing had gripped him with such intensity that by the time he arrived home last night, he lost his entire dinner. Deprived of sleep, he had watched the sky lighten. He continued the process of convincing himself that he could disguise his guilt and hide from Maryanne, and especially

Leila, what he had done and what he felt.

He made himself look at Leila, hoping to pull it off. Suspicion darted from her eyes.

"Oh my gosh …," she said under her breath.

He lowered his head. "What?"

"You and Maryanne …."

He couldn't deny what she had obviously deduced. He simply said, "Yeah, well, quit gawking. I'm not going to talk about it."

"Yeah, well, no one's asking."

"Good. Let's run."

That day, Kyle took the lead and Leila hung back as he ran hard, always just a pace ahead, never glancing back.

The bleakness of November had set in.

🐉 LEILA SAT IN HOMEROOM ON MONDAY MORNING, hoping Kyle might have lightened up. When he entered, he didn't look at her or nudge her or anything.

"Hey, Kyle," she said.

He grunted, "Hi."

Leila slumped in her seat. It didn't take too much imagination to figure that things had changed. Maryanne and Kyle had solidified their relationship and her situation with Kyle had shifted. She couldn't blame either Kyle or Maryanne, but Leila didn't really understand why sex should throw things so out of kilter between her and Kyle. Sure, they'd had their flustered little moment in his room, but it was fleeting and meant nothing. Typical teenage hormones. Just the same, Kyle's withdrawal cut into her heart.

She didn't leave with the rest of the class at homeroom dismissal; she couldn't stand the idea of Kyle ignoring her at their locker. And she didn't even want to think about seeing Maryanne, though she was curious if she would look any different, now that they had *done it*.

Mr. Myles laid down his *Rolling Stone* and folded his arms as he leaned back in his chair. "So what's up?"

"Nothing. I just don't feel like getting up."

Pulling the glasses from his nose, he squinted but said nothing.

"What?" she said, not masking her irritation.

"You tell me."

She rolled her eyes. She hated that he made her talk. "It's just stupid teenage stuff—nothing of concern to you."

He stared a moment longer. "Interesting that Mr. Schultz seems to be in the same funk."

"He and I are fine. I'm fine."

"Well, just don't let it affect your grade now that it's finally coming up."

🌿 CHAPTER 17

O N THE WEDNESDAY BEFORE THANKSGIVING, A bitter wind picked up. Ian flipped the collar of his peacoat against a gust and shoved his hands in his pockets. As he walked to his car in the parking lot, he squinted at the gray-bellied clouds above him. In the distance, Leila headed his way in a swirl of leaves and sand, her cheeks ruddy. She pulled her stocking cap over her ears and slung her pack over her shoulder as if it contained a cement block. A fine drizzle sprinkled his windshield as she approached and then paused in front of his car.

"Why didn't you drive today?" He shook his head. "Don't you ever listen to the weather forecast?"

Her gloved hand wiped her nose. "Apparently not this morning."

"They say it's supposed to be like this all weekend."

She shrugged. "It's all the same to me."

"You have plans for Thanksgiving?"

"Yes, I'm fixing dinner for Artie."

"Good."

"What about you? Do you have plans?"

"No, actually, I don't." Every holiday celebration Ian had attended since leaving home had been as a sorority party date or as an escort to some gathering where he rarely knew the host. But at least he'd had plans. This year would be different. He had no plans and no woman.

Leila cocked her brow. "Miss Weiss won't be fixing you a bird?"

"More like flipping me a bird," he smirked.

"Oh, I thought the two of you were—"

"Well, we're not."

She offered a brief smile. "I'm glad."

He returned her smile. "You know you shouldn't be running in this kind of weather. It's not good for your lungs."

"I've always run in this kind of weather."

"Well, I wish you wouldn't." He wished he could offer her a ride. Before he dismissed the irrational idea, she spoke up.

"Then perhaps you'd like to give me a ride home."

Emotion overrode logic. "Yeah, I would. Get in."

He scanned the lot for observers as she obeyed.

With the start of his engine, Clapton's singing blared from the speakers. He turned the volume way down and shifted into reverse as Leila fidgeted with her backpack and pulled off her stocking cap. As her hair came down, he had a hard time focusing on the road.

Impressions of Leila in his studio flashed from memory, but not just the photo shoot—everything that accompanied it. The confidences they had shared. The novel emotion she evoked. The way he had found himself thinking of her over the past weeks, quashing impulses to call and simply talk to someone who shared his interests, to someone who made him feel like talking, someone who didn't judge. He spent idle time imagining conversations and then spent as much time reminding himself that she was ten years his junior—a student. The injustice of it! And why on earth was he driving her home right now?

Without prompting, he headed north. As he drove without a word, the song "Layla" began playing. He let it run for a minute and then hit the eject button. He let out a sigh.

She looked at him. "Why are you driving me home, Ian?"

He pondered the question again. Yes, why? In fact, he knew why. Ian had experienced the upheaval of a date marked by death, and Leila was coming upon an anniversary.

Something in the change of the season, the smell of the atmosphere, even the subtle shifts in light from day to day, could conjure emotions and distort time, bringing on a flood of memories. Sometimes, he felt as though he were right in the midst of all the turmoil of his father's death. He hated to think of Leila going through all that—going through it alone. Yes, that's why he had offered to drive her home. Support. Empathy. Camaraderie. He genuinely cared about her.

"I'm concerned. I know you're coming up on the one-year anniversary ...." He stared ahead. "I just remember that for me, a year after my dad died, it was a lot harder than I expected. And I didn't have the long months of build-up that you had. I know you must be going through some really difficult stuff right now and—"

"I appreciate what you're saying, Ian. I do. But I really don't want to talk about it."

"I just want you to know that it does get easier."

"And that if I ever want to talk about it, you'll be there for me?"

"Leila," he said, his guard slipping. "I wish I could be there whenever you need someone, but—"

"I know. But you can't. I get it."

Perhaps he was the one who needed the support and camaraderie more than her. He shifted to a neutral subject. "How are things going with Mr. Myles?"

"Nothing's changed—except he made Kyle tutor me." She pointed ahead. "Two lefts and a right."

"So you're doing better in math?"

"Couldn't do much worse."

"And running together—how's that going?"

"Okay I guess ... a little weird lately."

"How so?"

"Ever since Kyle and Maryanne—well—things have just gotten weird, that's all. It's not a big deal. Take this left."

He glanced at her. "It kind of sounds like a big deal."

She shrugged. "At least we're still running, right?"

"Sure." He turned down her street. "The two of you seem

well paired."

"Yeah … well paired …." She pointed at her house. "This is it."

Pulling up in front, he shifted into neutral and pulled the emergency brake. They both looked straight ahead. He sighed and glanced at her. Time for her to climb out.

Leila did not move. After a moment, she said, "Do you want to come up and see my watercolors—and we could talk?"

His brow arched, now sensing her desire to open up, that indeed she did want to—need to—talk. For a brief moment, he considered her offer, but all the possible repercussions charged in on him. He no longer trusted himself, neither his judgment nor his restraint.

He shook his head. "I don't think that would be a good idea, Leila."

"Why not? I went to your place."

He exhaled. Offering her a ride had exposed his weakness. Just the same, sitting near her compensated for his feelings of guilt. He wanted nothing more than to be with her, alone in her apartment. He stared ahead, gripping his steering wheel, trying to get his yearning under control. "Going up to your apartment is not going to make things any easier."

"I don't care," she blurted.

He closed his eyes and mustered just enough moral strength to utter, "Well *I* have to."

"Is that why you listen to this—?" She shoved the cassette back in, and it picked up playing where it left off. "Because it makes it easier for you?"

He jabbed at the player, ejecting the tape, and tossed it onto the dashboard. His err in judgment punched him in the gut. He exhaled. "Leila, I'm so sorry … this was a bad idea …."

"I guess so." She flung open the car door, pulled herself out, ran to her staircase, and disappeared.

LEILA HADN'T INTENTIONALLY ARRIVED EARLY FOR school on Monday morning, but having slept away most of the holiday weekend, she woke sooner than usual. Preparing a dinner and playing with Artie and the boys had provided some diversion, but she had felt like the odd one out. Leila would never admit to anyone that she looked forward to seeing Mr. Myles, but the notion of being in his company—with someone who had demonstrated a genuine, unselfish interest in her—stirred something like hope as she headed down the sparsely populated hallway.

She opened his door slowly and waited until his attention settled on her. She needed him to invite her in.

"Miss Sanders. You're particularly early this morning."

She nodded.

"Do you intend to simply darken my doorway, or grace me with your company?"

"I don't want to impose. I know you like your private time."

"You are no imposition. Sit."

Leila slipped into her chair.

Myles pushed back in his usual repose. "And how was your holiday weekend?"

"How do you think?"

"From the looks of you, I'd say it was about as wretched as mine."

"I doubt it."

"What? You think you're the only one who hates the holiday season?"

"No. But you're the perpetual Grinch. Why would the holidays be different from any other time of year for you?"

He stared at her for a second, studying her. "They just are."

It took a moment to muster courage enough to ask, "Why?"

It took just as long for him to respond, "Divorce."

Although aware that she had likely overstepped her boundary, she had to ask, "Yours? Or your parents?"

"Both."

"Divorce was kind of unusual back then, wasn't it?"

"Indeed."

She gathered from the finality of his tone that whatever led to his parents' divorce must have been grave. She wouldn't press him on that. She had another interest. "Do you have any children?"

His gaze dropped and slowly came back to her. "I used to."

The pain that exuded from his eyes shot ice down her spine. She dared not ask any more about that, but his eyes never left hers, as if he was allowing some other question.

"So, what do you do on Christmas?" she asked.

"I go to the movies."

"That's what my dad and I used to do." Then, because, she desperately longed for a commiserator, she added, "That's when my father died, you know—on Christmas."

His eyes now beamed with the same emotion—a sort of torment—she had seen in her apartment. "No. I didn't know that."

Another student entered the room, ending their exchange. If Mr. Myles had meant to reach out to her, to offer consolation, he succeeded where Ian had not. Although, having even remotely common ground with Mr. Myles was not what she had initially hoped for, she at least found some comfort in his willingness to share his time. She missed talking with grown men—a different breed than Artie or Kyle or even Ian.

When Kyle arrived, he dropped to his seat, frowning.

"I guess I don't need to ask how your weekend went," she said.

He shook his head and rolled his eyes.

When homeroom ended, Leila remained in her seat. She never questioned whether Myles would allow it. He again turned his attention to her with his earlier tenderness.

"Do me a favor, Leila." That was the first time he called her Leila, in class.

"What's that?"

"Resist the temptation to isolate yourself."

His words carried the import of a man with too many regrets. Taking it as that, she acknowledged his counsel with a nod.

ᴂᴄᴳ THE FIRST OF DECEMBER ARRIVED AND LEILA longed for things to return to the way they were a month ago. With each passing day, Kyle had become increasingly distant. She missed how he couldn't wait to demonstrate his progress on the harmonica, the way he would nudge her for no reason, but especially his mischievous grin. She even missed the way he challenged her to a race every time they ran. It had been weeks since they did anything more than just run. No drills or exercises. No small talk. During their recent sessions, Leila tended to lag behind, however, this morning a mood struck her. As soon as they began running, she picked up her pace. Running abreast of him for a minute, she then advanced, glancing at him as she passed.

"Wanna race?" she baited with a grin.

He glared at her.

"Come on," she said while jogging backwards. "You know you want to."

He exhaled with a scowl.

"I can whup you so bad, and you know it."

He squinted. "Oh, you think so?"

"Why don't you find out? You know you want to."

A slow smile came over his face as she wiggled her fingers, taunting him.

He didn't say a word, he simply enlivened his stride. When he caught up beside her, they set off. Running neck and neck for about 100 yards, they both pushed hard, yet she pushed harder and pulled ahead just a bit but not for long.

Weeks of conditioning paid off for Kyle as he gained on her, keeping pace and even outrunning her after several yards. With a little more exertion, she reclaimed her lead and accelerated, pushing beyond him. Now she gave it her final kick. As her heart pounded and her body exceeded her wind capacity, she took a three-yard advantage. Her clothes billowed and her bun unraveled under her body's percussion. As her hair came down, she no longer heard him behind her. She glanced back. Kyle had completely spent himself and had slowed. The race ended.

As he continued making his way toward her, he retrieved the fallen pick and smiled openly. Leila waited, arching her back and walking circles.

When they met, they panted without a word, trying to catch their breath. A strong breeze wrapped strands of hair around Leila's head as they faced each other.

"You are amazing," Kyle said, moving in closer than he had in a month.

He held out the pick, but when she took hold of it, he wouldn't let go. And he wouldn't take his eyes off hers. He drew the wayward strands from her forehead, then dropped his hand to her cheek, stroking hair from her face. All the while, their eyes fixed. Still breathing heavily, he moved closer. She thought he might kiss her, but then his eyes narrowed and he withdrew, releasing the stick to her grip.

"Aw, Leila," he exhaled, "I can't do this anymore."

"Can't do what?"

He shook his head. "You're messing stuff up between me and Maryanne."

"Me?"

"I'm feeling stuff for you I don't want to feel. I love Maryanne—a lot ... but every time I'm around you—like this—you make it really hard."

"But I haven't done anything."

"You don't understand. I can't be your best friend and keep Maryanne. I'm sorry. This just isn't working." He cast his gaze away and rushed past her, walking, then jogging toward the school.

Leila wandered to the bleachers and dropped to the bench, stunned. She had never even had a boyfriend, how could she have just been dumped?

LEILA MADE QUICK EYE CONTACT WITH MR. MYLES when she entered homeroom. She rubbed her eyes, probably still pink and puffy. Kyle followed her in and they both sat without speaking.

"Lovers' spat?" Myles said glancing from Kyle to Leila.

Neither responded.

Another tense homeroom. Another tense math class, but this time it had nothing to do with Mr. Myles. She hadn't joined Kyle at their locker between homeroom and math, but afterward she walked directly up to him. His downcast eyes made little contact.

"Are we running tomorrow?" she asked.

Color drained from his cheeks. "No, it's too cold."

"What about tutoring?"

"You just got a seventy-eight on your last test, you don't need tutoring anymore." He didn't wait for a response before walking off. One more unreliable guy. She pushed back a wave of disappointment before it turned to anger, and she then set off for art class. At least she had some control there.

🐉 LEILA APPROACHED MISS MICHAELS AT HER DESK, holding out the completed watercolor portrait she had painted. It wasn't fair to ask her subject, but she wanted a few pointers. "Would you mind looking at something?"

Miss Michaels glanced at the painting. "Oh, my."

"Do you have any suggestions on how to lay down darker colors without turning them to mud?"

"Well, try using the largest brush you can for the area, make sure your surface is good and dry before adding another quick layer of color without disrupting the pigment beneath it. Try using a color from the opposite side of the color wheel for a little more depth."

Leila nodded. "Thanks."

"Actually, on this one, I wouldn't touch a thing. It's a very flattering likeness."

"So, you can tell it's you?"

"Of course." She winked. "She's wearing my skirt."

Leila double-checked the likeness against Miss Michaels.

"Oh, Leila, I'm only kidding … may I have it?"

"I guess."

"Actually, I'd like to display it, if you don't mind. Principal Boyd has made the exhibit case in the lobby available for our art classes."

"Oh."

THAT AFTERNOON, AFTER EIGHTH PERIOD, LEILA spotted Micah at his locker. He practically blocked her way to the gymnasium corridor. She almost made a U-turn but opted to face him.

"Hi Micah," she said as she approached.

His smile did not come as easily as it used to. "Hey."

"Listen, Micah, I've been wanting to say … well, I'm sorry I was so rude to you a few weeks back. I was just kind of in a mood and took it out on you. Sorry."

His expression lightened and his head bobbed. "That's okay. We're cool."

Leila involuntarily mimicked his bob.

"So, I heard you did a painting of Miss Michaels and she's putting it on display," he rambled. "She says it's really good. I can't wait to see it."

"Oh, yeah … I guess."

"So, is there anything you don't do? I mean, like, you're an amazing runner. You improvise blues on the piano. You do watercolors, which are supposed to be really difficult. You are seriously gifted."

Her face heated. "I'm not what you think I am. I run fast only because I've been doing it since I was little. And the piano—I can't do a thing with it outside of blues. And I struggle with my paintings. It's just some weird compulsion I have."

"Oh, well, I'm not very good at art or anything, but I really like art class."

"Me too." She didn't know what else to say except, "Okay, well … I'll see ya."

As she turned to leave, he spoke up. "Leila, I'm having a party Saturday night—you could come if you were in the mood."

Perhaps she could have a social life outside of Kyle. "That sounds like fun."

CHAPTER 18

IN ONE OF THE OLDER NEIGHBORHOODS SOUTH OF Merrick Road, Leila pulled up to the curb of Micah's house. A warm glow showed through the large picture windows as Leila followed a few kids down the driveway. Moonlight reflected off the canal behind the house where the basement entrance came into sight. She stepped inside, met by a waft of smoke. Aside from the scent of marijuana, the room had nothing in common with the unfinished basements where her father jammed with his band. Plush sofas and chairs occupied the perimeter of the room. Tall stools sat in front of the wet bar off to the side. An elaborately carved pool table consumed the center of the room, where players and spectators hung around it.

In the back corner, Micah stood amidst his band equipment, fingering his guitar to the music playing on the stereo. In spite of all the guests, a crowd large enough to fill the entire room, Micah spotted her right off. Leila's gaze moved from Micah to the pool table. Kyle glanced up at her as he took aim at the cue ball, grazing the top of it and blowing his shot. Maryanne looked around, as if searching for the object of Kyle's distraction. Before Maryanne could give her the stare down, Leila returned her sights to Micah's makeshift stage; he was no longer there.

In a moment, he appeared at her side. "I'm glad you came. You want a beer?"

She nodded. If nothing else, it would give her something to do with her hands and help her blend. She followed him to the beer-packed refrigerator.

Twisting the cap, he handed her the bottle. "Steve brought his Yamaha keyboard. You wanna check it out?"

"Sure," she said, as Kyle half-sat on a bar stool, straddling his cue stick. They ignored each other as she passed by.

Micah introduced her to his pianist friend, Steve.

"We were just getting ready to start up," Micah said. "You could play if you wanted."

"No thanks, I'm happy to just sit and watch tonight."

"Okay."

Leila sipped her beer and sat in a nearby chair as they began. Several couples danced in front of the large speakers. She scanned the basement, keeping an eye on Kyle's whereabouts. Several times, she caught him looking at her from across the room, his eyes full of the same regret-filled yearning she had seen on the track. She didn't look away. She missed him, but she couldn't allow her eyes to mist. His gaze wavered, but it was Maryanne who cut off their silent interaction with a yank at Kyle's arm. He turned his back on Leila, wrapping his girlfriend in an embrace. The ache that wracked Leila's core surprised her—how could she feel so hurt when he had never even been her boyfriend? She watched with envy-tinged vexation as he led Maryanne to the other dancers.

Once they hit the floor, more joined in, crowding Leila. Someone she barely knew grabbed her hand.

"Come on, Leila!" He pulled her to her feet. Before she could protest, she was bumping into everyone around her, clenching her beer and dancing.

When the song ended, Micah handed his guitar to one of the other guys, and they continued playing something slower. He approached Leila. Setting aside her half-empty beer bottle, he pulled her close. She responded, moving with him, less and less aware of Kyle's whereabouts.

After a minute he whispered, "You wanna get high?"

"I don't smoke, Micah."

"Okay," he nodded. "You want another beer?"

She half-smiled. "I didn't finish my first, and I still have to drive home."

"Of course." He was in a full bob now. "Have you ever played on a Steinway Grand?"

She threw her head back with a laugh. "No."

"My parents have one upstairs. You wanna check it out?"

She smiled. "Is this just some ploy to get me alone?"

"No, no—" he said with a grin. "Okay, a bit."

She smiled at his candor. "I am getting a little claustrophobic, and I would like to see the piano."

"Come on." He grabbed her hand. "We'll go around front so we don't have to disrupt my parents in the kitchen."

"They don't mind that you party down here?"

"Nah—I party down here, they party upstairs."

"Pretty liberal."

"You have no idea," he chuckled and led her out the back door, up the well-lit driveway and past the window where she spied the piano. When they entered the living room, the hugeness of it—the piano and the room—enveloped her. Carpet muffled their footsteps as she walked the length of the instrument. She dared not run her hand along the black-lacquered finish for fear of leaving a smudge.

Micah pulled out the bench and sat to her right, at the treble end.

"Will your parents mind if I try it?" she asked.

"No, go ahead."

She hit several keys in a chord progression, starting in the bass register and ending in the treble. Perfect resonance. Perfect pitch.

"Wow, your parents keep it tuned."

"Yeah," he nodded. "Pretty nice, isn't it?"

He crossed his wrist over her hand, playing a chord in the tenor range. As she caressed the ivory beneath her fingertips, Micah's gaze coaxed her to face him. When their eyes met, he leaned in and kissed her full on the mouth. She didn't respond. He withdrew and then came back, but this time she stiffened and pulled away.

"I'm sorry," he said. "I shouldn't have kissed you ... you must think I'm a total jerk."

"No, Micah. You're not a jerk. I'm just ... I'm not ...." She shook her head. Even if she had wanted him to kiss her, that was not the way she wanted to be kissed. "You're a nice guy and an amazing musician, and I really like you ... I'm just ... this just isn't a good time for me ... I'm sorry."

"Okay," he nodded.

They rose from the piano together, and he led her outside. Leila didn't want to stick around to invite further awkwardness, even though Micah's good mood hadn't diminished in spite of her rebuff. Typical pothead. As he walked Leila to her car, Kyle and Maryanne leaned against his parents' car, making out as usual. Maryanne spotted Leila first and took Kyle by the hand, leading him back to the basement. As both couples passed each other under the yard light, Kyle glanced behind at Leila, the same apology in his eyes but said nothing as he slung his arm over Maryanne's shoulder and pulled her close.

Micah said, "Lovebirds—they're like the perfect couple."

Leila grabbed her car door latch. "Yeah, just perfect."

"Catch ya later," he said as she climbed inside and shut the door with a wave.

Disappointed and wrestling with angst, her heart withered as she pulled away from the curb.

The dashboard clock read ten-thirty. She didn't want to go home, but she didn't want to drive aimlessly through the streets of Millville. She turned around and headed toward the beach. At least she could park or walk along the jetty or whatever. As she headed south, the streets took on a familiar feel. When she came upon Canal Lane, such a sense of longing came over her that she slowed, almost stopping. Might Ian still be up, perhaps in his studio? As if in autopilot, she turned with no real intention of seeing him; she simply felt drawn to a memory of comfort.

IAN SAT AT HIS WORKTABLE IN THE SILENCE OF HIS studio, organizing his space after a day in the darkroom. Tonight he didn't listen to the blues, not because they were depressing in themselves, but because they reminded him of Leila. It had been ten days since he drove her home—not long enough to absolve himself of giving in to his weakness. Worse than that, his guilt made it too easy to yield to weakness again when he accepted a party invitation from Karen one week ago. At least he hadn't stayed the night. Perhaps Karen had moved on and they could go back to being just friends. Only time would tell how things would level out with Karen, but time had not quelled his feelings for Leila.

Ian had been too lenient with her and his imagination. For God's sake, she was only seventeen! A minor. He could no longer justify his interest in her simply because they had so much in common. So what if they both practiced art, enjoyed running, liked the same music, loved New Hampshire and shared thoughts and feelings more easily than he had experienced with any woman, younger or older than him. He, of all of people, knew the fallout when boundaries were violated. Grown men—or women—had no business messing with a minor.

Ian placed several proof sheets in a stack and closed his file cabinet as headlights reflected from his front windowpane. The flash paused and then quit. Now the streetlight shone on a Volkswagen Bug opposite his house. Leila. His stomach churned. It was time to take a stand.

Heading toward his front door, he grabbed his jacket on the way out. He drew a deep breath, exhaling a mist as his words slipped out in an undertone—*Just do it.*

Forcing his arms into sleeves, he approached her car. Leila's head leaned back and her eyes closed. Perhaps she had not intended to come to his door, but parking in front of his house was unacceptable. All of this needed to stop.

He neared the driver's door. She startled as her eyes shot open. Her window slowly rolled down. Even under mere streetlights, her eyes appeared red and puffy. He swallowed back indecision and leaned against her car, his gaze level with hers.

"Leila, you reek. Where have you been?" His words came out harsher than he intended.

She rubbed her eyes. "At Micah's—but I wasn't smoking."

"You've been drinking."

"Just half a beer."

He stepped back, folding his arms. He needed to get to the point before he backed out. "Leila, what are you doing here?"

She wavered. "I'm not really sure … I just …."

He sighed, rubbing his forehead. *Get a grip.* "Leila, I owe you an apology. I'm afraid I've given you the wrong impression. You're a nice girl, and I care about you—I do—but I don't feel for you the way you think I do." The lie seared.

"What do you mean?"

Follow through. "I mean that you need to accept the fact that you and I are not going to happen." His words tumbled in his head, making no sense.

She said nothing, but her wide eyes bespoke confusion.

He straightened his back and tightened his crossed arms. *Tell her.* "You need to get a boyfriend your own age."

"Really, just like you have a girlfriend your own age?"

He hesitated, and nearly gasped as he said, "Actually, I do."

"Who? Karen Weiss?"

He spoke fast, trying to get it over with. "I am not going to discuss my love life with you, Leila."

"Ian—"

"Don't call me Ian. You have to stop that." He closed his eyes and choked on the words, "You need to go home and stop wishing for something that is not going take place."

"Maybe not *now*—"

"No—" he tensed, "not ever."

"You don't mean it." She wiped tears.

"I have never been more serious." He could no longer meet her eyes. "I have a history …." He shook his head. "You're only *seventeen* … so why don't you do us both a favor. Just leave, and get on with your life."

She recoiled. "*Fine.* That's exactly what I'll do."

With a jerk, she yanked the stick shift, grinding gears and peeled away from the curb.

Ian's stomach cramped as he watched her drive away. It was the right thing to do—wasn't it?

ON HIS WAY FROM THE STAFF LOUNGE, IAN PAUSED at the display case in the front lobby. He hadn't seen any of Leila's artwork, but it didn't take long to pick it out. The product of her hand and mind ignited all his regrets afresh and challenged the stance he needed to maintain.

Miss Michaels came up behind him. "It's quite good, isn't it?"

He forced a smile and teased, "The one of you?"

"Of course."

"It's beautiful."

"Why thank you," she said, taking the bait.

In fact, he found Miss Michaels very attractive. Why hadn't he tried to get together with her, over Karen Weiss?

"Seriously, though," he said, turning to her. "It's a very good likeness. Even if it weren't, she has a way with perspective and paint."

Andrea Michaels had a pretty spark to her eyes. "She does. Though I'd like to see her loosen up her style a little bit—free up some of those creative energies."

"I like her attention to detail."

She glanced back at the painting and then at him.

It might be futile, but he would give her a try. "So, Andrea—do you still have that boyfriend?"

She chuckled. "In fact, I do, Ian. Why do you ask?"

"Just checking," he said and walked away.

It wasn't as if he were actively seeking a girlfriend since he told Leila he had one, but Karen Weiss didn't exactly fit the description. As much as he had needed to take a stand with Leila, it hadn't gone the way he would have planned. Perhaps she had seen through his half-hearted lecture. He hated that he had lied to her, had crushed someone he deeply cared for, but he had only himself to blame. He didn't deserve a girlfriend.

🜨 KYLE WALKED UP THE PATH TO ARTIE'S STOOP, glancing down both ends of the street. He hoped the cover of night colored him less white. Although feeling conspicuous, something about venturing completely out of his element eased his anguish. Part of him hoped Leila might have called in sick for work, that he would see her and could explain how bad he felt for pushing her away, but a larger part just wanted to see Artie. He tapped the front door.

Artie cracked the door and then opened it wide. "Angel ain't here, son. She's working tonight."

"Actually, sir, I came to see you." He pulled the harmonica from his pocket. "I hoped you could give me a few pointers."

Artie smiled toothlessly. "Well come on in, son."

Kyle stepped into the dim room. It felt much different without the other old men and Leila. It smelled different, too—much more like the closet and Vicks and less like pot.

"Let me go get my teef," Artie said.

Sinking into the sofa, Kyle waited.

When Artie returned with teeth and his harmonica, he sat beside Kyle. "Go on, then, let's hear it."

Kyle pulled himself to the edge of the cushion, inhaled and puckered, hitting all the notes of "Oh Susanna," nearly flawlessly. Artie grinned wide, the kitchen light reflecting off his big choppers. After a quick pause, Kyle led into the second tune, "Home on the Range," drawing out the notes with bluesy emphasis.

"Oh, you sure got some blues in your heart, son."

Kyle smiled, though his spirits had not lifted. "Yeah," he half-chuckled. "You've got to teach me a song about being in love with two women at the same time."

"Oh, there's plenty two-timing blues."

"I'm not exactly a two-timer. I'm in love with one, but

can't stop thinking about another."

"Oh that's a good one." Artie set his harp aside, picked up his guitar and put music to Kyle's words. Kyle attempted to play along on his harmonica.

Artie sat back and sighed. "I sure been there before ...."

"Two-timing?"

"Oh yeah, but that ain't what broke my heart—that ain't what made me sing the bluest blues." Artie wrestled himself free from the cushions and staggered toward a nearby dresser, supporting himself on chairs along the way. He chuckled. "Sittin' too long."

He pulled the top drawer. From an old shoebox, he lifted a worn square of paper and returned to Kyle. "Real pretty, ain't she?"

Kyle took the small faded, black-and-white photograph from his hand and glanced at the tall and slender beauty. She appeared fair skinned and blond. Kyle returned the dog-eared memento.

"That were back in the day when no Negro man dared touch a white girl ... but I sure did." Artie gazed at the photo as if slipping back in time. As he stroked the image, his lips curled with sad longing, and he shook his head. "It caused some awful trouble ... some things they just ain't no fixin', son. Sometimes love just ain't enough ... that's why you sing the blues ... 'cause that's all you can do."

Artie picked up his own harp and wailed on it, his eyes glistening. Kyle tried to play along, and even though he didn't play well, it did make him feel better, like he'd had a good cry.

After a few minutes, Artie started to cough. "Get me some water, son, and then I'll show you how to bend some notes."

Kyle fetched water. As promised, Artie guided him through the ins and outs of pouring his heart into the blues.

"That, son, is the way you make your harp cry."

🐉CHAPTER 19

L EILA PULLED HER BAG OF SMUGGLED POPCORN FROM beneath her parka and set it in the seat beside her. Only a handful of other movie viewers occupied the small theater. She didn't expect any different. Often, when she and her father had spent Christmas Day at the movies, they'd had the place to themselves.

She sank into her seat, reading the local ads and celebrity trivia flashing across the screen. She picked at her popcorn, trying to make it last.

I couldn't care less about John Travolta or Olivia Newton John!

Leila opted out on *Saturday Night Fever*—what self-respecting blues aficionado would be caught dead watching disco? And she couldn't imagine sitting through *The Goodbye Girl*—Richard Dryfus was not the romantic lead she cared to stare at for two hours. Not that Gene Wilder was a hunk, but she liked Alfred Hitchcock and a parody might lift her mood, so *High Anxiety* won out.

After the movie ended, she remained in her seat as the theater emptied. A different few viewers trickled in. As the lights dimmed a second time, a lanky figure entered the theater. She did a double take. As Mr. Myles scanned the empty seats and then navigated toward her, a surge of conflicting emotions swelled her chest. Had he planned this or simply picked the same movie by chance? She wanted both to be true. She choked up as he carried a large bucket of popcorn and two Cokes. How could such an invasion feel so welcome? Without a word, he sat one seat over, setting the refreshment caddy between them.

"I could sit somewhere else, if you'd prefer," he said.

She swallowed to repress a smile. "No, you're okay."

"How's the movie?"

"If you like ridiculous, it's pretty good—kind of clever in places."

Second time around, Leila picked up on more of the subtle humor. To her amazement, Mr. Myles actually chuckled. She even caught a glimpse of a smile. Her stare drew his attention for a few tentative moments before they returned to the movie.

As the lights came back up, so did Leila's apprehension. Would he now leave?

Myles sank deeper into his seat, crossing his ankle over his knee in repose. She stared at the screen but caught his glance in her peripheral vision. He likely hoped she would say something, but what?

"Rough month, huh?" he said.

She rolled her eyes, weighing gratitude against annoyance. "That's an understatement."

"Do you want to talk about it?"

She shrugged.

Myles said nothing, as if she would fill the silence.

She sighed. "I wouldn't even know where to begin."

"You could tell me what's going on between you and Kyle."

"Kyle seems to think I'm messing things up between him and Maryanne."

"I see."

"No you don't."

"Sure I do. You like Kyle and he likes you, and his girlfriend doesn't like that."

So, he did get it. "Why do I always have to get mixed up with unattainable guys?"

"This is a pattern for you, is it?"

"Apparently."

Myles' brow rose.

Leila chased a kernel around the bottom of the popcorn bucket.

"Well, I figured as much about you and Kyle," he folded his arms, "but I'm more concerned to hear that you might not be running with the track team this spring, after all."

"Where did you hear that?"

"In the staff lounge."

Her eyes gaped.

"Oh yes." His fingers drumrolled his arm. "It's quite the rumor mill."

"Who did you hear it from?"

"Why, Ms. Thorpe, of course. It has been her observation that Coach Brigham and you—I think the expression she used was—'scarcely acknowledge each other.'"

Her posture drooped.

"I won't ask if you'd rather I don't."

He had figured it out. Why did he bother to ask when he already knew the answers? "I'm not just some silly schoolgirl who goes around getting crushes on cute teachers, you know."

"I would never—ever—associate the word *silly* with you."

She didn't doubt his sincerity, but defiance straightened her shoulders. She would test his reaction to a blatant confession and looked him in the eye. "I'm in love with Ian Brigham." Even as the words slipped out, she doubted the truth of it. On the other hand, if she wasn't in love, how could it hurt so bad?

Myles said nothing, he simply studied her face.

"How pathetic is that?" she said.

"Love only feels pathetic when you can entertain no hope of seeing it through."

Leila matched his folded arms. "Well, I guess that's pretty much the story of my life."

He blew out a long breath. "I'll tell you what's pathetic. Sitting in a movie theater with your math teacher on Christmas Day with an empty popcorn bucket." He stood. "I'm going to make a pit stop and get some refills."

"I could use a restroom myself." She followed him out of the theater. He seemed like a different man than the one who had walked in.

When she returned, Myles had already claimed his seat. She sat right beside him this time. For the first few minutes she squirmed, wishing she had kept their comfortable distance, but as the next set of previews began, she didn't give it another thought. Every time he chuckled, it broadened her own smile.

"Well, I don't know about you," Myles said when the movie ended, "but I think if I watch this one more time I'll be ready for the 'Home for the Very, Very Nervous.' Let's get dinner somewhere."

"Is that allowed?" she whispered.

"Why wouldn't it be?"

"Because, you know. I'm your student."

"So, you think that makes it inappropriate?"

"I don't know—isn't it?"

"I suppose if you wanted to get technical, some might find fault with it, though I'm not given to arbitrary prohibitions that don't pertain to real life."

"We wouldn't get in trouble, would we?"

"Not unless one of us has a crush on the other, and I can assure you I don't."

"Yuck! Neither do I!"

"Then we're good."

"Is there even going to be a place that's open?"

"Yeah, there's a diner nearby that's run by Jehovah's Witnesses. They don't care if it's Christmas. Best part is, it won't be decorated, and there won't be any Christmas music playing. It's the favorite Grinch hangout."

"Yay," she said, happy to have him follow her out.

THE DINER BELL JINGLED AS LEILA AND MYLES entered together. She stifled self-conciousness, the thought of anyone drawing conclusions. Perhaps she and her teacher simply appeared as father and daughter.

"They serve an excellent quiche," he said as she claimed a booth. The waitress arrived with a coffee carafe, unaffected at the sight of them. Myles turned his cup upright. "Please."

Leila settled in. "I've never had quiche."

"No?"

"I kind of grew up on burgers and pizza."

"Feeling adventurous?"

"Of course."

"Two quiches," he told the waitress. "And a side salad."

"Salad for me, too."

Myles assumed his usual repose, his arms across his chest. He smiled faintly, deepening yet softening his crow's-feet, warming the blue of his eyes. He didn't look at her the way her father sometimes had as if trying to unlock some hidden trove to which he had lost the key. On occasion, when she had lent him access, he had slammed the lid shut with impatience and judgment. Instead, Myles' eyes coaxed her comfort, promising acceptance.

She matched his pose and stared, wishing he held the answers to all her uncertainties.

He studied her face. "Do you have something on your mind?"

Her gaze moved all around the table and then settled back on him. "Maybe."

"Shall I get out my dentistry tools and extract it?" He continued his stare.

"It's just that—" her eyes rolled "—it's not easy to talk about."

"Just say it."

"Okay. How come, you know—sex—changes things?"

His brow arched, but not as high as she expected. Now, his gaze moved all around the table but settled back on her.

"Oftentimes, the reality of a sexual experience does not measure up to the fantasy." He paused, as if allowing her a moment to grasp his words. "Unfulfilled expectations can change a relationship. Even if initially fulfilled, expectations don't always remain the same."

She twisted her mouth, trying to understand.

"Think of it as an equation, with expectations on one side and reality on the other. Reality is the constant. If the fantasy and expectations don't add up, one of them has to change."

"But why would sex between two people change things with someone else?"

"Because that third party, whether she wants to admit it or not, may be part of the equation."

Leila had inadvertently become part of Kyle and Maryanne's equation; she understood that. "I'll have to think on that."

"Anything else?"

"Actually, yes." She required no further coaxing. "Could I ask about your kid?"

He blinked slowly. "What did you want to know?"

"Did you have a son or daughter?"

He drew in an uneasy breath. "A daughter."

She wanted to ask what happened to her, but didn't want to throw off her objective. Instead, she asked, "Is that why you've taken an interest in me?"

He seemed to mull over the question. "I take an interest in you, Leila Sanders, because I like you."

"You do?"

"Is that so hard to fathom?"

"I guess I was under the impression that you didn't like anyone."

He bit his lip. "Generally speaking, I suppose it's true that I'm not a people person."

"So, then, why do you like me?"

"Because, Leila—you are a bright and intelligent young lady. You have a great deal of potential."

"Do all your bright and intelligent students with potential get this kind of attention?"

"No, but then, they don't have a need."

"You think I'm needy?"

"I think you have enough dignity and insight to know the answer to that question."

"I don't need your attention," she said, her self-sufficiency wrestling her loneliness. "But I appreciate it. I think I might even miss you after midterms."

"Are you sure you don't want to move on to calculus with Kyle?"

"I won't miss you that much. Besides, you can still torment me in homeroom."

"Indeed," he said as the waitress brought their meal. They ate in comfortable silence.

IAN ELBOWED HIS WAY THROUGH KAREN'S crowded living room, making his way toward the bathroom. He flipped the light switch, unzipped and relieved himself of more beers than he usually drank in one sitting. The shower stall to his side reminded him of the last time he and Karen had messed around in there. As he washed his hands, he ran cold water and splashed his numbing cheeks, hoping to cool off and sober up.

As he stepped back into the hall, Karen's guests were counting down to midnight. She approached with a fresh beer and handed it to him.

"Three ... two ... one," the crowd chanted and Karen moved in close and kissed him in that particular, irresistible way. He resisted, at least initially.

"Stick around," she breathed in his ear and retreated.

'Stick around'—*Do I want to stick around?* The taste of her lingered on his lips. He took a long swallow of beer to wash it away, but old images of her—of their lovemaking—lingered.

Setting his beer aside, he loosened his collar and then cracked the sliding-glass door of her balcony. Brisk air cooled his sweating forehead as he slipped outside. He'd had too much to drink. Just a few minutes of fresh air and a coffee should bring him around. He reentered the living room as guests began to thin.

"Mind if I start a pot of coffee," he said as Karen ushered a few others out the door.

She smiled, "You know your way around—help yourself."

He fumbled about her kitchen. Within minutes, the pot started percolating, and he headed for the living room. Tired and lethargic, he sank into the sofa, another place they had wrestled and tumbled. Across the room, Karen smoothed her little black dress over her hips as she bade her last guest goodnight. He intended to leave, but had he waited too long? The aroma of coffee brought him to the edge of the sofa, bracing himself to stand. Karen approached, unzipping her dress.

"I'll get the coffee …." Her dress slipped to the floor.

When he halfway came to his feet, she stood over him and pushed him back into the cushions.

He sighed. "This is not getting coffee—"

"What's your hurry, Ian?"

"I'm not sure this is a great idea," he said, his eyes all over her.

"A little one-night stand won't hurt." She came down on top of him, kissing him on the mouth and then his neck.

He wanted her—wanted intimacy—so bad. He exhaled, "Oh, Leila …."

She pushed herself up off him. "*What?*"

"What?" He suddenly realized his slip. "Oh, jeez, Karen, I'm so sorry, I didn't—"

"Don't you dare tell me you didn't mean it!" She sprung from the couch and grabbed her dress, trying to cover herself. "Get out!"

CHAPTER 20

MIDTERM EXAMS CONSUMED THE SECOND WEEK of January. On the day that regularly scheduled classes resumed, Leila checked the short-term forecast. Wind, rain, and plummeting temperatures. She drove to school instead of running.

Eighty-one percent earned her a passing grade in trigonometry, officially ending her tutoring with Kyle. After homeroom, she proceeded to home economics. Other than that, her schedule remained the same, except for the last class of the day; her semester-long reprieve from gym under Ms. Thorpe had expired.

In the gymnasium, Miss Weiss—now the eighth-period instructor—stood in front of the office windows; Ms. Thorpe disappeared behind lowering shades. A half-circle of sitting girls fanned out on newly polished floors as Miss Weiss paced in front of them. Leila inched her way behind a heavier girl, staring at strands of greasy hair rather than put herself in Weiss' line of sight.

"Rape!" Weiss said and paused. "Over sixty-seven thousand cases of rape and attempted rape in the United States in the past year. Six, right here in Millville. How many of you could fend off a rapist?"

Leila's fellow classmates sat forward with rapt attention. She knew the scare tactics and the drill—all of that had made an impression on her as a fourteen-year-old girl in a room full of militant feminists, but now it bored Leila. Just the same, it would be a good review. At least she wouldn't have to bat around a tennis ball with Maryanne, though she had spied her up front. Leila leaned back upon her arms, scooting further out of sight. Then, Coach Brigham entered from the back alcove and took center stage. The Assailant.

Oh crap.

Leila sat up and hugged her knees, staving off stomach pangs that rolled with the memory of how he had humiliated her and sent her off. She stared at the floor, fidgeting with the chopstick at the back of her head.

Miss Weiss recited the technique. "Jab, stomp, gouge, and groin."

The heavy girl shifted her weight to one side, exposing Leila. She snatched a view of her instructor. Ian's arms wrapped around the woman in a half-hearted 'attack'. Leila gazed off at the bleachers.

"Sanders!"

Leila's attention shot forward.

Miss Weiss glared. "Is this class too dull for you?"

"Not at all, ma'am." Her back straightened.

"You think because you wiggled your way out of Ms. Thorpe's class, that you don't have to learn self-defense? Or perhaps you think you already know everything about this subject."

If the class was silent before, it now stifled even a cough or a breath.

"No ma'am, not at all." Her next words strained in her throat, squeaking out, "I believe it's extremely important."

"Then perhaps you would like to be our first volunteer."

Leila's heart pounded as if she had run a mile. She flashed a look at Ian. His shoulders drew back, his chest expanding with a deep breath. Tension twitched at his brow. Blood congealed in her veins.

Weiss stared her down. "What are you waiting for, Sanders?"

Somehow, the words came out, "I'd really rather not."

Weiss's nostrils flared. "*I* don't negotiate!"

Leila pried herself from what felt like shackles, coming to her feet in slow motion. She searched out every empty space in the gym, anything she could focus on rather than look Ian—or anyone else—in the eye. When she stood before him, her gaze kept to the ground. He cleared his throat, drawing her eyes as far as his tense jaw. She turned, taking the victim's stance in front of him.

"We don't need to put his eye out," Miss Weiss removed Leila's chopstick. Her bun unraveled.

Ian moved closer. He draped an arm across her front, resting a lax hand on her shoulder. His breath warmed her ear. His other hand loosely held her arm. Their heavy breathing synchronized.

Weiss sneered, "Now what will you do, Sanders?"

Paralysis set in. Leila couldn't speak let alone move.

"Surely you have some trick up your sleeve."

Brigham squeezed her arm gently and whispered, "It's okay."

Even in all the awkwardness, his reassuring voice set her in motion. Leila turned her chin into his bent elbow. Faking a stomp at his foot, she swiveled and elbowed him lethargically in the stomach. Now facing him, she lifted her knee toward his groin, never looking directly at him. He allowed her to follow through on each maneuver and then released her.

"Well, that would be fine if you were actually being attacked by Coach Brigham. I'd like to see what you'd do if you had someone who wasn't a wuss grabbing you."

A few of the girls gasped and snickered.

"I think for the purpose of demonstration, she did a perfectly adequate job." Ian nudged Leila toward where she had been sitting, and she began moving.

Miss Weiss grabbed Leila's arm. "How is the class going to learn anything if the attack is not believable?"

Weiss yanked Leila toward her. Positioning herself behind, she put her student in a chokehold and gripped her wrist. Leila shot a glance at Ian whose jaw clenched. He stepped toward them.

"What will you do now, Sanders?" she whispered in Leila's ear.

Leila offered no resistance, although adrenaline pumped through her body as her heart pounded painfully fast. Her breath halted. Weiss tightened her hold and pressed Leila's wrist upward, pulling at her shoulder.

"Well, Sanders?"

A sharp twinge gripped her shoulder. Leila winced.

Ian seized Karen's arm. "That's enough."

All of a sudden, an excruciating pain shot through Leila's body. She reacted instinctively, the way she had been instructed. In a flash, Miss Weiss lay on her back, coughing, trying to get air and looking up at Leila in an offensive stance. The class gasped. It happened so quickly that Leila wasn't quite sure how Miss Weiss had ended up on the mat. The throbbing pain in her shoulder seemed inexplicable.

Ian came to her side, and she now realized that she had sent Miss Weiss to the floor. Leila covered her mouth.

"Oh my God. I am so sorry!" Leila extended her hand to Miss Weiss, who held her gut and panted.

Weiss slapped her hand aside as Ms. Thorpe flew out of her office. Leila held her left shoulder as Weiss came to her feet.

Thorpe's eyes bulged as she approached Leila. "Are you alright?"

Leila staved off tears and nodded.

"Brigham. Weiss. In my office," Thorpe ordered, and then shouted, "You girls, run laps until the bell."

Dispersing to the perimeter of the gym, the class jogged counterclockwise. Ms. Thorpe followed the two into her office, slamming the door behind them.

Bewildered, Leila mechanically moved with the group of girls as they made their way around the gym. Coming near the office window, she slowed to a walk along with the others trying to overhear Miss Weiss' high-pitched defense—though it sounded more like accusations. Leila barely registered that she had anything to do with it. The warmth she experienced earlier drained from her body. She felt light headed.

The heated exchange in the office, which for the most part remained unintelligible, now rang out in crisp words, "… Ian would rather be screwing Leila Sanders!"

Another surge of adrenaline screamed through Leila's body. Faces stared. Voices hushed and snickered. Classmates huddled. Her heart pounded in her ears, darkening her peripheral vision until they all vanished. Leila wanted out! Her feet continued moving and quickened as she headed toward the nearby front doors. She pushed her way through, into the gym lobby and then breached the second set of doors out into the cold. As she ran from the school grounds, she felt more aware of her rolling stomach than the rain and her numbing shoulder. She neared a row of shrubs and vomited into them.

Images whirled in her head, spiraling into a vortex of dire consequence. She kept running as rain turned to sleet. Icy pellets clung to her hair. Her adrenaline wore thin, leaving her shivering and on the verge of exhaustion.

🐾 IAN SAT AT HIS DESK, HIS DOOR SHUT. HE ACHED, blaming himself for Leila's turmoil. There was no way any of this could end well. The ongoing conversation between Thorpe and Karen would be only the beginning of it.

In the girls' office, Thorpe scolded, "Your behavior was completely unacceptable, Karen. You were out of control. To assault a student, especially in front of an entire class, and then to top it off, accuse a fellow teacher of sexual misconduct—Have you lost your mind?" Thorpe paused. Ian visualized her eye-popping anger. "I cannot shield you from the consequences of your behavior." Weiss said nothing. "You need to go home. Do not come to school tomorrow. I will contact you and let you know how the school board intends to handle this."

Thorpe then entered Brigham's office without knocking. She paced back and forth. Their eyes locked.

"I want to know exactly what has been going on between you and Leila."

Ian rubbed his forehead and pushed back in his seat. He had prepared his answer and offered it with conviction. "I am not having, nor have I ever had a sexual relationship with Leila Sanders. I have never been sexually suggestive, nor have I ever had any inappropriate physical contact with her. Does that sufficiently cover all the bases?"

"No. I want to know how you feel about her."

"My feelings for her are not relevant."

"I will decide if they are relevant!"

He folded his arms and stared her down. He'd had enough bullying for one day.

Thorpe's eyes narrowed. "What deal did you cut with her regarding track tryouts?"

"What possible difference could that make?"

"Your hedging the issue indicates it may make a big difference."

"Fine. She wanted to see my photography—then she would try out."

"And why was that so difficult to admit?"

It would all come out sooner or later. Now it was simply a matter of controlling the fallout. "Because she came to my house."

"Were her parents aware of that?"

"No." He hated the idea of giving away what Leila had divulged in confidence. "That afternoon when she came to my house, she confided that she has no parents and no guardian. She lives on her own."

"What?"

"Her father died a year ago. Since then she has been living independently."

"And you've known this for how long?"

"Since the first week of school."

"Who else knows?"

"Myles. And I wouldn't be surprised if Kyle Schultz knows, too."

"Well, this just keeps getting better. Am I the only one around here interested in proper protocol?"

🌿CHAPTER 21

MS. THORPE SHOWED UP IN MYLES' DOORWAY toward the end of eighth period. That meant trouble. He joined her in the corridor.

"There's been an incident in gym class involving Leila Sanders. She took off running. I understand you have her contact card and know where she lives."

Myles didn't need further explanation. He simply stepped back into the classroom.

"Page fifty-seven through nine. Do the math," he said and then exited.

Within minutes he had his parka and car keys, driving north in his old Volvo. His wipers pushed ice back and forth as he slid to a stop at the first intersection. His defroster finally kicked in as he spotted Leila walking along the sidewalk, wearing only shorts and a T-shirt, her arms wrapped around her. He pulled to the curb and rolled down his window.

"Leila! Get in."

She didn't acknowledge him and continued walking. Even his beeping horn solicited only a look. Pulling his car ahead to the curb, he stopped and grabbed his parka. He approached, draping the coat over her shoulders and maneuvered her lethargic body into the passenger seat. As he sped to her house in silence, she shivered convulsively.

Myles guided Leila up the stairwell. He could not imagine

what 'incident' had put her in such a state that she would try to run home in the freezing rain. Perhaps hypothermia had left her listless, or was it something more?

"Do you have a key?" he asked at the top stair, turning her face to his. "The key, Leila."

She moved a loose asbestos shingle, and Myles snatched the key from the nail. Inside, he directed her to the bedroom, then headed to her shower and turned the hot water all the way up.

"Get those wet clothes off and get in the shower." Leaving her in the bedroom, he shut the door on his way out.

In her kitchenette, his ears perked for sounds from her room as he drew water for the kettle. He scanned the cabinet above her sideboard. A box of Cheerios, a jar of peanut butter, and a tin of Earl Grey. Under a less stressful circumstance, her taste in tea would have prompted a smile. He dropped a teabag into two mismatched mugs as her water pipes ticked and hummed. Three steps landed him at her bedroom door.

He tapped. "How are you doing in there?"

With no response, he tapped again, louder this time. "Leila?"

When she did not respond a second time, he cracked the bedroom door and then approached the closed bathroom door. He knocked. "Are you okay in there?"

Again, no response. He pushed the door ajar without looking in, hoping to hear some activity over the running water. "Are you okay?"

"I'm fine," she said, almost inaudible. "I'll be out in a minute."

He retreated to the kitchen where the kettle whistled. Myles still could not imagine what had set her in such a tailspin, but the image of her shivering body and the word "incident" made every fatherly cell in his body writhe.

While tea bags steeped along with his agitation, he paced the tiny living room and paused at her drawing table. A tablet of paper lay opened to a sketch of her hand. He cocked his head, impressed with its accuracy. Thumbing through a series of pencil sketches and watercolors of household objects, he came across the likeness of Ian Brigham. Leila drew him running, bare-chested, with his shorts low on his hips. Although it appeared a true depiction, he wondered how she had developed such an acute eye for the male form. Flipping back a few more pages, a telling portrait caught him off guard. His own eyes stared back.

"Did you find the one of you?" she asked.

He spun toward her. "I'm sorry, that was rude of me."

"It's okay." She moved to his side, wrapped in her bathrobe. Her wet hair draped down her back. "Do you like it?"

He studied it a moment longer. "It's very ... precise."

"Yes, but do you like it?"

"I'm not sure." He stepped into the kitchen to retrieve tea. "Sit."

Myles brought two steaming cups on saucers to the love seat and passed a set to her. Wincing, she reached for it with her right hand, while her left remained limp on her lap.

She sipped tea, her heavy eyes peering over her cup. "So what did you hear?"

He sat on her left, saucer on his knee. "Only that there was an incident in gym class."

She shook her head. "I was so stupid. If only I had been paying closer attention. I shouldn't have irritated her ... I didn't mean to hurt her."

His chest swelled and he released a long, restrained breath. "*Who* did you not mean to hurt?"

"Miss Weiss. I just wanted her to stop ...." She shook her head. "I am *so* sorry ...."

"You wanted her to stop *what*?"

"I just wanted her to let go of me." Her cup clattered against the saucer. "She didn't realize she was hurting me. I should have said something—"

"Okay, Leila, you're going to have to back up." He took the cup and saucer from her and placed them on the crate coffee table in front of them. "Tell me what was going on in class?"

She stared off. "Self-defense instruction."

"And you volunteered to be part of the demonstration?"

"No. She picked me—you know, to go against Ian."

Myles cringed at the mention of Coach Brigham—at the way she freely called him by his first name. "And did you?"

"Yes. You know, 'Jab, stomp, gouge, and groin.' But she didn't think we were realistic enough or something. So then she wanted me to do it again, except with her. "

Another deep breath. "And that's when you hurt her?"

"No, I just stood there like a big dummy ... but then when she pulled my arm back ... I should have told her it hurt. She wouldn't have done it if I spoke up. I don't know, it all happened so fast ... I think I must have flipped her or punched her in the gut or something. The next thing I knew, she was on the floor holding her stomach. I told her I was sorry, but she was so mad ...." Tears filled her eyes. "And then Ms. Thorpe came out and she was really mad."

"And that's when you took off running?"

"No." She paused, rubbing her cheek. "Then we all heard them in the office. We could tell Miss Weiss and Ian were angry ... then everybody heard Miss Weiss—"

As tears slipped down her face, Myles grit his teeth. He choked back indignation and grabbed a box of tissue from the floor. Handing it over, he gave her a moment.

He persisted. "Everybody heard Miss Weiss, *what*?"

She winced, releasing more tears. He turned her face and made her look at him.

"Leila—it's okay." His thumb wiped her cheek. "You can tell me."

Her gaze dropped to her lap. "She said that Ian would rather be ..."—her pitch rose—"he'd rather be *screwing* ... me." She rubbed her shoulder and grimaced.

"Did she hurt you? Let me see."

She slipped the robe from her left side, revealing only her shoulder, swollen and discolored. He swore.

"You need to have this looked at." He went to the freezer and returned with a bag of ice. Pressing it against her shoulder, he held it there. Again, she began crying.

"It wasn't your fault." He put his arm around her. "You did nothing wrong. You are not in trouble. Do you understand? This was not your fault."

Her chest heaved as she sobbed into her hand. He pulled her close and held her until she quieted.

Myles sighed at the profundity of the incident and all its implications. Such abuse would not go unpunished. Unfortunately, Leila and everything she wanted to protect would be exposed and scrutinized. Brigham was not without culpability, and even if he would not be the focus of the official and sure-to-follow inquiry, Brigham's relationship with Leila would be thoroughly investigated.

Leila wiped tears and sank into the sofa.

Myles tempered his voice, "Have you warmed up?"

She nodded.

"Then you need to put clothes on. Can you do that?"

"I think so," she said and headed to her room, closing the door behind. After a few long minutes, she emerged in jeans and a sweatshirt, combing fingers through still-damp hair.

He patted the sofa. "Sit down."

She again took her place beside him.

"I'm going to ask you some questions." He drew in a long breath. "They might make you uncomfortable, but I need you to be one-hundred percent honest with me. Do you understand?"

"Yes."

He shifted to face her. "I need to know about your relationship with Coach Brigham."

"What about it do you need to know?"

"Everything."

Leila shrank back. Yes, Leila and Myles had talked about things that most teenage girls would never dream of discussing with a middle-aged man—a teacher, no less. Yet when they had discussed sex at the diner, it was all in theory, formulaic, and abstract. But now, he needed to talk about private issues and real feelings. He hated rousing the discomfort that showed on her face.

She winced. "Why is it important for you to know about my relationship with Ian?"

"Because of what Miss Weiss accused him of. I'm not trying to be intrusive. I only want to help. You need to understand that what happened to you in gym today will not be viewed lightly by the school board." Myles did not want to alarm her, but she needed to understand there was a storm gathering around her. "Incidents like these are investigated, especially when a teacher has been implicated in alleged sexual misconduct. I want to prepare you for the questions they will ask."

"I'm going to have to explain about Ian?" Tears again gathered as she drew her knees to her chest.

"Leila, I don't want to panic you, but you need—" Myles finished forcefully, "You need to get a grip."

She sat up, offering a weak nod.

Her answers might come with difficulty, but she had no idea how difficult the asking was. He inhaled. "Have you ever had a sexual relationship with Coach Brigham?"

"Sexual?"

He did not want to have to explain it. "Yes, sexual—have you ever had any kind of sex with the man?"

"No!"

"Has he ever kissed you or tried to kiss you?"

"No."

"Has he ever touched you in an inappropriate way?"

"Inappropriate?"

"In a sexual kind of way."

She hesitated and blushed. "No."

"Leila, I'm not trying to embarrass you, but it's important that you tell me everything."

"Do feelings count?"

He arched his brow. "Feelings?"

"Yes, sexual feelings."

"No. Sexual feelings don't count." He shook his head, as it dawned on him. "You've never had sex with anyone, have you."

"No."

"Good," he said, and continued. "Has Coach Brigham ever spoken to you in a sexually suggestive way?"

"No, not—No. No, he hasn't."

"Okay ...." He didn't like her hesitation. "Have you ever been alone with him outside of the school setting?"

"Yes."

Now we're getting somewhere. "Under what circumstances?"

Leila sighed.

Here it comes.

"The first time ...."

Myles tried not to roll his eyes.

She continued, "... was last July."

Myles calculated. This might be a mitigating factor. "Before you enrolled in school?"

"Yes." She explained about her flat tire and Ian's blues and the conversation they'd had and their immediate rapport. "He didn't know I was only seventeen. He thought I was older because I sounded like I knew about some of the blues clubs around, which I had been to with my father when I was a kid, but he didn't know that," she rambled. "He gave me his card and a cassette, but I never called him because I knew he was older. I just didn't know he was a teacher, I thought he was a photographer."

Myles nodded. That was not so bad. "And the next time?"

"It was at his house."

Oh great! Here we go. "And, did he invite you to his house?"

"No. I just showed up."

"Okay, how long were you there?"

"I don't know ... a long time, it was hours."

He tried to relax the tendons in his neck. "And what were you doing for hours?"

"I wanted to see his photography. He showed it to me ... *all* of it."

Something in the way she said 'all of it' made him uneasy.

He feared the answer to his next question. "Any sexually explicit content?"

"How do you mean 'sexually explicit'?"

"Naked people, Leila," he snapped at her. "People without their clothes or people engaged in sex acts."

"Well, there were some nudes, but no sex. They weren't like the ones in Playboy or Penthouse, if that's what you mean."

"Like you would know."

"Don't be condescending, Clarence. Just because I'm a virgin does not mean that you know what I have or have not been exposed to. I know the difference between pornography and Ian's art. And you're not going to twist that."

Now, Myles startled. "First of all, do not call me by my first name!" He then softened. "Second, I did not mean to be condescending, I'm sorry. Thirdly, I am not trying to twist anything. These are very real questions that may be asked of you, Leila."

"How do you even know they're going to ask these kinds of questions?"

"Because I have served on committees whose job it is to ask these kinds of questions. *I* have had to ask these kinds of questions."

She slumped back, her eyes exuding exhaustion. "Well, are you done?"

"No. I'm not." He replaced the ice bag onto her shoulder and tempered his tone. "Were there other times?"

"He drove me home before Thanksgiving when the weather was bad. He dropped me off and left. Then a couple of weeks afterward, I drove to his house and parked outside. He came out. We talked. I left. We haven't spoken or seen each other since. Until today."

"What did you talk about?"

Her chin quivered. "He said I needed to stop wishing for something that will never happen ... and that I need to get a boyfriend my own age."

That pleased Myles.

She wiped her face. "So why is it that you and I can be alone together, go to the movies, go out to eat, and nobody gets worked up?"

"Because neither of us is romantically attracted to the other."

"So what. You were in my apartment while I was naked in the other room. You were practically in my bathroom while I was in the shower. What's the difference?"

"Motives and circumstance, Leila."

"And do they always take motives and circumstances into account?"

He had to admit, "Not always."

"So, potentially, you could get in trouble?"

"It's not likely. Besides, no one is accusing me of anything. I'm a grouchy old math teacher and a very unlikely target." Myles understood how the system worked.

"Is Ian going to be in trouble?"

"Only if you keep calling him Ian. Don't ever call him by his first name. Not even when you're talking to me. Do you understand?"

"Yes." She yawned. "What's going to happen to me?"

Pulling the coverlet from the back of the sofa, he spread it over her shoulders and perched her chin on his fingertips.

He looked into her eyes. "Nothing bad is going to happen to you. I promise."

"What if I don't want to talk to—you know, whoever they are?"

"I'm afraid you don't have a choice. If they need to, they can get a court injunction to force you."

"Do I have to go by myself?"

"Normally it would be your parents or a guardian. You're entitled to bring an attorney if you want. However, you are not the one being accused of anything. This is not about finding fault with you, Leila. You haven't done anything wrong."

"But I fell in love with Coach Brigham."

"Falling in love with the wrong person is not a crime. If it were, better than half the population would be locked up, myself included."

"Who's going to be with me when they ask me questions?"

"Whoever you want."

"I want you."

"Then you'll have me." He stood, rubbing his stubbled face. "It's time for you to put your shoes on. I'm taking you to the emergency room."

She whined, "I'm not going to the emergency room."

"Oh, yes you are!" He went to her room and found her sneakers sitting in a damp spot. "Are you going to find some dry shoes, or do I need to start snooping through your closet?"

She slumped back into the sofa as he placed her sneakers on the doormat. Just then, a loud rap rattled glass in the outside door. Ms. Thorpe peered through the window. He half-expected her.

Leila rolled her eyes at the sight of Ms. Thorpe. "Oh great."

Myles opened the door.

Thorpe whispered, "How is she?"

"She's fine," Leila called from the sofa.

"Yes," Myles said. "Though we are having difficulty getting her dressed for the emergency room."

Thorpe's eyebrows arched. "Tell me you are not serious."

Myles stepped aside. "See for yourself."

She rounded the sofa and stood in front of Leila. "Let me see."

Stretching the neck of her sweatshirt, Leila exposed part of her shoulder as Thorpe shot an alarmed and disgusted glance at Myles. Both knew the repercussions of a teacher-inflicted injury.

Myles piped up, "Miss Sanders seems to think that she does not need to go to the emergency room."

"Oh, she's going." Ms. Thorpe marched into Leila's room and returned with socks and boots. She handed Leila a sock.

"Put it on."

Leila grabbed the limp sock and one-handedly tried to insert her toes.

"Give me that." Thorpe snatched the sock and forced it on Leila's foot.

Both teachers escorted Leila downstairs and to the curb. Thorpe opened her passenger door. "Get in."

Leila glanced at Myles.

"She'll drive over with me," he said, and Leila followed him to his car.

Over slick roads, they arrived at the emergency room ten minutes later. From the scarcity of seats, it was apparent that it had been a busy night. Two chairs became available on opposite sides of the room. Thorpe took one and Leila took the other while Myles stood at her side. After about a half hour, another seat opened up beside Leila. Myles took the vacancy. As Leila dozed, he put his arm around her to keep her from falling over. While she snored quietly, he held her close and watched Thorpe across the room.

What did Thorpe know of Leila and Brigham's relationship? More than that, when push came to shove, as it surely would, how exacting would Thorpe, and thus the school board, be regarding Leila's domestic situation? Thorpe met his stare. She would have just as many questions.

When the seat beside Myles opened up, Thorpe moved to sit beside him. She inched her seat even closer.

Myles spoke first, in an undertone. "I take it you realize there are neither parents nor guardian involved."

"Yes." She squinted, studying his face. "And so does the board."

"Of course. And the hearing?"

"Tomorrow night."

"Who's on the list?"

"Weiss, Brigham, myself, then later on, of course Leila. You're not officially on the list. However, I would make myself available, if I were you."

"I'll do better than that." He cocked his brow. "Miss

Sanders has asked me to accompany her."

Looking at him askance, she squinted harder. "I find it more than a little disturbing that you—in a position of authority and oversight of a student—took it upon yourself to conceal Miss Sander's unsupervised status. What could possibly be your motive?"

Myles looked directly at her. He'd had enough. "You do not want to go there, Ms. Thorpe."

"I'm sorry. I did not mean to imply anything. It's just that I've come from hours of interrogating, wondering if my people have come clean with me, or am I going to hear any surprises come tomorrow night. I'm just trying to cover all my bases."

"I understand you have a vested interest in your so-called people," he spoke evenly. "However, my only interest is Miss Sanders and what repercussions she will have to suffer at the hands of your board, as a result of the behavior of 'your people'."

"This is not my board and it's not my inquest."

"And this means that neither you or the board has any intention of pushing the issue of Miss Sander's unsupervised status?"

"That's not my decision."

"No, but your husband is on the school board."

Her nostrils flared. "He has recused himself and will not be hearing this case. I resent the implication that you think my husband would influence the outcome of this hearing."

He smirked. "What you should be resenting is the fact that I believe you capable of influencing your husband, who certainly has the ability to influence the outcome of this hearing."

Thorpe leaned into him and glared. "How dare you insinuate that I would protect my people at Leila's expense." She drew curious glances from those around them.

Myles lips pressed tight before he answered. "I am not the least bit interested in what outcome your people suffer—or whether they suffer at all." He kept his voice low yet forceful. "My concern is that Leila maintains her dignity and her autonomy."

"That is completely out of the board's jurisdiction."

"And they have no intention of contacting Children's Protective Services?"

"And why would they?"

"A minor has been assaulted. A minor with no parent or guardian." He watched her calculating the repercussions of involving the state. And yet it was bound to come up. If they concealed her status, it could be construed as subterfuge. Just the same, he preferred the issue not come up at all.

Leila stirred, wincing as she rubbed her shoulder.

"Isn't there someone who can see her?" Myles barked at a passing nurse, rousing Leila as he massaged the bridge of his nose.

In a minute, the nurse returned and called for Leila.

"Come on." He helped her up.

Thorpe accompanied them, until the nurse said, "I'm sorry. Only one can come in."

Thorpe had been excluded. After an exam and an X-ray, Leila received an icepack, sling, painkiller, and instructions. The sprain should heal if she kept her shoulder inactive for a few weeks.

Chapter 22

W HEN KYLE ENTERED HOMEROOM, HE DIDN'T think much about Mr. Myles' clean-shaven face. Then Leila didn't show up. Suddenly, something in the universe felt dreadfully out of balance. In his gut, he correlated the two anomalies.

By the end of homeroom, Leila still hadn't shown up. He began to worry.

At his locker, only Micah met him. "Hey man, did you hear about Leila?"

"Hear what?"

"Some sort of cat fight in gym."

"What? Between her and Maryanne?"

"No man, between Leila and Miss Weiss."

It took a second for Micah's words to register. "What?"

"Yeah. Apparently she and the coach have been, you know, messin' around."

"Everybody knows Weiss and Brigham have been messing around."

"Not Weiss, man. Brigham and Leila."

"There's no way that's true. Why do you even listen to crap like that?"

Micah backed down. "I didn't say it was true, but you know, she is kind of mixed up. It wouldn't really surprise me if it were true."

Kyle rolled his eyes. "You're just saying that because she

didn't want to jump your bones."

Micah shrugged. "Yeah, maybe, but you know, they kind of have a lot in common—running and art and junk. I could definitely see the two of them together."

"That's sick."

"Don't be so judgmental, man."

"I'm not," Kyle huffed—that coming from a kid whose parents were the biggest drug dealers south of Merrick Road. What did he know about morals? "But you make Coach out to be some kind of perv."

"It ain't perverse, man. People can't help who they fall in love with."

He couldn't refute that, given his own wayward heart. "You've been listening to too many love songs."

"Yeah, probably." Micah bobbed, walking off.

Returning to the classroom, Kyle approached Myles' desk. "What's going on with Leila, is she okay?"

"Leila will be fine."

"What happened?"

"I'm sorry, Kyle, I can't discuss that with you. Please take your seat."

"What do you mean?"

"Kyle—" He gave him a warning glare. "Take your seat, please."

Kyle obeyed, but he couldn't quit thinking about Leila and what Micah had said. Was it true in his own case, that people can't help whom they fall in love with? Was he even capable of true love, or was the intensity of his feelings for either Maryanne or Leila simply a matter of horniness? How would he even know when or if it was true love? All he did know was that he needed to see Leila. He spent the remainder of class weighing out the risk of going up to her apartment. Sure, Maryanne might find out, but he didn't care. Besides, he shouldn't have had to hear about all that from Micah. Maryanne should have told him.

KYLE ARRIVED AT LEILA'S APARTMENT DURING HIS lunch hour. She answered her door, cradling her arm in a sling and smiled.

"Leila, what happened to you?"

He stepped in as she opened her door wide. "I'm sure you must have heard."

"I've heard all kinds of things. Are you alright?"

"Yeah. Just a little shoulder thing."

"What happened?"

"Miss Weiss got a little carried away during the self-defense demonstration. I guess I got a little carried away too."

"Is it true that Miss Weiss accused Coach of—you know, messing around with you?"

Leila's face reddened and she turned away. "Is that what everyone's saying?"

"Pretty much."

She returned to his gaze. "It's not true."

"I know that."

"Then that's all I care about."

"Jeez, Leila. What are they going to do about it?"

"I don't know. There's some sort of hearing tonight. Mr. Myles is taking me, but I think maybe you're not supposed to know about it."

"You know I can keep your secrets." Kyle looked at her tenderly. "I am really sorry about the way I've been treating you. I'm such a jerk."

"Yeah, you kind of are." She grinned. "So, after this secret rendezvous, are you going to ignore me again?"

He shook his head. "No. Things are kind of fizzling between me and Maryanne, anyway …."

"Which has nothing to do with me, right?"

"I can't say it has nothing to do with you, but even though I know you and Coach aren't, you know, I can't compete with him. Besides that, I'm an unstable, horny teenage guy who's thinking about all the hot chicks I'm going to meet when I'm away at college next year."

"You're such a pig."

"Yeah. I am."

She touched his shirt. "I'm really glad you came."

"Do you think you'll be at school tomorrow? 'Cause I could come pick you up, you know, since your car is still at school and everything."

"Thanks, but I can get it tonight. My shifting arm still works—I'll drive myself tomorrow."

"Okay." Stepping closer, he stroked her tousled hair away from her face and gently kissed her forehead.

A THROBBING PAIN AND A WHISTLING TEAKETTLE roused Leila as she shifted on her sofa. The painkillers she had taken after Kyle left had worn off. She braced herself to rise, startling at the sound of three taps. Mr. Myles waited on the other side of her door.

She stood. "C'mon in—it's open."

He stepped inside. "How's the shoulder?"

"Hurts—time for another pill." She started for the kitchen.

"Sit," he said, now at the range, removing the kettle. "If you can stand the pain, it's best you don't get yourself doped up before the hearing."

She stretched her back. "Nice tie, by the way. What time's the hearing?"

"Six—it's four now."

"Ugh—"

"Think you can hang on?"

"I'm not a sissy."

"No. You're not." He chuckled for the first time since the theater and loosened his tie. "Tea?"

"Sure."

As he retrieved mugs from the cabinet, she scooted to the corner of the sofa. "So, I guess everyone at school is talking."

"Does that bother you?" Teabags dropped into cups.

"Not particularly. I was only concerned about what Kyle thought."

"He's a decent young man." He poured water.

"You'd liked to have seen the two of us together, wouldn't you?"

"What I think is not relevant."

"I want to know what you think."

He gave her his usual perusal. "Since you asked … I think given everything you are juggling, a romantic involvement with anyone right now would needlessly complicate your life."

"You don't think I'm mature enough to handle a romantic relationship?"

"Maturity has nothing to do with it." He carried their cups on saucers. "It's about emotional vulnerability."

"Well, you don't have to worry about me and Kyle."

"I was under the impression that Kyle is not the one you want."

"He's not." She sighed. "It would just be nice to feel cared about." She looked up into his face as he handed her a cup. The kindness in his eyes made her words ring hollow.

"You can fill that need without the complications of a romantic relationship." He sat, wedged into the opposite corner and sipped.

"You make love sound pretty awful."

"Awful? Sometimes. Complicated? Always."

"Isn't it ever wonderful?"

He peered over the brim of his cup the way he did with his *Rolling Stone*. "Sometimes."

She wanted to ask about his personal experience, but didn't dare—and he didn't give her a chance.

He sighed. "There are a few things I want to go over with you beforehand."

"Okay." She sat erect.

"When they talk to you, it's very important that you be honest and straightforward. Since you haven't been given an opportunity to collaborate with Coach Brigham, they will be looking for continuity in your testimony. Unless they press you on it, do not mention the nude photography. In fact, mention as little about the photography as possible. Don't lie, but do not offer information unless they ask for it. Do you understand?"

She nodded.

He continued, "Although the board will be concerned about your welfare, when it comes right down to it, their weightiest concern is whether or not you'll sue the district. Since Millville school board had an officious bent, and given they are aware you are without a guardian, they may likely feel freer to push issues that are not germane to the immediate case. Although your unsupervised status should not even come up, it may. If you get a bad gut feeling, you may respectfully decline answering those questions. If they persist, I will back you up."

Leila nodded gratefully. "Will I see him there?"

"Coach Brigham? Probably not."

CHAPTER 23

LEILA SAT WITH MYLES IN THE SMALL WAITING ROOM. It looked like one of the doctor's offices she had been to with her father—a residential house remodeled to accommodate office space—with an 'examination' room down the hall. A clock on the wall buzzed as its minute hand completed seven slow cycles. Leila cradled her arm in the sling and winced.

Myles stroked her back. "I'm sorry it hurts, but it's good for them to see a little pain in your face."

"It's okay. I'm okay."

A man stepped into the hall. "We're ready for you."

Leila took a deep breath, and Myles rose with her, his guiding hand at her back.

The man held the door open. Three gentlemen and a lady sat along the length of a large conference table, across from a single chair in which they asked Leila to sit. She glanced back at Myles as he took the seat behind her, near the door.

"Thank you for meeting with us this evening. I'm Superintendent Fitzgerald." He then introduced each member of the panel, including the attorney for the school district. "And, how are you doing tonight, Leila?"

She rubbed her sling. "I've been better."

"Of course." He glanced at her for only a second. "First, we would like to offer our sympathies regarding your father's passing."

"Thank you." Leila did not take her eyes off them. She studied each face, just as they were studying her. They didn't smile, but they didn't frown, either. She thought it odd that no one had acknowledged Mr. Myles.

Fitzgerald read from his notes for a moment. "We understand you're quite an athlete."

"No sir. I'm not."

He glanced again at his notes and back at her. "We were told that you are a runner."

"Yes, sir. I run."

"And you have plans to try out for track this year, don't you?"

"Yes, sir."

Fitzgerald pinched a smile and nodded.

"Well, let's get down to business." He again referred to his notes. "We'd like to start by having you explain what happened in your gym class yesterday."

Leila ran through the sequence of events, leading up to the moment that Miss Weiss accused Coach Brigham. In response to Leila's answers, each board member scribbled notes. Without pause, the chairman continued, "And would you please tell us about any previous interactions you may have had with Miss Weiss."

"Outside of usual gym-class stuff, we really haven't had any." She paused. "Though there was once at the beginning of the school year when she spoke to me about trying out for track."

"Would you tell us about that?"

"I was speaking to Coach Brigham in his office and she came in. She was curious if I would be trying out for track. That's all."

"And you had no interest in trying out for the track team at that time. Is that correct?"

"That's correct."

"Did she express any hostility toward you?"

"No."

"Did she ever indicate that she did not like you?"

"For the most part she ignored me. I don't know what that indicated."

The Chairman nodded and flipped over the top page of his notes. Referring to them, he began again. "We'd like to ask you about your relationship with Coach Brigham." Now he paused, looking at Leila. "How would you describe it?"

"As friendly."

"Please tell us about the first time you met him."

Leila recounted in superficial detail what she had told Mr. Myles about her flat at the beach.

"Aside from what you have already mentioned," Fitzgerald said, "has Coach Brigham ever been alone with you outside of the school setting?"

"Yes."

"Please tell us about that."

"He gave me a ride home just before Thanksgiving. He dropped me off, that's all."

"Were you alone at any other time?"

"I went to his house uninvited one Sunday afternoon."

"This was shortly after Coach Brigham tried to persuade you to try out for the track team—is that correct?"

"Yes." It had become obvious that they were informed, at the very least, that she had been there.

"Please continue."

"I was lonely. I asked if I could see his photography because I'm interested in art. He agreed. I saw his work, and then I left."

"How long were you there?"

"I don't know, a couple hours maybe."

"Did you agree to try out for the track team as a result of that visit?"

"Yes."

"Would you explain that?"

"It's kind of complicated."

"Miss Sanders—Leila—no one is enjoying this. Please just explain the situation."

Leila sighed. "Ms. Thorpe told me I didn't have to attend

gym class for the rest of the semester if I showed her how fast I could run. We traded. So, Coach Brigham thought I might be willing to bargain when it came to running track in the spring. The only thing I wanted was to see his photography. We traded. That's all."

"Did any of his photographs include sexual content?"

"No."

"There were no nudes?"

"There were, but they were not sexual—certainly no more so than Michelangelo's *David*."

The Chairman frowned. "Miss Sanders, we are not here to debate what constitutes art versus pornography." He referred back to the papers in front of him and jotted more notes. "Miss Sanders—Leila—I need to ask you some questions that may be a little uncomfortable."

She knew what would follow. The questions were almost word for word what Mr. Myles had asked the night before. She answered unflinchingly as each board member noted her replies. Exhaling, Chairman Fitzgerald flipped the top page of his notes, signaling the end of that series of questions.

"Please tell us about the last time you spoke privately with Coach Brigham."

"I was parked in front of his house and he came out. He told me that I needed to stop wishing for a relationship with him, because it was never going to happen. He said I needed to have a boyfriend my own age, and that I needed to go home and get on with my life—which is what I did."

"And, just for the record, Miss Sanders, when exactly did he become aware that you live on your own?"

She squinted at each one. "On the day that I saw his photography."

"And how long have you been on your own?"

Her eyes dropped and rebounded. "I'm not comfortable talking about that."

"Well, Miss Sanders," he folded his arms and cocked his head. "You are a minor and the state has an interest—"

Myles cut him off, "Chairman, Miss Sander's living

arrangements are not relevant to this hearing."

Fitzgerald finally acknowledged him. "Mr. Myles, as you well know, we are at liberty to determine what is relevant to this hearing."

"Yes, sir, and Miss Sanders is at liberty to have an attorney present during any questioning. She will, of course, need several days in order to retain legal counsel, at which time you may resume your questioning."

Fitzgerald gripped the folder in front of him. "And, Mr. Myles, what exactly is the nature of your relationship with Miss Sanders?"

"I would be very happy to disclose that in the presence of my attorney, at which time, if necessary, we can also address the issue of Miss Sander's injuries and what punitive damages might be pursued."

The attorney cleared his throat.

Fitzgerald lips puckered, his brows furrowing into a deep V. "We have no further questions at this time. You are both dismissed."

Myles followed Leila through the doorway and they walked silently down the hall and out the way they came in.

"Did I do okay?" Leila asked when they stepped into the cold night air.

Crows feet sprouted from the corners of Myles' eyes as he smiled and took her right elbow, steadying her as they walked the sanded, icy sidewalk. "I could not have put better words in your mouth."

He opened the passenger door and assisted her into the seat.

As soon as he climbed in, she asked, "Will Ian be in big trouble? Did I say too much?"

"You were honest. And Coach Brigham is a grown man. He is accountable for his own actions. What happens to him is not your concern."

She pouted. "It is of concern to me. I care about him … a lot."

"Caring for someone does not mean we can always shield

them from consequences, especially if he brings something upon himself."

"You don't like him."

"What I think of him has nothing to do with anything."

"It means something to me."

"And that's why I'll refrain from sharing my opinion of him." He pulled at his tie, loosening the knot.

She growled under her breath. "You are so annoying sometimes."

"Yes. I know." He started the engine but left it in park.

Leila sighed. "So, what happens to me now?"

"Well, don't be surprised if in a day or two a state social worker visits you. Just in case, I suggest you fill your refrigerator and cupboard with food. Can you do that?"

"Yes. What then?"

"Under the circumstances, there is a chance that your case may come before a judge. Which means there's a possibility that there may be a hearing."

"Will you go with me?"

"Of course." Myles hesitated and then looked at her. "Actually, there is something I would like to talk to you about."

"What is it?"

Now, he stared straight ahead. "I've made an appointment with my attorney."

"But I don't want to sue the school. It's pointless to drag this whole thing out."

"The attorney isn't for pressing charges against the school."

Now her shoulder ached worse. "Then why do I need an attorney?"

His hands slid down the steering wheel and up again. As he inhaled deeply, his thumb tapped an even rhythm. "The attorney—the attorney is not for you." He let go of the breath he had been holding. "It's for me."

"Why do *you* need a lawyer?" Her heart jumped into high gear. "You don't really think they're going to accuse you of a wrong relationship with me, do you?"

"No, Leila. The lawyer is not for that." He looked at her,

his thumb now tapping sporadically. "If it's agreeable to you …" he sucked in a short breath, as if winded, "I would like to be assigned as your guardian."

She heard the words, but it took a second to realize what he had just proposed. In the next moment, her chest clamped down on her heart. Tears filled her eyes. "You … you *want* me?"

He handed her his handkerchief before a tear dropped from her chin. "What I want is for you to be safe and cared for." Now, his breath evened out. "However, this is more about what *you* want. I can provide some measure of security for you. The question is, would you be willing to have *me* as your legal guardian?"

Leila couldn't speak. She could only wipe her cheeks.

"Leila, this cannot be some emotional decision. You need to give it serious consideration. What I would like to do is petition the court to grant you the right to live independently, with the stipulation that I be materially responsible for you and indirectly involved with your supervision until you graduate." He let her think on that for a second and then continued. "I would like you to come with me to speak with my attorney tomorrow, and we could discuss the details."

"I don't know what to say."

"I don't want you to say anything right now. Sleep on it and we'll talk tomorrow."

⟋ CLARENCE MYLES SAT ACROSS FROM HIS LAWYER, Ruben Feinberg. The husky man's leather chair creaked as he pushed a folder across his desk toward Myles. His lawyer had had a few days to draw up the paperwork, which had also given him plenty of time to speculate—Myles knew Ruben well enough to read the scrutiny behind his deep-set eyes.

"This is the rough draft, as per our telephone discussion." Feinberg turned his skewed brow to Leila. She squirmed in her seat. Myles held the opened file so Leila could read along. She rubbed her knees.

"Miss Sanders, please note that although Mr. Myles

wishes to acquire a limited guardianship over you, he is petitioning for full guardianship. The reason being, in case the judge feels you need full supervision, he may assign it to Mr. Myles rather than place you in foster care. Mr. Myles' willingness to assume financial responsibility for you may be a compelling reason for assigning him guardianship. However, you should know that his unmarried status is a strong strike against him."

Leila glanced at Myles, then at the paperwork, and back to the lawyer, her expression blank.

He continued, "Of course, you may independently submit a counter-petition for full emancipation. However, I could not represent you, due to the conflict of interests. Nonetheless, provision has been made in Mr. Myles' petition to have the judge grant an emancipated status, or some variation thereof, at the judge's discretion. Therefore, that base has essentially been covered for you. Any questions so far?"

"Who will represent me?"

"You will be appointed a guardian *ad litem*. Often a social worker, someone who represents your best interests as they see them."

"Oh."

"You should also note that Mr. Myles has a total of six stipulations to be met by you, should he be awarded guardianship. These are not strictly enforceable by the court. However, if proven in violation of them, you would essentially give Mr. Myles grounds for terminating the arrangement. Please note that they are as follows: You must not smoke tobacco. You must not consume alcoholic beverages. You must not use illicit drugs. You must remain sexually inactive. You must maintain a B average in all academic subjects, and finally, you must graduate from high school with a fully accredited diploma."

Leila's palm slid down her thigh. She took a deep breath. "I guess I'm not the only one who likes to control everything."

Myles caught Feinberg wrestling a smirk as Leila's eyes dropped back to her lap. Myles didn't expect she would care for his stipulations, but he had hoped for a more transparent reaction.

"Well?" Myles asked.

"I guess I can live with those."

"Of course, no decision need be made today," Myles said. "This meeting is just for drawing up preliminary paperwork."

Ruben Feinberg pushed his chair back and reclined, his gaze alternating between the two. Myles had sat across from his desk too many times in Philadelphia, negotiating and renegotiating his separation, custody, divorce, and then post-divorce issues. When Feinberg had moved to Long Island, it was he that referred Myles to a job opening in the Millville school district. Desperate for a change, Myles followed through. He trusted Ruben Feinberg as a lawyer and a friend.

Feinberg picked up where he left off, "Mr. Myles does not need your consent to follow through on this action. Nevertheless, it is his desire that you consent. Without that, the petition will be dropped. If you consent, I will petition the court for an expedited hearing. Given there is no one contesting, and it would more or less be a matter of filing paperwork, the expedition will likely be granted. If you decide sooner as opposed to later, it may preempt over-involvement of Child Protective Services, which is not necessarily a bad thing, although they will no doubt go ahead and assign a guardian *ad litem*."

Leila took a deep breath. "Let's just do it."

Feinberg leaned forward in his chair. "Young lady, do you understand how serious a matter this is?" He narrowed his bushy brows until they joined. "You will essentially be entering a contract with Clarence Myles, one that should not be entered lightly. I'm assuming that you understand how obnoxious Clarence can be, and how miserable he could make your life. At least for the next five months. These prohibitions he's stipulating may significantly cramp your style."

"I know he can be—obnoxious. And actually, his stipulations won't cramp my style as much as you might think. Besides, the alternatives could be worse."

He paused for effect, the way Myles often did. "Are you certain this is what you want?"

"Yes. This is what I want, if Mr. Myles still wants it."

Myles nodded, repressing a smile.

"I'll draw up the final papers and you can stop by tomorrow and sign them."

Myles rose and extended his hand. "Do it."

🐟 LEILA TRIED TO REMEMBER IF THERE WAS EVER A time when she felt as if someone had her best interest at heart, above their own. Even in all her father's trying to protect her, she sensed some ulterior instability, some outworking of his own helplessness and inability to control his moods.

"You need help!" she had overheard Joe arguing with her dad yet again. "You're not right in your head. You're making our lives hell."

"You're one to talk! You're no better than her mother!"

"Yeah, well, if you weren't so screwed up, she wouldn't have needed to get high, and neither would I!"

Most days, Leila would have taken 'high' Joe over depressed and erratic Daddy. She was accustomed to high. Not until she was older did she realize that high meant drug abuse, and she found the band members amusing until she realized it also made them sick. As far as she knew, Joe was only a light user for years, or maybe she just hadn't recognized his low-keyed, mellow ways as stoned.

Leila had only ever heard bits and pieces before Joe or her dad would say *keep it down or you'll wake her*, but she had overheard enough of their arguments to make the connection between 'stoned' and 'leaving'—and her mother. Within a month of their last quarrel, Joe had indeed packed up and left. Not that he hadn't done so a dozen times before, but he had always come back, although she never understood why—after all, her own mother had never come back. *It's 'cause I miss you, Baby,* he would say. Didn't her mother miss her? But finally, even that wasn't enough for Joe. He boarded a plane and flew so far away that she didn't know if he would ever come home. They all left. Her mother, Joe, and her father.

Now, Clarence Myles wanted her. He wanted to protect her. She had only known him for a few months, but he felt more permanent than anything or anyone she had ever known. Perhaps he simply liked control, but he had at least asked her permission. She sensed his desire to protect sprung from respect, not from his own insecurity or need to control her—at least she was willing to gamble on that. Besides, it would only be for a few short months. Just the thought of being under his guardian hand, safe and warm, made her hope for it.

CHAPTER 24

W HEN LEILA ENTERED HOMEROOM THE NEXT morning, Myles acknowledged her with a raised brow and grinned behind his magazine, visible only to Leila.

Taking her seat, stifling her own grin, she scanned the classroom. Staring eyes darted away—all except Kyle's. He smiled and leaned forward. "How's the arm?"

"Hurts."

With that, the perky office messenger entered the room. She handed Mr. Myles a folded paper and then exited.

Adjusting his readers, Myles perused the note. He rose from his desk and handed it to Leila. She read silently: *Please send Leila Sanders to the Principal's office.* It could mean only one thing. He signaled that she should go immediately. As she left the room, she was surprised to find Kyle behind her.

"Myles told me to follow you. Where are we going?" he asked.

"To the office."

"Yikes."

When they entered, Principal Boyd's secretary instructed her and Kyle to have a seat. Muffled voices traveled through Boyd's closed office door.

"Do you want me to go in with you?" he whispered, rubbing his neck.

"No, this is my thing."

The door opened. Ian Brigham walked through. He flinched at the sight of Leila.

Principal Boyd said, "Miss Sanders ... here already?"

Leila stood as Ian, pale and distraught, walked past without so much as a glance. Like a boulder plummeting through watery depths, Leila floundered in his wake. As he exited, her heart plunged with his, whirling downward. As though gasping for air, she sucked in shame and humiliation.

"... Miss Sanders," Boyd repeated, "would you please come in."

He held the door and shot a look at Kyle. "Is there something I can do for you, Mr. Schultz?"

"No. I'm with Leila."

"There's no need for you to wait. Please return to your class," he said and shut the door behind them.

With his pasted-on smile, Superintendent Fitzgerald stood to the side of Boyd's desk. He glanced at her sling. "How are you this morning, Leila?"

Her jaw tensed. "How do you think I am?"

"Please, sit down."

"I'd rather stand."

"Very well. We wanted to let you know the outcome of Wednesday night's hearing."

She braced herself.

He continued, "I won't bore you with the legalities. However you should know that Miss Weiss' position at this high school has been terminated."

"And Coach Brigham?"

"The extent of any repercussions affecting him is mostly contingent on you. As you know, we are obligated to provide you with the opportunity to run on the track team this season. However, if you choose to do so, Coach Brigham will be required to resign as track coach, although he will maintain all other duties and positions that he currently fills."

"I don't understand."

"Coach Brigham is to have no contact with you whatsoever.

Therefore it will be quite impossible for him to coach you."

"What do you mean *no contact*?"

"He may at no time approach you or speak to you or be alone with you. He may not contact you over the telephone or through writing, nor by any other means."

"Coach Brigham is no threat to me!"

"We feel it is in your best interest—"

"My best interest?" She squinted contempt. "You haven't the first notion of what is in my best interest!"

"Miss Sanders, please lower your voice." Fitzgerald scowled. "What you fail to appreciate is that we have more to consider than just your feelings. How do you suppose the parents of our female students feel, knowing there have been accusations against one of our male teachers?"

"*Unfounded* accusations."

"They are out there nonetheless and not without substance. What you fail to understand is the leniency with which we have dealt with Coach Brigham. Exposing a student to indecent photographs is a grave offense. In spite of what you may believe, or what Mr. Myles may have convinced you of, we have tried to take all things into consideration, including any mitigating factors that might spare Coach Brigham. We suggest you be grateful that we did not terminate his employment also."

"Well, you don't need to make him resign as the track coach. I have no intention of running on the team." She glared at one and then the other. "May I go now?"

"In a moment." Fitzgerald now addressed her firmly. "You need to realize that if you cause Coach Brigham to violate the sanctions placed upon him, by imposing yourself on him, you jeopardize his position at this high school or any other. Do you understand that?"

"Yes," she seethed.

"You may go now," Fitzgerald said, as Boyd opened the door and closed it behind her.

Leila stormed through the office and slammed the outer door, barely noticing Kyle's absence from his chair or him standing in the hallway as she rushed past.

"Leila, hold up!" Kyle said.

She kept moving down the hall and burst through the front entrance. She wanted to run and run hard, but once the bitter cold stung her face, she stopped at the bottom step. Frost shot from her nostrils as she paced.

Kyle stood beside her. "You're not going to take off again, are you?"

She panted, inspecting the gray, billowy clouds overhead.

"No. I want to. But I'm not." She continued to pace. "I just need a minute to cool down."

Kyle stepped in front of her as the sky released snowflakes that settled upon her arm. He grabbed her and pulled her close. If only she could disappear into the fold of his arms and disperse like his breath in her ear.

❦ LEILA WOULDN'T TELL KYLE WHAT WENT ON IN Boyd's office, but it didn't take too much imagination to figure it out. What he did know was that Coach Brigham was innocent even if he did have feelings for Leila; Kyle knew his coach well enough to realize he would never follow through on them.

Before heading home for the long Martin Luther King holiday weekend, Kyle came upon Brigham in the parking lot. He blew warmth into his cupped hands. "Hey, Coach."

"How you doin', Kyle?"

"I'm okay." He shivered. "I'm really sorry about all the crap that's been going down. It's wrong, Coach—"

"Kyle, don't worry about it. "

"Yeah, but it's so unfair."

"Life is full of unfair, man. Just gotta learn to roll with it."

Kyle shook his head. "That's bull—"

"No," he cut him off, "It's life."

Kyle let out an exasperated breath that crystallized as his gaze moved from Brigham's face to the back seat of his Saab, packed to the ceiling. "Looks as if you're taking off for the weekend."

"Yeah. Seems like a good weekend for some hiking."

"Really? Where you headed?"

"New Hampshire. Presidential Range."

Kyle chuckled. "You're nuts, man."

Brigham nodded. "Yeah. I kind of am."

"Well, stay warm," Kyle said, just about to walk off. "Oh, and I just want you to know that Leila and I are still going to run together just as soon as her arm's better."

"Good." His eyes dropped and then came back to Kyle. "How is she?"

Kyle shrugged. "It's sort of hard to tell with her. You know how she is, all private and everything."

"Yeah," Brigham said under his breath.

LEILA'S ASSIGNED SOCIAL WORKER SHOWED UP unexpectedly that afternoon—in fact, as Leila pulled into her driveway, a trim, dark-complexioned woman with close-cropped hair stood on Artie's doorstep, chatting.

"Leila, I'm Mrs. Greene," she said, offering her hand.

Leila invited the woman up to her apartment. Her warm and spontaneous smile put Leila at ease as they talked for about an hour, covering familiar ground. The only new questions were regarding her mother.

"When's the last time you heard from your mother?" Greene asked.

"I've never heard from her." In fact, Leila didn't have the faintest recollection of her mother. Only a small creased and faded photo, insufficient to sow even an imaginary memory.

"No Birthday cards or letters?"

"No." Leila shrugged, expecting gushing sympathies. Instead, Mrs. Greene simply nodded.

"Do you have any idea of where she resides?"

Check the vicinity of every rehab center in your databanks and you'd come up with a better clue than I've got. "No."

"Do you know of anyone who might know?"

The sad truth struck Leila at the worst times, splitting wide open the hole she refused to acknowledge—that void where at least a trace of a mother's scent should linger. Her breath caught in that vacuum as the word "Nope" slipped out.

🐛THE CAPRICIOUS WEATHER ON THE PRESIDENTIAL Range was at best challenging and at worst, deadly. Ian's agitation begged piercing, subzero temperatures. There was nothing like the burn and strain of slogging through knee-deep snow. During weekends, especially holiday weekends, one never had the trails to himself, and so Ian felt comfortable hiking solo. In fact, he preferred it.

Fresh snow had fallen midweek, leaving a heavy blanket of glistening white under clear skies. Ian started off in snowshoes where the trail climbed slowly at first, through a tunnel of white. Foot traffic had not yet packed the snow, providing an even more pristine visage, though it added to the initial challenge. Before long, he had worked up a sweat and stripped to his short-sleeved thermal shirt. Over the next several hours, the ascent steepened and he switched from snowshoes to crampons. Each time Leila came to mind, he pushed harder, driving her out. High winds whistled in his ears, burning his cheeks as he approached the Spur.

Temperatures dropped drastically—nearly thirty degrees —in a matter of minutes. He hustled to pull his layers back over himself. By three o'clock, he stood on the bluff of Crag Camp, overlooking King Ravine. The sun behind him illuminated the snow-crested headwall of Durand Ridge across the ravine, casting Mossy Fall in the shadows. It was unspeakably beautiful. Now, he no longer resisted the thought of Leila, a million miles away.

Standing at the crest, only inches from oblivion, he drew in a labored breath. One strong gust of wind and he would be over the edge. Alone on the mountain, a man could not help wondering—if his footing slipped and he slid away, who would miss him? If he found himself in a whiteout, unable to make it to shelter and fell asleep in the cold, who would mourn him? He hoped Leila might but doubted she would grieve for long. Given all the women he had been with, why was he without anyone to miss him? He stood in awestruck exhilaration, yet with whom could he share it, either in this moment or in the retelling of it?

Wind picked up with sudden fury. He had better save his soul-searching for the cabin if he planned to make it before dark. He repositioned his pack and headed toward Gray Knob.

Twenty degrees in the cabin felt like a heat wave. Several other hikers greeted him with perfunctory chatter that quickly dwindled; all shared one objective. Sleep. To lie in his bag after completely spending himself on the mountain was one of the best feelings. His body sang with exhaustion. In the intense darkness, with senses heightened, a mouse scampered up his sleeping bag and perched upon Ian's chest. Darkness sharpened his sight and he watched the mouse stare back until sleep overtook him.

Sometime during the night, he woke in discomfort. He would have to brave the elements and ease nature. A gust of wind caught his breath as he stepped outside; its constant howling whirled about him. The utter black of night dispersed under starlight. He moved to a clearing and relieved himself. The sliver of a crescent moon rested low on the western horizon and a slurry of stars smeared across the concave sphere above. His insignificance in this moment, in the vastness of unending time and space humbled him. For a suspended second, the wind died and absolute silence enveloped him but for the voice in his head, the question he had asked of Leila when they first met, and more poignantly, the question she offered in response—*Why does anyone move away from paradise?*

The reasons he was then unable to admit to himself now came with full admission. He was afraid of failure, of not being good enough, of his father's chastisement for chasing a silly dream. It was so cliché. Bad enough that he had abandoned his father's plan for him to be a doctor, but to foolishly forfeit a good job and solid strategy was unthinkable. According to his father's plan, dreams were inevitably sacrificed on the altar of real life, rendering the safety of a pre-plotted course to all who submit. Worse yet, Ian's immobilization and fear of disapproval from a man in the grave had deprived him of real purpose. What did his father, a drunk, know of living life to its fullest? Furthermore, not all dreams were foolish any more than all women were self-serving. In fact, none of the woes or injustices of his lot in Millville were of any lasting consequence. Ian had never been struck with such clarity in any moment—clarity of mind and purpose. With his eyes to the stars, he drank in all his senses could bear until the cold and elation nearly overtook him.

Back in the cabin, as Ian lay alone, he no longer pushed away the idea of Leila. Resisting the possibility of her was pointless. He closed his eyes and freely envisioned her face. He had never known a woman experienced in so many ways yet still innocent. He had to wonder if part of the draw was the virgin he imagined she was—pristine as an unconquered mountain—encompassing the innocence he had experienced for only a few pre-pubescent years. What would it be like, to be free of his past, to make love for the first time and to make it with someone he truly loved? Then to share it with her and her alone for the rest of their lives.

Only time kept he and Leila apart, and if he allowed, his own stubbornness and fear of moving forward with his life. The months ahead of him dwindled in view of the long term.

CHAPTER 25

A S MR. MYLES ASSISTED LEILA FROM HIS CAR AND up the front steps of the courthouse, the firmness of his arm at her back quelled her nerves, but only until he pushed open the doors. Feinberg and Leila's social worker, Mrs. Greene, stood in the lobby below the large clock. Eight-thirty. They shuffled through folders of paper.

"I don't feel so good," Leila said.

Myles patted her back. "You're fine."

"Are you sure I look okay?" She smoothed her new denim skirt.

"You're perfect," he said as they approached their counsel.

Echoing footsteps and slamming doors punctuated the atmosphere, heavy with hushed drama as several other groups huddled in corners. Myles directed her to a long bench under archival photographs of judges. Feinberg and Greene conferred off to the side. Leila sat, scrutinizing each cluster of litigants and tried not to obsess. She fidgeted with the stitched edge of the sling still strapped to her shoulder. Her worst-case scenario was, in reality, only a huge inconvenience for her, and temporary. Not so, she sensed, for all the other plaintiffs, petitioners, and defendants. Put in perspective, and compared to the school-board hearing where Ian's future had also been in the balance, this was of greater material consequence to Clarence Myles than to Leila.

She studied his face and the flexing tendons of his neck.

He met her stare. Neither spoke reassurances, yet an awkward and tender version of a smile passed between them. They each wanted this. They wanted—somehow needed—a judge to validate it, to tell them it was alright to want a father—to want a daughter.

Greene approached and sat beside Leila. "Judge Moore will be hearing your case this morning. I've dealt with him before. A reasonable man. He's not so much a stickler for rules as he is at getting to the root of a matter. He's fair and very thorough."

Thorough. Leila braced herself for more embarrassing questions. "How long before it's our turn?"

"It's hard to say. The docket almost always runs behind." In fact, two hours late, the bailiff called them in.

Myles claimed a seat beside Leila at a large conference table. Each counsel sat beside their client or charge. When Judge Moore stepped into the room, they rose with the bailiff's call. The judge made immediate eye contact with Leila.

"Good morning," he said, glancing at all present. Even while she stood, Leila had to look up at him. His dark, deep-set eyes peered through heavy eyelids. Creases engraved his forehead. He gestured toward the seat in front of him.

"Please sit, Miss Sanders." His voice resonated with mellowness. "May I call you Leila?"

"Yes, Your Honor."

He leaned forward, casually crossing his arms over the paperwork in front of him. "How are you today?"

"Fine, thank you."

"I'm terribly sorry about your father's death." He shook his head. "That's very sad."

"Yes, sir."

Without referencing the notes, he began. "I understand you've been living independently for over a year now, and you moved from New Hampshire about six months ago?"

"Yes."

"How has that been going for you?"

Leila thought before answering. "It's been challenging, but I feel like I've been successful."

Leaning back in his chair, he cocked his head. "Tell me about the ways in which you feel you have succeeded."

Moore drew out his words, not in an unnatural way, not the way Myles did for effect. Nonetheless, his question spurred apprehension.

"It's not a trick question," he said with a kind smile. "I'm simply curious about your successes."

Leila inhaled. "Well, I moved to my own apartment just after my father died. Then I moved down here on my own. I've had a steady job ever since. I worked full-time all last summer and saved a little money. I work after school everyday, but I have weekends off. I earn a little for looking in on an elderly man who lives downstairs from me. I meet all my expenses. I maintain my own car. I'm passing all my classes and I've made a few friends."

Moore nodded. "You certainly have a full plate."

She shrugged. "I suppose."

He smiled again. "How much sleep do you get?"

Embellishing the hours from eleven to six, she said, "Seven or eight hours. More on the weekend."

He nodded slowly without taking his eyes off her. "And Clarence Myles is your math teacher?"

"I had him for trigonometry last semester. Now I only have him for homeroom."

Moore nodded, pushing back into his seat. "How did you do in his class?"

"I was failing, but he assigned me a tutor and brought my grade up to a B."

"How would you describe him as a teacher?"

"He's not popular. He's very strict and gives a lot of homework. He makes everyone work for their grade, even if math is easy for them. I've had a lot of teachers in all the schools I've been to. He's the best one I've ever had."

"How so?"

"He doesn't care if he's unpopular. He seems to know

what's in a student's best interest, and if he can do something about it, he does."

"Could you give me an example, aside from the tutoring?"

Leila did not have to think long. "He knew the one-year anniversary of my dad's death was coming up. Since he sees me practically every day, he could tell I was having a bad time. Well, he knew that I was just going to sit at the movie theater all day, so he showed up with popcorn and drinks and sat with me."

His eyes narrowed.

A pang of protectiveness rose in her chest. "I know that sounds kind of weird—that is, I know teachers don't usually get involved with their student's after-school lives, but you have no idea how that helped me. I don't know how I would have got through all of that if he hadn't been there."

As Leila spoke, Moore glanced at Myles. Again, Moore nodded. "Do you have a boyfriend?"

"No."

"You mentioned you have friends. None of them knew you were going through a difficult time?"

"Well, Artie who lives below me—he's pretty old and we mostly just play music together. And Kyle, well he was going through his own thing with his girlfriend."

"No girls you consider friends?"

"Well, there's Maryanne, Kyle's girlfriend, but like I said they were going through some stuff and weren't really available."

"And how would you feel about having Mr. Myles as your guardian?"

"He already feels like my guardian. He's very protective of me, but I can tell he respects me as a person. He irritates me sometimes because he doesn't let me get away with being stupid. When he thinks I'm off base, he calls me on it. To tell you the truth, Your Honor, I've learned how to sidestep or evade people when I need to, just for my own privacy and protection. But I've never been able to pull anything over on him. In some weird way he makes me feel accountable."

"Accountable to him?"

Leila shook her head. "Just accountable in general."

"And what do you think of the stipulations he's proposed?"

"I think they're fair. Besides, I've never really been in a hurry to violate any of them anyway."

Moore continued nodding as he paused and studied his notes. He then addressed his entire audience.

"I'd like a few minutes alone with Leila." He then singled her out. "Would you be comfortable with that? You may have Mrs. Greene stay if you'd like."

"Just you and me is fine."

The room cleared of all but the bailiff who faded into the background. Moore pushed back in his chair, removing his glasses and smiled. The pounding in Leila's chest slowed.

He exhaled. "I guess you've had a lot of embarrassing questions asked of you lately, huh?"

"Yes."

"I guess you also know I would be remiss in my duties as a judge if I did not also ask some of those questions."

"I understand, sir."

"The track coach, Ian Brigham—would I be accurate in saying that you feel attracted to him as a man, in a romantic kind of way?"

Her eyes widened. Although her cheeks warmed, she did not look away when she replied, "Yes."

"Probably you've had crushes on other teachers before?"

Was he leading her, trying to establish some pattern? "Not since ninth grade."

"Have you ever had even remotely similar feelings for Mr. Myles?"

She shook her head adamantly, looking him straight in the eyes. "No, sir."

"Have you ever had even just some funny little feeling that Mr. Myles might have those kinds of feelings for you?"

"Absolutely not, sir."

Moore stared her in the eyes for several long, probing

seconds before continuing. "You must miss your father very much."

"Yes."

"What do you miss most about him?"

"His music. He played the piano and sang—I miss that."

He squinted. "You must miss the security of having him around—having someone to take care of you?"

"Sir, I mostly took care of him. And I feel as secure now as I've ever felt." Leila sat through another long stare.

"Do you want me to assign Clarence Myles as your guardian?"

"I'd rather you emancipate me. But if you have to assign me a guardian, he's who I want—very much."

He replaced his readers and scribbled a few lines. "That's all the questions I have for you. Would you mind stepping into the hall?"

"Thank you, Your Honor."

The bailiff opened the door and she exited. The judge summoned Mr. Myles.

🡐 MYLES INHALED DEEPLY, BRACING HIMSELF AS HE entered the conference room.

Judge Moore stated, "You are, of course, welcome to have your counsel present."

"That won't be necessary."

"Please. Sit."

Myles took his place, sitting rigidly compared to the Judge's continued informality.

"You are fifty-two years old and employed by the Millville School District for eight years and have been teaching for almost thirty years. Correct?"

"Yes, sir."

Moore referred to his notes. "You've been married only once. Divorced for fifteen years, with a daughter resulting from that marriage." He looked up. "Correct?"

"Yes, sir."

"How many relationships with women would you say

you've had in the past fifteen years?"

"I've dated several. One was a serious relationship."

"How long ago was that?"

"About nine years ago."

"Are you involved in any relationships currently?"

"No."

Moore's brow rose. "When was the last time you dated anyone?"

"Several years."

Moore now squared his shoulders and looked directly into Myles eyes. "You appear healthy. Is there some reason why you do not date women?"

Myles restrained his hand from loosening his tie. He wished to challenge the relevancy of the judge's questions, however, he knew better. "I am a—that is, I have been told, that I'm not an easy person to be around. I have a tendency to push most women away."

"Is this characteristic of your relationships in general?" Moore pinched his chin.

"Yes."

"And yet you have not pushed Leila Sanders away. I have to wonder why that is. Furthermore, I cannot make a ruling without that bit of information. So let me come right out and ask, do you have romantic interest in Leila Sanders?"

Myles flatly stated, "No."

"Then, describe your relationship with her?"

"We have a respectful and trusting relationship."

"The Millville School Board seems to feel you are overly involved with Leila."

"Would the Millville School Board have preferred that Leila walk three miles home in the sleet and freezing rain in nothing but a T-shirt and shorts? Or perhaps they would have preferred that no one insist on taking her to the emergency room with a teacher-inflicted injury." Myles could not conceal his indignation. "I have no doubt that the school board would have preferred she attend their hearing all by herself."

As Moore again reclined, he studied Myles. "When did you become aware of her living situation?"

"The first week in October, as a result of her lack of representation at parent-teacher conferences."

"And yet you did not notify the appropriate agencies. Why is that?"

"I had the opportunity to observe her over quite a number of weeks, both in her work environment and at school—"

"And how did you come to observe her in her work environment?"

"I frequently shopped at Sam Goody's—I have an interest in music—sometime in July, Leila began working there."

"Did you socialize?"

"No. I'm afraid I was—that is, she might have considered me rude."

"Did you know she'd be attending Millville high school come September?"

"No."

"And again, when you became aware of her situation, why did you keep it to yourself?"

"As I mentioned, from observing what I knew of her, I was convinced she was capable of living independently. Looking back on it, I realize that due to my own personal and disappointing experiences with the family legal system, I was concerned that a judge might make some arbitrary ruling and put her in foster care. Nonetheless, my primary concern was that her life not be disrupted any further."

"And at that point, why did you not petition for guardianship?"

"Our relationship had not yet progressed to the point whereby I would have considered it."

Moore sighed as he stared off into mid-space. He then flashed a look at his notes. He leaned forward again. "Tell me about your daughter. Tell me about your relationship with her."

Myles shifted uneasily. "I don't have one. That is, I don't have a relationship with her."

"Well, when was the last time you spoke to her?"

"About nine years ago."

The creases in Moore's forehead arched and deepened. "Please elaborate."

There was no avoiding the issue. Myles reorganized his thoughts and began. "My daughter Bonnie was thirteen when her mother and I divorced. We had many post-divorce issues regarding custody. My ex-wife moved Bonnie to California when she was sixteen, where they became heavily involved in a loose lifestyle—alcohol and drug abuse. In '69, Bonnie hitchhiked cross-country with friends. Her mother and I have not seen or heard from her since."

Moore exhaled sharply, pushing back into his seat. "I'm so sorry. That must be very difficult."

Myles' old wounds split open, leaving him raw and parched. He pulled his handkerchief from his pocket and wiped his brow.

Moore jotted several notes before continuing, "What bearing do you feel this may have on your relationship with Leila?"

"If Your Honor wouldn't mind, may I have a glass of water?" He gestured toward the insulated pitcher and plastic cups at the end of the conference table.

"By all means, help yourself."

Myles poured a cup and sat again, this time meeting Moore's gaze. Sipping water did little to cool the furnace in his chest. "I see Leila as a vulnerable young woman. If I can prevent more harm in her life and allow her a situation whereby she can become firmly grounded, I wish to provide her with that, because I feel it is within my power to do so. For me to shirk this opportunity would be negligent on my part, not only as an adult and an educator but as a father."

"Do you view Leila as some sort of a surrogate daughter?"

"She could never replace my Bonnie. And I know that Leila is not looking to replace her father. But neither has she experienced the kind of protection and security that I believe I can provide—that I was unable to provide my own daughter." Myles choked, but remained stoic. "I will not deny that I have fatherly feelings for Leila."

The two broke eye contact as Judge Moore's pen tapped sporadically. Permitting Myles a moment to collect himself, Moore then signaled the bailiff to allow the others reentry.

Leila again sat beside Myles, but he did not look at her.

Moore spoke up. "Unless anyone has anything further they would like to add, I have Mrs. Greene's written recommendation and sufficient supplemental information on which to base my decision."

No one came forward.

"Good, then. I will hand down my ruling by the end of the day. You may check back with the clerk between four and five o'clock."

🐚 MYLES, LEILA, AND FEINBERG WENT FOR LUNCH A few buildings down from the courthouse. No one spoke about the hearing. No one speculated on the outcome. Myles observed Leila as she picked at her food. He found his own sandwich to his disliking but did not make an issue of it.

Feinberg wiped his mouth. "I can stick around if you'd like, but Clarence, you already know how to decipher all the legal gobbledygook."

"We'll manage." Myles smirked. "And make sure you turned off your time clock when we left the courthouse."

Feinberg ignored his cantankerousness, as usual. "We'll talk later."

Setting her fork aside, Leila slipped her hands beneath the table. She stared at Myles who stared back. With a raised brow, he invited her to divulge her thoughts.

She said, "I felt like it went pretty good on my end. How did it go with you?"

He glanced at his roast beef. "It's hard to say."

"Come on, what did he ask about? I mean aside from the usual uncomfortable questions."

"Actually, most all of the questions were uncomfortable."

"Did he ask why you don't have a girlfriend?"

Myles shot back, "Did he ask why you don't have a boyfriend?"

Leila smirked. "Your answer is in your evasion of the question."

"So it is."

"So, why don't you have a girlfriend?"

"My observably flawed personality should make that obvious. At any rate, that is not a subject open for discussion."

She frowned.

Wiping his hands with the napkin, he suggested, "There's a musical instrument store next door. Let's go kill some time."

AT NEAR FOUR O'CLOCK, THEY HEADED BACK TO the courthouse. Ten minutes later, they sat in Myles' Volvo with a large envelope. His heart beat faster than he expected, almost as fast as those other times—too many times—when he had received unfavorable rulings. He steadied his breathing.

"You open it," Leila said.

Lifting the flap, Myles pulled its contents. He read under his breath. "In the case of Leila Sanders ...," he mumbled through a string of legalese and finally looked at her, his suppressed smile curling the corners of his mouth. "Say hello to your legal guardian."

Leila's eyes filled with tears. "Please tell me I don't have to move in with you!"

"No. You do not. It's basically exactly what Mrs. Greene recommended, with my stipulations included." He now translated from the document, "... the state finds you competent and capable of dwelling independently. You and I must reside separately. I am awarded legal guardianship, including, but not limited to financial responsibility."

He continued reading in a monotone, "Said minor—you—must abide by the petitioner's stipulations cited herein. A representative of Child Protective Services will pay monthly visits to ensure compliance with all stipulations ... You must receive biweekly counseling sessions with a therapist assigned by the court—petitioner must accompany said minor ... every other session for family counseling—*What?*"

"Ha! You have to get therapy too!" Leila laughed. "Oh, this is so perfect."

He reread the last sentence and shook his head.

She continued laughing. "So does this mean I get to call you Clarence, now?"

"Absolutely not."

Her laugh turned to a frown.

He snorted. "Maybe after graduation."

The corners of her mouth inverted. "Thank you so much. I'm truly grateful."

"Don't get all emotional on me."

"I can't help it."

They sat quietly for a moment and he added, "I think it would be good if we kept our arrangement confidential."

"Okay. But I'm going to tell Kyle. He's trustworthy."

"That's fine." He looked at her and hesitated.

"What?"

"I've also been thinking—there's really no need for you to keep your job. I'd like to cover your expenses so that you can concentrate on school."

"No way!"

"If you want to keep your job, that's fine, as long as it doesn't interfere with your school work. Just the same, I'd like you to put the money in a savings account. There's no reason why you should have to feel pressured about money."

"Mr. Myles, I would feel really weird taking money from you. How about we leave things as they are, and if I run into any unusual expenses or I can't buy groceries, then the social worker can let you know." She smirked. "Or we could bring it up as an issue in family counseling."

"Don't be unreasonable, Leila."

She stared him down. "Don't step on me, Mr. Myles."

"Just how hard are you going to fight me on this?"

"All the way! You know as well as I do this arrangement is more formality than anything. I'm self-sufficient. Don't try to take that away from me."

"I don't want to take anything away from you, Leila. I want to add to what you have. Can't you see that?"

"You have already provided me with more than I could ever ask for—my independence. You are the first real man I have ever been able to count on. If I need you, I really feel like I could come to you with anything. But in reality, my needs are pretty few. Please don't tell me this is news to you."

"No. It's not."

She looked at him, her eyes glassy. "Clarence, you're the kindest man I know."

Her tenderness played at his own emotion—rather than give in to it, he stated, "I told you not to call me Clarence."

"I know."

Myles exhaled. "Let's get you home."

When he pulled up in front of her place, she asked, "So, what are we going to do to celebrate?"

"What—you want a party or something? I'm sure there would be lots of people who would love to attend that. Why don't we start by inviting the school board?"

"Very funny. No, I was thinking you could invite me over to your house for dinner."

As much as the notion appealed to him, he said, "Now *you're* being funny."

"I'm serious. We could invite Kyle, and I could fix the three of us dinner."

"While all that sounds very cozy, that's simply not a path we're going to head down."

"So, our new arrangement is pretty much all one-sided?"

He didn't care for the sound of one-sided, but he held his ground. "If you were hoping for more than that, you should have negotiated it into the contract."

"Am I ever going to get to know you, Clarence Myles?"

"If I allowed that, I would only be setting you up for disappointment. So let's just leave things as they are. Alright?"

"So, no celebration?"

"How about I give you fifty bucks, and you can take Kyle out to dinner."

Leila rolled her eyes. "I told you, I don't want your money."

"I know, I just thought that might be some sort of consolation prize."

"Yeah, well, it's not."

"You see? Already I'm disappointing you."

Leila sighed through a frown. "Okay. Well, I guess then I'll just see you on Monday morning as usual."

"That sounds about right."

"Okay then. Thanks for the lift." She opened the car door. As she pulled herself out, she offered a lame smile.

Myles reciprocated and watched her walk away. A perplexing sadness came over him. Leila turned before heading up the staircase. Her wistful smile as she waved tightened his throat. He had not known what to expect, but sadness was not what he had imagined. Driving away, exhausted and emotionally skinned, he wanted only to be at home.

CLARENCE MYLES DROVE THROUGH HIS SHADED neighborhood and pulled into the driveway of his Arts and Craft style bungalow. Stepping onto the veranda, he selected the house key from his ring. As he entered through the heavy oak door, an old, gray tabby cat greeted him with a trill, informing him he was late. She extended her declawed paws halfway up his trousers. Setting his paperwork on the entrance table, he lifted the half-blind, rescue-shelter cat onto his shoulder.

"Okay George, time to eat." He stroked her back while she kneaded his shoulder and purred loudly in his ear. In the kitchen, he set her on the floor. At the sound of the can opener, she wound herself around and between his legs until he placed the food before her.

Today he would forgo his cup of hot tea. Given the hour

and the day he'd had, he poured a glass of Pinot noir and placed Sergei Rachmaninoff, Piano Concerto no. 3 on the turntable and boosted the volume. Sinking into his leather armchair, he waited for George.

Low ceilings and red oak woodwork provided a warm backdrop to his austere Mission style furniture. His leather chair contrasted with luxurious comfort. Window blinds allowed maximum privacy. Well-placed floor lamps provided ambient light.

George hopped into his lap. After satisfying her minimal feline need for attention, he headed to the kitchen. Strips of bacon fat seared in a casserole on the range as he cut, rinsed, and dried chicken quarters. After lightly browning the meat, he poured a healthy douse of Cognac atop it. As bubbling amber liquid spread around the meat, he tipped the skillet, and the flame engulfed its contents. The aroma filled his senses. Heavy and sweet.

Although pragmatic and mathematical, Myles fancied himself somewhat artistic—an appreciator of art, collector of music, player of the saxophone—but cooking was his passion, and tonight he would regale his senses in *Coq au Vin*.

While dinner simmered, he set the table. Plate. Fork. Knife. Spoon. Cloth napkin and water glass. Clarence Myles maintained the habit of civilized dining as a major holdout in the abandonment of decorum to which he could easily succumb, already evident in his rebellion against daily shaving. To give up the civility of fine dining was to edge one's way toward complete barbarism, though he justified his lax grooming as recalcitrance against stuffy white-shirted bureaucrats. Besides, it was not that he didn't shave regularly.

Every Saturday and Wednesday evening, he pulled the straight razor from his medicine cabinet, lathered up for his twice-weekly close shave, and donned a fresh-pressed shirt. Both evenings he crossed over from Long Island to Greenwich Village. At his favorite jazz nook, he awaited the sultry voice that soothed him like nothing else. Yet it was not just her voice but her company—her attention that he craved.

Twyla always joined him between sets and afterward. She indulged him with smiles, nearly as rare as his own. Voluptuous and black, her beauty was both in her countenance and facial features. Her dark eyes had lost some spark over the years, but they each understood heartache and shutting pain out, even if it meant pushing people away; though she never pushed him away. They didn't talk about anything in particular—in fact she did most of the talking. Myles wondered if the divergent nature of their worlds provided each with the anonymity they craved. Originally, he considered it a relationship of little consequence, but over the years, he had grown more than fond of her. Twyla didn't divulge much about her marriage, but she withered when her husband would pick her up from the club, and it made Myles' heart ache. Yet that was better than feeling nothing at all.

Myles always left the lounge alone. He usually landed in his driveway just after one AM, making his Thursday mornings in class a little more difficult.

That was Clarence Myles' Wednesday night routine.

Saturday morning started out with sleeping in and then grading Friday's math quizzes, followed by an afternoon nap, a light dinner, 'the shave' and subsequent drive to the city.

On Sundays, he undertook another gastronomical challenge—Beef Wellington would not defeat him—and then spent the remainder of his day playing saxophone.

Aside from the legal papers now lying on his hallway table, he did not imagine that anything in his life would change.

CHAPTER 26

WAITING ROOMS NEVER HAD ANY DECENT magazines, unless one found the lives of celebrities fascinating. Leila did not. She had met more than a few over the years but didn't realize their elevated status until she was older; they all seemed pretty ordinary to her. She browsed the reading heap for something even remotely recent. A March edition of *Good Housekeeping* promised to help her with spring-cleaning, but in the dead of February, that was her least concern. She scanned the room, her sights landing upon a wall of pamphlets. Mental Illness and You—now, that looked interesting. Alone in the room, Leila didn't hesitate to get an up-close view.

Standing before the rack of the half-dozen titles, she paused at Manic-Depressive Disorder. As she read an almost exact description of her father, the door to an adjoining room opened. Leila folded the leaflet and tucked it in her pocket. The woman extended her hand.

"I'm Dr. Jennings. You must be Leila." She offered a smile that deepened the creases around her eyes and mouth. "You may call me Valerie if you'd like."

Leila took her hand. At least it wasn't limp—though she didn't know why she expected that. Perhaps it was the woman's soft voice and her soft grayish-blue eyes. Even her sandy hair, which curled loosely over her ears, appeared soft. Leila had expected at least a suit—a sweater did not fit the profile.

Leila didn't intentionally withhold a smile; she simply had nothing to offer. In fact, she didn't want to be here at all.

As they entered the small office, Dr. Jennings said, "Please, sit wherever you'll be comfortable."

Leila centered herself on the sofa and folded her arms. Jennings sat in an overstuffed chair, opposite her. When Leila glared at the notepad and pencil on her lap, Jennings set them aside. She tilted her head. "Have you ever been in therapy before?"

"No."

Jennings said nothing. It would be a very long and boring session if she was waiting for Leila to start things off. Finally the doctor spoke.

"How do you feel about Mr. Myles sitting in on your next session?"

"Fine with me."

"Kathy Greene's report states the two of you have a unique relationship."

Leila frowned. "So how much do you already know about me?"

"Would you like to have a look at your file?"

"No."

"Would you like to know what I've gathered?"

"If you're planning on telling me, just say it."

"I think you are a determined young woman who has developed some very efficient coping mechanisms."

"What do you mean by efficient?"

"Functional and effective, especially in situations that call for an immediate reaction, such as the death of your father and some of the other recent issues. I think you've done remarkably well."

"Then why am I here?"

"Perhaps you would like to further develop your skills— round them out and expand them a little—possibly anticipate and diminish some of the long-term fallout that is often the result of trauma."

"I haven't been traumatized."

Jennings nodded. More silence. "Tell me, do you have any hobbies?"

Leila rolled her eyes. "I run."

"You enjoy running." It was more of an acknowledgment than a question.

"Yes," Leila retorted. "Otherwise I wouldn't do it."

"I started running when I was your age. I still do."

"Why?"

"I like the solitude—being alone with my thoughts. I also like the physical exertion. As I'm sure you already know, it's very helpful in dealing with stress."

Find common ground. That must be the first thing they teach at shrink school. Leila did not want anything in common with her therapist. She simply wanted their time to run out. *Just throw her something—anything.*

"I draw," Leila offered.

"What medium do you prefer?"

"Watercolor and pencil."

"How would you describe your artwork?"

"Meticulous and controlled."

"Oh. Why that particular style?"

"I don't know."

"Well, think about it. Who controls your brush?"

Leila would have rolled her eyes, but the notion all at once occurred to her. "Me."

"And what else in your life do you ultimately control?"

"Very little. I guess my paint and brush are the only things I have exclusive control of. So that's what I do. I control them to the extreme."

"Have you ever shown your work to anyone?"

"Just my art teacher. I don't paint for other people, I do it for me."

"Is there anyone you might enjoy sharing your work with?"

"Yes." Leila had no intention of getting into all that.

Jennings smiled, "But you'd rather not tell me who he is."

"Why do you assume it's a he?"

"I don't know, just an intuitive impression. Therapists tend to be that way."

Leila's gaze dropped to her hands as she dug at some viridian hue that stained her thumb cuticle. "I don't want to talk about him."

Her therapist said nothing, and Leila withheld on principle.

Jennings spoke up, "Mr. Myles—"

"It's not Mr. Myles!"

Jennings smiled and she began again, "What I was going to say, is that Mr. Myles is scheduled to join us for our next session. Are there any issues you'd like to cover?"

"We pretty much cover all our issues outside of therapy."

"Well, I'm looking forward to meeting him."

"You say that now—"

Jennings cast a quizzical look.

"You'll see," Leila said, glancing at the clock. "Do I need to stay for the entire session?"

"I'm certainly not going to force you to stay."

"But you have to give a report to the court."

"Yes."

Leila rolled her eyes.

"Leila, we both know the only reason you're here is because of the court's mandate. I simply want to help you meet that mandate. And since you have to at least show up, perhaps we could make the best of it. You needn't divulge to me anything you're not comfortable with. In fact, you don't have to talk at all. But you might find that it helps to talk things out."

Leila stood. "Maybe next time. I'm just not in the mood for any more today." When she reached the door, she turned back toward the doctor. "Is Manic-Depression hereditary?"

Jennings' brow rose. "Clinical studies show there may be a genetic link."

"Oh," Leila said, and left.

LEILA WALKED HER WAY TOWARD THE TRACK. KYLE stretched in preparation for the official tryouts. She had to admit, he was kind of a hunk, but in proximity with Ian, *Coach Brigham*, Kyle could never compete. And now that Coach was sporting a beard for the last month or so, Kyle could never measure up to that kind of manliness, though she wasn't certain if she liked the facial hair or not.

As she came up beside Kyle, he gave her a startled double take and smiled. "So, are you here to watch or tryout?"

Leila's shoulders squared. "Actually, I'm going to tryout."

His eyes widened. "Seriously?"

"Yeah, I'm serious. I didn't tell the school board I wouldn't tryout," she said though she was stretching it. "They just had an issue with my being on the team and being coached by Brigham."

"Okay, so you want me to go tell him?"

"Sure."

Kyle ran over to Coach Brigham who stood with his clipboard, whistle, and stopwatch. Kyle gestured toward her. Ian smiled and glanced at Ms. Thorpe, and then back at Kyle and nodded.

With that, Leila joined the other track-team hopefuls. Just as she anticipated, Brigham included her in a threesome with Kyle and Micah. Ms. Thorpe observed from the sidelines without intervening.

With one leg extended, Leila squatted between the two boys, waiting for the whistle. She glanced at one and then the other, exchanging smiles. Micah winked back. In an instant, they lunged forward in a full run. For the first 50 meters she and Kyle ran neck in neck, leaving Micah behind. At 75 and then at the 100-meter finish line, she was ahead by a meter, and then two, finishing just ahead of Kyle. All three scored excellent time.

Stretching a little between events, Leila waited for Kyle to report back. The numbers meant nothing to her, but Brigham's spontaneous smile made her want to try all the harder in the 800-meter run. Twice around the track would be a breeze.

Once again, all three poised, side by side at the starting line. With the whistle, they took off. At first, they all kept apace with each other, but after 200 meters, Leila advanced. Kyle moved behind, and Leila allowed him to draft off her, but not for long. She could not resist pushing her lead harder and stronger, egging him forward in all earnestness. To her surprise, he edged ahead. The sight of him provoked a novel feeling. Competitiveness. It impelled her forward without restraint as she made the 400-meter loop. Now extending herself beyond him again, she passed the 600-meter mark, fully in the lead. As she headed out of the curve of the last 100 meters, she spotted Brigham on the sidelines ahead, spiking her exertion further. She flew past him and in seconds, Kyle finished a breath behind her.

If Leila had impressed Brigham in September, she hoped for astonishment now. She wound down and jogged back toward him. Kyle approached, elated with their results. Apparently, she had shaved seconds off her time. Kyle came in just behind, outdoing his personal best and nearing a record himself. This would be a good year for Kyle. And Micah, well, he would make the team, but too much pot smoking cut his performance.

Leila headed toward Brigham, watching him as he watched her. She walked past, keeping her eyes on him and then stood before Ms. Thorpe.

"Please let Coach Brigham know that I am officially withdrawing my name from the tryout roster. As we both know, I won't be running with the team this year," Leila said. "It's really too bad, isn't it? How us girls just can't seem to get a team of our own. I wonder what the school board will resort to next year to avoid funding a girls' track team."

Leila returned to Kyle on the infield. Micah migrated toward Coach as other boys positioned themselves on the track. Leila and Kyle speculated on their performances and simultaneously sensed an ominous presence—Mr. Myles sitting halfway up the bleachers.

"Looks like your daddy longlegs is here," Kyle said.

"Don't call him that."

He grinned. "Well, we could call him a brown recluse."

Leila shoved him. "Shut up—I never should have told you about me and him."

"Sorry."

Leila bit her lip. Myles stared directly at her.

"So why's he here?" Kyle said. "He never shows up for extracurriculars."

"Beats me," she said. "Wait for me, okay?"

Leila headed toward the bleachers and ascended them in a bounding gait. Myles leaned forward, his elbows on his knees. She sat to his rear. Looking at her askance, he leaned on the bleacher behind. She waited.

"I thought I might find you watching in the stands. Didn't imagine you'd be trying out."

"Oh. You saw that?"

"Indeed. You certainly are an evasive runner."

"Yeah, well, I relinquished my spot on the team if that's what you're worried about."

"I wasn't worried."

"So why are you here?"

He inhaled. "I wanted to talk to you about a sensitive subject."

Leila rolled her eyes. "This isn't going to be a sex talk, is it?"

He glanced back. "You aren't in need of one, are you?"

"Good God, no."

"Well, that's a relief. Though I have the feeling this issue will rouse even more discomfort." He exhaled. "We need to talk about your future."

Leila's chest collapsed onto her knees, her arms limp at her sides for effect. "Ugh!" She exaggerated her eye roll. "Is this going to be about college?"

"Just hear me out."

"Fine."

"I realize you haven't taken the SATs, but it's not too late. In fact, there's a test date for latecomers in a few weeks."

"Mr. Myles, I obviously don't have the money and I'm not going into debt with student loans. My grades are mediocre, so there will be no scholarships coming my way. And any chance I may have had at an athletic scholarship has been completely flushed by the school board."

"What about your art?"

"What about it?"

"Perhaps you'd like to pursue that."

"I can pursue art without sitting in a classroom being told I need to loosen up my style."

"If it's only a matter of money, I'm in a position where I could help out."

"You already know how I feel about the whole money thing."

"You could pay me back if you want to, without interest."

"All of that's beside the point. You're assuming that I even want to continue going to school. The last thing I want to do for the next two to four years is spend time in a classroom, trying to figure out what I want to do with the rest of my life and frittering away resources while I try and get my act together. The only thing I'm certain about at this point is that as soon as I graduate, I want off Long Island."

He nodded slowly. It took a long moment for him to ask, "Have you given any thought to where off Long Island you might be heading?"

"I really like New Hampshire. I thought I might head back up to the lakes where I used to live. It's familiar, and I think it would be a good place for me to be."

"I see." He stared at the track.

She blurted, "Would you please stop giving Coach Brigham the stare down. It's rude."

"I'm doing no such thing."

"I don't know what you have against him. He's never caused me any harm and you know it."

"Have you forgotten that it was your involvement with him that precipitated the whole gym incident?"

"Oh—I guess we've forgotten that it was Miss Weiss' lack of self-control that precipitated the whole incident?"

"I didn't mean it that way. I'm sorry."

"So did you start out disliking him? Or is it just the fact

that you can't control my attraction to him?"

He glanced back at her and then at the track. "I have nothing personal against Ian Brigham. In fact, I initially found him the most tolerable of my colleagues. My concern is that the forbidden aspect of this relationship has become very enticing. Your romantic notions may be blinding you to the fact that he is a grown man with adult issues of his own." He paused. "Forbidden fruit when it is tasted can be very sweet, but afterward, very disappointing, even devastating. I'm not saying that Ian Brigham would intentionally hurt you. It's just that your expectations may be unrealistic."

"Well, right now I don't really have any expectations regarding Ian Brigham."

"You expect me to believe that?"

She could not refute it.

"You know what, Clarence?" She rose from her seat. "This is not a subject open for discussion."

She descended the bleachers, then paused and turned back toward him. "By the way, we have a therapy session scheduled a week from today at three o'clock."

"Is that right?"

"Yes. If that's a problem, I'll give you the therapist's number and you can reschedule. But as you already know, I can only make it on Saturday or Sunday."

He scowled. "Saturday is fine."

"You're not going to like the therapist, you know."

"And why is that?"

"Because she's pretty."

She continued her descent as Ian watched her. When he smiled, she smiled back, indifferent to Myles' judgments and still undecided about the beard.

LEILA FLIPPED THROUGH A MAGAZINE, GLANCING out the waiting room window. *Where is he?* Of course he would show up—he was nothing if not responsible, downright dependable. The notion of him missing his first appointment with Dr. Jennings stirred the same old discomforts of never knowing if or when her father would show up for things like school productions, parent-teacher conferences—or worse yet, if they would up and move when she had a part in an upcoming play or had worked for weeks on a science project she would never get to present. Joe had been more dependable that way—at least to begin with.

Leila hadn't known quite what to expect from Mr. Myles as her guardian, but she had hoped they would spend more time together—quality time, not lecturing time like on the bleachers. Leila had even fantasized about just hanging out with him, the way normal teenagers fantasized about the opposite sex—but without the romance. The possibility of her childish wishes coming out in therapy mortified her. She had already set herself up for disillusionment when she had suggested a celebration of their new status, though he likely had no idea that declining would disappoint her so.

The interior office door opened and Jennings made a welcoming gesture. "Are we alone today?"

"No. He'll be here."

"Shall we wait for him?"

"No." She shot another look out the window and stood. "He's probably delaying just for effect."

"I see." Jennings lifted her brow and led Leila into the office.

Leila took her seat on the sofa and Jennings sat, as expected, in the chair across from her.

"Tell me, does Mr. Myles often do things just for effect?"

"Sometimes. Mostly in class. It's just his way of maintaining control."

"Is it effective?"

"I think he thinks so."

The sound of Myles' arrival filtered in. Jennings opened the door.

"Mr. Myles. Please join us." In her affable way, she extended her hand. "Valerie Jennings."

Myles looked her over from head to toe. Had he noted her lack of a wedding band? He shook her hand.

Leila said, "You're late Mr. Myles. I certainly hope this is not indicative of what we can expect from you in the future."

He glared at Leila but softened as he looked Jennings in the face. "My apologies."

"Please, have a seat," Jennings said.

He sat in a chair nearest the exit, and Jennings sat paperless, opposite him.

Jennings began. "I hope you don't mind that we started without you Mr. Myles—or would you prefer I call you Clarence?"

Leila smirked as he tightly crossed his leg and arms.

"Myles is fine," he said.

Dr. Jennings no longer tilted her head in her inviting way, and much of her facial expressiveness disappeared as she looked at one and then the other. "Is there anything in particular that either of you would like to talk about today?"

Myles and Leila stated in unison, "No."

"So then, would you say things are going well?"

Again, in unison, "Everything is great."

"Well, Myles, you've been Leila's guardian for four weeks now. How has your guardianship altered your relationship?"

"It hasn't altered anything."

Jennings folded her hands in her lap. "And what about you Leila, do you think his guardianship has altered anything?"

"Nope. Pretty much status quo."

Jennings' relaxed smile thinned. "So, you're happy with the way things are going?"

Leila didn't feel inclined to incriminate Myles and she knew he didn't care to get all deep and intimate with their therapist. In the ensuing silence an alliance congealed as Myles cast a sly eye at Leila.

"Oh yes." Leila said, "I think they're going very well."

"Wonderful. Then lets talk about the things you appreciate in each other." Jennings addressed Myles. "Why don't you begin."

Following through on their unspoken collusion, he began

with a nod. "One thing I appreciate about Leila is that she's open minded and compliant."

"Do you have a specific example?"

He nodded. "A week ago, I suggested she take the SATs. Reasonable girl that she is, Leila agreed that it would indeed be a fine idea."

Leila suppressed her surprise and annoyance. "Yes, Mr. Myles can be very persuasive. I really like how he's always looking out for me."

"Well, that's wonderful. Now, Leila, why don't you tell Mr. Myles what you appreciate about him, aside from his looking out for you?"

"That's easy." She looked directly at him. "I appreciate the way he trusts me and respects my privacy. He knows I would never pursue a relationship he didn't approve of and that going to college would indeed be a fine way to spend the next four years of my life."

"I see." Jennings' gaze shifted from one to the other. "Tell me, Mr. Myles, what major would you like to see Leila pursue?"

"Her art, of course. She's very talented."

"Oh. You've actually seen Leila's artwork?"

Leila did not like being made a liar but refrained from letting on.

"Yes," he elaborated, "she's quite the portraitist."

Leila chimed in, "Mr. Myles especially likes my choice of subjects."

Jennings took the bait. "Have you ever painted Mr. Myles?"

"Of course."

"And you've seen it?" Jennings raised her brow at Myles.

"Indeed," he scowled. "It was delightful."

"Did you consider it an accurate portrayal?"

"Yes—all of her work is quite good. In fact, at my bidding, she intends to enter some of her work in a community-sponsored art exhibit. Isn't that right, Leila?"

Myles had pushed their imaginary rapport too far. Rather

than expose it, Leila agreed. "Yes, that's right—and I know exactly which painting I'll exhibit."

🐾 LEILA'S CASEWORKER VISITED ON THE FIFTEENTH OF the month. She came and went with minimal attention from Leila. All things had been found as expected and to the woman's satisfaction. A week-and-a-half later, and at the beginning of spring break, Leila followed through with another scheduled visit with Dr. Jennings.

"I was so pleased to see how well you and Mr. Myles get along. You're quite the happy little family," Jennings said.

Leila smirked. "Oh please. We both know that was such a ruse."

Jennings acknowledged her admission with a satisfied smile. "Do you even like Clarence Myles?"

She thought for a minute. "I do. But it's sort of ironic that the very thing I like most about him is what annoys me most."

Jennings waited for her to elaborate.

"It's not as though he actually knows what I'm thinking, of course that's impossible, but I feel like he anticipates my next step or knows what I'm up to. It's weird. I feel like he knows me better than I know myself."

"Would you consider your relationship with Clarence mutual?"

"I don't feel like our relationship is particularly two-sided, if that's what you mean. Even though I think we're very alike in some ways, he definitely has the upper hand. He just has a lot more age and experience, so I think he picks up on things with me a lot easier. But I don't really know that much about him."

"Would you like to?"

"Yes. Of course."

"Perhaps we could discuss that during our next session."

"Well, that'd be interesting."

CHAPTER 27

L EILA PUSHED OPEN HER KITCHEN WINDOW AND
then the one beside her art table. A warm breeze blew in
from the south, ruffling the photograph tacked to her
wall. She sat and studied the picture Ian had taken of her. If
only he had shot it in color, then she could reproduce it in
watercolor, no problem. But to translate it into color was a
new frontier. She simply didn't have the confidence.
Fortunately, when Miss Michaels announced the spring
project—a self-portrait in any medium—she had also
provided Leila with a supply of good paper. Arches
Aquarelle. But still, Leila loathed wasting supplies.
Unfortunately, the project deadline rapidly approached and
all she had was a sketch, albeit a good one. At least she could
transfer the sketch to her watercolor paper and call it progress
for the day.

Standing before the open window, she inhaled the scent of
spring. Her feet tingled from sitting too long. She glanced
around her room. The walls closed in.

IN IAN'S OPINION, EASTER SUNDAY WOULD BE THE
perfect day for running the beach. Southerly breezes had
already started warming the atmosphere, and most people
stayed at home hunting pastel-colored eggs. An all-but-vacant
parking lot promised the hoped-for solitude and reprieve from
Millville's congestion.

As he pulled into the parking lot, Leila's little blue car sat in the exact same place she had parked in July. He laughed at the irony of it. Everything seemed to have been falling into place lately, and this simply confirmed that all his plans might actually work out.

He pulled in beside her car, remembering the way she once looked in the setting July sun. He tightened the laces of his sneakers. What a stark difference in climate a few months made. As he pulled on a pair of gloves and baseball cap, he crossed the causeway and breathed the heavy, salt air. In spite of the sun peeking through the clouds, and the warmer temperatures inland, wind stung his cheeks. It whooshed in his ears, pushing against him as he hiked up the path. He stood at the peak of the dunes, savoring the smell of the ocean. Deep gray water undulated, whipping into the March winds and then crashed ferociously onto shore. He was glad he hadn't shaved the beard he had grown a month ago.

A cursory glance up and down the beach revealed no other occupants. He started a slow jog, making his way toward the firm, wet sand, where tracks headed east and west. One set had the gait of a runner—a light-footed runner, heading east. He veered off in that direction.

Two miles into his run, he peeled off his first layer; his gloves had come off a mile back. As the sun ascended, the air warmed and the wind died a little. He scanned the far end of the beach where a figure nearly blended with the dunes. As he neared, his heart pounded. She lay with her knees bent skyward. Her hands folded across her middle. Her loose hair nestled her head and lifted with the gentle breeze.

His breath caught in his chest. Blocking the sun from her face, he stood over her.

Her hand shielded her squinting eyes. It took a moment before she spoke. "Ian?"

"Hi."

She rubbed her eyes. "What are you doing here?"

"The same thing as you. I just haven't gotten to the napping part yet."

She propped herself onto her elbows.

"I saw your car in the lot. Same place as last summer," he said. "Then I just followed your tracks—and—here you are. I guess we're both creatures of habit."

Ian squatted beside her as she sat and gasped. "We're not supposed to be talking."

He laughed. "What do you think is going to happen? Is the school board going to come out from behind the dunes? Or maybe Mr. Myles?"

"No, but ... I don't want you to get in trouble."

He shook his head. "There's nothing to worry about."

"You mean, we can just sit here and talk?"

"Yeah, Leila. We can."

She stiffened and looked at him askance. "But I'm only *seventeen*."

He recalled his own words with regret. "I'm sorry I said that ... I didn't mean it the way it came out."

"Then why did you say it? Why did you say all those things?"

He wavered. How honest could he be without imposing himself or his needs upon her? The least he owed her was honesty. "I was desperate and I panicked. I realized my feelings for you were out of control and it was my pathetic attempt at convincing myself of things that weren't true."

She faced him. "You humiliated me, Ian."

He had that coming, but her directness stung. "I am so sorry. You have every right to be angry."

"I'm not angry," she said. "Is that what you thought, that I was angry and so I got you in trouble?" Tears filled her eyes.

He choked up. "I can't imagine what you must have been feeling."

Her gaze dropped to her hands and then met his. "I'm sorry I got you in trouble."

"Please tell me you haven't been worrying about that."

A tear trickled down her cheek. "I tried to explain things ...."

"Leila. None of that whole mess makes any difference." He wiped her tear. "Even if they fired me it wouldn't matter."

"You haven't been disappointed with me?"

He drew her forehead to his, examining her eyes up close. "Not at all. You've never done anything but impress me."

A smile broke through her tears. "You have no idea how relieved I am." She stroked his beard. "Your whiskers. They make you look like a French artist."

He chuckled. "It's supposed to make me look rugged and outdoorsy."

"Well, I suppose it does a little. But it definitely makes you look older."

He smiled and withdrew. He didn't want to look older. Shifting his body and closing the gap between them, he sank his hands into the sand behind him.

Leila moved closer, leaning into his shoulder. "There's about a million things I want to say to you, Ian."

"There's no hurry. If in three months from now you still feel the same, you'll have plenty of time to tell me."

"You mean after I graduate."

"Right."

"Why wouldn't I feel the same in three months?"

"I don't know that you will or won't, but for a while there, it seemed you and Kyle might have had something going on. It wouldn't be right for me to interfere with that."

"We don't. I mean, we kind of did, but not really. We've always been just friends."

"He's been a good friend to you."

"When he's been my friend, yeah, he's been good, but it's been a lot of up and down. Maybe it's just because he's a teenage boy."

"As a general rule, teenage guys aren't particularly dependable as love interests. The male species changes a lot between seventeen and twenty, and a whole lot more by the time they hit their mid-twenties."

"I guess that could just as easily be said about teenage girls."

"I suppose so. And that's why I'm not in any hurry, and you shouldn't be, either." He looked at her. "Time is on our side, Leila."

"I know."

He moved his arm behind her.

She tipped her face toward the sun. "I have a shrink now."

"No kidding. How is that going?"

"Weird at first. Mr. Myles has to go with me every other session. That's really weird."

Ian chuckled. "I'll bet. I'd like to be a fly on the wall for that show."

"What do you think of Mr. Myles—honestly?"

"I think … he's a passionate man who's found something worthwhile to latch onto. I think he's principled—and guarded—and believes that whatever he's been through gives him the right to treat others like crap."

Leila's lips pursed. "You don't like him."

"I don't know him well enough to like or dislike him. Do you like him?"

"I'm not sure that like is the right word, but, yes, I do."

Ian had to admit, "He's been good to you."

"Yes, he has. I love him."

Her words surprised him at first, but then they seemed not so unexpected. "He probably won't like the idea of you and me—if we happen. But of course you already know that."

"Yes, I know. But I think he also knows that won't stand in my way."

He grinned. She had such a will of her own—he loved that about her.

The sun dropped behind them now, and their shadow fell long in the sand before them. They had sat long enough.

Ian stood, offering his hand and pulled her up. "It's cooling off. We should go."

"We can't go yet," she said with urgency as she shoved her hand into her jacket pocket. "I almost forgot. There's something I need to do."

"What?"

She held out a white handkerchief. Its four corners gathered atop a bundle the size of a baseball.

"What is it?"

"What's left of my dad."

Ian's eyes grew wide. "Really?"

"Yeah. He made me promise to sprinkle a little of him whenever I went someplace new. I ran out of new places. Besides that, I'm tired of carrying him around."

She started toward the shore. Ian hesitated. He didn't want to intrude.

"Come on." She motioned for him to follow.

Alongside each other, they walked to the edge of the water. Without ostentation, she untied the knot and squatted.

"You might not want to stand downwind of this," she said. "It can get a little messy."

Ian moved to her other side as she emptied the ashes into the ebbing waters. They broke apart, moving away from her and then returning. She poked at them, breaking the water tension. They began to swirl. As she stood, one large wave came and dispersed them, wetting her sneakers.

"Now he's all gone," she said, shoving both hands in her pockets and staring out over the water.

Ian tried to comprehend the weight of the moment. He remembered burying his own father's ashes, without pomp or ritual, interring them at the cemetery. He hadn't been back to the Connecticut gravesite since. Leila appeared as stoic as he likely had, holding it all in, trying to make a brave show for the few who had attended. He hadn't wanted sympathy. He sensed she did not want it now. He said nothing. He would not move until she did.

She gasped as if it suddenly struck her. Tears streamed from her eyes. He moved her away from the encroaching waters and held her close. She sobbed like a child, her body warming his as his emotions pounded in his chest. He allowed his own tears to come, grieving for her and for his own loss.

When she pulled back, wiping her eyes, she whispered, "I didn't mean to put you through that. I'm sorry."

"Don't be sorry." He stroked her face. "Be glad we were

together. We both needed this."

He did not linger in her gaze, but neither did he relinquish her hand as they walked the two-and-a-half miles back to the parking lot in silence. When they arrived at their cars, he followed her to her door.

She smiled, her nose still pink. "No flat tire today."

"Too bad."

He thought of kissing her. If he hadn't just told her there was no hurry, that time was on their side, he would have kissed her without reservation. He simply pulled her close and held her tight as his lips grazed her hair. He breathed her in, amazed at the day fate had handed them. A strange and novel feeling washed over him, as undeniable as the waves rolling onto the beach.

🦋CHAPTER 28

M YLES SIPPED HIS COFFEE BEFORE HOMEROOM, contemplating his upcoming weekend. The afternoon he had spent in therapy had altered his Saturday evening outing in Greenwich Village, but an hour spent with Leila provided more emotional satisfaction than his jazz singer Twyla ever could. Besides, it was short term and he still had alternate Saturdays and Wednesday evenings to torment himself with Twyla. He had to wonder why he put himself through it, why he chose the unattainable, married woman as a romantic interest—though it didn't take a whole lot of guessing. Not that therapy made him ponder such things. In fact, Judge Moore's line of questioning gave him as much pause as sitting in front of an attractive therapist.

Noise from the hall distracted Myles from his musings, and when his door opened, Leila walked in. He smiled at the welcome intrusion—she hadn't shown up early in quite some time.

"Good morning," he leaned back in his chair. "To what do I owe this pleasure?"

Leila stood in front of his desk and smiled, waiting a moment before speaking. "Since Dr. Jennings' office is up in your neck of the woods, I was wondering if we could just drive over there together, tomorrow. It seems like we haven't spent any time together lately."

Myles squinted at her with suspicion. She had missed the

alternate SATs, and ever since their last therapy session, she had given him the distinct impression she was avoiding him. Perhaps their therapy cahoots had backfired.

He adjusted his glasses. "You want me to come down and pick you up?"

"I could just meet you at your place. We could go from there."

He tried to read her motive, but she seemed to have brushed up on her poker face.

"Alright," he said, with a measure of skepticism, though happy she had sought him out. As an afterthought, he added, "Wear your skirt. If you can behave, perhaps we'll eat out."

🐉 LEILA SAT TUCKED IN THE BACK CORNER OF ART class as always, clutching loosely rolled-up watercolor paper with one hand and wiping sweat from the palm of the other.

"I am looking forward to seeing the results of all your planning and hard work." Miss Michaels clasped her hands and smiled at her budding artists. "Please get them out. We'll start with William."

The first student stood front and center. Leila wished they could simply show and tell from their seat. One classmate did a nice clay bust, a moderately true yet more attractive rendition of herself, titled *Wishful Thinking*. Clever. Several sketched in pencil, one named *Daddy's Girl*. Leila could have used that, but in the plural rather than the possessive. Someone even attempted soft sculpture and called it *Bizarre*—it was difficult to tell which end was up.

At her seat, Leila flexed open her own work. It took a couple attempts but she was satisfied, even pleased with her result. She drew the lines of her likeness with precision, yet allowed her brush uncustomary liberty, not that anyone else would notice. Perhaps her satisfaction sprung from having to use her imagination with color or simply the inspiration of working from Ian's photograph; either way, she liked the painting even though she could point out every flaw.

"Leila?" Miss Michaels repeated.

Leila stood and took her place beside her instructor, looking off to nowhere as she held up her project.

She sighed discomfort. *"Girl Running."*

🐛CLUSTERS OF DAFFODILS AND TULIPS BLOOMED along the veranda and in front of a trellis where roses would burst in a month. Leila had not imagined Clarence Myles as a gardener. Perhaps he hired out the groundskeeping.

As she stood at the door, horizontal blinds in the large windows to her right prevented her from seeing in. She peered through the small row of leaded-glass windows high up on the door as she rapped the iron knocker.

The door opened wide.

"Come on in," Mr. Myles said, giving her a once-over. "You look very nice."

He wore a tweed blazer and khakis, and to her amazement, a tie. "You look pretty nice yourself. You even shaved."

He offered a quick smile and closed the door. "Let me just go turn off the music and lock the back door."

Quiet jazz played as Leila waited in the spacious though dimly lit entrance. It melded into his living space where bookcases, stereo, several chairs, and a couch nestled around a grand fireplace tucked off at the far right. Between that and a heavy-balustered stairway directly in front of her, six chairs gathered around a dining table. Beyond that, Myles had just disappeared through a door that provided a glimpse of a bright kitchen.

She smelled furniture polish and leather. The atmosphere felt heavy; it appeared almost smoky as thin shafts of light cut between slatted blinds. A rush of pleasure broadened her smile as he turned off the music and approached.

He cut a sweeping gesture. "Is this what you wanted to see?"

"You read me too well."

"You're not so opaque as you think you are, my dear." He squeezed her arm. "Shall we?"

As they drove, he asked, "So, have you ratted us out yet?"

"You know I have. It's not as though she hadn't already figured us out anyway."

"Yes. She seems—" his brow twitched, "astute."

"I was right, wasn't I?"

"About what?"

"That you wouldn't like her, especially because she's attractive."

"Why do you think I would dislike her based on her level of attractiveness?"

"I don't think that it's so much that you dislike her. I think it's more that you're irritated by the fact that her attractiveness is distracting."

"And I think that is a very far stretch of your imagination, Miss Sanders."

"Maybe so. But I think you would be far more comfortable in a therapy setting with an ugly old man. Then you could be your rude self without caring. But you're not as comfortable being your mean self with her. That's what I think."

He cleared his throat and stared straight ahead. "And what do you think of her?"

"I like her alright. She sort of gets me thinking."

🐉 LEILA AGAIN CHOSE THE SOFA IN JENNINGS' OFFICE but this time sat with her back snuggled into the corner.

"Sit with me." Leila patted the cushion beside her. She doubted he would be blatantly rude in front of Valerie Jennings.

Mr. Myles took his seat at her side, tightly crossing his arms and legs.

"So," Jennings began with a deep breath. "How have the two of you been doing?"

Myles said nothing; he only looked at Leila, who then spoke up. "I saw Mr. Myles' house for the first time today."

"Did you?" Jennings glanced at Myles and then back to Leila. "How did you feel about that?"

Leila directed her response to Myles. "He let me in because he knows that I'm curious about him, but I don't think he realizes how much it means to me."

"Elaborate on that for me, please."

"I would, but I don't want to embarrass him, so I won't say it to him right now. I'll just tell him later."

Jennings looked at him kindly. "Mr. Myles, Leila seems very hesitant to embarrass you. Why do you suppose that is?"

He looked directly at the therapist. "Leila and I speak very freely in private. Just because she chooses not to speak freely now, does not mean that our communication is inhibited."

"So, you're saying that in private, she's not afraid of embarrassing you."

"Yes, that's right."

"How do you feel about that, Leila?"

She thought for a moment. "I'm not afraid of embarrassing him, but …."

Jennings prodded, "Go ahead, finish your thought."

Leila glanced at Myles. "There are some subjects that aren't any of my business."

"For instance?" Jennings asked.

"About his relationships with women and about his daughter."

The therapist looked at Myles. "I wasn't aware that you have a daughter."

Clenching his jaw, he met her stare and turned his attention to Leila.

She quickly bailed him out. "He doesn't have a daughter anymore."

Jennings brow rose. Myles neither confirmed nor denied Leila's statement.

After a moment, he said, "Doctor Jennings, you don't have children, do you?"

"No, Mr. Myles. I don't." She smiled. "And if your daughter is an issue you don't care to explore, I don't intend to press you on it. Unless of course, Leila wishes to."

"No, I don't," Leila spoke up. "But I do wish Mr. Myles

would let me get to know him better."

Myles ankle now rested on his knee. "Leila, how much better do you know me now than when we first met?"

"Much better. But you know me a whole lot better than I know you."

Myles' hand dropped between them as he turned toward her. "And that, Leila, is the nature of relationships. Rarely, if ever, are they equal."

Leila stared at him, weighing his statement against all the relationships of her life. "I guess that's true …," she finally said. "Though the balance often shifts. Sometimes gradually. Sometimes abruptly."

"Yes. And the ones that shift frequently are usually the most interesting and stimulating. But the balance in one person's favor or against it is rarely constant. No one should ever hold all or most of the power all the time. If they do, the relationship stagnates and isn't much of a relationship at all."

"And what about our relationship, Clarence?"

"You have more power and control in this relationship than you realize."

Leila beheld Myles with such affection—it beamed from her eyes. The sight of his flushed face made her own eyes burn. Without measuring her reaction, she slipped her hand beneath his. He more than allowed it; he squeezed her fingers.

Finally, Myles spoke up. "Valerie—do you mind if I call you Valerie?"

"No, not at all."

"Valerie, do you enjoy music?"

Jennings smiled. "Yes, very much. What makes you ask?"

"Leila, in addition to being a fast runner and accomplished artist, is also quite the pianist."

Leila shot back, "You've never even heard me play."

"Yes, but I've heard the rumors." He glanced at Jennings. "The staff room is quite the rumor pit. Teachers can be nearly as preoccupied with their students' lives as their own."

"So I gather," Jennings grinned. "Leila, what is your

preference? Classical, jazz, rock or what?"

"I guess blues, some jazz."

"Blues—that's revealing."

"Do you like jazz or blues, Valerie?" Leila's fingers wiggled under Myles' large hand.

"I like some of most genres. Tell me, between running, art, and music, to which do you have a stronger connection, Leila?"

"Running and piano are just things I do, but art is something I pursue."

"And Mr. Myles, what do you pursue?"

"Peace and repose."

MYLES SMOOTHED HIS LINEN NAPKIN ACROSS HIS lap as the waiter approached. Therapy had not squashed his appetite.

"My friend will have a sparkling water with a wedge of lime, and I'll have a glass of the Gevrey-Chambertin." Returning his attention to Leila, he smiled at her excitement as she scanned the menu.

"I wasn't expecting something this nice," Leila said in a hushed tone. "Or this expensive."

His smile twitched. "Then I've succeeded."

"At what?"

"At surprising you yet another time."

"You're so weird. You're so—I think the word is tenacious—about appearing a certain way, but on the other hand, you really get off on dispelling it."

"Yes. And I believe the term for that is *walking contradiction*."

The waiter returned with their drinks. Lifting his glass, Myles examined the rich burgundy color. A sliver of refracted light burst through.

"It truly is a shame that you're not old enough to drink. You are missing out on one of the most pleasurable experiences of life."

"Yes, well, it is on the 'To Don't' list."

He breathed in the bouquet with pleasure and then sipped. Swirling the velvety liquid over his taste buds, he savored the full-bodied, spicy flavor and smiled with approval.

Leila's eyes sparkled like the wine.

He held it up. "Would you like to smell it?"

"Sure."

He passed the glass. She took a whiff.

"Well," he asked, "what do you smell?"

She sniffed again. "It's not sweet. It smells a little bit smoky and like some sort of fruit—and I don't mean grapes."

"Would you like to taste it?"

"Really?"

"A small sip. And hold it in your mouth—move your tongue around in it."

Leila followed his instructions and then swallowed.

"What did you taste?"

"I'm not sure, but what I taste now is sort of like black cherries."

"Very good. You have an unspoiled palate."

The waiter returned. "Are you ready to order or shall I come back?"

Myles looked at Leila.

She shrugged. "I like anything."

"We'll each have the smoked salmon, with the bib lettuce, Gorgonzola, and roasted pecans—and please bring the entrée and salad out all at once."

The waiter again departed.

Gradually, a little smirk curled Leila's lips.

"What?" Myles said.

"I can't believe you were interviewing Valerie Jennings for a date during my therapy session."

"I was doing no such thing," he lied. "Is that what you thought?"

She quoted his own words, "You're not so opaque as you think you are, my dear."

"Do you catalogue everything I say?"

"Only the good stuff." She smiled smugly. Then her

countenance turned serious.

"You realize that was your last session before I turn eighteen, when I'm no longer under obligation to some court order or—" she quit before referencing him, and raised her deviant brow. "Anyway, that's the last time you have to see her. Under the restraints of doctor-patient ethics, that is."

Myles scowled as the waiter brought their dinner.

Leila stared at her meal and then closed her eyes and inhaled. He forfeited his annoyance at the sight of her, lost in the moment. He sipped his wine once more before tasting his salmon.

"Oh, Clarence," she said after the first swallow. "This is where you should bring her."

He shot her a squinty look. In fact, he had contemplated the notion. "Miss Sanders, you are on the verge of spoiling a perfectly enchanted evening."

She backed off with a grin and took a bite of Gorgonzola. "Mmm."

Her gaze came back to his, this time with gravity. A hundred words passed from her eyes to his and back until she broke the silence. "I love you, Mr. Myles."

How could her words catch him so off guard? His eyes burned and his heart hammered, heating his entire body. He knew how to repeat the words but they wouldn't come out.

Leila bit her lip. "I'm sorry, I didn't mean to embarrass you."

"I'm not embarrassed. I'm just out of practice."

"You don't have to say it out loud. I already know you love me back."

🌿CHAPTER 29

L EILA JARRED AWAKE FROM DEEP SLEEP AS IF THE
alarm had sounded. She grabbed the clock, but only
gentle ticking announced the time. It wasn't yet five AM,
and it took a moment to shuffle through the days of the week
before she settled on Wednesday. Wednesday, May 3. A
slow smile came over her as she pushed covers back and sat
up. Minutes later, her teapot whistled. Ultramarine melded
with the soft glow of the gamboge horizon. Within minutes,
the sun pushed above treetops revealing a cloudless sky
under which she would mark her eighteenth birthday.

A year ago, her birthday had come and gone without
notice. Little more than four months had passed since her
father had died. Life had devolved into a series of daily
motions with no one to share the passing time. This year, she
had a small but significant few who would remember, the
first being Artie. Then again, he might not remember.

When she passed by his kitchen window on her way to his
front stoop, his absence at the table didn't alarm her until she
stepped into his apartment, into utter silence and darkness.

A tingle crept up her spine as she called out, "Artie."

No answer. Floorboards creaked as she made her way to
his bedroom door. It groaned as she pushed it open. From
between the window and its shade, a shard of light cut in,
dancing upon the blanket halfway up Artie's body. His hands
folded across his chest like a mummy—wearing tropical-

print, silk pajamas—as still as death.

The tingle up Leila's body shot to her extremities. She did not need to feel his cold flesh or lay her hand on his chest or check for a pulse. She simply knew he was dead. Even as she approached, she hadn't any notion of trying to rouse him. Her vision blurred as she stood at the foot of his bed. Tears escaped without hindrance and dripped from her chin to the floor.

She pulled a chair to his bedside and sat facing him. The drawn shade billowed. His room smelled a little musty, and a lot like Old Spice and Vicks. Just like Artie. He appeared neither distraught nor peaceful. He simply looked dead—but not dead, the way her father had looked.

If her father had appeared peaceful, she wouldn't have recognized him. Even with palliative measures, his pain had been so entrenched in his face and in her own mind that that was all she remembered. Hospice had left their apartment that afternoon and, as usual, she had sat with him for hours. That late December day, Leila had watched him drift in and out of sleep, each breath slowing, pausing for long moments. Her future with her father was slipping away—every hope and every secret. She had thought about the man she would never really get to know, but more than that, she lamented all the answers he would take to his grave. It struck her with such urgency that she was not only losing her father, but the connection to her mother. She prayed he would open his eyes one last time. She needed to know. She needed him to trust her with the truth.

His eyes fluttered and opened. Although they glazed over, he seemed more alert than he had for hours. Leila held his hand, and he smiled through his distress. She couldn't bring herself to ask.

"You're going to be fine—just like we planned," he whispered.

Leila drew a hard breath. "It's not that, Daddy …."

He squeezed her hand with little strength. "Then tell me."

"I need to know about my mother. Please—tell me why

she left."

Her father's eyes rolled behind his lids. "Leila ...."

"Please, Daddy. I need to know ...."

He stared off for a few moments. He barely had the strength to turn his head. "Your mother had ... problems ...."

"What problems?"

"She left to straighten out her life."

"Why couldn't she stay and do that?"

"She needed professional help .... She went into a rehab clinic."

Leila tried to comprehend it.

"Leila, your mother loved you—she loved you so much. But she couldn't take care of you ... she had to leave."

"Why didn't she come back?" she pleaded.

He seemed so far away when he replied, "I don't know ...."

"You have to know! How could she just leave her baby?"

"I don't know ...." Tears seeped from her father's eyes. "I don't know why she never came back to us ...." He took a haggard breath. "I don't know ...."

Leila sobbed at her father's bedside. He drifted back off to sleep. When she tried to wake him, to tell him she was sorry—that she didn't need to know why her mother had left her precious little girl, that she was grateful he had kept her and raised her the best he could, that she loved him for the father he tried to be, that nothing else mattered—but he never woke.

Now, as she sat beside Artie, an extraordinary heaviness forced her eyelids closed and she drifted into dreams where surreal images of Artie morphed into Joe into her father. She woke to the sound of a slamming door.

Buddy stood at the end of Artie's bed and groaned. His posture went slack. Neither spoke as he moved to Leila's side. He squeezed her shoulder, releasing another wave of her tears. After a silent minute, he left the room. Leila heard him call for an ambulance. Every time she closed her eyes, the past and present intertwined, transporting her back to her father's bedroom. The sound of medics entering the apartment.

Low voices and rolling casters. The stretcher bumping living room furniture on its way. Her stomach roiled.

"Excuse me miss," a voice said. Buddy helped her up from the chair. As she moved away from the bed, her father's tortured face stared back. Her chest constricted.

"Buddy, I need to call Joe."

"Now don't you worry, I already called Joe. His manager says he'll get the message ASAP."

Even as her heart was breaking, it welled with hope of seeing Joe. Her feet began to move. "Buddy, I need to run."

"You go and have your run. I'll close up."

She scribbled a note, tucked it in her apartment door in case Myles or Kyle came looking for her, and then headed south. She needed to feel the water.

ARTIE DIED—I'M RUNNING. MYLES TUCKED THE note in his breast pocket.

There would be a good reason why Leila had not shown up at school, breaking her near-perfect attendance record, but he had not anticipated this. What's more, the implicit desperation of the note charged him with concern. He could not head home without knowing she was alright.

After checking with Kyle and turning up nothing, Myles had only one other option. Ian Brigham. Resorting to his assistance galled Myles, but for Leila's sake he stifled his pride and headed toward the canals of South Millville. When he pulled into the short driveway, he spotted a realtor's placard in the front yard, with an attached Sale Pending sign. An interesting development. Myles approached the door, face drawn with anxiety, and rapped. In a few seconds, Brigham appeared in the open doorway.

"I'm looking for Leila. Is she here?"

"No. She's not. Why would she be here?"

"Artie, the old man who lives downstairs from her, died. She didn't show up at school and she's not at home. She left this." Myles passed him the note.

Ian rubbed his beardless chin. "Is her car in the driveway?"

"Yes."

"Then she's running. I'm sure she's fine."

"Just because she's running does not mean she's fine," Myles barked.

"And this is not a cold, sleeting January afternoon."

Myles had to concede that Ian's insights on Leila might rival his own. "Where might she go?"

"I don't know. Leila's as likely to come here as anywhere."

Myles heaved a sigh. The phone rang in the background.

"Why don't you step in?" Brigham opened the door wide and then went to the phone on the kitchen wall, just down the hall beyond them. Myles stepped into the foyer. Boxes—some packed and some not yet full and sealed—lined the hallway. With the phone to his ear, Ian looked back at him. Myles moved toward the kitchen.

"No, Kyle, she's not here … I'll let you know if I hear anything … Bye."

Myles' hope devolved into greater worry as Ian hung up.

"Listen, Myles, you can drive the streets of Millville, go home and wait for a call, camp out at her place, or stay here and have a beer with me." Ian went to his refrigerator and pulled a Heineken. "Maybe she'll show up or call."

If Myles went home and waited, what if she never called? What if he waited at her place and she never came—with no phone, even Brigham could not contact him. Perhaps he was overreacting and just needed to calm down. Perhaps he just needed a few minutes to catch his breath.

Ian popped the cap from the green bottle and offered it.

"Haven't you anything more stout?" Myles said.

"Nope."

Myles scowled and grabbed it. Ian pulled another and each took a long gulp.

"Just sit down long enough to drink it." Ian gestured to the small table at the back of the kitchen overlooking the canal. Myles sat as Ian leaned against the counter. The clock on the wall ticked. Five minutes until four, around the time that Myles would normally arrive home. They were nearly done with their beer when the phone rang again. Ian snatched it.

"Hello ... Leila ...." He glanced at Myles. "I know he did ... Mr. Myles told me ... he's sitting right here. Let me put him on." Ian handed off the phone to Myles.

🐚 THE SLAM OF A CAR DOOR ROUSED LEILA FROM LIGHT sleep. She glanced at her clock. One-fifty AM. By the time she bounded downstairs, Joe was bent over the trunk of a Lincoln Town car and hoisting his luggage. She gasped with excitement as he turned toward her. Lanky arms dropped suitcases at his side.

"Baby!" He opened his arms wide and Leila dashed into his solid chest, reaching up to fling her arms around his neck.

"Oh my God! I can't believe you're really here!"

He held her at a distance as her hands settled on his wide lapels. His *café-au-lait* complexion took a bluish tinge in the streetlight and accentuated a few lines she hadn't remembered seeing three years ago.

"Look at you. All grown up and so beautiful." His voice resounded, deep and mellow.

"And look at you, all fancy. What did you have to hock to get these threads?"

"Baby, Europe has been good to me."

She sunk her fingers into his Afro. "Are you getting gray hair, or is that just the streetlights?"

"Never mind that. Give me some more of that sugar."

Leila hugged him again and then took him by the hand, leading him into Artie's apartment.

"Let me fix you something to eat," she said as he carried his luggage to Artie's room.

"No." He placed his bag on the bed. "I already ate."

Leila came in behind him. He faced the bed and sniffed hard.

She moved to his side. "He was in his bed, like someone had laid him out, with his hands folded on his chest—very dignified in those nice silk pajamas you sent him."

Joe nodded. "I'm sorry you had to find him."

"I'm not. I'm glad it was me ... I sat with him a long time."

"Too bad it was on your birthday and everything."

She shrugged. "You know how I feel about birthdays and holidays. Cancer sure had a way of sucking all the fun out of them. Seems like having some special day roll around is a sure-fire way to provoke the angry gods of tragedy."

Joe turned to her and stroked the hair from her face. "You're a good girl, Leila. You deserved a whole lot better."

"Well, so did Artie. And you. And my dad. Life just doesn't seem to dish out according to what's deserved."

"Baby, you're too young to be saying stuff like that. Sounds like you been hanging around too many old blues musicians."

"No doubt." She moved toward Artie's guitar, leaning in the corner. "C'mon, let's go out in the living room."

She grabbed the guitar and perched it in the chair opposite the sofa where they both sat. Strings poked out of its headstock like cat whiskers, and the finish on its body had worn through like old floorboards under a rocker.

Joe yawned. "You better go on up and get some sleep, or you won't be able to get out of bed for school tomorrow."

"I'm not going to school tomorrow. I'm going to hang out with you."

"They'll be no hanging out tomorrow. I am completely beat, and I won't be getting out of bed till you get home from school. Then you can come on down and we'll do some stuff."

"Fine."

🐚 WHEN LEILA PULLED INTO THE DRIVEWAY AFTER school, Joe's Town car drove up to the curb after her. She dashed to his car door as he swung it wide open.

"You said you were going to wait for me." She grabbed him by the arm and snuggled closer.

He drew in a long nasally sniff and took her by the waist. "It was just a bunch of funeral stuff. You sure didn't need to be there for that."

"Yeah, I guess." They walked arm in arm to the house.

"What do you say I take you out for dinner? How would you like that? Eighteen is legal in New York, and I know a real nice little club in the Village."

"But I have no club clothes."

"Then first we'll stop at the mall and do some shopping."

She ended up with a sleek black dress, a pair of strappy sandals, and a cropped, black angora cardigan. She wore them like a Parisian model.

Nine o'clock found them seated in a smoky little offbeat joint whose reputation for innovative jazz had made its way to the Amsterdam night scene. While Joe seemed impressed with the club, the music, and musicians, to Leila it seemed like any other establishment they had ever played at. And the food wasn't all that great. She ordered her first legal beer. She would have ordered a nice burgundy wine, but that was her thing with Clarence. After dinner, and when the band took their break, Joe leaned to her ear.

"You okay for a minute?"

"Yeah, why?"

"Gotta make a pit stop." He came to his feet.

"Sure thing."

He walked through the haze and entered a narrow corridor, then disappeared. She lifted her beer bottle and wiped a wet ring from the table as a swarthy man with gold chains wove his way through the crowd toward her; she pulled her sweater tighter around, folded her arms, and slumped back into the seat with a scowl. He threw up a hand and detoured to the bar. Anyone who looked as if he might even think of approaching warranted the same deterring grimace. By the time Joe reappeared fifteen minutes later, she had picked the label clean off her beer bottle.

She sat upright as he walked to the table, rubbing his nose. She knew what that meant.

She glared. "I guess you must have really had to go."

"Yeah. Yeah, right." He talked fast. "And I ran into the

bassist—sorry I took so long. You been okay, right?"

"Yeah. I'm always okay," she said, miffed.

When he settled back into his seat, apparently unaffected by her mood change, she asked, "So what time's the funeral tomorrow?"

"Uh … right. Um, seven."

"Is your mom coming?"

He blew out a long breath. "Don't know. Said she'd try."

"So, you've been talking to her?"

"Once in a while."

"Do you even want her to come?"

"Don't matter to me."

"So, what was really the deal between Artie and her—how did they end up together?"

Joe stared at her for a moment and sank further into his seat. He folded his arms to match hers. "Oh, I guess you're old enough to hear about that." He let out a quick exhale and pinched the bridge of his nose. "She was twenty-five and a beautiful, proper Southern white girl who didn't like her daddy much. Best way to get even with a bigoted old rich man is to get tangled up with some older black dude who plays guitar for a living."

"Did she love Artie?"

He shrugged. "Who knows? Ol' Artie sure thought so."

"You didn't see her much when you were growing up."

"She passed me off to some fine Negro family in Delaware—came to see me every now and again. I didn't really get that she was my mom till later. I started acting up around then. She moved me to Artie's when I was 10." Joe stared off, rapidly tapping the table. His watery eyes darted. Leila didn't want to rake up bad memories.

"Is there as much prejudice in Europe?" she asked.

"Sure. But it's way different. They don't got the Southern issue we got here."

"Makes me mad."

A wide grin flashed across his face. "Don't be mad, Baby. Life is good—life is *real* good."

🐉 AS MYLES UNDERSTOOD IT, THERE WOULD BE neither sermon nor eulogy. Leila had explained that the service would be played out later, at Artie's place, with his friends. The old man had only one last wish—that an angel scatter his ashes on the Mississippi Delta.

Myles stepped through the funeral home doorway. Leila stood beside a tall stranger in an expensive-looking suit. Not quite what he had expected of the typical down-and-out blues musician. Myles adjusted his own silk tie as he strode toward the couple in front of a large bouquet beside a plain alabaster urn. Leila smiled at him. He had promised he would be nice to Joe, and he was determined to follow through.

Joe extended his hand and greeted him first. "Mr. Myles, I've heard so much about you."

Myles shook his hand. "I'm terribly sorry for your loss."

"Thank you."

Myles bent to kiss Leila's cheek and squeezed her shoulder.

"This is new," he said, looking her up and down. She appeared to have transformed from a girl into a woman.

"Do you like it?"

"It's far different than I'm accustomed to. But yes, it's lovely. You look lovely."

Joe spoke up. "I understand you're a jazz and blues aficionado."

Myles nodded.

"I hope you'll come by Artie's place right after we're done here."

Myles was about to decline when Leila begged, "Oh, please come."

"Perhaps for a few minutes." He looked directly at Joe. "How long will you be staying in the States?"

"I leave a week from Monday, just long enough to go through Artie's things and get the house on the market." He glanced at Leila. "Of course I won't set any closing dates till Leila has graduated."

At that moment, a small group of old men, mostly black

and Hispanic, entered and made their way toward Joe and Leila. Myles made to step aside, but Leila grabbed his hand, keeping him close. He didn't mind the gesture; in fact the naturalness of it surprised him. She kept her hand in his as she introduced Buddy, Pedro, and Artie's other regulars. Each offered their sympathies and huddled around the flowers. Shortly thereafter, Kyle entered with Micah and the Tailgate's bassist, bringing a smile to Leila's face. She introduced them to Joe, who extended the same invitation for afterward.

Myles remained quiet, scanning the room and its occupants. Might Ian show up? He supposed it didn't matter—the school board's prohibitions had little teeth at this point, and his own ambivalence toward Ian Brigham waned. Just the same he stood guard, and when Ian appeared in the draped doorway, Myles moved closer to Leila.

Ian walked down the center aisle, his line of sight firmly set on Leila. She let go of Myles' grip and stepped forward as Ian took her hand and whispered her name, keeping a respectable distance between them. Her chin quivered.

"I'm so sorry," Ian said. "I know how much you cared for Artie."

Myles passed Leila his handkerchief. Looking him in the eye, Ian extended his hand. "Myles."

"Brigham." Myles had difficulty rousing enough animosity to intensify his grip.

Joe stepped forward. Myles introduced the two men. Joe accepted Ian's hand and offered the same invitation for later. Ian hesitated. Leila's eyes begged yes.

"I'm honored," Ian said. "Thank you."

Myles shifted with annoyance as nearby Buddy talked loudly, recounting old tales. Pedro nudged the old codger, quieting him as all eyes turned toward the entryway. There paused a white-haired, fair-skinned woman. As she sauntered toward them, her swank navy-blue pantsuit played off her coral blouse. She tucked her bobbed hair behind her ear. The boys parted, making Joe and Leila more accessible. Standing before Joe, the woman clutched his hand in a lady-like manner. All were silent. Only Joe and Buddy seemed to know exactly who she was, though Myles had his suspicions.

Joe accepted a glancing kiss on the cheek. "Angela. I'm glad you came."

"Hello, Joseph," she said with a demure smile and dancing eyes.

She then turned to Buddy. "It's been such a long time ...." Her voice lilted with a distinctly southern accent. "How are you, Buddy?"

"Just fine, miss. And you sure look fine."

Smiling with more ease than politeness dictated, she brushed his sleeve since he did not offer his hand.

"Angela," Joe said, "this is Leila."

She stepped in front of Leila and slowly looked her over.

"Leila, this is—my mother. Miss Angela Phillips."

Leila grasped the woman's extended hand. "I'm very pleased to meet you."

A brief smile passed over Miss Phillips' face as she lingered with Leila's hand in hers and crooned, "Hmm ... you are lovely. I'm so pleased to meet you."

As soon as Myles caught her eye, she turned her attention to him. "And who is this gentleman?"

Myles did not have to force a smile, though he felt the need to subdue it. Angela was quite lovely, perhaps not much older than he was. When she smiled, it was hard for him to take his eyes off her. Something in her reserved manner seemed to be suppressing a liveliness, which beamed from her eyes.

Leila spoke up. "Miss Phillips, this is Clarence Myles. My guardian."

Myles took her hand—she placing hers on his in such a way that it was quite natural for him to bring her fingertips to his lips. Miss Phillips seemed surprised yet pleased.

"It's a pleasure to meet you, Miss Phillips," he said, enjoying the twinkle in her eyes.

"Please. Do call me Angela." She studied his face and

then glanced back at Leila. "Your *guardian*?"

"Yes. It's complicated."

"Life can be that way," she smiled wistfully and returned her gaze to Myles. A dimple appeared on each cheek. "I believe every girl should have a guardian—at least for a little while."

She lingered in his sight and then returned her attention to Leila. "Please, dear, let's sit."

Taking Leila by the hand, Miss Phillips led her to the front row of chairs.

"Angela—my mother—has come to take Artie's remains back to Natchez so they can be scattered by the Mississippi," Joe said, as Myles, still standing off to the side and eavesdropping, watched Leila and Angela. They sat symmetrically, facing each other. Their thighs tapered and met where each pair of hands neatly clasped their knees. The only gestures were in their corresponding facial expressions, each seeming to mimic the other, like matching bookends.

He looked at his watch. It was finally eight o'clock.

Joe picked up the urn and approached Angela. She rose to accept it.

"Thank you for coming, Angela. Are you sure you won't come back to the house?"

"As much as I would love to—" she glanced at Myles, "I have an early flight and I'm terribly exhausted. But I'll talk to you soon."

Joe kissed her and took Leila by the arm. Myles, having caught the woman's glance, came toward her.

"Allow me." He took the urn and offered his arm.

"Why, thank you, Clarence."

He did not mind her familiarity—he rather enjoyed it—and escorted her to the curb where she had parked a Mercedes Benz. She unlocked the front passenger door and stepped aside, allowing Clarence to open it.

"On the seat, if you wouldn't mind," she said.

Having placed Artie's remains as she wished, Myles pulled the seat belt to secure it. With an acknowledging nod to Artie Sparks—old Black & Bluesy—he closed the door and escorted Angela to the driver's side. He assisted her from the curb to the street. Her blue eyes smiled before her lips curled and extended.

"Why, Mr. Myles," she lilted, "I lament that I will not have the opportunity to know you better."

Lamentable indeed! "It's been a pleasure. Brief, but a pleasure nonetheless." He took her hand and again brought it to his lips with his eyes on her.

For the first time she offered a broad and beautiful smile that took him by surprise. They lingered a moment longer before he closed the door behind her. He wondered at the anomaly of emotion she evoked. As she drove off, he regretted the opportunity slipping away.

⟋⟍LEILA SAT ON THE PIANO BENCH, HER HANDS TUCKED beneath her thighs, surrounded by her people. Joe sat with Kyle and Buddy on the sofa, tuning his guitar. Micah and the Tailgate's bassist talked music with Pedro and the other old men. Myles poised himself near the exit. Ian stood in the kitchen doorway, drawing Leila's attention. Her cheeks burned.

Buddy had just finished adjusting the amp, the one Artie never got around to fixing. One of the boys rolled his fingers on the bongos as Joe looked at Ian, whose focus now shifted. Joe set his guitar aside and picked up Artie's, inviting Ian to sit beside him and take up his own guitar. Ian joined him.

Joe played an initial riff. "You know Robert's 'Cross Road Blues'?"

Ian nodded. "I do."

It was "Crossroads" that had been playing from Ian's Saab the day Leila and he first met. Had it not been that song at that moment, she surely would have refused Ian's assistance. When he looked up at her, she knew he was remembering, too. "Crossroads"—the irony of the title!

"One of Artie's favorites—" Joe smiled wistfully, sniffed, and began again, singing the verses. He played solo for the first refrain and then Ian joined in. Before long, all were adding their bit; except Leila. She could not bring herself to play, she just listened and remembered the first time she sat like this, sketching Artie as he noodled and grinned with his big new teeth. That very sketch now sat framed atop the piano.

All but Kyle—who sat off to the side, face drawn—played for about ten minutes. Myles caught Leila's eye and flashed a look toward the door. As he opened it, she rose and stepped outside with him.

"Thanks for sticking around for a few minutes." She squeezed his hand.

"I wouldn't have missed it."

"Yes you would have. But you did it for me, and I appreciate it." She smiled impishly. "At least the entire evening wasn't a complete bore for you."

"And what do you mean by that?"

"You seemed to enjoy Miss Angela Phillips."

"She was captivating."

"But I thought you liked Valerie Jennings."

"Oh, Leila," he patted her shoulder, "you have so much to learn about men."

"What—that all men are pigs?"

"That is a very derogatory way to put it—but yes."

"It's not really true though, is it?"

"That, my little Leila, is a discussion for another time."

CHAPTER 30

THE POURING RAIN WAS BAD ENOUGH, BUT LEILA fatigued quicker than usual on her run home. Last night, she had heard Joe downstairs, thumping around in Artie's room. He kept the strangest hours—jet lag, she assumed—but it had robbed her of sleep. This morning, when only a gentle rain fell, she found him sprawled out on the sofa, rousing only when she kissed his cheek.

Now, the darkened sky poured rain that streamed from her hooded poncho. She stepped onto the front stoop, shaking her rain gear and peeling it off as she opened the door. Thunder clamored as the door shut. Tossing aside her wet things, she rushed up behind Joe on the sofa and threw her arms around his neck in an embrace. He jumped.

"Sorry." She tucked her chin in the crook of his neck. "Didn't mean to startle you."

He held a lavender-colored paper in his hand and a picture in his other. She squinted—the photo seemed vaguely familiar.

"What are those, Joe?" She flew around the sofa to his side. Now she recognized her own face as a baby—and the woman holding her. "Is that me? Is that my mother? Where did you get that?"

He pushed her away and groaned, trying to tuck the folded notepaper under his thigh.

"What was that?" She reached to grab it as he tightened his grip. "What is it? Let me see."

"No, Leila … Baby."

Papers on the table distracted her and she relented, snatching a photograph from atop them. Two women. Her heart pounded. "Is this my mother? Where did you get this?"

Joe said nothing.

She refocused on the lavender paper in his hand. "Give me that," she demanded, pulling it free from his tight grip.

"No, Leila … Baby. Let me explain first."

"No." She yanked herself from his grasp and came to her feet, glaring at him. Unfolding the paper, she looked again at the photograph and then began reading.

> *My Dearest Joe,*
> *It has been such a terrible struggle for me, and I'm sure for you too, but I can't seem to escape what I'm about to do. Perhaps you've suspected it all along, but I feel I need to tell you myself, now before I go, that Leila Mae is your little girl …*

Leila's heart stopped. Her breath evaporated as Joe reached for her and the note. "Baby, wait!"

She shoved him away and continued reading under her breath.

> *… I know you remember when it happened. I was never with Marc that night, and I know that I have thought about it every day since then. I tried to pull myself together—you don't know how hard I've tried. And not just once—over and over again. And now I'm just so tired, and I can't stand the pain anymore.*

Joe touched her shoulder. She flinched with fury. "Don't!" Through blurring vision, she continued reading …

> *I have always loved you as much as Marc, I think sometimes more. I am so sorry for all the pain I have caused—please forgive me and kiss our baby for me. I will love you both, always.*
>
> *Marilyn*

Leila caught enough breath to say, "This isn't from my mother. Who wrote this?"

"Leila ...."

"Who wrote it? Did you?"

"Leila, no—you know I'd never do that." His eyes welled. "Your mother did write it ... I'm so sorry."

Her disbelief turned to anger. "Where did this come from?"

"A friend of your mother's—I only found it and these other papers just now, unopened—Artie must have misplaced the envelope."

"What does this letter mean? Why did she write it?"

"She was messed up."

Tears streamed down her overheated face. "She killed herself? This is a suicide note?"

"Baby ...."

"It's not true ... She never slept with you .... You're not my father!"

He hung his head and looked away, saying nothing.

She yanked him to face her. "Is it true, Joe?"

He stood motionless, anguish distorting his face.

"You both lied to me!" She shook the letter at him. "You did this to her! You turned my mother into a whore!"

She flung around, grabbed her poncho. The door slammed behind her.

🌴IAN'S ANXIETY INCREASED ALONG WITH THE DRIVING rain. His wipers beat frantically. Bolts of lightning out over the Atlantic increased in frequency, turning his concern for Leila's state of mind into worry for her safety. Nearly forty-five minutes had passed since he left his house after a call from Myles who had just received a call from Joe Phillips. As Ian advanced toward the second causeway bridge, he hoped for Leila's predictability.

He approached the parking lot where her solitary Bug parked in her usual spot. He pulled in on her driver's side. She was nowhere in sight. Zipping his hooded rain slicker, he headed against the wind, toward the oceanside path. Rain pelted his face, more raw than cold. From the top of the dune, Ian scanned from east to west. With visibility less than three-quarters of a mile, he headed east where he had once found her.

The surf was high. Rain poured in sheets over the dark churning sea that merged with the sky, splitting as lightening streaked across it. Rumbling thunder followed. His breath mingled with precipitation as he ran nearly half the length of the beach. The rain had let up just enough to discern her sitting figure in drab green amidst the grassy dunes. Leila's body moved in a heaving rhythm as she sobbed. He approached and called her name. She did not respond.

"Leila," he repeated as he crouched beside her, his hand on her shoulder. She startled violently.

Her red face and eyes contorted with anguish. She shrugged him off.

"Leila." He replaced his hand. "Let's get out of here before the storm rolls around again."

"I'm not going anywhere," she cried, burying her face.

He sat close beside her. She recoiled with a jerk.

"Leila, it's not safe to be out here. Let's go back and sit in the car."

"*You* go sit in the car if you want," she shot back through her tears. "*I'm* not going anywhere."

"And I'm not going anywhere without you." Lightning flashed again. He cringed at the instantaneous thunder. "Let's just go to the car and talk."

She threw her head back as a gust of wind caught her hood and whipped it behind her. She burst out, "Talk!— Talking isn't going to change anything—it won't bring my father back. It won't change the fact that my mother was a junkie whore—and it won't bring *her* back either." Her breathing deepened and quickened, her face now colorless.

He moved to put his arm around her. She shoved him away.

"Don't touch me—" She wept into her hands.

Hoping to stall hysteria, he stroked her back.

"Get away from me!" she gasped.

"Just calm down, stop breathing so fast. *Slow down*."

Sobbing out of control, she could barely articulate, "I think I'm losing my mind—" she panted "—I feel so—so—I'm losing my mind—"

"You're not losing your mind. You're hyperventilating. Slow down."

"I can't!"

Rain returned in a torrent.

"Put your head between your knees."

With unexpected obedience, she parted her legs and plunged her head into her lap, then threw herself back. "—I can't breathe."

Pulling his raincoat off, he made a pouch from the hood and cupped it in front of her. "Put your face in it."

She resisted at first but then submitted, placing her mouth over the hood. He massaged her neck and the back of her head. In a second, she pulled up, throwing her head back.

Thoroughly drenched, Ian grabbed his slicker and came to his feet, slipping his arms back into it.

"You need to get moving to use up your oxygen—come on. It's time to run." Grabbing her hand before she had a chance to resist, he pulled her lethargic body up. Once standing, her defiance returned. He gripped her tighter, moving her forward.

"Come on—" he said, jogging toward the firm sand nearer the shore, heading west with her beside him.

They ran together, nearing the path back to the parking lot when an earsplitting peal of thunder and simultaneous bolt of lightning touched down on the beach ahead of them. Like a violent slap in the face, it jarred them, leaving his ears ringing. They stopped in their tracks.

"No more running, Leila."

He prodded her up the dune and down the other side.

As they neared her car, he kept her moving. "Where are your keys?"

She shook her head, searching her pockets beneath her poncho. Spotting them in her ignition, he reached her car first, flung the door open and pulled the keys.

As he straightened, she grabbed at him. "Give me my keys!"

"I'm not letting you drive, Leila. We'll come back for your car tomorrow." He reached behind himself to open his front passenger door. "I'm taking you home."

"I am *not* going back there. Now *give* me my keys!" She tried to pry them from his tight grip.

"Fine," he said, exasperated. "We don't need to go back to your place, we can just spend the entire night right here."

"I've got a better idea. Why don't we just go back to your place! Isn't that all you really want anyway? Isn't that why you're really here? Hoping that I'm just like my mother, all screwed up and willing to do it with anyone?" Her nostrils flared. "Why don't we just climb in the back seat and do it right here?"

He recoiled. She covered her face and whirled around, then rushed toward her car. Ian grabbed her arm. She yanked herself free.

"Leila, don't be difficult—just get in and let's go." He gripped both her shoulders from behind, maneuvering her toward the car as Leila drove her elbow, full force into his ribs. He gasped, releasing her. Without breath, he bent over, bracing himself on his car. "Jeez, Leila."

She whirled toward him, and again bringing her hands to her face, she sobbed.

He winced and stepped forward, pulling her into his embrace. She sobbed and, without a fight, dropped into the seat. He pressed the lock button, shut her door, and then locked up the Volkswagen. Wringing water from his hair to the pavement, he slipped into his seat and shut his door. She wilted as he sat back and sighed. His ribcage ached. He tried to take her hand, but she withdrew, slumping into the door.

As they crossed the bridge, rain streamed down his windshield. Ian's head pounded along with the wipers.

"I'll take you to Myles' house. I'm sure you can spend the night there."

🌿 "CUT THE CRAP, PHILLIPS." MYLES SPOKE INTO HIS phone. "What did her mother confess? That you're Leila's father?" It was not an imaginative deduction. The similarity between Angela Phillips and Leila sparked the possibility that there might have been added reasons why Angela had shown up and seemed especially preoccupied with Leila.

"Yes," Joe finally admitted. "I always wondered, but the letter confirmed it."

"Well, that's helpful information. I'll let you know if I hear anything."

George the cat wound herself around Myles' legs until he lifted her to his shoulder.

"Yes, I know," he said as headlights rounded the corner and pulled into his driveway. He breathed relief as Ian opened the passenger door and Leila climbed out. "Looks like we have company."

He set her down. As the front door opened, the cat scampered to her hiding place.

Stepping in, Leila would barely meet Myles' eyes. His attention turned to sopping and vanquished Ian.

"I told her she could stay here tonight." Ian said without any hint of apology.

Having already anticipated that possibility, and scrambling for at least some semblance of propriety—when in fact all propriety was null the moment he allowed both Leila and Ian into his home—Myles said, "Indeed. And of course, you will also be staying."

At least, if he were called on it, Leila and he would not be spending the night alone, as if Ian qualified as any sort of chaperone. Oh, the irony of it!

Pulling hair from his face, Ian raised a reluctant brow and removed his wet sneakers and socks.

Myles pulled the poncho over Leila's head and hung it on the rack. "You're soaked."

"I'm just damp," she said, squeezing a drip from her braid.

Myles led her to his bedroom, behind the staircase and pulled two T-shirts from his dresser drawer. He passed one to Leila. "Put this on and come on out to the kitchen."

Myles tossed the other shirt to Ian in the open dining area and gestured for him to follow. Leila joined them.

"Sit." Myles dragged a tall chair toward the end of the butcher-block island.

Leila sat, staring at the floor.

"Get those wet things off her feet," he said, stepping into the adjoining laundry room, and grabbed towels.

"I can take care of my own feet," Leila snapped as he handed her a towel. Ian threw his hands up and backed off. As she removed her own shoes, Ian pulled his shirt overhead. A patch of purplish-red welted above his ribs. Apparently, it had been no easy task getting Leila there.

Grabbing the phone from the wall mount, Myles dialed Joe and then Kyle from the privacy of the living room. When he returned to the kitchen, shirted Ian sat staring off into mid-space. He appeared nearly as dazed as Leila. Neither would look at the other. It was not difficult to imagine what had transpired. Myles faced them both from his side of the island. Ian slumped back in his seat and met his stare, shaking his head.

Myles reached for his wine rack, pulling a dark green bottle, and set it on the butcher block. With the cork dislodged, he retrieved three crystal goblets. After pouring, he set the bottle in front of Leila. The label faced her.

"Gevrey-Chambertin," he said to her. "Do you remember?"

It took a moment, but she reached for her glass and sipped, swishing the wine in her mouth the way he had taught her. "Yes. I remember."

"Good then. Enjoy."

Ian sipped with a nod. "This is really good."

"Yes. It is." *It better be for the price of it!*

Sipping his own wine, Myles studied Leila, contemplating

his next tactic. Sharing wine could soften an adversary. Breaking bread would level her wall of resistance.

Myles placed a wedge of Brie cheese on the counter. He would allow a few minutes to take the chill off it and Leila. Meanwhile, he handed Leila a long crusty French baguette and refilled her glass.

He said, "Tear off a piece and give it to Ian."

Ian looked perplexed. Leila squinted at Myles but obeyed. Having pulled off a small portion, she begrudgingly pushed the remaining loaf toward Ian, refusing to look at him.

"No," Myles said. "Give him the piece you intended for yourself."

She frowned at Ian and shoved the bit of bread toward him.

Myles now held out a knife. "Spread cheese on it for him."

She pushed his hand away. "He can spread his own cheese."

Myles grabbed her hand, pressing the knife to her palm. "Do it."

She accepted the knife and dug off a clump of rind and cheese, then smashed it onto his bread. "There!"

"Now hand it to him."

She hesitated.

"Trust me," he said.

As soon as she picked it up, her eyes met Ian's and filled with tears. He didn't take the bread right away but kept his gaze upon her.

"Here," she said, her hard face flinching. "I'm ... I'm so sorry I said those things ...."

"Leila ...," Ian said.

She wiped her face. "... and I'm sorry I hurt you."

Ian half-smirked. "I should have seen that coming—but I'll be fine."

Myles next served Leila and finally himself. He then returned to the refrigerator and pulled leftover Beef Wellington, some mayonnaise, and Dijon mustard. He set them in front of Ian. "You must be hungry."

"Yes. Thank you."

When Leila finally emptied her glass, she was primed.

Myles waited patiently. Meeting his eyes, she thrust her hand in her pocket and pulled out a lavender paper. She laid it before him.

Perching his reading glasses, he read it, careful not to react. He then passed it to Ian.

"I'm very sorry about your mother," Myles said, his hand on hers.

Ian's eyes grew wide as he read. "How is that possible?"

Myles cocked his brow. "You did see her grandmother, didn't you?"

"Of course."

Leila slumped back into her seat, her eyes heavy.

"How did you come across this?" Myles asked.

"Joe was reading it when I got home from school. I guess some friend of my mother sent it—only Artie must have misplaced it or something. I'm not sure." She yawned. "I don't want to talk about it tonight—I'm so tired. I want to sleep."

"Of course. I'll get you some pajamas."

Myles led her back to his bedroom and showed her the adjoining bathroom. Laying a pair of his own pajamas at the foot of the bed, he said, "Bring your wet clothes out when you're done."

When Myles emerged from the bedroom, he invited Ian to sit at the dining room table.

"Do you want ice for your ribs?" Myles asked.

"Nah."

"I hope you won't be too uncomfortable tonight."

Ian glanced up from his plate but said nothing.

Myles sighed. "Ironic."

"No kidding."

At that moment, Leila stepped into the room. Myles collected her armful of clothes as she laid a photograph on the table.

"It's my mother and her friend," she said as he exited.

When he returned, Ian passed the photo, pointing to the figure on the right.

Myles adjusted his readers and squinted, then tipped it

toward better light. He flipped the photo over and read *Me and BJ*. All at once, Myles' breath left him, and all warmth drained from his temples down. "Where did you get this?"

Leila replied, "It was with the note and some other papers that came with it."

He flipped back to the images and nearly choked. "Time for bed, Leila."

She offered a half-smile and returned to the bedroom, closing the door behind her.

Myles rubbed his eyes—he couldn't believe what he was looking at. It couldn't be true.

"What's wrong?" Ian asked.

Myles' focus darted from the picture to his keys on the entryway table. "Stay here. I'll be right back."

"Where are you going?"

He hustled to the door. "Just stay here. I'll be back in a half hour."

Before Ian could protest, Myles was out the door and headed south. He would not allow himself to indulge in frivolous speculation as he sped to Artie's old apartment.

CLARENCE SAT IN HIS DRIVEWAY FOR A MINUTE, pulling himself together. He stared at the large envelope for a moment before peering inside. His heart pounded as he patted his shirt pocket. He had forgotten his readers inside. He sighed and tucked the envelope under his raincoat and dashed for the porch.

When he came through the door, Ian stood in front of Myles' music selection, in his boxer shorts and T-shirt. The dryer hummed in the background. Myles glared and Ian headed toward the laundry room.

Standing at the maple island, Myles emptied the envelope, spreading the papers under the bright lights. Several drawings, a picture of Marilynn and Leila, and another letter.

As Clarence read the first line, *My name is BJ Kerns. I was a good friend of Marilynn for a few years*, his heart burst. Bonnie Jane.

He read quickly …

> *… I met her in rehab in Oregon, and she told me all about you and her little girl, Leila. It took some time to track down an address for you. I'm so sorry to have to inform you, nine months after the fact, that Marilynn took her life on February 1, 1976. I just want you to know that she tried very hard, but she just couldn't seem to stay clean. It finally got the best of her.*
>
> *I know she wanted you to have this letter, and these other things are all of what she left behind. I thought you should have them also. I'm very sorry to have to bring this bad news to you, and if you want to talk to me about it, you can call me or write to me at the address and phone number below.*
>
> *Again, I'm so sorry,*
> *BJ*

Myles swallowed, choking down the knot in his throat.

Ian entered the room wearing jeans as Myles snatched the envelope and inspected the return address and postmark.

"October 26, 1976." He looked up at Ian. "Only one-and-a-half years ago."

Ian glanced at the pictures and letter. "What am I missing?"

Myles spoke but not so much to Ian. "BJ is my Bonnie Jane. Kerns is her mother's maiden name."

Controlling his emotion and imagination, Clarence considered dialing the phone number. But what if no one answered or the number belonged to someone else now? And what if she did answer? He was unprepared for that. He then pulled his wallet from his hip pocket, checking his watch. Six o'clock, California time. He removed a well-worn card and dialed the telephone. He waited and prayed. Finally, an answer.

"It's Clarence Myles … Yes, it has—listen, I have recent information on my daughter … yes, Bonnie … a telephone number and address. Also an associate … No, I haven't—I was hoping you would …." He then relayed all of the information. "Yes, as soon as you know anything, please."

When he turned to hang up the telephone, Leila stood in the shadows of the doorway. She stepped forward.

She looked at him with puzzlement. "I thought your daughter was dead."

"I never said she was dead."

"Yes, but—"

"I simply didn't know. I've been preparing for the worst for years. This is the only glimmer I've had that she might still be alive."

Leila moved to the counter and looked at the letter, and then the picture. "BJ is your daughter?"

Myles nodded. "Yes. I'm sure of it."

With tears in her eyes, she stared at him. "Clarence ...."

She approached. Slipping her arms around his waist, she held him tightly, crying softly into his chest. It was beyond his control to do anything but reciprocate as he pressed his chin to her head, stroking her hair. His vision blurred. When Leila finally pulled away, Ian had left the room.

"You should get some rest," he whispered.

"Tuck me in."

As she slid between the sheets, he pulled them up under her chin and kissed her forehead.

"I love you, Clarence," she said in a sleepy voice.

He whispered back, "And I love you ...."

❧ IAN TOPPED OFF HIS WINE GLASS AND WANDERED back to Myles' album collection. He couldn't remember a more awkward time than when Leila and Myles shared their little moment. Ian scanned the room as he had earlier. Everything was meticulous and tasteful. No articles of clothing or messy stacks of paper out of place. No film of dust on the polished furniture. And no photographs. He liked Myles' house and his taste in furnishings. Even more, he liked his sound system. How could a schoolteacher afford a state-of-the-art stereo and expensive bottles of wine? There was obviously money, but one would never know it to look at him or the old Volvo he drove. Perhaps it was simply that Clarence Myles chose to spend his money on only a few things in which he placed value. Music, food, and his cloistered environment.

Ian dropped into an old Mission rocker opposite what was obviously Myles' own chair. He swallowed the last of his wine and pulled at his neck muscles. His side throbbed. In a few days, the welt would be a substantial bruise. He sighed, wishing he could just turn in—if only he knew where he would be sleeping.

Just then, Myles returned and went to the liquor cabinet. He pulled out a bottle of Hennessy cognac and poured a little into two snifters. Without a word, he passed one to Ian. Then, setting the needle on a record as the turntable revolved, some mellow jazz began playing. He finally took his seat in his leather chair.

Ian said nothing. It wasn't that he was uninterested, he was simply too spent to pry. They exchanged nothing more than pensive looks until Ian emptied his drink.

Myles spoke up. "Pretty rough going with Leila, today?"

"Yeah ... you could say that."

Myles stared at him, his eyes calculating. "You do realize it's not too late for you to back out."

"Why would I back out?"

"Leila is not going to be an easy young woman."

"I realize that."

"The question is ... are you man enough to do the right thing by her?"

Ian did not flinch. He felt no compunction nor any need to explain or justify his feelings for Leila or any of his decisions. If Myles wanted to spar, he wouldn't find a participant in Ian.

Ian rose, gesturing toward the stairs. "Where to?"

"Upstairs to the left. Bathroom's the middle door."

CHAPTER 31

LEILA WOKE TO THE AROMA OF STRONG COFFEE AND muffled voices. It took a moment to remember where she was, and even then, to believe she was lying in Mr. Myles' bed. As she rolled over, hugging the pillow, her body ached and her mind spun. The little girl in her wanted to stay wrapped in the security of Clarence Myles, but the young woman felt disconcerted in a man's bed. She lingered for only a moment, collecting fragments of yesterday's upheaval. When Leila stepped through the bedroom door and into the kitchen, she squinted in the bright light, rubbing her eyes.

"Good morning," Myles said.

Myles' pajamas hung from her shoulders and past her fingertips. She forced a half-smile as she glanced from him to Ian, trying to smooth what little remained of her braid. "I need my clothes and a comb or something."

As Myles retrieved her things from the laundry room, Leila avoided Ian's stare. Flashes of memory continued to swirl. The letter. Harsh words with Joe. Myles' discovery. And how badly she had treated Ian.

Ian downed the last of his coffee and rose as Myles stepped back into the room. He handed Leila the folded clothing, a comb, and a toothbrush.

"I have an appointment. I'll let myself out." Ian stepped past Leila in the doorway. Glancing at her, he offered a subdued smile.

She followed to where he sat on the steps tying shoelaces. Standing before him, she hugged her clean laundry, absorbing the warmth and scent of Clarence's home.

He paused with a sigh and met her gaze.

"I wish you hadn't seen me like this. And the way I was yesterday …," she began. "I wouldn't blame you if—"

"If what? If I decided to bail on you? If I decided I wanted to back out? That maybe you no longer interest me?"

She said nothing, but that was what she had been thinking.

"Well, either you have far worse problems than you're letting on, or you think I'm so emotionally inept that I don't realize people are complicated and come with baggage. Is that what you think?"

"It's just that I was so mean to you. And said awful things."

"I didn't take it personally and I won't unless you want me to."

"No … I would just rather you forget that yesterday ever happened."

"Well, I have no intention of forgetting it. I pay attention to everything. Every interaction I have with you teaches me something about you and helps me understand you better." He stood. "You know, you're not the only one with baggage. You might actually want to ask yourself if *I'm* the person *you* want to be involved with."

How could he have any worse baggage than she had?

Looking into her eyes, he tucked stray hairs behind her ear.

"I gotta go." He kissed her cheek and left.

Leila dressed and then returned to the kitchen. Myles stood at the range, sautéing onions and mushrooms. He asked, "How did you sleep?"

"I don't remember. How about you?"

"Not a wink." He cracked several eggs into a bowl.

"I guess you were probably thinking about your daughter."

He nodded, beating the eggs and then dumping them into

the pan

"Could I ask you a question, Clarence?"

"You may."

"Why would your daughter—Bonnie—not contact you for all these years? I mean, if she was all messed up on drugs and stuff, I guess that would sort of make sense. But it sounds like she was clean. At least a year-and-a-half ago. Why wouldn't she call you or something?"

Myles remained silent as he flipped an omelet and laid plates before them. "Toast?"

"No, thank you." She waited.

He cleared his throat. "I suppose there are several possibilities. It might be the distorted things her mother told her. Or the drugs may have scrambled her brain." He looked at Leila as he placed the omelet neatly on her plate with a sprig of parsley beside it. "Or ... it could just be me."

She breathed in the aroma. "I was wondering if she's sort of like you in some ways."

"What do you mean?"

"I mean, does she have really high expectations about other people and herself?"

"I don't know. I never really got to know her."

"Well, how old was she when you divorced?"

"She was thirteen. Unfortunately, we were never particularly close. I guess we never really clicked as father and daughter."

She took a bite. "But she probably knows what you're like."

He swallowed. "What? That I'm *difficult*?"

She did not want to agree so readily. "You know, ever since I found out that you had a kid—who I thought was dead—I sort of wondered if that's what made you, you know, the way you are. But now, I wonder if you've just always been this way. I just wonder, 'cause if Bonnie knows you aren't easy to please, maybe she figured that she wasn't good enough yet."

🐦 MYLES READ THE NO OVERNIGHT PARKING SIGN AS
they pulled into the state park lot. When they climbed out of
his Volvo, he snatched the ticket from her windshield and
pocketed it.

"Let's walk the beach," he said.

It was Saturday, and many people sat or walked the shore,
but none ventured into the frigid water. At Leila's direction,
they headed west. Myles' windbreaker billowed as he tucked
his hands in his pockets. She locked her arm in his. After a
mile or so of silence, they stood, looking out beyond the
crashing waves. He had been trying to round up courage
enough to risk a question. "Leila, may I ask you something?"

"Sure."

"You once asked of me what it was I liked about you. I'd
like to ask the same question."

"You want to know what *I* like about *you*?"

He swallowed with difficulty. "Yes."

She seemed to be weighing her words, taking longer than
his comfort allowed. "I like your honesty. I like that you
understand human nature—I like that a lot. You're very wise.
And you know how to give in. I think you're very generous."
She glanced at him sideways. "It's just that being your friend
requires a lot of patience. But I don't think that's a bad thing.
You're seriously worth it."

Myles nodded. He appreciated her honesty. He also hoped
Bonnie might someday feel the same way.

Leila leaned into him and squeezed his arm. After a
minute, she asked, "So, did you ever go looking for her?"

"Of course. After I reported her missing, and when her
trail turned up cold, I hired a private investigator.
Occasionally a dead body would turn up, but thankfully, it
was never Bonnie. Eventually I just started expecting that
one day it would be her. A couple times there were hopeful
leads, but they turned up nothing. As of five years ago, her
trail went completely cold. People go missing all the time. I
just figured that she was never coming home …." He pushed
back his welling emotion. "… hoping was just too hard."

"When was the last time you talked to her?

"Eight years, ten months and twenty-two days ago."

"You know, if you don't find her, you'll always have me."

He removed his hand from his pocket and put his arm around her as they continued walking.

"SO, I GUESS EVERYTHING IS GOING TO BE ALL WEIRD between us now?" Leila said to Joe as he fidgeted with an alarm clock, ready to put it in the box on Artie's sofa.

His voice pleaded, "Baby, that's up to you."

Leila didn't smile. She remained quiet, staring at him.

"Goodwill? Or do you want it?"

She blinked slowly. "So, how long did you know that I was—you know … ?"

Joe rubbed the bridge of his nose. "I guess I always wondered if it was me, especially when you got older and started looking just like Angela. That's why I stuck around all those years—I couldn't help but love you, even if I didn't know for sure—not until the letter, anyway."

He placed the clock in the box.

She shook her head. "How well did you even know my mother?"

"I knew her as well as anyone. Probably better. What you have to understand about her was that she had some bad things happen when she was a little girl."

"What kinds of things?"

"Really bad things. Things she could never shake. But she was real sweet. She always managed to look for the good in people. She just couldn't see the good in herself."

"Am I like her?"

"Baby, you have her sweetness, her artistic ways, and her eyes, but you're a lot different from her—you're a lot stronger and not insecure."

Leila turned away, weighing his words. He came up behind her and touched her shoulder. She remained aloof.

"Baby, I know it was difficult for you growing up. Your daddy—he had a hard time being one—we tried real hard, but we had no idea what we were doing. We had no business dragging you around all those years, keeping you from kids your own age. Never giving you a proper home. I'm sorry."

"It's a little late for that."

"I know. But you need to let it go. Trust me. Carrying around resentment toward me and your dad will only eat you up."

She turned to him. "What do you want me to say?"

"That you forgive us." Anguish filled his eyes. "*Please.* Not just for me, but more for yourself."

She wagged her head, feeling pity for him. If anyone truly understood what a screwed-up childhood was, Joe did.

"I think we did okay," she said. "I know you tried hard. I remember how kind you always were to me. I wish you hadn't left."

His eyes darted from hers. "I know. It was bad timing."

"I missed you so much."

"I would have come home if you'd asked—but you never did." He took her hand. "I should have come back anyway, but I can't change that now. Leila, Baby … come back to Amsterdam with me."

Leila's eyes welled. "I can't, Joe."

"Why not? You'd love it there."

She shook her head. "I need someone I can count on. I can't count on you."

He looked at her with bewilderment.

"Do you honestly think I don't know?"

"What are you talking about?"

She continued shaking her head. "You raised me around a bunch of worldly musicians—I know the lifestyle. You think I don't know what drug abuse looks like?"

He licked his lips and rubbed his cheek, his eyes evading hers.

"I love you Joe—but no. I won't have any part of it."

❧CHAPTER 32

THE WAITRESS GAVE MYLES AN INQUISITIVE LOOK when he again turned down a coffee refill. He refused to check his watch for the tenth time in thirty minutes. Bonnie had said, "At the old diner on the corner of Snyder and South 15th Street, where we used to go after my orthodontist appointments when I was a kid ...."

This was the only diner he ever remembered taking her to. And the triangular intersection was the only corner at Snyder and South 15th. Perhaps she had changed her mind. She hadn't seemed eager to meet with him, but she knew he would be driving all the way to Philadelphia just to see her. True, his making contact after so many years had upset her, but hadn't she softened a little when she called him back a few days later? She hadn't wanted him to come to her home but "the old diner"—she had said—"at noon."

He caved and glanced at his watch. Forty-five minutes late.

He understood that children of divorce often had justifiable anger. He pledged not to make excuses or defend the decisions he had made, although in the end, after all the divorce and post-divorce proceedings, there was very little in the outcome that reflected what he would have chosen. He did not want the divorce. And he did not want his daughter moved to the West Coast.

As the minutes ticked by, he thought of Bonnie when she

was little, the perfect crown jewel, born only a year after he married Michelle, before his wife turned restless. For a time, she continued to present herself as the perfectly beautiful wife in a perfectly happy marriage, with a perfectly behaved little daughter, in a perfectly predictable ticky-tacky neighborhood. But something in Michelle had been changing, or at least surfacing. Society clung to stability by a thread, back just before JFK had been assassinated, and before the first organized Vietnam War protests.

Michelle Myles had made her husband believe he was lovable, that she relished his complexities. She had broken through his walls and made him vulnerable. He loved her so much, he had even forgiven her infidelity. He should have picked up on her underlying selfishness, but all the while, she appeared the epitome of domesticity and devotion. In the end, it was all too cliché. She had dreams of stardom and Hollywood. Myles never imagined she would follow through—not until the court served divorce documents.

He regretted that he hadn't fought harder for custody of Bonnie, but courts did not separate a child from her mother back in those days. And what did he know of raising a thirteen-year-old girl?

"Decaf," Myles said as the waitress again approached his table.

"You know," she said, pouring and chomping gum. "If you're waiting for someone, maybe they just aren't going to show up."

Myles glared. She backed off.

When three hours had passed, he retrieved his billfold and pressed a ten on the table. As he rose in defeat, tucking his wallet into his hip pocket, he turned and stood face to face with a striking blond woman who could have been Michelle's twin. It were as if twenty-five years condensed. His heart leapt into his throat, bringing a sting to his eyes.

"Bonnie."

She didn't quite smile. "I was wondering how long you'd wait."

He swallowed his heart back down. "I'm glad you came. Would you like to sit?"

"No. Let's walk."

He followed her out, stunned at how grown up she was, though at twenty-eight he should have expected as much. She could have stepped off the cover of *Cosmopolitan* in her clingy dress and heels. As he held the door for her, she slung her designer bag over her shoulder.

As they strode side by side past storefronts, he said, "I know this is awkward for you."

She glanced at him, and then fixed her gaze straight ahead. "Probably more awkward for you. I doubt you've been in therapy preparing for this moment."

He nodded. In fact, nothing could have prepared him for the sight of his daughter, for the loss he mourned in that moment, knowing how little he'd had to do with the self-assured woman she had become.

She fluffed her hair. "So, how did you find me?"

"Your friend Marilyn Sanders was the mother of one of my students—Leila. She and her father—that is, Joe, only last week received the envelope you sent."

Her step faltered as she flashed a look at Myles. For the first time, her countenance wavered. She covered her mouth.

"Oh my God." She wiped a tear and breathed deep. It took a moment before she continued. "Is she alright? I had hoped I would hear from Joe." She shook her head. "I wish there had been something I could have done …."

"Leila is a fine young woman. And resilient."

She folded her arms across her full bosom. "Do you have such close rapport with all your students, that they share such personal tragedies with you?"

"No. Leila is special." As soon as the words left his mouth, he wished he could retract them.

"How nice for her."

Myles remained silent, hoping he might coax her tender side again. They continued walking as she glanced into the occasional storefront and again fluffed her hair.

"So, tell me about your life." He shoved his hands in his pockets. "I mean, what do you do?"

"I went to FIT for fashion design, and currently I'm working for an interior designer." She looked at him as they rounded the block. "I have a three-year-old son."

"You have a *son*?"

"Yes. His name is Peter."

The notion both startled and pleased him. "Is there a father in his life?—I'm sorry, I didn't mean to pry."

"No. There isn't."

"I'd like to meet Peter."

"Perhaps in time."

He stopped walking, hoping she would pause with him. When he had her full attention, he said, "I know you don't need me in your life. You've made a life of your own, all on your own. I'm proud of you for that."

She kept her eyes on his, her rigid demeanor softening.

He continued, "If this is the last time you'll allow me to see you, I'll have to accept that, but I have never stopped loving you, Bonnie."

"Dad—stop. Please."

"Bonnie, I—"

"I'm not ready for this. I thought I was." Her eyes misted. "Seeing you after so long … this is hard for me. I hoped it wouldn't be this hard."

"I know I wasn't the best father. I know I was aloof and didn't spend enough time—"

"No you didn't, in fact I have very few good memories of you. You didn't know who I was then, not any more than you do now. You had no idea what my life was like. The endless auditions. The disappointments. Being paraded around at parties, in front of agents—the alcohol and drug scene. I was a child, for God's sake." She shook her head with disgust, reclaiming her composure. "But none of that matters now. I've moved on. I'm clean and I've made a life. I have a beautiful child. *I'm* in control now."

Myles couldn't bring himself to say another word. If she

meant her words to cause injury and to silence him, she had succeeded. What more was there to say? He simply nodded as they again walked, now in silence, and turned another corner.

They arrived back at the diner parking lot and she stopped beside a cherry-red Camaro. "This is my ride."

He nodded. "Thank you for meeting with me."

Her eyes darted away from his and back. She clutched her bag. "Thank you for waiting for hours. And for letting me say my piece."

He wanted so badly to reach out and hold her—to at least take her hand or touch her arm, but he didn't dare.

Her eyes misted again. "Okay, then ... Well ... maybe I'll call sometime."

CHAPTER 33

LEILA SEEMED TO HIT EVERY LIGHT AS SHE HEADED
south. It had been a difficult three weeks between
finding out about her mother—about Joe, and then
saying goodbye again. And then there was Mr. Clarence
Myles. He too seemed so very out of sorts since he had met
with his daughter. In homeroom, he hadn't wanted to talk
about his trip to Philadelphia. When Leila asked about
Bonnie, he would only say, "It was difficult." She wondered
if or how Bonnie might alter Leila's relationship with
Clarence. Everything seemed on the crest of change. She
found herself holding her breath as she tapped her steering
wheel. She hoped Ian might be at home on a Saturday
morning.

In three weeks she would graduate, and Ian would no
longer be under any prohibitions, but given everything she
had been through, she didn't much care about school-board-
imposed sanctions. She simply needed a new plan—or two.

Pulling up in front of his house, her attention vacillated
between the strange car parked beside his Saab and the Sale
Pending sign. When Ian answered the door, his surprise
matched her apprehension. An attractive, professional-
looking young woman walked behind him, toward the
kitchen.

"That's my realtor," he said.

"I see." She cast her eyes to the placard on the lawn. "This is a new development."

"Actually, it's been in the works for a little while." He sighed. "Listen, this isn't a good time for me to break away. I'm sort of in the middle of stuff. When can we talk?"

"I don't know. I'm going to the ocean for a run. Maybe you need a run on the beach."

He smiled.

✿ SUNNY AND NEAR-SEVENTY-DEGREE WEATHER HAD drawn a crowd to the ocean. A stiff easterly breeze whipped hair around Ian's face; he gathered it into a ponytail and rolled up the hem of his jeans. As he dodged children and sand castles on his way to the shoreline, he scanned the beach for Leila. Down at the water, she stood out amidst the crowd. The sun beat upon her back, covered by only her tank top.

He came up behind her. "Sorry it took me so long. I'm glad you're still here."

"You know I would have waited all day," she said, without looking at him.

He pocketed his hands and dug his toes into the sand beside her. Water licked their ankles, as he stood just close enough that his bare arm brushed hers.

"I'm sorry I didn't say something sooner about moving. It never seemed like the right time." In fact, he had decided to move while hiking through mountain snow, but he had wanted a more solid plan before presenting it to her.

"I guess it's not really any of my business, and I suppose it doesn't really matter to me that you're selling your house. I'm just wondering why you're selling it and where you're moving to."

"I'm not selling it because of what happened this winter, if that's what you mean."

"That had nothing to do with it?"

"Well, actually, all of that did give me a little more clarity on what I want. And where I want to be."

"So, where are you headed?"

"I've got some leads on several fixer-upper properties in

New Hampshire." The sale of his pretty waterfront house would more than pay for a small cabin and renovations on a new place.

Leila smiled. "So when are you closing on your house?"

"Right after finals, I'll be headed up north. That'll give me a week before your graduation."

"You'll be back for that?"

"Yeah. It's a big day for you. Any idea what you're doing after graduation?"

"Well, my plan B was to maybe visit my grandmother in Natchez, but suddenly plan A sounds better."

"What's plan A?"

"Go back to New Hampshire."

"Any particular area?"

"The Sunapee Lake Region."

He hoped she would say that. "No kidding. One of the properties I'll be looking at is on Pleasant Lake."

"I know right where that is." She smiled. "I don't suppose you'd want some kid following you up there."

"What kid?"

"Me."

"You're no kid."

She looked at him askance. "Ian, how old *are* you?"

"I'm twenty-seven. I'll be twenty-eight next month. Does that bother you—I mean, our age difference?"

"No. Not really. I just know you're a lot more experienced than me."

"That's just a by-product of age."

"I don't mean *life* experience."

He looked at her. His head bobbed. "I know." Someday, perhaps he would go into more detail, but he wasn't sure what point there would be in telling her that one of his father's floozy girlfriends had seduced him on his thirteenth birthday—that that was only the beginning, and that all of his 'experience' was not an asset.

"Have you ever been in love?"

"No."

"Never?"

He shook his head. He had thought he was in love a couple of times, but he never felt the connection he had with Leila.

"I've never been with anybody."

He looked directly at her. "Your virginity is a beautiful thing, Leila."

"It just feels awkward to me."

"It shouldn't. You should feel proud of it. I'd do anything to get my virginity back, to offer it to—well … all I'm saying is you shouldn't be in a hurry to give it up."

"What if I want to?"

He turned to her, taking her hands. "Leila, if we both happen to end up in New Hampshire, we are each going to have our own place. We'll date, like a regular dating couple, but I'm not in any hurry for sex. That's not what I want this relationship to be about."

Her brow furrowed with bewilderment.

"Trust me on this."

She nodded.

He tugged her belt loop. "You want to walk?"

"Sure."

As they strolled, they picked up the occasional polished stone and kicked at tumbling shells. For now, Ian wouldn't elaborate on how important waiting was to him, though if their relationship progressed, his reluctance to sleep with her would probably become an issue. Halfway to the point, he glanced at her faraway eyes. Did she think he wasn't interested, that she didn't turn him on? He paused and faced her.

"What?" she said.

He pulled her closer, studying her face for a moment before his lips brushed hers, caressing more than kissing, tentative and light, a small token of his affection.

CHAPTER 34

L EILA STOOD BEFORE MISS MICHAELS AFTER CLASS AND unfurled the watercolor canvas. She smiled at the satisfaction beaming from her teacher's face.

"That's an insightful depiction. So sinister." She chuckled at the portrait of Mr. Myles.

In Leila's estimation, the depth in his eyes revealed unexpected softness, and his lips looked to be on the verge of breaking not his typical scowl but his almost-smile.

"This will look lovely beside your self-portrait at the Historical Society's art show," Michaels said.

Unbeknownst to Michaels, Leila intended to swap her self-portrait with the one she had painted of Coach Ian Brigham. The one that showed off his masculinity.

IAN ENTERED THE OLD BANK BUILDING, HIS SNEAKERS squeaking on the polished marble floors. A Millville Historical Society Art Show banner hung overhead. He had been packing all afternoon and this would be a good break, but he didn't have time to view the entire exhibit, so he followed the arrows to the high school display. As he turned the corner, he came upon Myles, which meant he had also found Leila's artwork.

Myles pinched his chin, staring straight ahead.

As Ian claimed a place beside him, Myles glanced at him with a spiked brow.

Ian's gaze first fell upon Myles' portrait, and heat came up from his chest when his own physique caught his eye.

Myles remarked, "Interesting portrayals."

"Yes. It's amazing what she's able to produce from her imagination."

"I certainly hope yours sprung from imagination only."

"I think she may have stretched it in my case, but there's no doubt she did with you. Why, you look downright human."

"In the eyes of the beholder." Staring straight ahead, Myles asked, "So, do you have plans for the summer?"

"I close on my house this week, and then I'll be heading north."

"Any job prospects?"

"As a matter of fact, yes. An assistant coaching position at a small college, contingent on a letter of recommendation."

"I wouldn't worry too much about that. The board will be glad to be rid of you, especially as they know you and Leila have a connection they can't control."

"And that's going to get me a good letter of recommendation?"

"Their fear of Leila suing sometime down the line will. Right now, a happy Leila is good insurance. And they likely consider a happily employed Ian as a happy Leila."

None of that had occurred to Ian. Even better, Myles showed a glimmer of support, albeit faint. Ian ventured, "And what about you? What are your plans for the summer?"

"All depends upon my daughter."

He was genuinely curious—and concerned. Did he dare ask? "Have you been in contact with her?"

Myles exhaled. "I have. She's invited me down for a few days. I leave right after graduation."

"I hope it goes the way you want."

Sooner than Myles had a chance to respond, Leila came up from behind. "Well, this is certainly a frame-worthy picture."

"Yes," Myles said, "we were just enjoying your embellishments."

"The only one I embellished is you, Mr. Myles." She squeezed his arm affectionately. "Coach Brigham stands on his own merits."

Myles scowled as they all three noted the award ribbons hanging from her work. Myles had taken first place in the student division, and Ian, the peoples' choice award, which he attributed to the large percentage of high-school-girl voters. Myles looked from Leila to Ian and dismissed himself, leaving the two standing before the paintings.

"Walk with me," Ian said, keeping a discreet distance between them.

The two made their way out of the building and to the side street where Ian had parked his Saab.

As they stood on the curb, he said, "I have a lot to pack between now and closing. I should probably get going."

"I guess I'll see you at school, then."

"At least till the end of the week," he glanced from side to side, "but we'd probably better not push it."

"So, then, I guess we'll talk at graduation?"

"We'll do better than talk," he said, matching the longing in her eyes.

🐉 LEILA SMOOTHED THE SKIRT OF HER LITTLE BLACK dress and clasped her hands in her lap. She stared at Myles as the waiter approached with the bottle of Gevrey-Chambertin and began inserting the corkscrew.

"Please—" Myles took the bottle from the waiter's grasp. "Like a virgin, only the one intent on imbibing her through to the finish should be allowed to uncork her bottle."

"Clarence Myles." Leila blushed. "How *risqué*."

He eased the cork from the bottle's slender neck.

"My apologies—but there is simply no analogy more fitting."

"For a man I suppose."

He conceded. Myles' implication was not lost on her. She hoped that whoever 'uncorked' her would indeed see her through to the finish. Every small thing Clarence had taught her she treasured, and now, their time together was drawing to a close. She could not express all her heart was bursting with.

"I don't know what to say, Clarence."

He smiled with a squint. "Let's not make this all sappy and sentimental. Agreed?"

"Yes, but you'll be headed to Philadelphia at the same time I'll be—"

He finished, "Leaving with Ian—I know."

"I want you to be happy for me."

"I will be happy for you in a year from now when you let me know that it was not a mistake."

He lifted his glass, waiting for her to do likewise. Instead, she averted her eyes, staring at the ruddy liquid in her glass, unable to smile.

Myles sighed. "This is what you really want? You believe you'll be happy with him?"

"I believe I will."

"Then I'm happy for you."

Leila's gaze begged his sincerity.

He sighed. "If my blessing is what you want ... you have it."

Her eyes welled.

"Don't you dare start crying. Have another sip of wine."

His sanction was a concession in the moment, but it warmed her heart. As he ate, she glanced at him from time to time. How different he seemed since their first encounter at Sam Goody's. Had he simply allowed her to see his softer side, or had he changed as a person since they first met?

He wiped his mouth and pushed his plate to the side. "I have something for you."

Leila's face lit up. "A present?"

"Yes. It occurs to me that a young lady with expanding tastes should also broaden her musical boundaries. I think you'll find this agreeable." He placed before her a tape.

"Wolfgang Amadeus Mozart."

"I think you'll especially like Symphony no. 25. It's the

first track."

"Thank you." She had never really considered or listened to the classical genre. "I didn't know you like this sort of music."

"Yes, well, you've always seen to my blues. However, for any true music lover, no one genre can satisfy the thirst. If you like this, I'll introduce you to my friend, Sergei Rachmaninoff."

LEILA RAN THE WARM IRON OVER HER GRADUATION gown, her last chore before leaving for the high school. She had already schlepped most of her belongings down the stairway and into her Volkswagen, now packed with little more than what it had transported nearly a year ago—a couple new clothing items and an expanded portfolio of watercolors and sketches. Her disassembled drawing table fit snugly in the back seat. She would leave Artie's apartment vacant but for the furnishings, in preparation for the change of ownership.

Pulling into the schoolyard at three-thirty, she scanned the parking lot for Ian's Saab. As far as she could tell, he hadn't arrived yet. Locating Kyle, she headed toward him, all the while surveying those nearby or approaching. Her skin felt clammy and hypersensitive. As she came up next to Kyle, she detected the aroma of pot.

"Big day, huh?" he said.

"Yeah," she glanced over his shoulder.

"I haven't seen him anywhere."

"Who?"

"You know who."

She said nothing, and continued scanning the passing faces. *He'll be here—he promised he would be here.*

Principal Boyd herded the group of seniors with his clipboard. "Please find your places and straighten out the line."

Myles came up beside Leila and patted her arm. "I'll see you in a little while." He turned his attention to Kyle. "You're looking, or shall I say, *smelling* very relaxed today."

Kyle grinned. As Myles walked away, Leila shifted her cap and then smoothed her gown.

"You look tense," Kyle said, his eyelids heavy. "I could hook you up, Micah's treat."

She frowned and shook her head.

"So, where is he?"

She snapped back, "Shut up, Kyle."

"Make me."

"Jerk."

"You're a jerk."

Leila stared ahead as the procession began, trying to look around without Kyle noticing. Now focusing her attention on the bleachers, they marched two by two down the track that she and Kyle had so many times run together. Even though they hadn't spent much time together lately, she felt it all slipping away. She missed Kyle already.

"Remember, Leila?" he said, with his crooked smile.

"How could I forget?" she whispered back. His fingers slipped between hers and she gripped him tightly. Her heart raced as she forced tears back and they took their seats, side by side, as always. He never let go of her hand while they waited their turn to receive diplomas.

Ian was nowhere on the bleachers, nor anywhere within her peripheral vision. The noon heat baked their bodies, trapped inside draped crimson-and-gray polyester ovens. As she stood in line with Kyle behind her, she hoped her lightheadedness would not give way to nausea or worse. Not a moment too soon, Principal Boyd called her name.

Finally, with diploma in hand, and the Principal congratulating the class of 1978, her fellow graduates flung their caps in the air as hers dropped from her grip. She grabbed Kyle's hand. "I don't feel so good."

"Just sit back down." He stood beside her, fanning her face. The group of students began to collect and re-form into a disorganized procession, heading back off the athletic field. "Are you going to be okay?"

"Yeah—" she nodded, slowly coming to her feet and

pulling at her robe's zipper.

Converging into one muddled mass, the graduates and attendees trickled off the bleachers and from the field, leaving a few stragglers.

"I gotta go say goodbye to my parents," Kyle said. "I'll catch up with you."

Myles appeared at Leila's side. "You look a little pale. You okay?"

"Yeah." She pulled off her robe, leaving only her denim skirt and tank top. "Just too hot."

"Shall we?" He nudged her toward the school. He also appeared to be searching out Coach Brigham. "So, what now?"

"I get in my car and drive."

"Still headed up north?"

"Yup." Sweat stung her eyes.

"Do you have enough cash?"

She rolled her eyes. "Yes. I have my savings and Joe wired me a very generous graduation gift."

They neared the school building. "Do you want to catch a bite before you take off?"

She shook her head. "No. I don't want to drag out the goodbyes. I've never been any good with these. Usually I just up and leave."

Kyle bounded up behind them and came to Leila's side.

Just then, Micah approached.

"It looks like the only one missing is Coach Brigham. Guess he got hung up somewhere." He turned his attention to Leila. "Good luck, man."

Leila offered him a weak smile.

He nudged her. "You sure you don't want to tag along with me and Kyle on our cross-country adventure?"

"Thanks for the invite, but no." She kissed his cheek.

Micah grinned and turned to Kyle. "You coming, man?"

"Go ahead, I'll be right there." Kyle looked at Myles who seemed to take the hint and stepped aside.

Kyle turned to Leila and drew in a quick breath. "So.

You're headed to New Hampshire?"

She nodded.

"Well, I'm taking off with Micah for a few weeks."

"What about Maryanne?"

"She's going with her parents to Maine ... Maybe sometime I could look you up."

"That would be nice."

Kyle hesitated but then leaned to kiss her. She kissed him back.

Holding him tight she whispered, "Be good."

Withdrawing, he bobbed his head like Micah and turned away. She would miss her partner.

Myles stepped back into her peripheral. A few picture-takers lingered nearby, but most everyone else had moved to the parking lot. A steady stream of vehicles flowed toward the exits.

"Might as well wait till the traffic clears a little," Myles said, urging her toward an umbrella of a tree beside the asphalt.

Leila stood at his side in the shade and grabbed his wrist to check the time. Neither said a word.

"So, when will you be leaving?" she asked.

"Tomorrow morning. First thing."

She forced a smile. "Kind of crazy how things worked out."

"It is amazing how one unexpected person can show up in your life and change everything."

Leila slipped her hand in his. She still stared straight ahead looking for Ian through blurred eyes. "I'm going to miss you so much Clarence. Please don't disappear from my life."

"Don't you worry about that. I'll come visit, I promise."

She wiped her eyes. "Looks as if you'll be visiting just me."

Irritation permeated his deep, grating breath. They both scanned the nearly empty lot.

"He's beyond late," she said.

"Have you talked to him since he left?"

"No."

"No updates at all?"

She shook her head. "I feel so stupid. I actually thought he'd come. That we'd ride off into the sunset together."

"Leila …."

"Maybe my dad was right about men." She looked at Clarence. "Well, not all men, anyway."

"How long do you plan to wait?"

"I don't know. All night?"

"You're better off just going now. If the two of you are meant to be, you'll find each other."

"Do you think Ian and I are meant to be?"

"I don't know. I only know that you'll be fine on your own. You don't need Ian to be happy." He tucked her hand in the crook of his elbow and led her toward her waiting Beetle.

As she pulled her keys from her skirt pocket, they turned at the grinding sound of a clutch. A forest green Saab hugged the corner's curb, sporting a crumpled front driver's door and fender, and a donut tire. Ian's car rasped and jolted to a stop, blocking Leila's Volkswagen.

As he struggled over the console, across the front seats, Myles opened the passenger door. Ian pulled himself out, looking exhausted, disheveled, and elated.

"Hey lady," he grinned. "Help me change a tire?"

THE END

OTHER NOVELS
BY
J. B. CHICOINE

Portrait

of a

P R O T É G É

FOUR YEARS AFTER the close of *Portrait of a Girl Running*, Leila is twenty-two and living on a pretty, little lake in New Hampshire. A new set of circumstances throws her into a repeating cycle of grief that twists and morphs into unexpected and powerful emotions. Leila must finally confront her fears and learn to let go while navigating the field of cutting-edge psychology, protecting herself from the capricious winds of Southern hospitality, playing in the backyard of big-money art, and taming her unruly heart. Even her 'guardian' has a thing or two he must learn about love and letting go.

Straw Hill Publishing

Available as a trade paperback and e-book from your favorite online bookstore

SPILLED COFFEE

BENJAMIN HUGHES IS ON A MISSION. He has just bought back the New Hampshire lake cottage his family lost eighteen summers ago, in 1969, just before he turned fourteen—just before his life blew apart.

Still reeling from a broken engagement, Ben has committed himself to relive that momentous summer for the next twenty-four hours.

Every summer as a boy, Ben has gawked at the pretty redhead Amelia, granddaughter to the richest man on the lake, Doc Burns—owner of a Cessna floatplane and the Whispering Narrows estate. During the summer of '69, Ben not only sneaks around with Amelia, but he learns how to fly with Doc, and meets an eclectic cast of characters that will change him forever. The best summer of Ben's life turns out to be the worst as the Burns' family dysfunction collides with his own family's skeletons.

Straw
Hill
Publishing

Available as a trade paperback and e-book from your favorite online bookstore

Story *for a* Shipwright

WHEN A PECULIAR YOUNG WOMAN shows up at the Wesley House Bed and Breakfast with a battered suitcase and stories to tell, shipwright Sam Wesley isn't sure if she's incredibly imaginative or just plain delusional. He soon realizes that Marlena is like no other woman he has ever met. Her strange behavior and far-fetched tales of shipwrecks and survival are a fresh breeze in Sam's stagnant life.

Sam isn't the only one enchanted by Marlena. With his best friend putting the moves on her and a man from her past coming back into her life, the competition for Marlena's heart is fierce. In the midst of it all, a misunderstanding sends Marlena running, and by the time Sam learns what his heart really wants, it may be too late to win her back.

> "*Uncharted* tells a story within a story. Readers will be forced to skate along the edge of suspended belief, eagerly turning the pages, hoping it all turns out to be true. A great read that will appeal to armchair sailors, romantics, and real adventurers."
> ~Carol Newman Cronin, author of *Cape Cod Surprise*

Straw Hill Publishing

Available as a trade paperback, e-book, and audio book from your favorite online bookstore

ABOUT THE AUTHOR

J. B. CHICOINE WAS BORN ON LONG ISLAND, New York, and grew up in Amityville during the 1960s and '70s. Since then, she has lived in New Hampshire, Kansas City and Michigan. New England is her favorite setting for her stories.

When she's not writing or painting, she enjoys volunteer work, baking crusty breads and working on various projects with her husband.

She blogs about her painting and writing, and can be contacted via her website, www.JBChicoine.com and her J.B. Chicoine author page on Facebook.

Made in the USA
Charleston, SC
24 December 2013